"THE BESTSELLING NOVELIST
IN AMERICA"
Washington Post

ROSEMARY ROGERS

SWEET SAVAGE LOVE

DARK FIRES

LOST LOVE, LAST LOVE

WICKED LOVING LIES

SURRENDER TO LOVE

FOLLOWING HER 30-MILLION-COPY
SUCCESS WITH 9 STRAIGHT *NEW YORK
TIMES* BESTSELLERS, NOW COMES THE
TRIUMPH OF HER ROMANTIC ART...

THE WANTON

The adventures and passions of a woman too
beautiful to ever be alone.

Other Avon Books by
Rosemary Rogers

Avon Books are available at special quantity discounts for bulk purchases for sales promotions, premiums, fund raising or educational use. Special books, or book excerpts, can also be created to fit specific needs.

For details write or telephone the office of the Director of Special Markets, Avon Books, Dept. FP, 1790 Broadway, New York, New York 10019, 212-399-1357. *IN CANADA:* Director of Special Sales, Avon Books of Canada, Suite 210, 2061 McCowan Rd., Scarborough, Ontario M1S 3Y6, 416-293-9404.

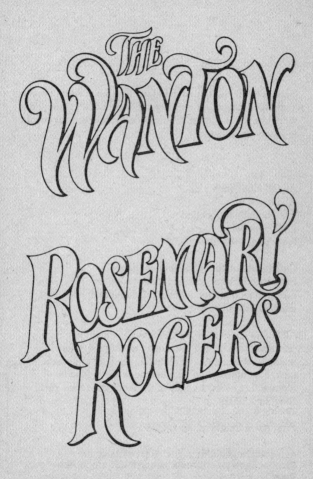

THE WANTON

ROSEMARY ROGERS

AVON
PUBLISHERS OF BARD, CAMELOT, DISCUS AND FLARE BOOKS

AVON BOOKS
A division of
The Hearst Corporation
1790 Broadway
New York, New York 10019

Copyright © 1985 by Rosemary Rogers
Published by arrangement with the author
Library of Congress Catalog Card Number: 83-091121
ISBN: 0-380-86165-8

First Avon Printing, April 1985

Printed in the U.S.A.

WFH 10 9 8 7 6 5 4 3 2 1

To my men:
Mike and Adam—my sons, and finally,
Chris—my man, my mate, my lover, and
my husband.

Prologue ⤳

The place where the old woman dwelled was a house surrounded by sounds as well as silence. The sounds were the sounds of bullfrogs and crickets and lapping water—against the sides of the pirogue and when the oar cut into the thick greenness that was a mixture of water and weeds. The silence seemed to come from nowhere and everywhere, to press against the thin, dilapidated walls of what had once been a mansion of sorts—at least at the time in which it had been built, very long ago. Most people had, by now, forgotten the Island in the Swamp; and those who did remember chose to pretend they had forgotten.

The people who lived there were descendants of ancient pirates and their captive women—or of the Old People who had traveled there (as they had traveled everywhere else) in makeshift wooden boats before the continent they had known exploded and sank below the seas. These were the legends that were handed down from one generation to the next. Stories to be told over dying campfires. Folktales . . . the stuff of ballads and fables, to be sure. But in the swamps nothing was sure and anything was possible if you had the magic in you and *knew* you had it! And then . . . and then . . . ?

The old woman said, "You will *know* your answers when you are ready to accept them. It is not for me to tell you—it

1

is for you to find out. You will know shame and pride; sorrow and happiness. Which will prevail and which will be the ultimate is left to you, and you alone. *That* is the magic and the charm."

The swamp was dead and alive at the same time—gave both death and life. Its stagnant waters sighed with the ooze of mud, and the tiny, sun-rippled streams that escaped occasionally from the constricting grasp of water weeds and sucking green moss chuckled to be free.

"Always remember what you have been taught, my child; and never misuse what you have learned. Seek to gain only—understanding."

"But of what? Please tell me . . . of *what?*"

"Trista! Trista!"

"What . . . ? What am I supposed to understand?"

"If every human being has but one eternal question, this must be mine—especially after I have dreamed the swamp-dream, which is always subtly different each time. Each time the setting is the same and the swamp is the same, but . . . but each time I am told something else; there is something new added on, so to speak, for me to puzzle over in my waking thoughts. Or, perhaps, *not* to, if I feel strong enough.

"I *don't* feel strong at all today, although I know inside myself that I will be if I must be. Today, precisely at noon, my best friend, Marie-Claire, is to marry my brother Fernando, who is not really my brother, and whom I have always . . ."

Fortunately, the next word in that last entry I must have made in that particular diary was blotted out by what might have been a tear or a drop of water. It could have been "loved" or it might well have been "hated." I think I felt both emotions at the time, in addition to being utterly devastated, as sixteen-year-olds are apt to be when they imagine their hearts broken. But in the end, who broke whose heart? And does it matter? A short while ago Fernando gave back to me at last my tattered and violated diary—open at that last, blotted page I had written. "Love or hate—it makes no difference, eh? Sometimes I feel as if they are the same thing!" Is he right? I should *hate* it if he's right. He was smiling in a certain fashion while he said those words . . . a smile that made me frightened, and that still frightens me in retrospect. I could read in it both anger and violence and . . . something more. God, something even more terrifying, that I would rather not think of—not until I might have to face it.

I am imprisoned, held helpless captive. By these four windowless walls that cut off all sound and the heavy wooden door banded with metal and a keyhole in which a key turns to remind me that I am locked in. And by my own fears that scamper even now like rats on a treadmill within my mind. I feel stifled, unable to breathe. I want to beat my fists hysterically against the walls that seem suddenly to press in on me; squeezing me, *crushing* me . . . No! I must stay calm. Force my mind to think coolly. Detach my mind from my body, if I have to, in order to survive. And I will survive—I must survive; if only to say to those who matter everything I should have said to them before.

Think—think about the past. Even about Fernando, as he was before. Remember? Sighing, I lean my back against the wall and close my eyes, forcing my mind to go backward to the past instead of forward to what could only be unpleasant speculation. The past . . . how much of it do I *really* remember? At first it returns to me in fragments— then, suddenly, in a floodtide of memories that overwhelm and almost drown me.

There are certain things that I would rather *not* remember; and others that I want to go over and over, savoring. Anything to escape from the unpleasant present and what might lie in the immediate future. I keep going back to the swamp, and the things the old woman told me with her mind; much more important than the muttered words and incantations she said aloud to please Tante Ninette, who had brought me there. Begin there, when I was . . . perhaps two years old?

BOOK ONE: *Trista*

Chapter 1 ⌁

I was born in Louisiana, and have been told that I am half-Spanish and half-French. My mother was fifteen when my natural father, only twenty himself, was killed in a duel, leaving her both widowed and pregnant. All this is only what I have been *told*. But the man I always knew and thought of as Papa was my *real* father, and the first and only time he betrayed and hurt me was by dying.

We must have arrived in California when I was about three or four years old; and in less than a year I felt as if I had always been there—had always known the sprawling old house, and the valley of the seven streams, and the rounded hills that rose in tiers around it in every direction. I had two older brothers, Fernando and Miguel; and there were servants everywhere to spoil me and wait on my every whim. It was easy, then, to push everything I didn't want to think about out of my mind; and to concentrate only upon the present.

In the beginning . . . I never needed to ask myself searching questions, as I do now! Why should I? I accepted things as they were on the surface and thought only of myself and my wants and well-being. I was taught to ride almost before I could walk; and I could use (and respect) a gun or a knife with equal ease by the time I was ten. I learned (as I now learn) everything quickly; numbers and letters as well as swimming and how to snare and hold at bay even the fiercest bull. I used to wish, in those days, that I had been born à boy. That I did not have to go away to school—especially not a *convent* school! Those were the days when I used to follow Fernando about—doing every stupid, daring thing I did in the hope that he would notice me, and perhaps give me even a grudging word of approval. How childish, how silly! Now, I despise myself for what I was; and for not wanting to see what was before my eyes all the time.

Papa's marriage to my mother (if they ever *were* married) was his second. His first wife, the mother of Fernando and Miguel, had been the spoiled only daughter of a prominent Spanish-Californian family—closely related to General Vallejo. He had been a ship's captain in those days, sailing from Boston to put in at Monterey to trade for hides. And then the beautiful Josefa had seen him and whispered to her best friend: "That is the man I am going to marry!" It's a romantic story, I suppose! Like another one I was told once, when I was still in the convent school in Benicia.

Love . . . romance . . . hate . . . jealousy . . . are all these emotions really tied together? I have been called a witch, a *bruja*; and sometimes without the nervous, deprecating laugh that usually follows such a statement. And so? At least they do not burn witches any longer. Perhaps it is because witches tend to burn themselves up—usually by flying too close to the twin flames of danger and challenge.

Challenge—I have always been exhilarated by any kind of challenge, or wager. And purposely blind, perhaps, to those things I do not wish to see. Why didn't I see, for instance, that Fernando used to trail behind my mother in much the same fashion that I trailed behind *him?* He called her names after she ran away from us with a red-headed Irishman who had his own gold mine and several millions of dollars to throw away on whatever he chose. *"Puta!* Whore!" Sometimes it seemed as if he was saying those words at *me,* and that they were meant for me and were not about my mother at all. So, frightened without quite knowing why, I started to stay away from Fernando and to avoid him as much as I could. I even agreed, willingly, to a convent school; and when, eighteen months later, I sailed for Boston and yet another school, I was almost relieved. I needed discipline, and a disciplined way of life—I can see that now. There was so much I had to learn!

Marie-Claire taught me a great deal during those years we were at school together. We had a great deal in common, too. Her father was French; her mother American. And *her* mother too had gone away with another man. . . . There had been the unpleasantness of a divorce, and then her father had remarried and they didn't want her around, in the way. So—here she was!

"And I am bored, bored, *bored!* Why did my papa put me in such a prison? Oh yes. It's because of his new wife, who is jealous of me. But I'll teach her—and *him* too! I'll marry the first man I encounter next—I swear it! Anything to get out of this ugly place, this prison!"

Papa brought Fernando with him to Boston the year I turned sixteen. And within the week they were engaged to be married—he and Marie-Claire. *She* was desperate to be free, and he and I had been brought up as brother and sister. In any case, and in all honesty, Marie-Claire is pretty, and I am not. She has hair the color of freshly minted gold, wide blue eyes, and *breasts.* My hair is night-black and my eyes silver-gray. I am too tall for a woman, and I do *not* have large breasts. All the same, I have been called "striking"—whatever that means. I know only that it does *not* mean beautiful, or even pretty. My face is more triangular shaped than oval . . . my cheekbones too high and too wide . . . my eyebrows too upward slanting. But what is the point of all this dwelling on detail? I am what I am *inside* myself, and I can be anything I choose to be. Witch!

"You are very much like your mother . . . ," I have been told. Leaving me wondering—in what ways? We were never very close, but when I remember her I remember a beautiful woman who always sparkled with the brilliance of the jewels she wore. I hated her at times, and I loved her at times—but did I ever really understand her?

When I think back . . . I did not spend very much time with my mother at all. I got on her nerves—I was too wild and boisterous. Or was I merely in her way? No matter. It made no difference to me whether she was there or not; because I always had Papa, who loved me, and Miguel, who understood me.

Miguel is Father Michael now. And it was just before he

entered the seminary that Papa brought Fernando with
him to Boston. We had all the time we wanted to spend together, because I attended Windham Academy for Young
Ladies, and Miss Charity Windham was Papa's sister.

We visited museums; went on walks and boat rides.
Papa and I had long talks every evening, with Miss Charity sometimes joining in. Fernando and Marie-Claire merely *looked* at each other while the rest of us were engaged in
conversation. I suppose I had guessed the outcome even before Marie-Claire told me late one night, her voice an excited whisper, that they were going to be married,
Fernando and she.

"Are you? Of course, no one would have guessed . . . ! In
any case, I'm happy for you both."

"Fernando and Captain Windham are to speak to my father tomorrow. I am sure he'll say yes and feel relieved
that I am off his hands! Just think—I shall be a respectable
married woman soon, and then we will truly be like sisters!"

"Fernando will expect a virgin, you know." I hoped my
voice sounded dispassionate. "He is very old-fashioned in
some ways, like most *Californios.*"

Marie-Claire gave a soft gurgle of laughter. "I know! He
has only kissed me twice—nothing else! But I can promise
you that on our wedding night there will be blood on the
sheets to attest to my . . . *pure* state; and I'll make sure he
finds it difficult to enter me—at first, that is!"

I was no longer shocked at anything Marie-Claire said.
She had told me her whole life story already, sparing no
detail. Grooms, servants, any man who was well built and
lusty enough to match her appetites. I actually found myself hoping that Fernando would be able to satisfy her and
to keep her sated.

"He has a terrible temper—do be careful, won't you?"

"Oh *pouf!* But of course I will be cautious—and very,
very discreet, don't worry! Only—tell me—is he *big?* Does
he make love well?"

I was thankful for the darkness that hid the burning
flush I felt mounting in my cheeks. Sometimes, she *did* go
too far!

"I'm sure it won't take *you* too long to find that out for

yourself!" I remember snapping as I turned my back to her, pulling the covers firmly over my head before I added, my voice sounding muffled: "In any case, how would *I* know anything like that about Fernando? He's my *brother,* do remember."

"Only your stepbrother, which means that you're not really related at all! I wouldn't blame you at all for . . . *experimenting* with the best-looking man who happens to be nearest at hand—I know *I* have done so, and you are silly, *silly* if *you* did not!"

Well, I had not, and that was that. Marie-Claire enjoyed the adventure of "experimenting," as she called it, whereas I—I had never been invited to do so. Everything is high drama when one is sixteen, and Marie-Claire's mocking, scornful words made me toss all night with hateful dreams of things I would much rather *not* have thought about, and didn't know I knew.

It rained all the next day, and I remember feeling glad because the weather matched my mood and gave me an excuse to sit by the fireplace in the library, reading. I had my favorite chair there—red plush, with a worn seat, and big enough to allow me to curl my feet up under me. I had been allowed a small glass of sherry with which to drink the health of the happy couple, and I suppose it was the unaccustomed alcohol that made me feel drowsy after a while. I had to fight to keep my eyes open, and my limbs felt heavy. "Silly . . . ," I remember thinking, lowering my book to stare into the fire. Was I?

It would be silly indeed to fall asleep here when I had a perfectly good bed upstairs. I suppose I really should bestir myself, I remember thinking almost regretfully, for it was pleasantly warm and cozy here by the fire. Comfortable, more than half-asleep, I was hardly aware of time, or its passing. The flickering fire seemed to have mesmerized me, for I thought I saw pictures in it—caught within tongues of flame that made them grow larger and then smaller, only to change again and again into something else, something different.

I saw, even through the green and yellow underbrush, the tiger that stalked me without sound. The beast's eyes were sungolded green that gleamed in the darkness; its muscles moved with beautiful symmetry under its sleek, black-and-gold striped skin. No matter how fast I ran down the endless, twisting paths of the forest, the tiger kept abreast of me—constantly watching me, *watching* me. And at my heels, so close behind I could feel its hot breath, ran the puma. *El gato,* the mountain lion. I was prey. Who would have me first?

"Ah!"

Had I screamed aloud? I could not remember. What I do remember was opening my eyes with a start; to find Fernando gazing at me through narrowed eyes in a most *peculiar* way that made me feel awkward and uncomfortable as I sat upright, trying to untangle my bare legs from beneath me.

"I . . . I'm sorry, I didn't mean to fall asleep here! I suppose you wanted to smoke . . . and I . . ."

Fernando cut off my stuttering with a wave of his hand that warned me that he had probably imbibed far too much liquor.

"I have already smoked too many cigars and have had too many bottles of wine, I think. My respected *padre* has been safely helped to bed by Tía—and my *novia* has also retired for the night. She suggested that I might find you here, fallen asleep over some ridiculous book as usual. Medical books instead of novels? Keep it up, little sister, and you will end up like poor Tía—without a man!"

Sheer rage almost overcame me for a few seconds, urging me to strike out at him with any weapon I could think of; and then I managed to say in as cold a voice as I could muster: "I think Aunt Charity is *lucky* not to be saddled with some stupid, unreasonable man! And as for the books I choose to read . . . I am *not* your sister, Fernando, and I owe you no explanations!"

"You are younger, and not half as beautiful as *she* was, of course," Fernando said brutally, as if he had not heard anything I had said, adding contemplatively: "But there are times, you know, when you resemble your mother almost *too* much. Especially *now,* when I can see fire-devils in your eyes. Is that why you reminded me that you are not my sister? *Is* it? Are you a *puta,* like her?"

I tried to struggle to my feet, but I was angry, frightened, and confused, my legs without feeling.

"You don't answer? Or cannot *deny,* is that it? Eh?"

He was standing before me now, blocking out the firelight and all its cozy warmth, so that I was suddenly cold— and even worse than that, afraid. I had to grit my teeth together so that they wouldn't chatter while I sought for words that would be cutting enough and cold enough to bring him back to his senses. If Papa or Aunt Charity could have known what he had just said—*implied* . . . !

I was quite unaware that I had huddled back into my chair as if I wanted to melt into it until I felt my cheek sting from the flick of his fingers against it, making me gasp out loud with shock as well as pain.

"You're afraid to answer me, eh, little *bruja?* Oh *sí,* I have heard them all whisper that that is what you are! And don't think that I haven't noticed the way you talk to horses to make them tame—even to that fierce bull that nobody else could go near! You have witch's eyes; I used to try to escape from them, and from *you!* What a nuisance you were, always following us about . . ."

I had felt fury surge through me, wiping out fear. And then a thankful return to sanity. Fernando was drunk. He did not know, and would probably not remember, any of his words or actions tonight. I had seen him become violent in the past with any animal or man that thwarted him— and I could almost *smell* the barely leashed violence that was in him now, under the reek of liquor. "Careful!" a voice in my mind warned me. "Be very careful!"

Still rubbing my cheek, I took refuge in the obvious. Confusion. Disbelief. A pretense of not having heard, or understood, most of what he had said.

"Fernando . . . why did you hurt me? What do you mean by all these terrible things you have been saying? You know very well that *I* am not to blame for anything my mother—"

This time, he literally hauled me to my feet, holding me by the upper arms while he snarled into my face: "So tell me—how many men have had you so far? Have you matched your mother yet?" He shook me so hard that my carelessly pinned-up hair came loose about my face and shoulders; and then, releasing me as suddenly as he had seized me, he gave a strange laugh and put his hands on me in a different way—one squeezing my breast painfully, and the other . . .

"No!" I suppose my rage was as hot as the end of the poker I suddenly found myself holding—keeping him at bay, I think, because something in my eyes and my look must have warned him that I would either maim or kill him if he attempted to touch me again. "No, and no!" I repeated, almost breathless, all but voiceless with the force of my fury and humiliation. "Understand this, Fernando—I am *not* Laurette, *not* my mother! I am *myself,* understand? I am *Trista*—and I don't care what you or anyone else might say or think. *I* know what I have done and not done, and that is all that matters to me. When I . . . if I let a man *touch* me . . . come close enough to me even to *kiss* me, it will be I who will choose both the man . . . and the time . . . and . . . and *where!* But at this particular moment, I think . . . I *know* that I would much rather remain the way I am . . . or become a nun like Concepcion Arguello. And if . . . if the manner in which you just treated me is usual between a man and a woman, then I don't choose to experience such a thing again. Not *ever!*"

"You're still a virgin then? No other man . . ."

By then I was sniffling from sheer anger and frustration. I hated myself for such a show of weakness, and I hated Fernando for what he had done while feeling *sorry* for him at the same time, because he must have loved my butterfly mother very much, with all the passion of a young boy.

"Fernando—please *go!* You're to be married in less than a week to Marie-Claire, who is my closest friend; and *she* should be your only concern, not I!" I hoped I did not sound desperate and that my voice did not shake as I rushed on, "And since I . . . we *both* realize by now, I'm sure, that you are not yourself, I think it might be best if we forgot everything that just took place."

"Your weapon is no longer hot enough to burn me—and I think your newfound defiance is merely pretense! *More* pretense! Perhaps, as your older brother, I should find out for myself if what you have just implied is true or not? There have already been marriage offers for you, did you know that? A husband will expect—"

"If you take one step closer, Fernando, I will maim you.

The 'ridiculous' books that I am so fond of reading have taught me a great deal about anatomy—and in addition, I am also capable of screaming very loudly. Shall I do so now?"

My voice might have been shaking, but I meant every word that I had said, and I think he knew it. There was a split second of hesitation while I poised myself; and then Fernando shrugged, and even managed a twisted sort of smile.

"I believe you really *would* do what you just threatened! Well, well! You've turned into quite a vixen! Perhaps some man, sometime, might think you worth taming—if he has the stomach for it!" He sketched me a sarcastic travesty of a bow before he turned to walk, not very steadily, to the door.

I stayed where I was, watching him, and before the door closed behind him he looked over his shoulder at me, saying with an odd kind of laugh: "I hope you continue to guard your virtue carefully, my little *adopted* sister! Because one of these days, when *I* am head of the family, I might insist on being certain that it won't be damaged goods I hand over in marriage to one of my friends. You take my meaning, I'm sure? *Buenas noches, Trista querida!*"

I almost fell against the door in my haste to lock it after he was finally gone; and after that, I found that I could not seem to stop shaking as if I had the chills. I could spend the rest of the night in here, and explain in the morning that I had fallen asleep over a book as usual. Aunt Charity would understand . . . and I did not care any longer what Fernando thought, or how he might smirk. He was to marry Marie-Claire, and I . . . what would my future hold?

Chapter 2 ❧

I cannot remember now how long I stayed leaning against that door as if it were my only support in all the world, my forehead pressed hard against it, as if to ward off all the thoughts and longings I didn't want to think of. My breathing sounded far too loud, even to myself, almost drowning out the loud, regular ticking of the Seth Thomas clock that sat squatly on the mantelpiece, loftily ignoring all the bric-a-brac that surrounded it.

"That's it! Hold on to detachment. The clock ticks, and time is forever. Moments and incidents pass—and are finished. You learn . . . or you do not. No matter, for time never moves backward, only forward. Time is not for wasting on regrets—it is for *doing*—it is for *feeling*—it is the *now* that colors your afterward . . . and your memories."

I thought: Oh God, perhaps I *am* a witch after all! Why else would I hear the old swamp-woman's voice so clearly in my purposefully emptied-out mind? The *meaning* of the words—warning against weakness or affirmation of it? For I had already, stealthily, slyly, begun to wonder: What if I had *not* resisted? What might have happened then? Would he still be marrying Marie-Claire next month . . . or *me*?

"I thought you handled him very well—and wisely too, if you mean to have him later. He's one of those men who will always want the unattainable—or what seems to be difficult to obtain! So if you want my advice, I wouldn't unlock that door too quickly. Make him wait on *your* whims; I can assure you that he'll be all the more inflamed by both desire and curiosity. If that is what you really want . . . ?"

I felt the light, and yet somehow firm, pressure of hands on my shoulders and heard and understood every word that was said to me—every nuance, including that odd, questioning inflection at the end of an unfinished sentence. And yet it was as if—at least for some moments—as if time itself had paused, suspending me in a frozen vacuum where I alone was incapable of words or motion. Of everything but . . . remembering. It is something that the French call *déjà vu*—"already seen"; and it can be frightening, like anything else that one does not quite understand and cannot quite explain.

But . . . ! The touch of a certain pair of hands . . . the sound and timbre of a certain voice . . . How can it be possible to *know* what you cannot possibly know? To *recognize*, without seeing, someone you cannot possibly have met before? And how can I explain something that cannot *be* explained—only *felt?*

In the end, that certain moment dissolved as if it had never been. Vanishing with the exhalation of my snatched-in breath as I spun around and let anger replace whatever had been in my mind some seconds earlier.

"Who . . . *how* . . ."

I knew I stuttered like the village idiot, and I despised myself for doing so almost as much as I disliked the cause of my natural confusion—especially after I had discerned that he, a stranger who had appeared from nowhere, actually seemed amused at having startled me. Why, even his all-too-perfunctory "apology" was phrased as condescendingly as if it had been addressed to a child!

"As to *who*—I'm a friend of Charity's. And how . . . ? I came up the secret stairway from the cellar, of course. Sorry I didn't warn you by coughing loudly or anything like that, but I must confess to being quite . . . well, quite intrigued by the little scene I could not help overhearing. Isn't he a trifle *old* for you, this not-quite-brother of yours?"

"You are . . . quite *despicable!* To eavesdrop deliberately on a *private* conversation, and then presume to give me *advice* on . . . on matters that are no concern of yours . . . even if you *are* a friend of Aunt—Miss Windham, I mean—that cannot possibly excuse your lamentable lack of . . . of . . ."

"Of manners—or of tact? I have to admit I've been accused before of possessing neither! But as for you, young Miss . . . if you were *my* niece—or daughter, God forbid—I'd certainly make sure you were locked into your room every night like a Spanish virgin; with a *dueña* to attend your every step during the day. Your precious Fernando could have raped you if he had been determined enough, and less drunk. Don't you understand that yet? Or is that what you really wanted?"

There was a wolf snarl underlying those last words, and I knew it, felt it, and wanted to claw back at him, but I wasn't experienced enough to know just *how* to do so effectively—at least, not then. Attempting to deal with Fernando and my half-felt regrets afterward had been bad enough; but facing nasty, ugly accusations from a man who was a complete stranger to me was too much— "friend" of Aunt Charity's or not!

I did not realize that my fisted hands had come up to strike him until he seized my wrists.

"Well?" he repeated annoyingly, while he grinned down into my face. And then, compounding the insolence he had already shown me, and in spite of my angry struggles, he said the *worst* thing he could possibly have said. "Aren't you a little *young* to be indulging in the kind of games you were playing with the unfortunate—and patient—Fernando? For God's sake, you can't be over twelve or thirteen at the most! I shall have to speak to Charity about you . . . after I and the friends I brought with me have been fed. Where is she?"

His eyes were the kind of gold-green that reminded me of the swamps, and his hair the color of dark mahogany that was almost black. There was a cleft in his chin, and small sunburst lines at the corners of his eyes to prove that he either squinted against the sun or scowled quite often. He was, in fact, dark complexioned enough to be taken for a Spaniard, or . . . what and who *was* he, anyhow, this tall and arrogant man who presumed far too much?

I had ceased my useless attempts to free myself by now, and resorted to haughty disdain; although I could not help remaining curious about the man—and even a little bit afraid of him. He was certainly very different from all the other so-called couriers of what was known then as the Liberty Line, or the Underground Railroad. Aunt Charity's exclusive academy was but one of the many stations along the difficult and arduous path to freedom; and only she and I (or so I had thought all this time) knew of the small, cramped little cellar beneath the cellar, or the narrow, spiraling secret stairway concealed by walls within walls, leading from the cellar to the library. If he knew about and had used it, only Aunt Charity could have told him—and in that case, why hadn't I met the wretch before?

"I wish you would . . . would be good enough to *unhand* me, *sir!*" I managed to say in response to the painful, warning pressure of his fingers as they tightened very slightly about my wrists. "You should have made yourself and your business here known to me at the beginning instead of taking it upon yourself to *preach* at me about something that is *my* private business!"

At least he did release me; but to my added annoyance, he had to give vent to a burst of soft but spontaneous laughter.

I must have looked daggers at him (and wished I had them to throw!) because he said in a choked kind of voice: " 'Unhand me, sir!' I never thought to hear the words *off* the boards! So you're a budding Thespian, are you? You and your desperately intense Fernando should make a good pair someday, whether he's still conveniently married to this friend of yours or not! But as you reminded me—it *is* none of my business, is it? And I'm sure you have plenty of time in which to grow up into a woman—perhaps!" The suggestively insolent condescension of his words, coupled with the tone of his voice, left me breathless and almost speechless with such rage that if I had had the poker or even a gun within reach, I could easily have killed him without the slightest qualm. Especially when, in a dismissing kind of fashion, he had the audacity to say that I should hurry up and tell Aunt Charity that he was here—and *then* go to the kitchen and find some victuals. That is—if I was capable of cooking . . . ?

I knew somehow that I was being deliberately baited for some obscure reason of his own. Or was this perhaps just a hobby with this man—a cat-and-mouse kind of game he enjoyed playing at times?

"Hurry along now, my girl—I'm ravenously hungry, and so are my friends! I'm surprised that Charity wasn't here herself, if at least to supervise *your* nocturnal adventures!"

As far as I was concerned he could have stayed hungry forever. ". . . my girl . . ." indeed. As if I were a child or a chambermaid! How I hated him and longed to be able to tell him so! I would certainly tell Aunt Charity exactly what I thought of this latest courier and his lack of manners and breeding. How could she possibly *know* such a person?

I had to force myself to speak to him with a certain degree of civility, but with my voice as frosty as I could make it.

"I'll go up and try to rouse Aunt Charity if it's a matter of real urgency, of course. But if all you need is food, or directions to the next—"

He cut me off there, those green-golden animal eyes of his narrowing as he studied me like a poor botanical specimen.

"So there's some fire there beneath the icicles? What a surprising child you are!" And then, surprising *me,* he suddenly gave me a rather lopsided smile that deepened the grooves beside his mouth, and brushed a finger under my chin, raising my stormy face to confront his.

"I am *not* a child, I'd have you know!" My temper, always volatile, was past containing now. "I am past sixteen, and quite old enough to be married and have children if I should want to do so!" If it would not have seemed far too childish, I would have stamped my foot to emphasize my statement. "And speaking as a *woman,* Mister whatever-your-name-is, let me tell you that you are the *rudest,* most boorish, unmannerly and *crude* man it has ever been my misfortune to encounter! And if you weren't a friend . . . an *acquaintance* of my aunt, I would . . ."

"I can well imagine, judging from what I happened to overhear, that you would indeed!"

"Happened to . . . ? You eavesdropped deliberately! And

then, as if *that* wasn't low and contemptible enough, you proceeded to insult and to . . . to taunt and provoke me. *Damn* you and your smiling hypocrisy and your cruel games of words and ugly insinuations! Fine things to say to a mere *child,* don't you think? You have made it very obvious that you are no gentleman, of course; but even worse—"

"Stop . . . enough. You should learn not to belabor a point once you have made it. And to curb that wildcat temper of yours too, if you want to get anywhere." He had the impudence to smile at me mockingly again before his voice turned coaxing for a change. "Oh, very well, then! If you don't appreciate my well-meant advice, will my abject apologies mollify you instead? My friends and I *are* extremely hungry and thirsty, you know! I believe the last time we ate was over two days ago . . . or was it three? Listen—if your Fernando isn't still lurking about, I could forage for food myself. I think I still remember where the kitchen is. Or perhaps *I* should go upstairs to wake Charity up."

I had placed my back against the door without realizing I had done so, my hands, with fingers outspread, pressed palms down against the polished wooden door panels on either side of me. And I wasn't taken in by his sudden change of attitude—any more than I trusted anything at all about him.

"If you'll go back down to the cellar I'll bring down food, and fresh water and milk to drink. But I won't let you wake Aunt Charity; not if she's already fallen asleep." I faced him defiantly, this time without flinching, for I knew that this time, at least, it was I who had the advantage over him. In all except that infernally ironic, pretentiously knowing, crooked grin of his that already seemed far too familiar to me.

"Your eyes remind me of lightning bolts at this moment. I suppose it's a good thing they are not!" He shrugged then in a fashion that made me think he was still playing with me . . . or *along* with me—but only for as long as it suited him. "Would you really banish me to that cellar again? Perhaps if you were to bribe me with wine instead of water . . ."

"I would *not*—," I had begun hotly, when I heard the soft

tapping from the other side of the door and Aunt Charity's voice speaking my name softly.

"Trista? Trista, please *do* unlock the door if you hear me, I beg of you. Trista . . . !"

"Your aunt sounds real worried. Don't you think you should open up like she says?" The words were an illiterate drawl all of a sudden, but the *look* he gave me through lazy-lidded green-amber eyes seemed to flatten me against the door for a few moments before I summoned up the strength to open it and let my aunt in.

"Trista my *dear!* I saw Fernando to bed too, and then I noticed that you were not in your . . . *Blaze?*"

Aunt Charity's hair, which she usually wore in a severe knot, hung loosely down to just below her shoulders. She looked, in that moment when she said his name, like a young girl with unguarded responses.

"Yes, it's me all right, Charity love. The bad penny, I guess."

It was as if I, and my very presence there, had suddenly been erased, just as if I had only been a picture drawn on a slate.

"You're not . . . ! Oh, Blaze, I had begun to *worry,* especially after that last time . . ."

"My dear, you should have known better! I'm good at shaking off pursuers—and better yet when it comes to self-preservation. I don't want you worrying about me—ever."

His voice, even the harsh planes of his face, seemed to soften when he looked at my aunt, taking her impulsively outstretched hands in his and holding them tightly; and *she* could not seem to take her eyes from him. I felt like an unwanted, unwelcome intruder standing awkwardly rooted in place. Like a child left to suck my thumb to console myself for not being allowed to join the grown-ups for dinner.

But *why,* for heaven's sake? I had already decided to dislike this man Blaze—if that really was his name. Why then did I feel a pang of . . . something close to pain shoot through me as I watched them together? I wouldn't—I couldn't possibly *bear* to stand there any longer while they looked into each other's eyes and seemed to carry on a conversation without words.

"I suppose I might as well go upstairs to bed since you

are up, Aunt Charity—unless you need me? I fell asleep. I'm sorry if my thoughtlessness prevented *you* from sleeping."

"Trista? Oh!" Aunt Charity looked as if she had just been awakened out of a trance, and I almost wanted to shake her.

At least I did not encounter Fernando again that night; but even after I was safely in my own bed, I found my mind seething with a strange mixture of emotions, some of which I did not quite understand. Fernando . . . I had always, as long as I could remember, nourished a secret (or so I thought) infatuation for him. He was handsome in almost a classic fashion, and had inherited his mother's brown-gold hair and Papa's blue eyes. Well built, and with a quick smile, he had always endeared himself to women of all ages. Marie-Claire and he were a perfect match in every way, and their children would be beautiful, of course. *I* was usually referred to as "unusual looking" because of the startling contrast between my hair and eyes; but I had never, ever, been called *beautiful.*

Ah—but I had never thought of Aunt Charity as a still-young, beautiful woman until that night either. Why had she remained single? Because of this man she called Blaze, who could make her face glow and her eyes shine with a brilliance I had never seen before? Why had they not married if they loved each other?

I tossed and turned uneasily in my narrow bed, tossing off blankets and comforters at one moment and pulling them up to my neck the next. I did not want to think of what might have happened if Aunt Charity had not come looking for me. *Nothing,* of course, I told myself angrily. And because I did not want to think of *him* any longer, I thought of Fernando instead, and wondered . . . and didn't know how I really felt or what I wanted.

Fernando? Or the unknown? The unattainable, perhaps? Like being a doctor with a real medical degree. Finding . . . myself—or someone? Myself first! Who am I? *What* am I? Along what paths and to what end will my strange dreams and secret ambitions, and my deepest, darkest feelings lead me?

Chapter 3 ~ℋ~

How strange! I remember thinking that the next day, when everyone and everything seemed exactly the same as before. Fernando treated me just as he used to, with exaggerated patience—nothing in his manner betraying anything that had passed between us. Aunt Charity, with her hair pulled back in a spinsterish bun as usual and wearing her severely high-necked alpaca gown, bore no resemblance to the vital, glowing woman I had suddenly perceived in the library the previous night. I presumed that the man she had called Blaze had gone on his way by now with the "friends" he was helping to freedom and safety. I would probably not see him again, and nor did I want to!

In the days that followed I was glad of every small detail that had to be attended to before the wedding took place. I packed Marie-Claire's clothes for her because she could never have managed to do so herself, and I listened to her confidences and answered as many questions as I could about life in California. "Things have changed, I'm sure," I warned her, and explained that although slavery did not exist there, she would have servants—as many as she needed.

"My stepmother is from the Carolinas—North or South; I forget which, exactly! But her family is very rich; they have plantations and many slaves. That's why, probably, my father married her! At any rate, as long as I have servants to wait on me and as many beautiful gowns and jewels as I might crave, I suppose I will be happy enough. At least I will have *freedom* of a sort, a husband—position . . . !"

"And children?" I put in tartly. "You'll be expected to produce heirs to carry on the family name, you know. Miguel is a priest and I am only an adopted relative, so that leaves Fernando the only one."

"Children? I want to go out, to enjoy myself and do as *I* please for a change! I am only seventeen—I'm not ready to have wet, whining babies yet! If Fernando must have an heir I will give him one, I suppose—but only when *I* am ready, and only if I am sure there will be a wet-nurse to feed and take care of it. But why speak of such unpleasant things? Just think—I am actually to be married within two weeks, and my papa has promised that I may purchase my trousseau in Paris, while we are on our honeymoon. Gowns by Worth—imagine! And of course Papa will arrange that we will be presented to the Emperor and Empress. Oh, Trista—I wish you were coming with us too! I need someone to share it all with, and you're the only female I've ever really liked, or felt I could be close to. Can't you come? Once I'm married I can chaperone you, you know! You could go to university in Paris, study medicine if your heart is still set on such dull stuff!—and stay with us for as long as you want. Wouldn't it be fun? When Fernando is out with his cronies, you and I could chaperone each other—and enjoy ourselves at the same time. I'm going to talk to your papa and to Fernando about it. He wouldn't mind—he'd give me anything in the world I want!"

Marie-Claire had been whirling about, admiring her image in the mirror while *she* talked and *I* tried not to pay too much attention to her babbling. Go to Paris . . . travel to new places where I would meet different people and learn more about the world I lived in . . . It wasn't possible, of course; so why think about such things? I would continue to be a champion of causes and of underdogs, read whatever medical books I could lay my hands on, and I would probably end up a disillusioned, vinegar-tongued spinster!

"Yes—yes! You're my best friend, after all, as well as my sister-in-law. I might *need* you!"

"Well, if you do, you'll always know where to find me! But you do *not* need a third party when you're on your honeymoon! Invite me to visit you after you have come back from Europe and have quite settled down, and I promise I'll come."

"You will? I'll need somebody to talk to and confide in, you know. I suppose we'll get bored with each other after a while, Fernando and I. And then . . . who knows?"

How vividly all of that time stands out in my mind! All the preparations for our leaving, by locomotive no less, for Washington, where we would be met by Marie-Claire's parents. Then they would travel on to Richmond for the wedding, and from there to Charleston in South Carolina; and then by sea to France.

"We'll go to Italy too, of course. I've always wanted to see Rome. And then to England . . . Greece . . . and perhaps to Spain as well. I want to travel *everywhere!*"

Why should I spoil my friend's excitement with dour reminders that she could not expect to go on traveling all over Europe forever, and would sooner or later have to settle down? She was like a bright, gay butterfly just emerging from her chrysalis-prison: impatient to fly everywhere and try as many new things as she could. And how could I blame her for that? Given the chance, might not I too want to travel all over the world without giving a thought to settling down for too long in any one place because there was always the next new experience to look forward to?

All I said at the time was: "Well, I hope that you will remind Fernando that you will need a personal maid to accompany you on your travels, for you know very well you can never remember where you have put anything—and you are quite hopeless at packing or unpacking for yourself. But for now, I need to know which gowns you have decided on for traveling to Washington so that I may make sure that they are pressed and do not have missing buttons or ripped hems."

"There are times, I vow, when you sound almost exactly like Miss Charity! Lost buttons . . . ripped hems . . . Do you never think of something—*doing* anything—that is not at all practical but might well prove to be terribly *exciting?* Have you ever taken risks? Well, you know *I* have! And I don't regret anything; at least I've learned a great deal about men—and I think *you* need to, or you'll end up a spinster like Miss Charity!"

I remember that day very clearly. The sun sending slanted gold light through the open window to reflect almost dazzlingly off the matching brightness of Marie-Claire's ringlets as she shook her head at me exasperatedly. I don't know why. Perhaps because she had put into words certain things that I myself had almost been afraid to *think* of? What *did* I want—and what did *wanting* itself mean? And when I found out . . . what then?

Perhaps it is just as well that I did not have time for too much introspection during the days that followed. All the last-minute details to be taken care of; and the long and cindery train ride to Washington with its many overnight stops "for the comfort of the weary traveler" . . . or so our guidebook stated. I, for one, felt far too weary and hot to need any other comfort but a cool bath and a dreamless night's sleep. Once we are safely arrived in Washington, I used to console myself, then I will surely not have to share a bed with Marie-Claire, who tosses and turns so much in her sleep that sleep becomes impossible for *me!* Not only that, but during the night we spent in New York she insisted on keeping me up by demanding from me details of how much I knew about men, and how to please them, and how to please myself as well as encourage *them* to please me. I suppose I learned a great deal; but oddly enough, I would much rather have been allowed to sleep!

I slept right through the dinner hour that first night I spent in Washington, for Papa, bless his heart, would not allow them to disturb me. I think I slept for ten hours or more. I would probably have slept for much longer if I had not been startled bolt upright out of a heavy sleep by having my shoulder shaken urgently, only to find myself thrust into the middle of some deep intrigue of which I knew or comprehended nothing—for all that I was expected to play my part in it.

"Hush!" Marie-Claire's urgent whisper came out of the darkness as I felt her slide into my bed and push me back down. *"Please,* Trista! You *must* pretend you're sound asleep, and that I've been here with you for the past few hours, because I said I could not sleep and wanted to gossip with you. Promise you'll say so? I swear I'll explain everything to you later, but for now . . ." The way her words rattled on I was hardly surprised at how breathless she sounded. And also, it didn't take me long to realize that she was wearing nothing more than a sheer chemise under the thin silk wrapper she slipped out of while she was talking, dropping it carelessly on the floor a moment later.

I have never been at my best when I first awaken, and this time proved no exception. My mind seemed clogged and dull with the debris left behind by an unusually deep slumber, and at first all I seemed capable of doing was to mumble something unintelligible like, "Wha . . . ? Hunh?"

"Never *mind!* When they don't find me in my room, only my clothes scattered everywhere and my bed . . . Sshh! You remember what you must say? Trista . . . !"

"Sshh yourself!" I mumbled ungraciously, turning my back on her. "I'm supposed to be sound asleep, am I not?"

I had barely finished saying so when, after no more than a cursory knock, the door was practically *flung* open to admit not only Marie-Claire's father and her stepmother, but her glowering fiancé as well, with poor Papa, who had obviously been *forced* along, trailing as far behind this militant group as he could and patting awkwardly at the shoulder of one of the maids, who sobbed through her apron that the young miss had told her to go off to bed long ago—had said she wouldn't need any help to undress. What a scene! One that might have been written by Mr. Sheridan, or William Shakespeare himself!

"Marie-Claire! Is she here?"

As a candle was held up to illuminate peering faces, it was Marie-Claire, this time, who pretended to mumble sleepily, while I, feeling like a jack-in-the-box, bolted upright again to contribute my playacting talents to this Gothic farce.

"Good heavens! Is anything wrong? Is there a *fire?* Ohh!" This last as I pulled the covers up to my neck with a properly dismayed show of maidenly modesty.

"It's Marie-Claire!" her stepmother said in a quivering voice. "I thought I heard something . . . someone on the staircase . . . Or perhaps it was a door closing? And when I looked she wasn't in her room! I . . ."

Under the covers, I'd kicked Marie-Claire to warn her

that it was her cue now, and with a smothered exclamation she propped herself up on one elbow to demand what on earth everyone was *doing*—for surely it wasn't morning yet!

After all the mutual explanations and apologies had been made and the door, like the curtain in a theater, had closed behind the rest of the cast, I turned wrathfully upon my reckless friend, only to find that she had burrowed herself, head and all, under the covers.

"Very well! You owe me an explanation, I think! And I hope you are thinking as well of the foolish, dangerous risks you are taking, and how much you stand to lose—especially now. Marie-Claire . . . really!"

"Oh . . . there you go, scolding at me again!" Marie-Claire mumbled sulkily in a muffled voice. "Didn't I tell you before how you are getting to sound exactly like Miss Charity? And I'm far too tired and sleepy now to explain anything, in any case. After all, *you've* done nothing but sleep since we arrived here, while I've had to be . . . on *exhibition*, smiling and being charming to my parents' dull friends and distant relatives I have not even *heard* of! I'll tell you tomorrow, I promise, if you'll just let me go to sleep now instead of being so . . . *prickly* about everything!"

"Prickly," she had called me. Was *that* how everybody else saw me too? Horrid, ugly word—with its even more detestable connotations. Making me bite back everything else I had been about to say.

I lay down again with my back rigid, as far away from Marie-Claire as the bed would allow. Prickly, was I? Vinegar-tongued . . . spinsterish, too blunt . . . We'd see!

I said aloud in a stiffly indifferent voice: "But you're right, of course; and what *you* choose to do is none of my affair, is it?"

After a short silence I heard Marie-Claire grumble: "Oh, very well then! There is no need to sound so *icy* . . . ! I'll tell you everything if you'll promise to let me sleep afterwards—with no more sermons? *Please?*"

For almost the first time since we had become friends, I found myself able to resist that coaxing, little-girl tone that had crept into her voice.

"Do go to sleep, since that is what you need! I don't want to know anything about your latest escapade now I've had

second thoughts—especially if he happens be one of the
footmen or a muscular young gardener! So spare me, do!"

"It *wasn't* a servant or anyone like that at all! And it
wasn't Fernando either—after I had made him all excited
by letting him kiss me *very* passionately and by leaning
against his body as if his passion had made me weak!" Marie-Claire gave a soft, amused chuckle before she whispered triumphantly, "No, my dearest Trista, the *he* that I
took such risks to . . . meet, shall we say? . . . He is . . .
But, since you are obviously not at all interested, why
should I tell you? I had probably better not, in any case,
since he . . . well, good night, then!"

Her blithe dismissal had me almost grinding my teeth
with frustration, although I silently vowed I'd never give
her the satisfaction of begging her to tell me who *he* was.

In any case, I was soon to discover that my strength of
will would probably not be tested after all; or so it appeared the following morning, when we were all summoned
together for breakfast and *planning*.

Madame la Comtesse Bertrand de Martineau, soon to be
privately referred to by all of us as "The Stepmother," had
everything in hand, she informed us. All she would require
was cooperation from all those concerned, and it would all
go off without a hitch. "Of course I have already whispered
to every one of my friends that this wedding is the culmi-
nation of a secret engagement of long standing . . . and it
would be as well if the *families* support what I have said?
Good! And now, to begin with the bride . . ."

Fittings every day! There was not only the bridal gown
to be considered but a going-away ensemble: clothes for
traveling in, for the daytime when one had to make calls
on all the right people, and for the evening. For formal dinner parties, levees, balls . . . "For of course you will need
an adequate and fashionable wardrobe, my dear, to serve
you until you are in Paris!"

Poor Marie-Claire! Innumerable fittings every morning
and a round of social calls to be paid in the afternoons before resting an hour or two in order to look fresh in the
evenings. I remember thinking, How I should *hate* to be
forced to suffer through such an ordeal, just to have what
they call a "fashionable wedding"!

Chapter 4 ❧

After that day I hardly saw Marie-Claire; and when we did encounter each other there was never any time for us to speak in private, or confide in each other as we used to do.

Papa, who liked neither turmoil nor bossy women, had accepted the loan for two weeks of a gracefully classical and magnificently furnished home not far outside the city, belonging to an old friend of his who called it, so Papa informed us, his "country cottage."

I missed the gaiety and excitement that Marie-Claire had always seemed to create for those around her, and I felt almost guilty at deserting her, as she once accused me of doing. But I loved the feeling of being in the country again—of being able to *ride* once more! This friend of Papa's obviously knew horseflesh, as I discovered when I visited the stables; and once I had made friends with them and had convinced the grooms that I was capable of controlling a frisky, spirited mount . . . why, I was allowed to have my pick of them and enjoyed exploring the countryside. In fact, there was even a prettily winding stream that meandered through the property; and on a few occasions, when I felt daring enough, I would tether my horse and play in the clear, mountain-cool water—pretending sometimes that I was a mermaid, or an Indian maiden who had bathed in this same stream very long ago, hoping that her chosen lover would surprise her.

Whenever I used to study myself in a mirror, clothed (and in my right mind, Aunt Charity would have added tartly), I could never like what I saw. My hair was too thick, far too unruly to tame with hairpins or combs or pretty ribbons. My face—well, I had grown used to my face; but why did my body not fill out to give me the voluptuous curves that all men seemed to admire so much? Ah, but I discovered the water a much kinder mirror! And when I had thrown aside all the layers of clothing beneath which I was forced to conceal my body . . . then, and only then, with my hair dripping wet and lying along my shoulders, touching my breasts, hanging heavily down my back . . . yes, only then did I *know,* and *believe,* that I was beautiful! My body might be slender, but I was naturally small-waisted and long-legged. My breasts could never be called *ample,* of course, but at least they were adequate! Will a man ever see me like this? Will I allow it? Would it feel very strange and different if a man were to touch my body in certain places? Languid half-thoughts under leaf-filtered sunlight. So much to *learn.* But for myself now, and not secondhand from someone else. Dare I?

How I always hated the time when I had to get dressed again and leave behind my secret fantasies! And there would not be many more times when I could come here and be transformed into a naked water nymph. How much I hated the thought and tried to avoid it! Especially when I had to return to the house early in order to change for dinner, or because we had been invited to visit our nearest neighbors for a musical evening.

I suppose that in looking back on those days, I tend to dwell almost deliberately on all the peaceful times and the small details that go to make up a quiet and uneventful existence. I didn't *want* anything to change, God knows; or to be changed myself either. I had been taught, both by the circumstances of my life and by Aunt Charity, to think and act rationally as well as reasonably. And yet . . . I had suddenly begun to wonder about that *other* side of my nature: the dark side that was ruled by passion and emotion. Worst of all, I had begun to become curious about the purely sensual feelings that could be evoked in the

body—in *my* body—for instance when I felt the cool stroking motion of running water between my parted thighs
and about my hips and breasts as I lay back in the shallow
part of the stream with my eyes closed against the brightness of the sun and did not *think*, nor want to; only *felt* and
did not question. Not then, at least.

I did not realize how those few free days I spent riding
hatless and astride under the sun, and then giving myself
up to the flowing water, must have changed me—and in
others' eyes as well. Papa did not seem to have noticed; but
then, he had been resting a lot in the afternoons and
seemed preoccupied with paperwork and in writing letters
when we were not occupied with the usual social obligations. I almost felt glad that Aunt Charity was not with us,
for she would never have allowed me as much freedom and
as much time as I had to myself during those days when
everyone else was busy with preparations for the wedding
and the traveling afterward.

"I'm afraid . . . well, there are so many things I have to
attend to before I can leave, you see, and just not enough
time. I have to be sure that Miss Graham knows exactly
how everything is to be managed while I am away . . . the
accounts, for instance. And you know I cannot abide smoke
and cinders! No—I shall need another week at least to set
everything in order; and then I plan to travel sensibly, by
coach, directly to my friend's home in Virginia. Of *course* I
would not dream of missing my nephew's wedding!"

Aunt Charity's speech had taken us all by surprise, coming as it did at almost the last moment during our preparations to leave Boston. I was probably the only person who
wondered if she had had any *other* reasons left unmen-
tioned for not wanting to leave right away . . . but then I
took myself sternly to task for being petty and small-
minded. If she *did* have her private reasons for wanting to
stay behind in Boston, they were certainly none of my
business—*whoever* her reasons might concern! *I*, certainly,
would much prefer to forget my encounter with that detestable, condescending man she had called Blaze, a certain note in her voice I had never heard before or since.

Were they lovers? Had they been for a long time? What
did it *feel* like to have a man make love to you? Marie-
Claire seemed to enjoy it. Perhaps I should have encour-

aged her to tell me more—to *teach* me more. I want to learn
. . . to know . . . or am I still too afraid to experience everything? Those were the strange thoughts that ran through
my head on that particularly hot afternoon I remember almost too well.

I had almost fallen asleep lying in the water—and almost drowned! Now, I knew I had to hurry back to the
house before someone was sent to look for me and I would
be in disgrace. I'd promised Papa that I'd be back early
enough to make sure that everything was just right before
our guests arrived, even though we both knew that the
well-trained staff would take care of all the arrangements
better than either of us could.

Still, I could not escape the feelings of guilt that assailed
me as I dressed myself hurriedly and wound my dripping-
wet hair up in a careless knot. I looked a fright, and this
time I did not need a mirror to tell me so. My skin had
turned from pale marble to olive-gold under the sun—
unfashionably dark, in fact; especially for *this* part of the
country! No doubt Marie-Claire would take me aside and
scold me for being so careless—just before her wedding,
too! And as for Madame la Comtesse, "The Stepmother"
. . . I was almost positive she would soon make sure that
everyone knew I was no more than a poor adopted relative
of dubious origin who had been taken in out of charity—
and certainly not to be considered as a *bridesmaid,* of all
things, even if dear Marie-Claire was as softhearted as she
was!

The scenes I had just imagined had me smiling for just a
few seconds—until I discovered that I had been deserted by
my horse and would have to *walk* back to the house. And as
if that weren't bad enough, there was my appearance,
which was even worse. I had dressed like a gypsy in a full,
patterned skirt and a peasant blouse that fell off one shoulder. It was so much cooler, I had told myself that morning,
and there was no one to criticize or lift eyebrows. In any
case, I had meant to return at least two hours earlier, well
before any guests might be expected to arrive. But there
was no point *now* in thinking of what my intentions had
been, was there? I must just hope for the best—and *run* as
fast as I could back to the house.

At that time I did not know as many swear words as I

have learned since—in at least five different languages. As it was, every time I tripped or caught my skirt in a bramble I would say, "Damn!" or, more daringly, "Hell!"—until I was out of breath.

Since I had always ridden back and forth to the stream, it had never seemed such a long way before. Now, when I was on foot, the distance seemed interminable, and I could easily have sat down and cried with frustration if I had dared let myself do so. I remember thinking that perhaps I should just sit down under some shady tree and wait to be rescued . . . for surely when my independent mount returned to the stables without *me* I would be searched for. But I didn't want that either. It would be too humiliating—not only for me, but for Papa as well. So I kept running—or stumbling forward, rather—while I heard each breath I took sound too much like a sob, and forced my legs to move even when I could no longer feel them.

I have always been stubborn, and even after I had stopped thinking of where I was going and why, my instincts alone, like those of an animal, must have taken me in the right direction, for I *would* go on and *had* to—although I had almost forgotten why. And then . . . I cannot remember now whether I tripped over something and fell or whether I lost consciousness from sheer lack of breath. I *do* remember, however, that when I came back to my senses it was only to feel that I had truly lost them, or was caught up in the throes of some frightening dream that was both real and unreal at the same time.

I could not seem to move. Perhaps I did not really *want* to move. Not my suddenly nerveless body from under the weight that straddled it, nor my open mouth from under that other mouth that covered mine and gave me back the power to breathe again on my own. At that point, thinking and reasoning had not yet returned and I was only half-awake and half-aware, and not all the way back from wherever I had been before. But what, or *when*, was before? And did I care, when there was *now* and I was only feeling instead of thinking? How did I know, without it being possible for me to know, who he was—this man who had given me his breath to help me find mine again?

Perhaps I had only imagined I had regained my senses—only to lose them again soon afterward. Perhaps . . . ah, why do I feel, even now, compelled to make excuses for my-self, and for what happened? There *are* no excuses to ex-plain my actions at that time—or my *yearnings* either.

I only know that I wanted something . . . something I knew nothing about and had never experienced before. And that I was without shame or embarrassment and un-able to fight any longer against whatever it was that drew me to this man and had drawn me to him against my will from the first time I had met him—and disliked him. *Him.* A man I knew nothing about except for his name—Blaze—which did not sound like a *real* name and was probably an alias. I didn't care! I suppose I was past thinking by then, past reason, gone beyond everything but feeling and de-sire.

When he knew that I was conscious again, he would have moved away to a safe distance, but I would not let him. Even now I do not know what demon possessed me and made me clasp my arms about his neck, pulling his mouth down to meet mine again. Not for the kiss—the breath—of *life* this time, but for something else that could mean death and destruction instead, although I didn't care at the moment about anything but the assuagement of a hunger I felt take control of all my senses, blinding me to everything else.

He could not have known that I had not kissed a man be-fore. Everything I did, every motion of my body as I arched it up against his, came from something, some primitive in-stinct beyond myself. That afternoon I was no sixteen-year-old girl; I was a woman—*female*—exulting in the feeling of power I had suddenly discovered I could wield. Perhaps I really *am* a witch, as I have been told many times. Or was I only bewitched myself? I remember that I felt as if we had kissed before, this stranger who was not a stranger and I. As if . . .

It had to happen. He and I, out there in the open with the green smell of crushed grass under my back and the blue-ness of the sky and the white-gold heat of the sun above us. I *wanted* it to happen, and with *him*. His eyes were the deep, dark ambered green of the swamp-water under the sun; his body was hard and strong and as lean as whipcord. I wanted, for some inexplicable reason, to see him naked—to have him see *me* naked too. I was *possessed*—

perhaps by the soul of some ancient Druid priestess. And how suddenly, and yet seemingly inevitably, this had happened!

We both spoke at different times, I remember—God, so clearly!—but said very few words. I remember more of the *feeling*. I suppose now that, while I lay naked in the water, letting it play with my body and my senses, I was getting ready for what happened that afternoon. And I recall . . . the feel of his lips over mine first, and then—everywhere on my body. On my temples, my earlobes; lingering on all the pulse spots along my neck, my throat, and down from there; but so very slowly . . .

His hands pushed my skirt up over my thighs and began another maddeningly slow exploration of my body from below, while his lips, and then his tongue, made my nipples so taut and so sensitive that I almost cried out aloud—and had to stop myself by taking in a deep breath that sounded too much like a sigh.

His head rose, and those infernal tiger's eyes narrowed as they searched mine, making me feel again as if I were drowning. In passion—in lust—in whatever it was that had driven us together that afternoon.

"You're bored?"

I almost hated him at that moment for making me articulate what I had been feeling—what I *felt*.

"No—damn you!"

"Well! At least you show some signs of being spirited. I had begun to wonder if your estimable Fernando had tamed you to the point of complete submission by now."

I hated the drawling, sarcastic tone of his voice, and the way in which he *looked* at me, lying all but naked under the length and weight of his body. How could he have made such tender love to me a few moments before and talk to me now as if I had been some cheap . . . *whore* he'd picked up off the streets? And yet . . . wasn't I acting like one? And then again, why had he made love to me . . . caressed me . . . deliberately excited my senses if he didn't desire me?

Trapped, I resorted to honesty—perhaps the most powerful weapon of all. And I was able to look unfalteringly back into his eyes as I answered him, too.

"You're the first man I have ever been with in . . . this

way. And I want you to *be* the first to . . ." And then, the
spiritedness of which he'd accused me rising up in me, I
added with what I hoped was an unconcerned shrug: "But
as you reminded me, there's always Fernando . . . in case
you do not feel up to the task of—"

As I had hoped and half expected, he cut off the rest of
my words with his kiss, this time harsh and demanding
like the feel of his hands on my body, and no longer tender.
I would have preferred the tenderness he had shown me
earlier, I suppose, but I was ready for him all the same. He
was fighting himself, and I wasn't.

"So you're a virgin who is impatient to learn? But you
know exactly the right goads to use, don't you? Or else,
God help us both, you're someone—some*thing*—too much
like myself!" The words he snarled at me came from between his teeth, but I had no time then to ponder on their
meaning before he began to strip me of what scanty garments I wore—and then to take his time in exploring every
part of my body with deliberately insolent slowness. I
think that he wanted, at first, to hurt and humiliate me because I had all but forced him into this. Into . . . *deflowering* me, in fact!

That *word!* Deflowering, indeed! Who could have in-
vented it? I must have laughed, or given vent to a nervous
chuckle at least, because suddenly I found myself jerked
up painfully into a sitting position by my hair.

"You find something amusing!" The voice was deceptively soft; the narrowed eyes and tightened muscles
alerted me to danger. He reminded me of a tiger, this man
Blaze: the golden greenness of his eyes, the movement of
muscle under skin revealed by his open shirt; just the way
in which he *looked* at me, forcing me to meet his uncompromising gaze with my hair still wrapped around his fist.

I blurted out, almost without thinking: "It was only because . . . well, because I suddenly thought that I was
about to be ... . deflowered! I couldn't help it . . . I have
never understood why . . . the expression . . ."

"Why, you little . . ." And then I saw the smile crinkles
deepen at the corners of his eyes and mouth before he released me, but only long enough to make sure I was lying
on my back again, with him kneeling between my parted
thighs.

"Are you sure, Trista?" And now he was no longer smiling. "For God's sake! I have to keep reminding myself that you're . . ."

I reached out and touched him—tentatively at first, and then, as I felt the swelling hardness under my hand, more boldly, more surely, when I heard his quickened, indrawn breath.

"Now—am I still a child? I had finished his sentence for him, and he displayed no surprise that I had done so—only looked down at me consideringly while his fingers resumed at last their magical stroking of my body. For a few moments only—long enough to drive me half-wild with wanting before he stood up to rid himself of the encumbrance of his clothes.

He did not ask me after that whether I was sure or not . . . or anything else, for that matter. He made me no false promises, told me no smiling lies. Only took me after that as I wanted to be taken for the first time—with touches and exploring fingers and with surprising tenderness.

It did not hurt as much as I had expected, this deflowering. A short, stabbing pain that made me gasp, and then it was over; but right afterward he began to move more slowly and more deliberately inside me—touching me, caressing me all the while until I felt something . . . a kind of gathering and spiraling upward of a myriad different sensations all swirling together and pushing outward and inward at the same time until I felt myself burst into a million pieces—hearing myself cry out at the same time with a primitive woman-cry of joy and fulfillment while my arms clasped his body fiercely and even more closely against mine.

Chapter 5 ⁊

I remember feeling as if I had been pierced and shot through by the sheer force of my emotions after it was all over. I had *wanted* this to happen—I had let myself be carried away by the wild, primeval side of my nature. *I* had been the one to choose the man who would make me a whole woman. So why then, after it was all over, did I have to keep on clinging to him while I wept like an abandoned child against his shoulder?

"Did I hurt you? Trista . . . sweeting . . ." His use of that old-fashioned word I had only read before made me sob all the louder and cling all the harder. Why did he have to be *nice* to me, even after he had had me? Why did I feel as if everything had gone awry and I was a stranger in strange territory where every step I took might lead me deeper and even further into the swamp—the uncharted places of the heart and the mind?

I knew he was the man who was meant to have me first. I knew that this was the time and the place for it . . . with the bloody proof of my virginity already lost in the grass-grown earth I lay on. It was over—it was done with; and *I* had been the one to decide when, and with whom. Why, then, did I sniffle and sob instead of feeling triumphant and even stronger within myself? He should have raped me instead of making love to me. He should not have known without being told exactly how and where I was most sensitive, most vulnerable. Fernando should have been the one—and then I would not *feel* as I did now.

"Trista—Trista?" He wove from my name both a statement and a question; and it was only when he caught me by my bare shoulders and shook me back into reality that I was able to push away (for the moment, at least) the dangerous emotions that threatened to overwhelm me . . . *drown* me if I didn't retrieve myself.

"It . . . it's nothing, after all! Is it? You don't have to worry, because it had to happen sometime . . . and now . . . now I feel . . ."

Why did he have to *look* at me that way, his hands dropping from my shoulders and his eyes piercing me like green-flamed daggers? "Yes?" he drawled in an infuriatingly indifferent voice that was quite at odds with the tone I had detected in it earlier. "And how *do* you feel now, little ex-virgin witch? Disappointed that the earth didn't shake or a magic carpet appear to whisk you off into rainbow-land?"

My sense of euphoria disappeared as my earlier dislike for him returned, and I tilted my chin at him with as much arrogance as I could muster, trying to keep my voice as unconcerned as his had been. "I expected nothing of the kind—naturally! I was just tired of not having experienced anything, that's all! And I must admit that this has been a most interesting experiment! I wonder what the next one will be like?"

I had gone too far in my goading of him; I knew it while I was speaking, and yet I could not seem to stop myself. I wonder now . . . did I deliberately set out to seek some reaction?

I cannot cower behind excuses. I deserve the blame for what happened next. And, God knows, perhaps I *wanted* it, too, for some perverse reason. I learned, at least, not to play little-girls' games with grown men, although to begin with I thought I had managed to get away with my jauntily delivered speech, after all—and wondered why I felt slightly disappointed at such an easy triumph.

I remember reaching for my hastily discarded garments, and then . . . then I was to learn that there was another side to the man who had made love to me only some moments ago. A side that was as hard and unyielding as his tense-jawed, tight-lipped face when he seized my wrist, twisting it and me around so that I was forced to my knees with a cry of pain I could not bite back.

Instinctively, I brought up my free hand to claw at his dark, enigmatic face, only to find myself held captive and almost paralyzed by the strength of his fingers gripping both of my wrists now. "You . . . you . . . ! Let me *go,* damn you! You're . . . hurting me!"

"Am I?" The sudden force he used to fling me around as if I was nothing more than a rag doll belied the casually offhand tone of his voice. I found myself lying facedown on the grass with my wrists held uncomfortably pinioned behind my back; and in fact, when I attempted to struggle, I thought for a moment that both my arms would be broken—and they would have been, I'm sure, if I had continued to resist.

When I had ceased my useless struggles and simply *lay* there, my whole body burning with humiliation and frustrated rage, my breath coming in short, sobbing gasps, I felt the heat of his body behind me as he casually nudged my thighs apart—still holding my wrists in a cruelly painful grasp.

Without a word at first, he began to caress me with one hand, his hold on my wrists warning me not to resist.

"So you enjoy experimenting, Trista? Better learn, then, that there is another side to sexuality, and to a man's nature; especially when he's been teased, and aroused, and challenged." His fingers probed deeply inside me—searching, exploring, *moving;* and in spite of my efforts I could not help moaning—both with humiliation and with some other shameful emotion that seemed to grow and expand, ring upon ring, like ripples in a pool after a pebble has been flung in its center. I knew that he meant to punish me for what I had said, and to degrade me—making me *feel* degraded—and yet there was something almost diabolical in the way he was doing this, forcing a reaction from me against my will.

I was sobbing, squirming, begging him in a voice that did not seem to belong to me to stop—please—and yet there was a demon inside myself that did not *want* him to stop, that wanted everything he was doing to me and making me feel.

"Get up on your knees, Trista. You've made me want you again. Quickly now!"

"No—damn you, no! You cannot make me—" I broke off, biting my lower lip, as he simply jerked me up into the position he desired. A stinging slap across my bottom warned me that I had better comply with his demands.

"There are some women, I've found, who enjoy being spanked. Do you?" When I could not answer such a lewd question, I was jerked back unpleasantly to awareness of my plight by another smack on my derriere, this one a trifle more purposeful than before. I felt as if I was in the clutches of a madman—and it was all my fault. I'd *asked* for this. I'd even thought I *wanted* this man-turned-into-monster! I knew I had read somewhere that it was safest not to attempt arguing with a maniac; nevertheless, I could not refrain from commenting bitterly:

"And *you* have shown me that there are men who enjoy striking helpless females!" It was all I could do to stop myself from weeping tears of sheer humiliation at being forced to endure such degradation, being alternately spanked like a naughty child or—as he had begun to do now—being played with in the most intimate and familiar fashion, as if I'd been some . . . harlot!

Instead of responding to my taunt, the monster merely chuckled, his long fingers alternately touching and probing within me until I began to writhe and cry out in an agony of frustration; but his implacable grip on my bruised, aching wrists only tightened, pushing me down until my face was being pressed against the scratchy grass that irritated my already sore nipples as well. How *could* he use me this way, force me to kneel and—exhibit myself to him—be subject to the casual inspection of his devilish fingers that continued to probe into me everywhere—*touch* me in certain ways and in certain places until I felt I could no longer stand it and sobbingly begged him in a hoarse voice that did not seem to belong to me: *"Please—*oh please, *please,* no more—no . . ." And then the length and the hardness of him rammed deeply, deeply into me without warning, and I cried out against the damp grass while his hand under me and his fingers *in* me lifted me to meet his every long thrust.

"Is this pleasure for you too, my lovely little wanton

with the golden skin? Do you know what pleasure it gives me to sheathe myself in you while I feel and watch you quiver? Is this as good for you as it is for me?"

Like Lucifer himself, he whispered in my ear, using words I had never heard before while he moved, and moved and moved on me and in me, *sheathing* himself, he had said, inside me while his fingers touched me on my tiny, hidden mound until I could not *think* any longer but could only give myself up to the madness, the pure lust that boiled in us both like molten lava, like a forest fire, like . . . "Blaze—Blaze!" I cried out, not even realizing I had done so as he took me to peak after peak after peak until I could no longer contain myself and felt myself soar so high I dissolved into a thousand shimmery light-crystals.

How could a man change so quickly from tenderness to brutality and back again to tenderness? When I had returned to earth from whatever sphere I had floated to before, with my body still quivering with the aftermath of passion, it was to realize that I was being cradled against his body and stroked gently while his lips first nuzzled at the nape of my neck and then traveled up teasingly to pull lightly on my earlobe.

"Come, sweeting," he murmured huskily, coaxingly. "It wasn't all that bad, was it? I'm sorry if I lost my temper and acted harshly a while ago, but you must admit you're a mighty provocative little baggage, to say the least! Say you'll forgive me for losing my head over your undeniably charming little . . . uh . . . body? I should like to paint you sometime. If you'll let me, that is. Like this . . ." And his fingertips traced the outline of my body with tiny, tender brushstrokes that made me quiver again in spite of myself.

I did not know what to make of this man! Was he playing with me again? Were the words he whispered in my ear meant to be ironic—or not?" All I knew was that I was not yet ready to turn my head and *face* him—not quite yet. For else I would certainly have torn myself from his . . . his vile *clutches,* dressed myself, and . . . And then the jarring realization struck me that I would be expected back at the house to greet our guests, and instead I was still lying out here in the open, naked and brazen and held fast in the arms of the man who had just taken my virginity and taken *me* as well—several times!

Madness! That's what it had to have been. Sunstroke . . . yes, that's what must have addled my senses, made me delirious. Supposing someone had been dispatched to look for me when my horse returned riderless? Oh God, what was I doing here with a stranger, a man I had thought of as a maniac only a few minutes ago? And what had he meant by saying . . . No! I couldn't remain here, with his fingers brushing as lightly as feathers over my breasts, my belly, my thighs . . . I did not know that I'd had my eyes tightly closed until I forced them open, meeting the sun and being almost blinded by it.

"No!" I burst out, almost desperately. "No, *don't* . . . can't you *understand?* They'll be looking for me—Papa, the servants . . . *please* let me go!" There was no need, in the end, for me to struggle to get free. He surprised me by releasing me immediately with a short, ugly-sounding laugh that made me pause in the act of scrambling to my feet to look over my shoulder at him almost fearfully; to find that I could discern only indifference on those dark, sardonic features and in the hard green-gold eyes that flickered over me casually.

Catching my almost startled look, he cocked one eyebrow at me before drawling in an almost *bored* fashion: "Well? Changed your mind? Or are you still afraid that stepbrother Fernando might discover his carefully nurtured little maiden is no longer a maid? Do make up your mind, sweetheart!"

"Ohh!" I gasped out angrily, and had whirled to run from him and his barbed words when I found myself seized about the ankle, so that I was falling headlong in an ignominious sprawl of bare limbs—and having most of the breath knocked out of my body as well. When I was able to speak again, I was so furious that all I could do at first was sputter.

"Why . . . you . . . ho-how *dare* . . . I *hate* you! I'd . . . I'd like to . . . to . . ."

"Why don't you shut up?" It was said in a casual, matter-of-fact kind of tone; and before I could give vent to any of the angry words that jostled about in my mind, he made *quite* sure of my keeping silent by positively jamming his mouth down over mine and kissing me, hard and almost hurtfully—and, the devil take him, *purposefully*—

until I was breathless again. I remember thinking despairingly, What does he want with me? Why is he doing this to me? I remembered suddenly an old ballad poem I had once come across, "The Demon Lover," and I could not prevent the shudder that went through me. Dear Lord, was the demon I should fear most my own lust or the man who had aroused it in me? What would come of my own act of folly? And yet, even while all these thoughts skittered nervously through my mind, I could feel the response of my flesh and my senses and the burning of my skin as I pressed myself, kneeling now facing him, against the hardness and *differentness* of his man's body. I clung to him (I told myself almost desperately) only in order to keep my balance while he kissed me so fiercely, pulling my head back with fingers tangled in my hair until I felt my neck might snap if I did not give in.

Give in . . . Was what I was doing really giving in, or was it *greed?* Greed for more . . . to feel at least once more the sensation that built up to such unutterable delight that I felt as if I were flying out of myself. I heard myself moan deep in my throat, like an animal. I *felt* like one then, as I began touching him as he was touching me— eagerly, hungrily. I felt, oddly, as if things I had once known (and could not possibly have known, of course) had surged to the surface of my consciousness, so that suddenly I knew where and in what fashion to caress him. Now I touched him, held him, moved my hand on him boldly, exulting in the reaction I could feel. I wanted to *look*, to watch as well as feel . . . and I felt caught in a daze, a time-stopped trance; or held in the center of an enchanted circle that kept out everyone and everything else—including reality.

"You learn fast, don't you? Or perhaps you've been practicing?" He'd raised his mouth from mine to almost *snarl* the words at me; but before my bruised lips could form an answer, he had already caught me about the hips, lifting me onto him and lying back in the same fluid motion, and catching me off guard. I looked down at his darkly unreadable face with, I'm ashamed to say, my mouth hanging open with shock. "Since you lost your mount earlier, and *I* have already mounted *you* . . . may I offer myself? Or haven't you practiced *this* kind of riding yet, sweet wanton?"

I felt impaled as he impatiently began to move me over him by the hips. "I will *not* . . . !" I began, my voice rising with pure fury and my fingers all claws as they reached for his eyes. But he caught my wrists with an unbelievably swift motion and held me pinioned for what seemed an endless moment while our eyes met and clashed in a silent battle. And then he pulled me down to him, spreading his arms as wide as mine could reach on either side; and we continued to look into each other's eyes—but this time almost consideringly.

I shall never know what went through *his* mind during those few seconds, and I will never tell him what went through mine. There are certain thoughts and feelings, as I know now, that do not need to be enunciated—are only communicated. All my righteous anger seemed to drain out of me in a sudden rush as I understood some little, minuscule part of the complex puzzle he was, and realized painfully the dark deepness and vastness of the depths of his self that I did not—and might never, perhaps—fathom.

How he continued to surprise and . . . unbalance me! All of a sudden, with his eyes still locked together with mine, he brought my wrists against his lips and kissed each bruise, each spot that throbbed painfully, with infinite tenderness while he murmured against them: "Oh God . . . poor little Trista! Poor, eager young novice! Someone should have warned you against recklessness . . . and against wicked and unscrupulous ogres such as I am! You see what the consequences are? You have been ravished, raped, and mistreated—all in one single afternoon; and I think you are about to be ravished yet again. Damn, but you're so tight and so silky feeling! And you know far too much about teasing a man for a virgin of less than two hours ago. You're . . ."

I was exultant with a sense of power when I heard his sudden, sharply indrawn breath as I moved slowly and almost languorously over him—teasing him by pausing for an infinitesimal moment before I lowered my hips to take him deep, deep within myself again. And on my own, I leaned down to him to rub my nipples against his chest, feeling the tightening inside myself that held him all the closer. My parted lips hovered provocatively over his frowning look until his arms dragged me down roughly to meet his stabbing tongue while our bodies suddenly discovered a rhythm of their own—a rising and falling like the sea, thrust and counterthrust—becoming damp and slippery with sweat as we became two ocean waves that meld together and build up and up to unbelievable heights before cresting, poising before smashing down against the shore in a violently shattering white-foamed explosion of fury and wildly windblown spume.

Then, limp and spent, I collapsed against his body, feeling his pounding heartbeat which matched my own. I did not want to think or wonder about consequences yet. I did not *care* . . . not yet! And I was not ready to bestir myself quite yet either. Why couldn't I continue to lie as I was, with my lover's arm across my back still bonding my body to his, and his shoulder pillowing my head?

I could not, of course—and I knew it and he knew it. I had already stretched my borrowed time to beyond the breaking point; and if someone should discover us here, like *this* . . . then what? Would there be a duel—or a murder? Perhaps he would offer to *marry* me to make amends— although I would most certainly turn him down no matter what anybody said! I could never endure living with the uncertainty of his changing moods and his arrogant attitude—not to mention his dangerously volatile temper and his insistence on having his own way without regard for *my* feelings.

"No!" I said aloud, and looked into lazy-lidded amber-green eyes that narrowed contemplatively as they studied my frowning face.

"No? I'm afraid I can't seem to recall asking a question! But . . . as delightful as it's been, I'm afraid . . ." Sitting up abruptly, he lifted me to my feet as he rose, his body uncoiling as easily as that of a great cat—or a cobra rearing to strike. For an instant his eyes looked into mine with, I thought, almost a regretful look; and then, tilting my chin up with his fingers, he brushed a light and far-from-loverlike kiss across my lips. "Be more careful in your choice of men next time, Trista. You might arouse some wild beast that could devour you whole—or destroy you." And then he turned away from me to find his clothes and put them on—leaving me no alternative but to bite my lip sullenly and follow suit.

Chapter 6 ❧

Too much exposure to the hot afternoon sun for a young lady's naturally delicate constitution. And to go bareheaded, without the protection of a hat—that had been very foolish indeed, to say the least, for people had been known to die from sunstroke! So the hastily summoned Doctor Wise had told me sternly in a ponderous kind of voice I detested. How unendurable life with him must be for his poor wife and daughters who would *never* (he also informed me frowningly) have entertained even the *thought* of going riding unaccompanied by a groom.

I am ashamed to admit that I made a childish grimace at his frock-coated back when he turned away to write some instructions for my "treatment"—and was caught doing so by one of the maids, who was forced, poor thing, to hide her giggles by going into a paroxysm of coughing, for which ailment the good doctor promptly wrote out another prescription!

Finally, *thankfully*, I was left alone at last to "get some sleep" in my darkened room. I hated dark, airless rooms even then; and if I didn't know I would be caught out, I would have flung open all those heavy shutters and drapes myself. And oh, if only I *could* have slept after all and shut out all the dark, angry, *confused* thoughts and thought-pictures that kept flashing into my mind!

Blaze . . . no, I didn't want to think about *that* part of it

49

yet. Perhaps I really *had* been suffering from sunstroke after all, which had brought on a temporary derangement of
my senses. Why, at the time when I opened my eyes into
his, I had not even thought to ask what strange coinci-
dence (or *mischance*) had brought him there—to that particular place of all places. I had simply accepted the fact
that he was *there,* just as if . . . No! I told myself crossly.
Foreordained—there is no such thing except in ancient
myths! And perhaps I had been devouring too many of
those musty old calfskin-bound volumes on Norse and
Greek mythology I had discovered on one of the very top
shelves in the library. What had I expected? Zeus himself
in a shower of gold light? Apollo? I had found Hades—
Pluto, the dark god of the underworld, instead, like foolish
Persephone!

It had been *his* idea to tell everyone I had been accidentally thrown from my horse and had begun to walk back to
the house when I started to feel dizzy. . . .

"And then you must have fainted. Women always faint
very conveniently, I've noticed—or have attacks of the
vapors, whatever the hell *that* means!"

"I won't say anything of the kind! I've never been
thrown from a horse yet, and I *never* faint—or indulge in
vapors either!"

"Really? Well, I suppose there is a first time for everything, my dear, and you will be able to count having *three*
such experiences during the same afternoon, then, won't
you?"

How I longed, at that moment, to be able to slap his
dark, sardonic face as hard as I could for saying what he
had! But unfortunately that was almost impossible, since I
was at that moment riding *his* horse, and almost *forced* to
lean far too closely against his chest. But what a low, vile
brute he was all the same, and I should never have—

He interrupted my black thoughts by drawling
smoothly: "Of course, if you can think of a better story to
account for your rather . . . well . . . disheveled, shall we
say, appearance, not to mention the rips and grass stains
on your gown . . . ?"

My gown was a crushed and crumpled mess, of course,
and my hair would not stay pinned but kept slipping down
in unruly strands—in fact, I did not *want* to wonder what I

must look like. He was right, I was forced to concede, gritting my teeth; but why did he have to be?

Blaze Davenant. *Afterward,* as he assisted me politely and distantly to where his horse was tethered in a grove of trees, he finally deigned to tell me his full name. "At your service always, of course, Miss . . . er . . . Windham, is it?"

I know he was warning me subtly that we were not supposed to have met before today, but I was *not* as stupid as that; and besides, the sudden, exaggerated formality of his manner had begun to grate infuriatingly upon my nerves. And how was it that his words—even his very *presence*— could affect me so strongly?

I remember trying to cover my strange jumble of emotions by demanding rather ungraciously: "And how, pray, will you explain your trespassing on this property when you take me home? Why *are* you here at all?" No sooner had I spoken than I suddenly thought of Aunt Charity— and wondered if he had thought to find *her* here. A sharp pang shot through me for an instant; I did not know if it was from jealousy or guilt.

Of course! I thought, tossing restlessly about in bed in that too-hot room. I should have guessed that he would be armed with a perfectly legitimate excuse for his presence here, no matter what his real reason for turning up might be. If only I had never met him before . . . had not encountered him as I did this afternoon! "You were running like a wild thing," he'd said. Why did I have to wonder, suddenly, if perhaps some deeply primitive instinct had sent me running headlong to find *him?*

He's here now, in this house, I thought. Downstairs with Papa. Showing Papa some of the sketches he'd made that morning. Blaze, of all people—an *artist?* "Even if you do get away with saying that you are an acquaintance of these friends of Papa who own this property, you will never get away with *that* part of your story!" I remember snapping at him. "You don't look in the *least* like . . . like someone who has the sensitivity or the talent for anything artistic, you know! You're more like—like one of those Moorish corsairs who pillaged and sacked half the seaports of Europe!"

The last thing I had expected was that he would laugh— with what sounded like genuine amusement.

"And did your history books also tell you that these Moorish corsairs would also carry off the prettiest girls from those cities they—pillaged and sacked, did you say?" And then, while my shoulders were still rigid with indignation, I heard him add with a completely different note in his voice: "Perhaps—if it's true that all of us have lived before in different times and different places—then *that* is how we met for the very first time. And I'm sure, if we had, that I would have ravished you a countless number of times, and in every conceivable fashion—until I tired of you, of course!"

He had almost made me feel as if I were in some kind of a trance until that last offhanded statement jerked me back to unpleasant reality. "You really *are* quite despicable!" I said with as much coldness as I could muster, while I tried to forget the fact of his too-close body and the brush of his arms against my breasts.

"Of course I am, my dearest Miss Windham! But I think you knew *that* already, didn't you? And yet . . . you offer your virgin body and your untried passions to *me,* of all the men you might have chosen? For God's sake, you little idiot—*why?* And what in hell will you do if you should become pregnant? Or if you should get married to a man who'd expect a virgin bride? Either you should have been kept locked up at night and followed by a *dueña* all day, or you should have had the sense to choose someone more chivalrous than I am—the kind of *gentleman* who would have patted you gently on the shoulder and told you that you were obviously not yourself, and that you could trust him of course not to take advantage of a lady!"

"Don't . . . don't!" If it was possible, I would have clapped my hands over his mouth to stop him from saying what he was saying. Why—*why?* And how could any one man be so changeable from one moment to another? "There's no need to *remind* me of . . . of . . ." Dragging in a deep breath, I was able to continue in a more even tone of voice: "In any case, the possible consequences to me could hardly be of any concern to you, I should think, since . . . since as you have reminded me again, you are . . . the kind of person you are! I'd rather not talk about it—about anything that happened between us—if you please?"

I thought I heard *him* suck his breath in too, and then he

said with a return to expressionless formality: "I beg your pardon, Miss Windham. You're quite right, of course; and I can assure you that I will not be so presumptuous again." And then, when I was still silent: "You're not too uncomfortable, I hope? We are almost in sight of the house now."

"Have you *really* been here before?" I couldn't prevent myself from asking, and then added quickly, for the sake of keeping up a normal kind of conversation before we reached the house, "We are supposed to have several guests for dinner tonight, but I'm sure Papa will want you to have a glass of sherry with him, at least. . . ."

"Oh, but I'm supposed to be staying for dinner. Didn't you draw up a guest list? I'm a distant cousin, several times removed or something of the sort, of the Comtesse—who is, I believe, your girlfriend's stepmother? In any case, I had called on them in Washington and I believe *she* arranged that I should be invited. Quite a formidable lady, my cousin Cornelia, don't you agree?"

To say that I was shocked is an understatement. I was closer to being *stunned* by this perfunctorily delivered piece of information. This man—an abolitionist, a courier for what was becoming informally referred to as the Underground Railroad—how could such a thing be possible? Unless Blaze Davenant was another man's identity that he had assumed. . . . Unless . . .

"But . . . but The Stepmother's family is from South Carolina!" I cried out accusingly, this time risking both life and limb to twist around far enough to see his expression. "Why, they own *slaves,* and so do all their friends, while *you* . . ."

"Careful!" I had nearly slipped from the saddle and his arms tightened about me, almost cutting off my breath. "You're one of the most reckless . . . Sit *still,* dammit! I thought you said you were a horsewoman!"

"But I don't understand! How *could* you be . . . ?"

"There isn't enough time for lengthy explanations, I'm afraid, Miss Windham." His voice was dry. "Especially with a search party almost upon us . . . Ham and Rex, I think. But I can tell you this much, I suppose, since you would find out soon enough! My family *is* from the South. On my father's side, that is. And any Southern lady can prove that most of us are related in some way or other.

Rather incestuous, I've always thought! But I—I don't believe in anybody owning *anyone*, Trista. And that's all I'm
going to tell you."

That last, flatly uttered statement cut me off; and then
two of the grooms rode up to us, looks of relief spreading
over their faces when they saw me, and they recognized,
obviously, my so-called rescuer.

"Mr. Blaze! Welcome back! And you, miss—your pa's
been gettin' mighty worried . . . although I didn't tell him
for long as I could 'bout your horse coming back without
you."

I thought Ham's eyes avoided mine, and I could not help
the flush that heated my face. He'd probably come out to
search for me himself and had seen . . . Oh God—seen
what?

"Didn't 'spect to see you back so soon, Mister Blaze. We
all thought . . ."

"What you thinkin' 'bout, Rex, keepin' Mr. Blaze and
the young miss out here talkin' when they're been looked
for back at the house?"

There was no more conversation as I recall. Blaze Davenant, a distant stranger I had just met, took me back to the
refreshing coolness of the house and obligingly made all
my explanations for me to poor Papa, who looked really
worried and upset.

Thank goodness none of the other dinner guests had arrived in time to comment on my bedraggled appearance!
That, I supposed, was the only thing I could be thankful
for. Had they arrived yet? The Stepmother—how could
Blaze be related to a woman like that? No doubt she'd put
up her long nose and join that pompous Doctor Wise in disapproving of my riding out unescorted. And Fernando—no,
I had enough to think about already, my thoughts circling
about like buzzing flies in my head. I was hot, the closed
room made me feel stifled, and my whole body, every part
of it, had begun to ache as well. *My* fault, of course, as he
had reminded me caustically. I had *offered* myself up to
him—and being the unprincipled ruffian he was, he had
not hesitated to take me and to *use* me.

"I would have ravished you a countless number of times,
and in every conceivable fashion. . . ." Why did I have to
remember even the deepening harshness of his voice when

he had said that to me? And now that I had been deflowered *and* ravished . . . had he tired of me already?

You're a fool, a stupid fool! an inner voice kept repeating in my tired mind. *He'd* said so too. Had reminded me pitilessly of *consequences.* All to me. He, of course, had no conscience, as he had clearly demonstrated. I got up and walked over to the dresser, where the doctor had left the dark brown bottle labeled "Laudanum. Two drops as needed to be taken in a medicine glass of water or weak tea." Well, water would have to do! Two drops—there! And now perhaps I could sleep as I had been instructed to do, and not have to keep on *thinking* over and over of what had happened and could never be changed or forgotten.

Chapter 7 ⁊

I was dreaming the tiger-dream again, and I was running, panting, terrified because it was night and I could only see the gold streaks on that sleek-muscled skin while the tiger, the beast, kept up with me—green eyes glowing luminously in the living, breathing darkness that surrounded me and pressed in upon me until I thought, despairingly: Why does he not take me now and have it over with? And I felt myself falling, whirling through space and emptiness shot through with streaks and needle-stabs of light until suddenly I was face-to-face with him—the "Tyger burning bright" of Blake's poem; and I was suddenly meshed with my tiger, and knew suddenly that I had already been taken and devoured and absorbed into him so that at last we were one—I and the tiger . . . together in one skin . . . . "I shall always be yours, and you will always be mine. And if we lose each other we will always find each other again, for we can change without changing and yet remain One." Unuttered words in minds that moved together, wove together, *became.* And I knew I had always been the tiger—and he, me.

I woke up in a bath of sweat, shaking and nauseated. I had always known, I suppose, that sometimes I *knew* things—although I soon learned not to tell anyone when "certain pictures," as I used to call them when I was younger, came to me. No one really wants to know the future, after all! They are more afraid of what will be than of what might be—and how in any case could a child ever explain such things? They started called me a *bruja*, a witch, and crossing themselves when they saw me; and I soon refrained from speaking about any of my dreams, even when I was asked by the few people who dared to be curious. Was *I* curious enough to want to know what this particular dream meant for me . . . or did I already know?

After some time the nausea and the shivering went away, as they always did . . . and I realized only then that I had kicked off all my covers and lay curled up into myself, with my forehead pressed against my knees. No more opium drops—never again! Straightening my cramped limbs, I stretched every muscle in my body, taking a deep breath as I did so. And then I got out of bed and went to the windows, drawing back the heavy curtains and throwing open slatted wooden shutters before I opened the windows themselves and let in the cool night air with all its sounds and fragrances. Kneeling on the padded window seat and looking down, I could see the orange swaths of light that spilled out onto the green lawns from the rooms downstairs; and I heard a clock chime the hour and realized with a shock that it was quite early yet. How long did it take to dream a dream? Or had I myself created this particular dream?

"What on *earth* are you doing perched up on that windowsill with the shutters all open? Of course I knew you couldn't possibly be as ill as they said you were; you are never ill!"

"Marie-Claire!"

"I am sorry I didn't knock first, but I had to see you! I cannot really talk to anybody else, as you well know—and there is so *much* I must tell you! Why didn't you come down for dinner? I can't imagine *you* getting sunstroke . . . or being thrown from a horse either! Was it Fernando you didn't want to face?"

Lighting lamps, grimacing at the array of medicines on my dresser, Marie-Claire was like a whirlwind, hardly giving me time to answer one question before she asked me another. Used to her volatile ways, I stayed where I was on my window seat, watching her move restlessly about—a gorgeous butterfly in her swishing taffeta gown.

"Well?" Marie-Claire demanded finally, when she had rearranged everything in the room to her satisfaction. "You don't *look* very ill, I must say! What have you been doing with yourself while you've been stuck out here in the country? And aren't you anxious to hear what *I* have been up to?"

I would much rather hear about *her* adventures than continue to dwell on my crazed moments of folly, I thought, and shrugged my shoulders. "Of course! But you know you've hardly given me an opportunity to—"

"I know—I know! But you know what I'm like by now, don't you? I can't help the way I am; and you don't understand *feeling* yet! Don't you want to find out? Is it because you're afraid?"

"You are talking so fast that I cannot understand half of what you are saying! And what should I be afraid of? *You* are the one who should be cautious, I think! That night . . ."

"Yes . . . that night! It was wonderful, and I enjoyed the danger. And *tonight* . . . ! That's why I had to make sure you were not *really* ill, you know. And I'll forgive you for not joining us for dinner if you'll keep your door unlocked—just in case!" Marie-Claire, her eyes shining with mischief, gave me a sly look before she added: "But if you can keep Fernando occupied . . ." Catching my look, she giggled. "Did you really think I'd *mind?* Of course I don't— and you were silly not to encourage him that night I sent him down to find you in the library!"

"Stop!" I had almost put my hands up against my ears. "Marie-Claire, I don't know what you're talking about— and I look on Fernando as a *brother,* for . . ."

"He doesn't feel that way! Do you think I haven't noticed the way he looks at you? Or you at him? Anyway, it doesn't matter, and *I* won't mind as long as I can start really doing as I please—although I *will* be very careful about not making a scandal, of course. So . . . please, Trista . . . you are my only *real* friend, as you know, and the only female of my acquaintance who isn't jealous of me. I can *trust* you— and you *will* help, won't you?" Lowering her voice belatedly, Marie-Claire came as close to me as her crinolined skirts would allow; and I could smell the perfume of violets that matched the color of her lace-trimmed gown.

"Please, Trista," she wheedled as she had done so many times before. "He's actually *here,* and under the same roof, and who knows when we shall next see each other before I am married and must go away on my honeymoon?"

"Must go away?" I felt goaded, somehow, and my head had begun to ache. "On the last occasion we talked about your honeymoon, you said you did not wish to return here from Europe. If you have finally encountered a man that you really want, why don't you marry *him* instead?"

"You could never understand," Marie-Claire pronounced dramatically before she added: "But you will help? Say you will, do! And I'll go down and inform them all that I woke you and you're feeling very much better—I can *tell* you are. And I promise that I will explain everything just as soon as ever I can; and—"

"No!" I said uncompromisingly, and met her shocked, widening gaze without flinching. "If I don't know from the beginning what I am supposed to be involved in, and understand why, then I refuse to become entangled in the dangerous kind of intrigue you're thinking of. Why can't you change your mind? You don't *have* to marry Fernando; you can choose—"

"I *can?* You don't know anything, do you? Ah—you are so naive! You see nothing—understand nothing that is not between the covers of one of your silly books! Well, life is not always like books—and I learned that a long time ago! I enjoy what I want to enjoy—you understand?—because I do what I have to do. Like my papa, I suppose . . . He has a title but no money, so what else is there for him to do but marry a rich woman? One has to be *practical,* after all— and I have no desire to live a pauper's existence! Life is like a marketplace: Those who bargain shrewdly make off with the profits; and as for the rest . . ." Marie-Claire's shoulders lifted in an impatient shrug, while she looked at me almost defiantly. "Well? Will you help me or not? Tell me *now!*"

For the first time since we had known each other and become friends she had been bluntly honest with me, I thought, meeting her glittering blue eyes. "I'll help—as you probably know already. But is he *worth* the risks you are running, whoever this man is? *He,* at least, should know better than to jeopardize your whole future . . . whoever he is!"

"You haven't guessed? But of course—that night you were sleeping as soundly as a baby, weren't you? Overtired . . ." Marie-Claire gave a brittle laugh that sounded like that of a stranger. "And thank goodness you were in your bed where you were supposed to be, or . . . who knows what might have happened? In any case, perhaps I might not have cared! How should I know? I want him . . . and I mean to keep him even after Fernando and I are married. I suppose I should be thankful that my future husband thinks my lover is no more than an effeminate weakling who writes poetry and draws pictures and prefers the company of men to that of women! It leaves us room—"

"Draws pictures?" my voice said from somewhere outside of myself. "And do I happen to know this paragon?"

Even when I asked the question, I already knew the answer to it, even before Marie-Claire said, with a bubble of laughter underlying her voice: "You should, of a certainty! For I understand that *he* was the one who found you unconscious and brought you back here. What do *you* think of him? Do you remember anything? *Him?*" Her eyes searched my face before she added abruptly: "There's no need to look so *stunned,* after all! Or is your look supposed to be disapproving? You should count yourself lucky that he followed me here; after all, your case of sunstroke could have been much worse if he hadn't found you! Don't you think you owe us both *something?* Some gratitude perhaps?"

I had never come so close to hating my best friend as I did then. *"Us,"* she'd said. And he had arranged to be here in order to see Marie-Claire and be with her. All *I* had meant to him, obviously, was an afternoon's diversion—a cheap, silly slut who had thrown herself at his head. I had asked . . . no, almost *begged* for the treatment I'd received; and now I could not blame anyone but myself for it.

All the dream images that had continued to linger in my mind were dissolved by the heat of the raging anger and self-disgust that welled up in me, almost choking me. It was just as well that I had retained enough presence of mind to turn my face away from Marie-Claire's inquisitive eyes, pretending to look out of the window, while I considered what answer I would give her. Damn him; damn him to hell for a liar, a hypocrite, and a conscienceless reprobate! Once he had *had* me—or what I had offered too freely—there was no excuse for his going much further and taking much more . . . whether I liked it or not. I hated him almost as much as I was ashamed of my own weakness.

"Oh, *ciel!* Sometimes, Trista, I wonder if you are capable of any feeling or emotion! Why can't you *say* something instead of turning your head away from me to look out of the window?" I could hardly avoid Marie-Claire's accusing voice or her look when she came up to me and thrust her face close to mine. "Well? And I might as well tell you that if you won't help, I'll find some way in any case—or Blaze will!"

"Oh, very well then! You know that when it comes to making up plausible excuses, I am much more inventive than you are!" I seemed to hear my calm, almost indifferent voice from somewhere beyond myself, and even marveled that I was capable of being such a good actress. "But what kind of excuses will I be supposed to make? And how . . ."

Marie-Claire hugged me, all smiles and dimples now that she had achieved her object. "I *knew* you'd come around in the end, in spite of all your growls and grumbles! Oh, Trista—you are the best and dearest friend in all the world, and the only person I can really *trust!* I must go back downstairs in just a minute of course—but before then I suppose I should tell you something about the scheme we cooked up, Blaze and I!"

"Blaze and I . . ." Why should it matter to me at all? I could not escape from the scent of violets that pervaded my room long after Marie-Claire had left—nor from the echo of her words, either. I remember telling myself cynically that I should really laugh over the whole farcical situation instead of feeling so *angry.* My fingers shook as I arranged my hair as well as I could contrive by myself, in an old-fashioned knot high at the back of my head that set some unruly curls free to brush my shoulders and the back of my neck. "Blaze and I . . ." It took minutes to put on my favorite garnet earrings, which I usually wore with my golden brown watered-silk gown with black trimming that Papa had brought back from Paris for me a year before. In fact, I was hardly aware of what I was doing—even when I threw off my high-necked and long-sleeved nightgown and stood in front of the mirror wearing only my sheerest cotton chemise, which was threaded through with pale blue ribbons.

Why did I trouble to do up my hair . . . to wear my prettiest earrings? For whose benefit? Marie-Claire had promised to have one of the maids bring a tray up to me; and she had also reminded me again, with a mischievous smile, that she had been allotted the room adjoining mine. I had seen to that myself when I learned she was coming, because I'd thought we might *talk* as we used to before, in school. But there would be no long, whispered confidences interspersed with giggles tonight; for she had already planned to be with Blaze, and he would make love to her—over and over again in different ways. . . . I hated him!

I can see now that, most of all, I disliked myself and that physical, purely sensual part of me that had overcome every thought that was rational and balanced, and had reduced me to animal level—to acting, in fact, like a bitch in heat. Even worse, I could not explain even to myself *why* it had happened or what had driven me to it.

It had only seemed, at the time, something both inescapable and inevitable. I had surrendered to what was perhaps my true self—my real nature. And what was that? What was *I*?

I ask myself the same questions even now—but I can remember almost too clearly that on that particular evening I had already advanced from soul-searching to angry defiance. *Blaze*—and Marie-Claire. I, obviously, had been nothing more than an incident that helped while away the hours he had to wait in order to be with *her*. I had been used as callously and indifferently as a . . . a *harlot!* I know what I'll do! I remember thinking, studying myself in the mirror. And I'll do it, too—why not? And make sure he knows it—low-down *wretch* that he is! Oh yes, I knew exactly what I was about! Or *thought* I did.

Chapter 8 ✒

I seemed to have become bold suddenly, shrugging aside both morals and scruples during the space of that one day as if such things did not exist. After all, I was already a fallen woman, wasn't I? Like my mother. And Fernando must have sensed it that night when we encountered each other in the library and he had said what he had said and tried to do more than I would allow. The same night I'd had the misfortune to encounter Blaze Davenant.

That thought alone was sufficient to make me rub the crimson rose petals even harder along my cheekbones until they stung, glowing with an almost feverish color that matched my lips. I looked like someone different . . . like a whore waiting for a customer, perhaps. Even my eyes seemed to glitter, like splinters of shattered crystal when they caught the light.

If only I really were a witch, and could make anything I really wanted happen merely by willing it to *be*, I remember thinking just as a light tap on the door made me turn quickly and almost ashamedly from my contemplation of my own reflection. Susy, no doubt, with my long-delayed supper—and I hoped it wouldn't be the usual invalid fare: watery gruel or some vile-tasting herbal tea.

"At *last!* Thank goodness . . . I had begun to wonder if—" And then I felt as if I had been transfixed, my breath cut off with my first involuntary gasp of sheer, unbelieving shock.

It wasn't poor Susy who had just invaded my room but the one person I had least expected—or *wanted*, for that matter—to encounter once more that day.

"My apologies for *not* being the lucky man you have been waiting for with such obvious impatience!"

That deceptively silky, insinuating tone of voice—a growl beneath its surface purr. How well I had learned to know it in the space of less than two hours, even if I did not know *him* at all. Blaze Davenant—to whom I had meant nothing, *been* nothing! And now he dared to walk uninvited into my bedroom, and even go so far as to lock the door behind him?

"Get *out!*" My fingers had curled into claws that longed to rip and tear him to bloody shreds, and I could hear my voice rise almost stridently. "That you should *dare*, after . . . If you do not leave at once I shall start *screaming*, I assure you; and then you would not be able to keep your assignation with Marie-Claire, would you?"

His ironically twisted smile and lifted eyebrow showed me to myself as *he* must have seen me. A vindictive, jealous female who had been spurned and could not bear the thought.

"I only came to ask how you were feeling after your attack of sunstroke, my dear! And in view of my later . . . assignation, as you called it . . . why, I'm sorry, sweeting, but I did not pay you this visit with the idea of a repetition of this afternoon. Far from it. I merely wished to make sure which doors and windows I could use in case . . . the need should arise!"

I could not help but notice the obvious, almost ugly way his narrowing eyes had surveyed every detail of my appearance while he was delivering that drawlingly sarcastic speech, with every deliberately hurtful word *meant* to be a barb. I suppose that sudden realization was all that kept me from being either crushed or pushed beyond endurance. It was the only reason that I found myself able to answer him in a tight voice that sounded reasonably controlled, at least.

"In that case—and since you have already intruded yourself upon my privacy—pray *do* make sure of how you might need to . . . *escape* from the consequences of being found out! But please be quick about it, will you? Because—as I'm sure you have already guessed—I too have have an appointment tonight." I could not only *see* it in his eyes and the tautening of his lips and jaw muscles, I could almost *feel*, as if they had been something physical, the waves of fury emanating from the coiled-spring tension of his body. I had actually, quite amazingly, managed to make him angry; and how I reveled in the fleeting feeling of power the thought gave me before we began to duel in earnest.

"There are also windows that lead onto the same gallery in the room next to mine—where Marie-Claire will be sleeping. Shall I let you in there so that you can make sure of *escaping* if necessary? Although I hardly think you need to take such elaborate precautions, because I have already promised to do all I can to occupy Fernando's attention while the two of you are preoccupied with each other!" I even went so far as to dare an exaggerated sigh before I bent my neck in mock humility and added in a little-girl voice: "And I'm sorry for all the nasty, unpleasant things I might have said to you instead of being grateful for your *instruction* in certain matters. I think I understand things better now that I have them in perspective, you know!"

I had already dared to go much further than I should have; and one quick, flickering glance from behind the cover of my lashes served to warn me of that fact, making me back off instinctively from what I could read in Blaze Davenant's dark, uncompromising countenance and glowering frown.

He smiled, however, within the next instant—the kind of smile I could neither trust nor like because it reminded me more of a predator's curled-lip snarl. "You flatter me indeed, sweeting; especially since I could not possibly claim to have instructed someone as practiced as you seem to be in both playing at passion—and passionate abandon as well! Do accept my congratulations, Miss Windham, on a magnificent performance—and your many *other* talents!"

I *hated* the mocking caricature of a bow he awarded me, still wearing that ugly, infernal smile that taunted my self-control. Damn him! I wanted to . . .

There must have been something in my expression that

was easy to read, I suppose. *"No!* I wouldn't try it if I were you, my dear," he warned me in a softly menacing voice.

Did I strike out wildly at his sneering face . . . or was it he who seized my wrists first? I don't recall. Only his harshly whispered "Damn you, bitch! Damn your eyes!" before he dragged me roughly up against his body and choked back my startled gasp with the assault of his mouth over mine—hurting, taking, ravaging, pillaging . . . and merciless. I felt as if he meant to snap my neck as it strained backward under the force and fury of his kisses. I could not breathe any longer. I felt his hate and his rage and his lust and . . . his *wanting* of me, too, that matched mine for him and was something that neither of us could help or fight against. I might die under cruel kisses like these and from the punishing embrace of arms that held me so hard and so closely that I almost felt as if my body was going to be crushed into his to become a part of it . . . and yet, strangely enough, I was past fear by then and merely let myself yield against him instead of straining to be free. I remember opening my eyes wide to stare into the amber-green swamp-depths of his, thinking, Is this how it feels to drown? And then . . . then for a little while I felt nothing and remembered nothing except the swamp, and sinking into its depths all wrapped around with water-weeds until my breathing was stopped and silenced.

"Miss? Miss Trista, is you feeling bad? I kep' knocking an' knocking at your door, Miss Trista, and I sho didn't want to wake you up, 'cept the other young lady said you was hungry, an' when I saw Mister Blaze jes now he tol' me . . ."

I sat up to find myself in bed once more, with everything seemingly normal until Susy mentioned his name and my memory returned. "Mister Blaze," was it? No doubt he was in the habit of bribing servants in the houses where he was entertained, to make sure they remained close-mouthed over his liaisons with the opposite sex . . . which were probably countless by now! And what had he *done* to me to render me unconscious? Had he meant to kill me with his kisses in order to prevent me from saying something to Papa or to Fernando? Perhaps it had only been Susy's knocking that had saved me at the last minute!

"Miss Trista, you sho you ain't got a *fever* or somep'n?

You look real flushed in the face to *me,* if you'll 'scuse me
for saying so, miss. Would you want for the doctor to be
sent for again?"

"No!" I said almost violently before I caught myself and
shook my head apologetically. "Oh, Susy, I'm sorry! I know
you're worried and so is everyone else, but I really am feeling
much better now—and very hungry too! It was just that I . . .
probably slept too soundly for a few minutes."

Had I actually drifted from unconsciousness into sleep,
or had I only *dreamed* everything I thought I had experienced a short while ago? Whispered words as ephemeral as
smoke rings drifting through the further reaches of my
memory . . . had I dreamed those too or only imagined
them? "Trista! For God's sake—*why?* Why *you* . . . witch-
wanton creature? Why *me?* And why in the devil's name
did we ever have to meet?"

I know that Susy looked at me strangely and almost
warily before she left my room that night. I must have
seemed changed: more highly strung—more inquisitive.
Poor girl, I made her wait while I ate as much as I could of
the remnants of the elaborate feast they'd enjoyed downstairs. There was even, surprisingly, a bottle of chilled
white wine to accompany my repast. How thoughtful—of
someone!

"Does Mr. Davenant—Mr. Blaze, that is—does he visit
very often? It's just that he seems to be so familiar with
everything and everyone around here!"

Susy's face suddenly assumed a blank expression when I
began asking my "casual" questions while I ate; and I soon
realized that I would learn nothing from her that I did not
know already. Yes, he visited sometimes. And some of his
sketches had been in a magazine, too—Susy remembered
seeing them but could not recall the name of the journal.
And it had been Mister Blaze, whom she'd encountered on
the stairs (or so she said), who had suggested the wine; for
"medicinal purposes," of course! Perhaps he thought I'd
choke on it—or drink enough of it to put me into a drunken
stupor so that I couldn't know how long he spent making
love to beautiful, golden-haired Marie-Claire! And would
be in no condition to receive Fernando either? Well—he'd
find himself proven wrong. He'd find that two people could
play the same game. And perhaps *I* might be able to free

myself from whatever had drawn me to him in the first place. I remember thinking: Perhaps I *am* like my mother after all, and have her volatile nature and her strong desires. And why not, since I am her daughter? She always found—and *took*—whatever or whomever she desired, I suppose, and then discarded what she no longer wanted. She was strong enough to survive anything she had to face—and at the same time, to live by her own set of rules. Why can't I?

I had not thought of my mother for a very long time before then; and I had certainly never missed her. I suppose it was only because of the strange, tightly strung mood I was in that I suddenly remembered, from out of nowhere, something she had said to me once when I was very young and tried to cling to her, wanting her warmth and her love and needing to hide my face and dry my tears against her skirts. She had held me close for no more than a moment before putting me away firmly and setting me on my uncertain feet at what seemed to be then, and still is, an unbridgeable distance from her.

"No, Trista. But it is for *your* sake more than for mine, *p'tite!* If I allow you to become too attached to me, I will only wound you terribly . . . and myself as well. It is better for you to learn to live for yourself and *in* yourself, so that you will never, *ever* have to depend on some other person for your happiness and be hurt . . . hurt like a knife twisting and twisting inside while you have to smile and go through life as if nothing of any consequence had happened at all . . . !"

My Tante Ninette had carried me away then, and shortly after that she took me to see the Old One. The witch-woman of the swamp. She had talked to me out of her mind, and I had too—but it was still part of something I didn't want to, or perhaps wasn't ready to, think of yet. But my mother's voice, and every word she had uttered, had suddenly burst into my mind with almost startling clarity, perhaps because that was the only time she revealed something of her *real* self to me. The rest of my memories are of a beautiful, surface-shallow woman who could have any man she chose dancing to her tune or following in her perfumed wake. *I* was the only one kept at a distance—the only person who was not a recipient of her easily given kisses and hugs. And perhaps that was why both Papa and Aunt Charity had found it easy to love me and still protected me. Perhaps *that* was why I did not feel any tearing sense of loss when she left us all, my flighty, unfeeling mother—the *puta*, Fernando had called her contemptuously. Fernando—my childhood idol who had been infatuated by her teasing, butterfly ways and the way she would reach out with a laugh to stroke his angry frowns away, or put her fingers at the corners of his mouth when he was in a sullen mood and try to push them up into a smile. "Smile, please! Don't you know life is far too uncertain to waste time on being sad? Come, smile for *me*, my sulky little boy—for your bad, *wicked* stepmother, yes?"

Oh God! I pressed my palms against my temples, pushing back any more memories that might haunt or hurt me. No more of the past or of my mother unless I needed to *learn* something!

Had my wine been drugged, or was the strangeness of my mood only the result of having imbibed too much of it? I felt so strange—almost disembodied. As if I had become my mother now that I suddenly understood her better. And every man the lovely Laurette had ever decided was worth playing with for a while had found her irresistible. "There was, in spite of all you saw on the surface, something almost inviolate . . . or perhaps beyond feeling . . . deep beneath. She played games—but only, perhaps, to occupy her mind and keep from thinking. But with all of her faults, and whatever others might say, you must never think of her as *bad*, Trista. Thoughtless and sometimes selfish perhaps—but never bad. Remember that always, little sister!"

Brother Michael—my stepbrother who was a Jesuit priest now, as hard as that was to imagine. Even he had fallen under my mother's spell. And as for me—did I really understand her? Hate her? Or wish I was more like her?

At that moment—but how can I possibly recall *now* the thoughts that raced through my mind before I decided, recklessly, to find out if I had inherited any of my mother's traits: that quality the French call *"mystique,"* which drew people to her . . . and above all, her ability to control without being controlled.

The wine? Perhaps. But I know I was hell-bent to discover *myself*—if nothing else!

Chapter 9 ~℀

"He's decided to take a stroll outside with his cigar and wanted *me* to come, but fortunately my stepmother would not hear of it unless *she* could chaperone us! Imagine what she would do if she even *suspected* . . .? In any case, *she's* safely tucked in bed and snoring already, and so is my papa, I'm glad to say." Marie-Claire had burst into my room without as much as a perfunctory tap at the connecting door, and I noticed that under a sheer silk wrapper she wore nothing at all. *"Everyone's* in bed but Fernando, in fact—so . . ." She smiled mischievously at me and winked before adding with a gurgle of laughter underlying her whisper: "I hope, *chérie,* that *your* night is as enjoyable as mine will be! And then tomorrow we can compare notes before we leave! But *do* keep him busy for as long as you can—and do try to remember everything I've told you!"

I wondered, as she whirled away and the door closed softly behind her breathless, perfumed figure, if she was in such a hurry because Blaze was already in her bed, naked and hard with desire as he waited for her. And why did that thought have the power to make me furious all over again and strengthen my resolve to find out if . . . if . . .

Not wanting to think or hesitate any longer, I slipped swiftly and quietly on my bare feet through the open shutters that led onto the gallery. Very well—I *would* discover for myself if another man could exorcise this crazy feeling of being drawn, suddenly and frighteningly, into a vortex of emotions I could neither control nor comprehend. Fernando . . . why not? After all, I had already thrown my so-called virtue to the winds and had nothing left to lose now but my pride.

I remember the feel of warm weathered wood under my feet as I sped down the length of the gallery. The faint, faltering light of a waning moon barely allowed me to see my way as I told myself fiercely that I knew very well what I was about. I was my mother's daughter, wasn't I? It didn't matter what men *called* her, because they had all continued to want her just the same. Like Fernando—who had also shown he wanted *me*. I slowed my steps and then paused for a moment, my eyes searching for the glow of a cigar in the garden below. Had he gone to his room already? And why did I feel almost relieved at not having to answer the defiant challenge I had thrown out to myself?

Before I had time to analyze my contradictory thoughts, I felt my hair ruffled by a warm puff of breeze that carried the aroma of cigar smoke on its feathertips. He must be standing right underneath me, I remember thinking, and held on to the railing that ran the length of the gallery with both hands while I wondered what I would do. Go meekly back to my room and lie awake imagining how they must be making love on the other side of the door? Or—since *I* had allotted all the guest rooms—should I perhaps let Fernando discover me in his bed? And then? I felt my teeth worry uncertainly at my lower lip while I hesitated, poised on the balls of my feet. Shall I—or not?

I first heard the sounds during the instant when both my breath and decision were suspended. They came from below me, like the cigar smell . . . soft scuffling; muffled words.

"Please! Oh please, sir, no! I *begs* you . . . ahh!"

"That's better! And if you keep struggling I'll break you arm, understand? Damn nigger wench . . . who do you think you are, telling me no? You should feel proud if I so much as put my hand on your body, bitch! Eh? *Comprende?* So now you will do as I say—*exactly* as I say—or I'll have you hung upside down and whipped, while that buck you were sneaking out to meet watches the skin taken off your back! So now . . ."

"But I'm *free!* I don't belong to no one but myself . . . and
. . . and you can't have me hung up and whipped, or use me
like you wants to do . . . no! Ohh . . ."

All this time I had felt as if I were paralyzed—unbelieving. But that last desperate cry of pain and the ugly laugh
that followed on its heels brought me to my senses at last.
"Fernando? Fernando, I thought I heard voices! What are
you doing down there? Who are you talking to? Shall I call
Papa?" If I ever *acted,* I acted then, although I was sick and
shaking inside. It is not a pleasant thing to surprise the
darkest, most twisted side of a man—and not the *safest*
thing either.

I had to listen to all of the obscenities he growled—in
English as well as Spanish. But at least he was forced to
set the girl free. Mary. I recognized her as she fled across
the lawn to the haven of the servants' quarters, clutching
her torn blouse across her full breasts. She was young—
perhaps a year younger than I; light-skinned and very
pretty. Susy's daughter, who helped out when there was
extra company. She should have known better, perhaps,
than to go wandering off by herself at this hour of the
night. But Fernando—the terrible, *ugly* things he had said
and threatened the poor girl with—I could find no excuses
for *him!*

I had almost forgotten the steps leading down from the
gallery to the lawn until he seemed to vault up them, two
at a time, to stand threateningly before me, making me
suddenly aware of how scantily clad I was. Nevertheless, I
faced him with as much insouciance and bluster as I could
summon.

"How *disgusting* that was! You're no better than an animal! And if my poor Marie-Claire only *knew* the depths of
your—"

"Of my *what?* My future wife understands, or will soon
understand I think, that a nigger wench is—no more than
just that; and if a man uses one of them as a receptacle for
his masculine needs now and then, it doesn't mean a damn
thing! But as for *you,* meddling little *step*sister . . . can you
explain how you can be a victim of severe sunstroke this
afternoon and be suddenly well enough to lurk out here
eavesdropping on me wearing little less than a—"

"What I wear or don't wear is hardly any concern of

yours is it? But if you must know, I woke feeling stifled and came out here for a breath of fresh air. And then I heard you. How *could* you? To say the filthy, degrading things you said to that poor child, and to try to—" My defiant words were cut off by fingers that bit cruelly into the flesh of my bare shoulders as Fernando brought his face down to mine, making me flinch back involuntarily with a gasp of pain and indignation.

"And you, I think, try *me* too far—just as your devil-damned mother did! All kisses and promises and yielding softness at one moment—and distant indifference the next. Especially when there was another man about, sniffing at her skirts the way a dog scents a bitch! And you—even when you would follow me around as a child—I think I knew even then that you were like her. Aren't you? A *puta*—a bitch in heat! Isn't that why you left your room to-night dressed like a whore?" He shook me savagely, almost driving the breath from my body as he demanded: "Isn't that so? You're ripe for a man—and you were looking for one, weren't you? Which man did you have in mind? *Tell* me, *puta*, before I . . ."

Finding a strength and power I had not known I possessed until then, I managed to wrench myself away from his grip, my fisted hands striking out at his throat and the vulnerable spot that lies just below the rib cage. I could have killed him if I had struck harder; but all I wanted was to free myself of his hands and his words. He took a few staggering steps backward before he recovered himself; but I had already made sure of putting enough distance to feel safe before I turned to say in a shaking, almost breathless voice: "It was *you!* I was looking for *you*, Fernando, until . . ."

Mistrusting both my ability to utter another coherent word and his almost crouched and waiting stance, I had barely turned in order to flee to safety when he caught up with me and *flung* me about-face, slamming my spine up against the railing with a force that could easily have broken it.

"You were looking for *me*, were you? I think you have inherited all of your mother's teasing tricks! And what will the next one be, I wonder? You can think about it while I sample what you *meant* to offer me, eh?"

"No, Fernando! No! I won't . . ." It was as far as he let me go before I felt a shocking pain that stunned me and left me uncomprehending for some seconds until the taste of blood from a cut lip and the pressure of his hand over my mouth made me realize, almost unbelievingly, that he had slapped me across the face with his open hand—the same hand that now kept me virtually gagged while his other hand made lewdly free with my desperately twisting, shrinking body.

He hurt me—and I know he *wanted* to hurt me—to punish my mother through me, perhaps. "So you liked that?" He'd grin every time I moaned helpless behind the cruel pressure of his hand. "Laurette would enjoy being touched and held that way too. She used to give me instructions, the bitch! 'Touch me *here,* 'Nando—and now *here.* Like this . . .' And you, Trista?" He'd made sure I couldn't answer him, of course. All that I could do was to glare up at him through my tear-filled but resolutely open eyes. "Do you also enjoy being touched in the same places? And if you attempt to strike out at me again, my little *sister,* I might be forced to—"

"A little family squabble? Sorry if I've barged in, so to speak, but you see . . . I'm not used to drinking as much as I did tonight, and I'm afraid . . . 'fraid I'm hopelessly lost! Can't seem to find my own room . . . think I woke everybody up looking for it . . . sorry!"

Blaze? Fernando had released me abruptly with a smothered oath; but in spite of it, I could not seem to move as I stared at a caricature of the man I *thought* I had known. Unsteady on his feet, floppy tie askew, a foolish, vacuous grin on his face. How could he possibly be the same person?

It was only when Fernando snarled an ugly and insulting phrase in Spanish, and Blaze, almost falling on top of him, mumbled apologetically: "Sorry, m'dear fellow! Don't know any French, I'm afraid!"—only *then,* at last, that I felt my rooted feet capable of moving again as I ran without a word or a backward glance to the safety of my room, making sure the shutters and windows were bolted behind me before I allowed myself to fall across my bed, to lie there shaking with the reaction that came with the memory of stark terror and the thought of what might have happened.

It seemed as if I could not stop the shudders that ran through my body as I lay there clutching at the edges of the velvet bedspread that adorned the old-fashioned four-poster bed, with its satin and velvet tester and matching curtains knotted back with golden, silken cords. A medieval kind of room—why had I chosen it for my own? Medieval women had been kept under lock and key and married off for the convenience of their fathers or brothers. Not allowed—not *supposed* to think for themselves. I, on the other hand, had recklessly acted on my own childish impulses today instead of thinking, and had ended up the sorrier for having done so.

"Ohh . . . ! Oh *damn, damn, damn!*" I pounded my fists against the covers now, as anger became mixed in with all the other emotions that threatened to overwhelm me. What an utter fool I had made of myself! How Marie-Claire would laugh at me . . . and Blaze . . . Blaze?

Blaze should have been making love to Marie-Claire— *not* staggering along the gallery pretending to be inebriated and . . . and *ignorant!* Rescuing me from the consequences of my own folly, in fact. But why did *he* have to be the one to do so?

My thoughts were as jumpy as my nerves. I didn't *want* to think; nor to remember. I had locked myself securely in—and by now, surely, Fernando had gone sullenly back to his room and I could feel safe. I should force myself to get up and wash my face, perhaps read for a while until I became sleepy.

I think I had started to raise myself up into a sitting position before I was *tugged* upright and twisted around roughly to find my widening eyes blinking into Blaze Davenant's dark, angry face while he snarled at me: "What in *hell* did you think you were doing out there? Is that the kind of treatment you really enjoy? Because you should have *told* me so in that case, *ma petite,* and I would have endeavored to oblige!"

"Blaze . . . ?" I had *thought* him, and I had even *felt* him, I think, before he put his hands on me. And now there was an instinct that rose in me that was much, much older than I—and had nothing to do with reason as I tipped my head back to look directly into his eyes without flinching. "I was out there because—because I knew you were with Marie-Claire, and I—I wanted to . . ."

"I know," he said surprisingly, shocking me into momentary silence. "Trista . . . damn your witch's soul . . . I *know!* I wasn't with Marie-Claire tonight because I was too preoccupied with wondering what *you* might be up to with your precious Fernando." And then, as if to relieve the intensity of those words, he gave a short, cynical laugh. "Hell! I guess every man's entitled to turn into a damned fool at least once—and I'm no exception. I cannot, at the moment, decide if my protective instinct toward you is paternal or—otherwise! And I wish to hell you hadn't decided to bestow your precious virginity upon *me*—and that I hadn't taken it."

Even while he was speaking he had begun to snatch almost angrily at the silken cords that held the bed-curtains back; and when they fell together we were enclosed, the two of us, in the half-light of a separate world where time no longer existed; nor limitations on any form of sensual pleasure that was both given and accepted freely.

I found it easier to be bold and to explore and taste and experience his body in our private darkness; while at the same time, I was surrendering myself to the touch and feel of his fingers and lips and tongue on me and in me. We felt each other as the blind feel—discovering worlds and shapes, undulations and hollows by touch alone at first, and then in a different fashion and a different dimension when I felt him fit himself inside me to wait, poised for an instant during which I waited too, before he moved in me— filling every emptiness that had existed until that moment when I felt myself flow and crest and burst beyond all boundaries like a river gone wild after too much rain.

Chapter 10 ~

I must have been floating in that indeterminate half-state that lies between deep sleep and dreaming when Blaze left me. Or had I only imagined his sudden appearance in my room through a door I'd made sure of locking myself? And everything else that had happened as well? Perhaps it was because I preferred not to have to face the coldness of reality just then that I let myself keep drifting after I had given a sleepy murmur of protest.

"Mmm-hmm?"

"Sleep . . . love." Had he *really* whispered those words, or had they been part of a dream like the softly given kisses that barely grazed my lips and temples? And would I ever learn what kind of man this was who could be hard and unfeeling and almost cruel at one moment . . . and so gently tender the next? And I—what wild impulse (or deeply primitive instinct) had led me to him and made me feel that my offering myself to a stranger I did not even *like* was something natural and even foreordained? Perhaps I had been immersing myself too much in musty books that told of ancient myths and legends of a time before civilization existed. Perhaps I *was* a kind of witch after all; because I *felt* certain things I did not *know* consciously.

I was still too much of a girl-child then—for all that my

soul was Woman. We had met—and mated—too early, Blaze and I; and *he* realized it long before I did.

Of course! Because he was *older,* and so much more experienced—as he had taught me only too well. And because he was incapable of any true feeling, for he was too busy with his games of masquerade and playing roles to become real himself! And I was better off being disillusioned now, while I was still young enough to learn, than later . . . perhaps when it was too late, and I was already committed.

How different waking, *rational* thoughts are from dream images, which are gossamer thin and woven only of imagination. Dreams were dreams—and reality was what one had to live with from day to day. The sooner I realized that, the better off I'd be!

It was my friend Marie-Claire who was the first to remind me of these pragmatic but inescapable facts of life. I had been lying sprawled across my woefully rumpled bed, naked but for the sheet that *he* must have pulled up over me to cover me up to the waist at least. Fast asleep there in my curtained haven of lust and sweet forgetfulness . . . until the curtains were wrenched apart and I was jerked back into reality by Marie-Claire's accusing voice.

"Ah! So now I see for myself! And I tell you, it is a good thing that it is *I,* and not your Tante Charity who has just arrived with much fuss, who has discovered you—*so!"*

"Please, Marie-Claire! Must you be so *French* this early in the morning? And . . ."

"And? And what? It is a good thing, Trista, that I am truly your friend—even though you did play a nasty little jealous trick on me last night, eh? You could have told me that you've been lying under more than just the *sun* these last few afternoons, my dear, for surely you know me better than to think I'd feel *jealous?* Or were you afraid of what I could have told you about the lying *bâtard?* For *me,* I understand men; and especially men of *his* type— although from that stricken look on your face, *pauvre petite,* I doubt that *you* do! Surely you could not have taken him seriously just because he seduced you?"

"Stop! Stop it this instant, Marie-Claire! What on earth are you talking about? And I didn't . . . I hadn't planned to . . . you're making assumptions without . . ." I had put my hands over my ears involuntarily, as if to shut out her sharply pointed words; and now I could hear myself stutter like a child caught out in some mischief—hating the feeling of guilt and shame that suddenly rose in me like bile.

"Oh, for goodness' sake, Trista! There's no need to invent excuses for *me*, you know! I am not angry that you have been lying with Blaze Davenant. Only because you did not tell me, your best friend! Did you think I'd mind? Why, knowing Blaze, I rather think he would have enjoyed very much the prospect of having us both in the same bed—and in every conceivable way. He's like a satyr, that man! Don't you agree?" Sitting on the edge of my bed, Marie-Claire studied me with a mocking gleam in her eyes and an amused smile on her pink lips.

God knows what she read in my face—what I had *let* her read, as unprepared as I had been when she burst into my room. I only knew that even if I wanted to double over and be violently sick I could not give in—nor let her see what blows she had delivered me with her scornful, carelessly flung words. She was watching me, one eyebrow arching now, and I had to . . . I *had* to say something, or she'd really begin to think that . . .

"Have you quite finished yet?" I heard my own voice; it sounded strangely disembodied and—thank God—quite expressionless. "Heavens—you've been rattling on for so long about the most ridiculous things that I can't seem to make up my mind as to whether I'm being accused or commiserated with. And as for . . . for him . . ." I could not bring myself to say his name, and Marie-Claire pounced on my slight hesitation.

"Hah! *Ridiculous* things, you say? *Ciel!* You ought to have seen your own face, my girl! But why should I care if you want to make a fool of yourself? At least I've warned you, haven't I?" Marie-Claire had jumped to her feet while she was speaking; and now, looking down at me, she gave a short, throaty laugh. *"Ma pauvre amie!* Were you preparing yourself for a jealous scene and did I disappoint you? Ah, bah! Blaze, I think, understands me better than you do. Why else should he ask *me* to give you this little souvenir of your pleasant afternoons together in such a romantic setting? Here!"

I hardly paid heed to the flat, clumsily wrapped packet

she had tossed carelessly at me as a sudden spurt of anger
stiffened my spine, enabling me to say coldly: "I have
never attempted to pass judgment on *your* activities, Marie-Claire—nor discuss them with anyone else! And I don't
feel obliged to explain or answer to you for any action of
mine, or how I may choose to spend my afternoons—except
to say that they were *not* spent with . . . with your Mr. Davenant! Yesterday was the first time I encountered the
wretched man." No wonder Marie-Claire looked disbelievingly, almost contemptuously, at me as my words trailed
away and I realized how it must sound—how it would *seem*
to anyone else.

I thought for a moment that Marie-Claire had become as
angry as I had been only seconds ago; her eyes narrowed
and her nostrils seemed to dilate. But then she shrugged
almost indifferently and shook her head at me before saying admonishingly: "Please, Trista! I thought I had made
it clear that you can trust me. After all, I've always trusted
you ever since we became friends, haven't I? *Chérie,* he is
not worth a quarrel between us—and before you burst into
any more denials, you should look at the little package I
just gave you. Even Blaze, I suppose, is a gentleman in
some ways!"

It was only after Marie-Claire had left, without giving
me the chance to question or protest further, that I remembered the brown-paper-wrapped packet and tore it open
with shaking fingers, teeth caught in my lip. What new
game was *this?*

And then, when I saw what he had sent me, I could have
screamed aloud with the rage that bubbled up like liquid
fire in my veins. No wonder Marie-Claire had drawn her
conclusions! The sketches, drawn on rough-textured art
paper, were all of *me,* and in all of them I was naked, pos-
ing unposed in what I had always thought of as my own private place and quite unaware of prying, watching eyes
that violated my secret fantasies—my secret self that I,
fool that I was, had given up willingly to another kind of
violation. Oh God . . . God! And he had let Marie-Claire
see these too—that was worse still! Had he gone straight to
her bed from mine once I was safely asleep, and made love
to her before he'd shown her, laughing, the sketches he'd
made of me? Had he compared my body to hers?

Damn him, I thought. Damn him to hell! So he'd been skulking about all week without showing himself. *Spying*—and especially on me when I thought I was alone. I should tear each sketch into shreds—I should . . . But in spite of myself, I could not help studying them, still frowning and breathing fast with anger. Here I was standing on a sun-warmed rock with my face turned up to the sun and my arms uplifted to hold the weight of my dripping hair away from my neck. And in the next I was lying half in and half out of the water with my hair spread out behind me . . . fantasizing. The remembrance made me blush now as I stared down at the dreamlike look on my own face and felt that somehow he had known what I was imagining—what I was *feeling* just then.

Hastily, wanting to avoid the implications of that last thought, I leafed through the three or four other sketches he'd made. Here I was climbing out of the water with my back to him. And in this one I was shaking the hair out of my face. And then I turned to the last one and felt my heart almost stop. He had turned everything around, changing without changing, so that the pretty stream with its scattered rocks and boulders had become sinister and the trees growing beside it seemed to bend more closely toward the water, reaching over it with gnarled, leafy arms that shadowed the stone in the center around which the water swirled and splashed upward. And I, or my image, was the center of this vortex, standing spread-legged and naked except for wide bands around my ankles and wrists and snake bracelets circling my upper arms. My head was flung back, and my hair swirled about me as if each strand had a life of its own. My arms were outflung as if in invocation—and in one hand I held a dagger and in the other a bow.

Dear God! I could ask myself once I could breathe again: Is *this* how he really sees me? As some pagan priestess waiting poised on the sacrificial stone for her next sacrifice? What does it mean, this symbolism he has used to mock me with? I hated it. It turned everything I had thought peaceful and pretty into something wild and even sinister. I should burn it—and yet I could not stop staring down at this strange picture as if I had been mesmerized

by its aliveness and its violence as my pictured image
laughed defiance at the gods.

That's not . . . yes it *is* me! The inside me that dwells
hidden within myself. Wild, pagan, primitive cat-creature
that had stayed crouching within me, hidden behind all
the polite tissue-thin conventions—the lessons in proper
etiquette and deportment and how a young lady was supposed to comport herself. Blaze Davenant, damn his devil-
soul, had seen through all those veneered layers to the
leopardess even before I'd set it free myself.

Only he has seen me as I really am, or has known what I
am as *myself*. As I have known *him*—whether he might
like the idea or not! He watched me and drew my body on
paper but had made no move to touch me until . . .

I heard myself laugh suddenly as I stretched my bare
arms over my head. After all, it had been *I* who had chosen
him—not the other way around. I'd been the one to take
the initiative—and since I had, why feel shame or guilt for
having done so? I should learn to become amoral, like Marie-Claire. Like—Blaze Davenant with those strange eyes
of his that looked sometimes dark green and sometimes
amber. A man of several talents, it seemed. But a *man*—
and he had wanted me. No matter what Marie-Claire had
said to make me feel stupidly naive and too impression-
able, I *knew* that while we had lain together Blaze had
wanted me just as strongly as I had wanted him. I knew he
hadn't liked it one bit when I spoke of "entertaining" Fernando . . . ! Fernando. Last night. I could not help the cold
chill that seemed to crawl up my spine, my self-confidence
vanishing with my shudder.

What was I going to do about Fernando? I dreaded the
thought of having to face him again, remembering as clearly
as I did what had passed between us. I shuddered again without being able to help it. My feelings for Fernando had always
been so mixed-up and so confusing! Sometimes I would hate
him because it was he and not I who had most of my mother's
attention and affection; and at other times I loved him and
thought I wanted to be *her*, so that he'd smile at me in the
same way he smiled at her—look at me with the same passionate gaze he used to fix on her. Even a very young child no-
tices and remembers such things, and can sense without
understanding what is *there* between two people. My mother—

Fernando. Had Papa ever known or suspected? Had he sent me to a school as far away as possible because he'd noticed my growing infatuation for my oldest stepbrother and because— because I looked too much like my mother?

I heard the soft tap on my bedroom door that usually heralded Susy's appearance with my tray of coffee and hot, buttery biscuits spread lavishly with peach or apricot jam, and I barely had time to push the portfolio containing those incriminating sketches under a pillow before the door opened.

"Mornin', Miss Trista! They said I was to wake you up if you wasn't already—and you got a surprise visitor to see you too!"

"Aunt Charity! Oh, Aunt, I am so *very* glad to see you!"

I felt, as she crossed the room to hug me warmly, as if I could go back thankfully to being a child again, a child who had blundered into adulthood too fast and had found its way back to what was comfortable and familiar. If only I could have stayed in that old, safe world! But it was I who had deliberately broken out of my chrysalis, after all—and I who had to come to the bitter realization that nothing could, or would, ever be the same again, no matter how hard I wished it to be so.

"My dear! What *is* this I hear about sunstroke? Were you indeed very ill?" Aunt Charity held me away from her for some moments while she studied me, making me suddenly and guiltily conscious of my nudity, so that I could feel my face grow warm under her calm, cool regard. "I must say that you certainly do not *look* ill—although it's clear you've been communing with the sun a great deal! We shall have to bathe you in buttermilk and cucumber lotions to lighten your skin before the wedding, my love, or you're likely to be taken for some planter's by-blow, I'm afraid! But tell me—are you really sick enough to stay abed all day, even when I have just arrived with several trunks full of surprises?" She gave me a smile that was both affectionate and mischievous, patting my flushed cheek lightly before adding: "I've been shopping in New York for us both. Wait until you see my purchases! But that is *my* excuse for delaying my arrival. What is yours for being so lazy when it is such a beautiful day—and I have just arrived? Didn't Marie-Claire tell you?"

Chapter 11 ～

The rest of that particular day comes back to me in snatches of conversation—in remembered feelings I did not know what to make of at the time.

"Well, Trista! Suddenly it seems that they are all in a great hurry to leave at *once* so that we may try to reach the outskirts of Richmond by nightfall; but I couldn't leave without saying *au 'voir* to you, *petite.* You're not angry with me? I was a nasty scold only because you are my dearest friend, and I could not bear for you to be hurt by a . . . oh, very well! I know that forbidding look of yours, and will not say another word on the subject, I promise! And . . . oh, I promise also that I will find out who are the richest and most eligible young men—and make sure they are presented to you! There! Will that make up for my runaway tongue? Ah, *merde!* I hear my stepmother calling out for me in that piercing screech of a voice. . . . I *must* go at once! We shall see each other again soon, shall we not? Don't go out in the sun too much!"

I had been attempting to comb out my tangled mass of curls when Marie-Claire burst into my room, and had not been given an opportunity to say one word to her before she whirled away and was gone—leaving only the fragrance of her perfume behind her as proof that she had indeed been there at all. Now there's no need for me to take extra pains with my appearance, or to dress up too much, I remember thinking; and I wondered even then why I should suddenly feel so listless.

"And here is Trista at last—now that all our guests have departed! I am beginning to wonder, my girl, if your 'sunstroke' was not merely an excuse to avoid a dull and extremely boring dinner party!" The twinkle in Papa's eyes belied the mock severity of his tone; but I could not help the involuntary flush that heated my cheeks, and he must have thought that he had upset me because he added hastily: "Come, come, puss, there's no need to look so crushed! I only meant to tease you a little! And now that Charity's come at last, I'm sure that dinner tonight will be a much more enjoyable occasion, eh, Charity?"

"We're going to be homely tonight and eat out on the porch; don't you think that will be fun? How I love the fragrance of magnolias and honeysuckle and all the other night smells and night sounds! It makes me think almost nostalgically of the South, and warm nights with firefly sparkles everywhere you looked . . . that is, until I think of their reprehensible institutions!"

Aunt Charity's face looked softer, younger, in the half-light, and in spite of what must have been a long and tiring journey, she actually seemed unusually vivacious. Looking at her, I felt uncomfortably guilty remembering the last occasion I had seen her like this. She's in love with Blaze. Did they meet and talk before he left? Did they walk together to find the small, wisteria-hung gazebo that was tucked away in the furthest corner of the overgrown rose garden?

I was angry with myself and my treacherous thoughts only a moment later. It should not matter to me in the least. And I should never have betrayed Aunt Charity, always so kind and affectionate to me, with her lover—even if he *did* happen to be a conscienceless philanderer. Where, for the matter, had *my* conscience been hiding before I deliberately stifled it? I'm going to do everything I can to please her and show her how very much I love and appreciate her, I remember vowing to myself; and all through our *al fresco* dinner I joined with as much vivacity as I could muster in the lively discussion and friendly argument that Papa and his sister so enjoyed. War! I remember thinking with an inward grimace. Why is it that everyone I've heard recently talks as if conflict between the states is inevitable? Such a ridiculous thought! Men just seem to enjoy quarreling and making loud, blustering threats; and even the most hotheaded politicians must surely realize that there is nothing that can possibly be gained by internecine warfare.

It was easy to brush away all thought of politics soon afterward, when Aunt Charity asked me if I was no longer curious about the surprises she had brought me. "You make me feel as if it's Christmas already! Am I allowed to guess?"

"No, indeed you're not! All you may do is close your eyes when I tell you to, and count to five. Oh dear—I *do* hope you will like what I've chosen for you!"

Clothes! One of the larger guest bedrooms had been transformed into what seemed to my bedazzled eyes a pirates' market hung with every conceivable kind of feminine frippery ranging from a variety of hats and bonnets down to clocked silk stockings, pretty kid boots, and dainty evening slippers. There were lace-trimmed underwear and ribbon-bedecked corsets, and the prettiest flounced petticoats I had ever set eyes on, to go over the very latest lightweight crinoline—a wired contraption meant to make sure that the skirts of a fashionable female belled out from waist to ankle without touching any part of her anatomy below her waist. And the gowns! There were gowns for each particular time of day: morning gowns, afternoon gowns, gowns meant to be worn at tea parties, and at least four dazzling evening gowns. Two riding habits—one pale gray trimmed with black grosgrain ribbon, and the other black velvet, to be worn with a lacy white jabot that matched the undersleeves and petticoat. There was even a luxuriously fur-lined pelisse with a matching hat and muff, and shawls and mantles of all kinds from Indian cashmere to fringed, jewel-colored silks—some of them heavily embroidered.

"Well?" Aunt Charity demanded nervously, while my eyes felt as if they were growing wider and wider and my throat became constricted so that I could do no more than croak at first—and point. "Trista, dear, you will not be angry with me or think that I have—gone too far? It's just that—well, you cannot imagine what *pleasure* it gave me to shop for you!"

"I f-feel like . . . Cinderella! But . . . but you *must* see that I cannot let you . . . why, these things must have cost a *fortune!*" Guilt twisted like a knife inside me, plunging even deeper when my feeble arguments were insouciantly brushed aside and I was informed that it had all been previously arranged, and that Papa, if I approached him with my objections, would prove just as insistent. I was going to do more than hold my own among the daughters of the planter aristocracy of the South—I was going to outshine them all and be known as a belle.

"I know it might sound silly and stupidly frivolous to you *now,* dear, but—when we arrive in Richmond and the giddying round of dinners and receptions and *soirees* is in full swing, you'll have no reason to hide away like some poor mousy little governess! If you won't think of yourself, at least think of the satisfaction my brother and I will derive from seeing you put some arrogant noses out of joint! And tell me this; what good is it possessing a small fortune if one cannot enjoy spending it in any way one chooses to do so? In any case, I had not meant to tell you until you were at least eighteen years old, but since you have shown yourself to be remarkably mature and self-possessed for a female of your age . . ." I heard the grandfather clock on the landing outside the room ticking loudly and inexorably when Aunt Charity paused for a few telling seconds before saying slowly and with emphasis: "Trista dear—when you attain twenty-one years of age you will be inheriting a sizable amount of money. Quite a fortune, in fact! And if you do not start learning certain things *now,* while you're still young and not too set in your ways—why then, don't you see my love, there'd be no point in having money at all. Not if you let *it* own *you* instead of the other way around! And, oh, I do hope you will understand someday that *giving* can bring as much enjoyment as receiving—and that you will learn to accept easily and joyously those gifts, no matter how small or large, that are freely given out of love and for no other reason." Aunt Charity's smile was loving as she added coaxingly, "Trista? Can't you tell me if you *like* them or not? I know it's difficult to choose for someone else—everyone has their own individual taste, I know; but there is time to have some things altered if you wish it."

I wanted to weep. I wished that I could throw myself into her arms and tell her everything, even while I knew I could not bear to wipe all of the happiness out of her face with the cruelty of disillusionment. I suppose I was just beginning to grow up, and to learn that being adult also meant containing your own pain—never letting it show.

"I . . . it's just that I never expected . . . oh, Aunt Charity! How could you even imagine that I might not . . . not . . . it's just that I feel quite overwhelmed! It *is* like something out of a fairy tale, you know—fairy godmother! But I don't deserve such—"

"Oh, hush!" Aunt Charity scolded in her old, schoolmarmish (as Papa used to tease her) voice. "Try everything on, do—we haven't much time for alterations if any are needed. I took one of the old gowns you left behind—and your shabby, *favorite* shoes that I persuaded you to leave behind—to New York with me."

"How can I thank you and Papa enough? And you know I'll never be known as a belle. I'm too . . . different! But I do want to do you credit—and I promise to be on my best behavior."

It was only some time later, when the two tired maids who had been helping me to dress and undress had been dismissed for the night and Aunt Charity was unlacing my whalebone corset herself, that I remembered. In all of the talk and all of the confusion of trying on this and that and being pinned and turned about like a doll, I had forgotten to ask her what she could possibly have meant when she informed me that . . . Or had I only imagined that she'd said I was to inherit a lot of money when I became twenty-one years old? I thought she meant she was going to leave her own money to me . . . but more than she had already done and was doing now, I could *not* accept!

I let out the breath I had been holding in a gusty sigh of relief when the corset was off at last. "Thank goodness! Do you think there will ever be a time when women will not have to resort to lacings and whalebone and wire cages in order to be thought fashionable, and will be only themselves instead?" I suppose I hesitated, practicing insouciance, before turning about to meet her level eyes and say as steadily as I could: "There is something I forgot to ask you, in all this excitement, that I *would* like to ask now if you're not too tired. Did you tell me earlier something about . . . an inheritance of some kind? I have no relatives that I know of except for . . ." And I could not say my mother's name, but felt the heat rise in my face instead.

"Trista dear—your mother is your mother, and you are *you.* Always remember that! She is what she is, and you are—you can be whatever you want to be, don't you see that? The past and other people in it must never be allowed to drag at your skirts to pull *you* down with them—do you hear me?"

Aunt Charity's voice contained in it an unaccustomed, almost violent tone I had never heard before, as she held me by the shoulders and almost shook me before her hands dropped and she clasped them together tightly, giving me an apologetic headshake as she visibly attempted to regain her usual composure.

I said fiercely: *"You* have been more of a mother to me than *she* ever was. And Papa is to me my *real* father—not that man whose name I used to bear and never saw, never *knew.* Why, *you* are my only *real* family, and the only people who cared what became of me and . . ."

"If we both become emotional and start to weep, then we'll get nothing accomplished!" Charity said tartly, although I thought that she too blinked back tears. "And since there's no room left for sitting down in here, we might as well repair to my bedchamber, which is large enough to accommodate several comfortable chairs that are not all crowded with clothes. I bought several new gowns and other fripperies for myself too, I'm afraid! I couldn't resist the temptation—and I shall probably be encountering several people I used to know in the old days, when I was about your age and was sent to school in Charleston."

Chapter 12 ✒︎

I had always known, and had accepted casually and unquestioningly, as a child accepts such things, that the Windhams had had their early roots in England, and later in the South. I myself had been born in Louisiana. But I had not realized until that night the intricate and almost incestuous web of relationships and family ties that seemed to bond so many unlike people together—especially in the South, where such things were considered important. I had never thought to ask about my own roots either, until Aunt Charity began patiently to explain everything to me, leading up with painstaking detail to the amazing and almost incredible fact that I was indeed an heiress—being now the only living *direct* descendant of my unknown father's family.

"But they never cared about me—never bothered to find out if I was alive or not, or . . ."

"They were a very old and very proud family who cared more for their family *name* than for flesh and blood, my dear. They were very angry when your father made his own choice and married your mother. But in the end it was their own pride that killed them off. Their men died in duels fought over trivialities, and their women died unmarried rather than marry beneath themselves. At the last there was only one very old man—an uncle of your father's, I believe—and since he was clever enough to let

90

them think he was somewhat eccentric, they let him be. He never married, and the gossips said it was because he preferred—" Seeming to recollect herself, Aunt Chairty cut herself short before going on hastily: "Well, all that doesn't matter in any case! What *does* is that he inherited everything—and left it to *you*. There are certain stipulations, though, that you should be aware of. And there are always risks as well as responsibilities to go along with the acceptance of a . . . well, shall we say a *considerable* amount of money in addition to the other assets that are a part of the Villarreal estate."

I was packed off to bed soon afterward, when Aunt Charity decided that I had had more than enough to assimilate for one night; but I lay wakeful and restless for what seemed hours on end, and when I slept at last, I was tormented by strange dreams of people and places I had never known before—and dreams of running, running, with my feet sinking into what was sometimes sand and sometimes swamp as I tried to escape from frightening, faceless pursuers.

I woke up thankfully, to find myself drenched to the skin with perspiration and almost wishing that everything I had been told the night before would turn out to be only a dream. An heiress—I did not *want* to be an heiress. Those proud and arrogant ancestors of mine who had cast off my father and refused to acknowledge my existence had no right to pass their burdens on to me—*only because there was no one else left!*

"And if I had died, or should die; then who would inherit? How can a whole family become extinct?"

"I have already explained how. And as to your first question—I do not know! There might be some very distant cousins somewhere; the lawyer did not say. But he has seen you himself and admits that you resemble your father's family—no, don't ask me where, or when, for I do not know myself; nor do I understand the need for such secrecy—unless it is meant to protect you from fortune hunters!"

"Well, at least . . . for the next five years, anyhow, I suppose I can be myself, can't I? And as for their silly old stipulations, whatever they are—I don't care if I fulfill them or not!"

I can still remember myself then—how defiant I felt, and must have sounded. In any case, it all sounded too much like a fairy tale, and quite as unreal. Five years seemed an eternity. Why, by the time I was twenty-one I would either be a married woman or a confirmed old maid. Stipulations indeed!

"You'll change, my dear," Aunt Charity said quietly when I faced her with my rebellious outbursts. "And in the end you will do what is expedient—as we all learn to do."

I didn't realize it at the time, but I can see now that I had already begun to learn. Feeling for the first time the caress of silk against my skin and hearing the froufrou of wide, swishing taffeta petticoats under my English velveteen walking dress, I felt—no, I *knew*—that for the first time in my life I was beautiful.

Who is this strange, exotic young woman I see staring back at me from the mirror? She wears a silvery-gray velveteen gown banded with black over her dark blue petticoats, and a silver-gray straw bonnet trimmed with dark blue velvet ribbons and tassels. Her black hair is caught up at the back of her neck, imprisoned in a silken net, and bright spots of color flame high on her cheekbones. She is a belle!

I remember laughing out loud, seeing sparkles in my reflected eyes, and then practicing flirtatious, seductive smiles to show off the dimple at the left corner of my mouth. Is it possible, I thought wonderingly, that this is *me?* Or that fashionable clothes could make such a difference—even in the way I *feel?* I will always wear beautiful things that make me feel beautiful, I promised myself. And underneath, against my skin, never anything but the finest, sheerest silks. Soon—or soon enough if you're *sensible,* a sly voice whispered in my mind—you will be able to afford to buy anything you want for yourself. And why shouldn't you enjoy what is rightly yours? Think of how your father's stiff-necked family would turn in their coffins! Think of being independent—*free!* Money's only for enjoying, after all; and there could be nothing wrong about wanting to *look* well at all times!

"Trista! Do hurry, dear—we're all waiting for you!"

"I'm coming, Aunt Charity!" I twirled before the mirror for one last time, and suddenly the thought came unbidden: I wonder how he will look at me *now?* And my breathing quickened.

"Well, well! So our little Trista has blossomed overnight into a beauty! Charity and you will be the loveliest and most stylish ladies there, I'm sure—and I will be envied the privilege of escorting both of you! Dear me, I hope I will not be challenged to a duel by some jealous swain before our stay in Richmond is over!" Papa's eyes twinkled quizzically as he handed us into the light, open-sided carriage—known, I believe, as a rockaway. The more conservative perch coach meant for city use was piled high with our luggage and trailed behind us at a maddeningly slow pace that made me want to grit my teeth with exasperation and— *Why* was I so impatient? We had chosen a beautiful day on which to travel—sun-warm, but not uncomfortably so thanks to the light puffs of blossom-scented breeze that fanned my flushed cheeks.

Forcing an air of composure I hardly felt, I listened to Aunt Charity's ironic discourse on what she termed "the manners and mores of our Southern aristocrats," and which turned out to be a horrendously long list of regulations governing the behavior, dress, and deportment of *ladies*—especially those who were young and unmarried. "But how very *Gothic!*" I interpolated once. "Why do these downtrodden females accept such a system with its double standard? And how could *you* endure living under such tyranny?"

"As you see, I did not! I was always an independent thinker, a questioner—with a rebellious nature besides! And after I had discovered the writings of Miss Grimke and Mrs. Beecher Stowe, to name but two brave women, I *knew* I had to travel north—supposedly to act as housekeeper for my brother!"

"Hmm, yes!" Papa interjected at this point, smiling. "And she threatened to play havoc with my happy bachelor existence if I did not help her with this school she was intent on founding! Blackmail, *I* call it!"

"You might have helped find a suitable place, my dear Hugh," Aunt Charity retorted with some asperity, "but don't forget that I had just come into Grandmother's legacy and could afford everything that had to be done!" With color in her cheeks she looked positively pretty, and—and

young, the bronze-gold and brown watered silk she wore
complementing her fair complexion and brown-gold hair
that showed no strands of gray in it yet. Why, she's really a
very attractive woman! I thought suddenly—and wondered
why I felt a sharp pang of something I did not want to acknowledge shoot through me. *Blaze!* I thought. Her new,
stylish gowns and the young, happy look on her face—all
for him!

"Tell me again, please, Aunt Charity!" I said, leaning
forward. "I must practice flirting and simpering in just the
right way so that I might find myself a string of adoring
beaux before we leave Charleston. And if Papa would be
obliging enough to stay awake, perhaps I could practice on
him? *Please,* Papa? And you must promise to be quite honest with me and tell me if I am doing well or not!"

I will not think of him unless it is with detachment. I
will *ignore* him except for a frosty nod when I have to, and I
shall be so busy flirting and enjoying myself that our paths
need never cross. Perhaps I shall even become *engaged*
—for a few days, at least! And I *won't* allow him to hurt
Aunt Charity, no matter what I might have to do to prevent it!

I closed my eyes when the road we were traveling grew
wider and there were fewer bumps and potholes to jolt us
about, and I must have fallen asleep . . . for when I opened
my eyes again we were traveling along the tree-lined carriage drive leading to the magnificent Grecian-style mansion that was Hartswood.

To say that I was *impressed* cannot possibly convey what
I felt during those first moments that were filled with
warm welcomes and greetings—all the hustle and bustle
that accompanies the arrival of guests. To tell the truth, I
was almost *overwhelmed,* for even the columned classical
beauty of its exterior paled in comparison with the magnif-
icence within. Enormous chandeliers that had to have
been imported from European palaces lit rooms whose
walls were lined with silk and gold and silver patterned
brocade, and every exquisite item of furniture could easily
have found a place of honor in a museum. Smiling liveried
servants (or were they *slaves?* I was to wonder uneasily
later) were everywhere to make sure that every guest had
anything he wished, and even I had begun to feel before

the night was over that I had been drawn into a warm, magical circle of acceptance and genuine friendship.

"Well, goodness! Charity honey—where *have* you been hiding this pretty young thing? Just *look* at her! Why, she's a beauty—and mercy, I've a feeling that my poor sons are liable to fall head over heels in love with her just as soon as they set eyes on her!" Our hostess, Mrs. Hartford, kissed me on both cheeks.

I was enveloped by hugs and kisses from ladies I had never met before, and was awarded extravagant compliments I knew I didn't deserve—but what of it? In spite of the fact that I had been traveling all day and must have looked rumpled and untidy and tired, I was soon made to feel beautiful again.

"Now, I know *very* well how you must feel right now, finding yourself right in the middle of a crowd of strangers! But I do hope you won't think of us that way any longer, now that you've met almost everybody! Mr. Hartford and I both hope that you'll come to feel at home here—and we've heard so much about you from your pretty little friend that it's not hard at all to feel as if I know you already!" My hostess was a short, rather plump woman with a round face that looked plain until her dimpled, genuinely merry smile transformed it, and you could see that she must have been considered a sparklingly pretty girl once. I had liked her at once, and she, surprisingly, seemed to have conceived a liking for me, taking pains to make me feel comfortable.

"I'm sure you must be just *longing* to wash off all the nasty travel dust and change out of those clothes. I'll send some hot water upstairs to you, and you just tell Lilith what you need to have done and she'll see to it. She's been taking care of my Clarissa since they were both children, and she's been positively *moping* since we enrolled Clarissa in that famous school in Paris—I keep forgetting the name, but Mr. Hartford will be able to tell you what it is! In any case, Lilith will be looking after *you* while you're here—I suppose 'taking charge' would be more to the point! And I've given you Clarissa's rooms. We had them done over for her the month before she left for Paris, and even though Mr. Hartford growled a great deal, he gave in and let her have her way as he always does! He won't admit he spoils her, of course; but at any rate, I have three sons who spoil *me,* and I must admit I enjoy being made to feel pampered and protected by three tall, hulking young men who treat me as if I'm made of glass! I cannot wait for you to meet them—or for them to see *you!* Just promise me you won't break their hearts?"

I wondered dazedly, after she had left me in Lilith's capable hands, how on earth Mrs. Hartford managed to keep rattling on without so much as pausing to catch her breath. At least I had certainly learned a great deal in the space of a few minutes! All the "young people," she'd told me apologetically, had left early for a barbecue at Amherst, a neighboring plantation belonging to the Amersons, who were old friends.

"But they'll all be back here in time for late supper, with the younger Amersons as well. They have six grown children, but the two older girls are married now and so is Brett, their oldest son—the serious one! You'll meet the two younger girls and Farland—we all call him 'the wild son,' and I'm sure you'll soon see why!"

As I soaked away the stiffness in my muscles in warm, scented water, I still seemed to hear my well-meaning hostess's voice echoing and reechoing in my head. It's not at all as I expected it would be, I found myself admitting reluctantly. They all seem so very nice, and so kind and *friendly,* even to strangers! And their servants—not *slaves,* surely!—seem happy and not at all discontented. After all, these are educated, enlightened people who travel all over the civilized world! Surely things have changed since Aunt Charity left the South?

I had given Lilith, a spare-boned, bustling young woman with smooth, velvet-dark skin, one of my prettier silk gowns to press while I reveled in the unusual luxury of feeling pampered and waited upon. I had over an hour before I should go down for supper, I thought lazily as I stretched like a sleek, contented young cat, extending my legs in front of me so that my heels balanced on either edge of the tub before I leaned forward to soap my feet and ankles.

"Do the white missy need her back scrubbed and soaped? I been told I do ladies' backs real good so dey's satisfied."

I heard myself gasp out loud before I twisted about,

water splashing everywhere. "How dare . . . ! Will you leave my room this *instant,* before I start to scream as loudly as I can?"

"I rather think, sweeting, that I could manage to hold your head underwater long enough to . . . *dampen* any such ideas, shall we say?" Infuriatingly, Blaze ducked just in time to avoid being hit squarely in the face by the dripping-wet sponge I threw at him, and he straightened up with a taunting grin on his face as his eyes looked me up and down with slow, obvious insolence that made my face burn with rage.

"Get out—this very *minute,* you . . . you *lecher!* I swear that if you do not I will . . . I'll . . ."

"But never forswear yourself, witch-eyes! Surely you must know better than that?" His lifted eyebrow and satirical tone of voice taunted me so that I was almost beside myself and choked over the angry words I wanted to sling at him like pointed stones, shaming him into a realization of his base perfidiousness.

Instead of his showing, even belatedly, some vestiges of *decency,* my widening, horrified eyes discovered that the wretch had actually begun to unbutton his shirt—as casually as if he had been undressing in his own bedroom, not mine. "No!" I managed to utter despairingly at last, drawing my knees up against my body as I slid as far as I could under the tepid water. *"Please!"* I heard my shameful, imploring whisper only moments before he leaned over me, twisting his fingers in my dripping-wet hair to pull my head back painfully and force me to endure his savagely ruthless kiss until my lips felt bruised and swollen—until I was no longer capable of protest—nor of thought either, under his hands touching me, fingers finding all of the places in all of the ways that I secretly longed to be touched. I was no longer capable of resistance, and I knew it! Not even when the tub overflowed with a splashing surge of soapy water as he lowered his body into it and over mine, and I felt his hands slide over and then under me as he lifted my hips up to meet the fierce, almost savage sword thrust of his body, which impaled me, pierced me, penetrated so far inside me that I would have screamed if his mouth had not taken possession of mine and stopped up my involuntary cries as he took me, and took me, and took me until the

world was all motion and whirling silver dust in the
blackness of space forming changing patterns—coming together, pulling apart, joining, coalescing, expanding,
tightening, funneling upward and upward and filling the
universe for a blinding-bright silver moment of eternities
before the bursting—the starburst—star-flung silver fragments—whirling, floating dust motes glittering against
night-dark void.

"Blaze—I had such a strange—it was like a . . . a *vision!*
It was—beautiful and frightening and . . . even a little sad,
I suppose. I wonder . . . *Blaze!* Oh God! I must be mad . . .
and *you* are inquestionably insane. Let me up this *minute!*
Don't you realize what would happen if we are found . . .
like *this?*" In my agitation, I had started to beat at his
chest wildly, picturing the scene that would ensue if someone else walked in at that moment. Aunt Charity—Marie-
Claire! Or Lilith . . . hadn't she promised to return in a
few minutes? Suppose she had *seen?*

"Enough!" I found myself looking into dangerously narrowed amber-green eyes as Blaze captured both my wrists
in a harshly painful grip, pushing them roughly up between my breasts with enough force to make me gasp for
breath and remain speechless under the weight of his body
and his sardonic look that seemed to reduce me to childhood. "Now that's better!" he had to say unnecessarily, his
upper lip curling up on one side in the travesty of a smile
that made me squirm angrily. "You know, you're beginning to remind me too much of your friend, the bride-to-be!
And especially when you won't stop gabbling on and on—
asking a string of questions without pausing to listen for
answers! Also, I must inform you that *I* am no more comfortable on my aching knees in such a cramped-up position
than you are, my pet!" His voice growing caustic, he
added: "The next time you find yourself in a similar position, may I suggest that you try saying, 'Please,' or even,
'Would you mind allowing me to rise, sir, now that our
business dealings are concluded?' I can assure you, sweeting, that a polite request, rather than flailing fists and
hysterical outbursts *after* the fact, would have been quite
sufficient!"

He stood up then, hauling me precariously to my feet as
he did so, then freeing my aching wrists to pull me closely

against himself in almost the same motion—hard hands cupping my buttocks to bring me even closer. I only clung to him with my arms wrapped about his neck because I was in danger of losing my balance—and for no other reason, of course! The bath water was cold at my ankles—but where our bodies touched there was warmth, spreading like fire until I felt as if every inch of my skin burned hotly, and the heat sank through my pores to concentrate within me, flame flaring and licking upward and everywhere until all of me burned and there was no sense, no sanity, left anywhere in a world where rational thought, like mythical Atlantis, became submerged by the primeval force of pure *feeling*. Like Atlantis, I was lost—helplessly carried along upon the crest of the vast tidal wave that soared skyward, shaking off rainbowed spume and streamers of frothy white foam, blocking out even the sun before I was crushed beneath the sound of shattering thunder as it flung itself against the earth—and *took* it.

Chapter 13 ♌

I have never been able to forget anything that happened on that first night I spent at Hartswood Plantation. I have learned since then that some memories can never be erased—no matter how hard one tries to wipe them away. And there was a time when I wished *not* to remember— especially the feeling of having lost all sense of balance or reason as I let myself be swept along and almost drowned in a flood tide of passion and emotion I could neither understand nor withstand at the time.

"Never make the mistake again, sweet innocent, of awakening the sleeping primitive beast that dwells in all men!" Blaze whispered against my ear, his voice a low, rough animal growl. He had taken me again, but this time lying across my bed, with both of us still dripping wet.

He had all but *thrown* me facedown across the quilted satin spread before; and because by then I had begun to want and even to need the wild, unthinking fulfillment his touch, his body promised and brought me to, I was able to turn my head and whisper back: "And what of *women?* Is there a sleeping beast inside me to, Blaze Davenant, that *you* have forced into the open?" I felt the weight and pressure of his body leave mine as he turned on his side and moved me with him so that we faced each other eye to eye, and I was finally able to ask: "*Why?* Why the other night . . . why now, and *this,* with the risk of . . . What *would* happen, do you think, if someone should discover us like this?"

He kissed me into silence like any smiling betrayer, before he began to put his clothes back on with surprising swiftness. "No one will, I hope, since I had the forethought to lock the door behind me." He paused halfway through drawing on his boots to look at me, and I could not read the expression on his shadowed face when he said: "If you're really a witch, you should look to your magic charms and spells! For I am the last man on earth you should draw to yourself—and the worst—if you are looking for happiness, or even some measure of contentment from life. And try to remember too, for your own sake, that there can be certain consequences that women must bear the brunt of and men escape—no matter where the fault lies. It's a damned unfair world, even for a sweetly beguiling enchantress with eyes like depthless silver-surfaced pools, making me wonder . . . what *does* lie beneath? Is it forgetfulness you offer, or oblivion?"

"Damn you, Blaze! Don't evade me with riddles and poesy!" I sprang to my feet to face him angrily, pricked by his words and their implication. "So it's an unfair world, is it? And I, being a *woman,* am to blame for enticing you, for *enchanting* you—poor helpless male! Why, you're even more contemptible than—than Fernando! And it is I who have allowed myself to be stupidly oblivious to—to the plain, unvarnished truth . . . to *everything,* including my own conscience. But I, at least, can face the truth about myself. Can *you?* Or are you too much of a coward and a hypocrite for that? You mouth platitudes and deceive with poetic phrases while you . . . you do exactly as you please without regard for anyone else, or their feelings, or . . . Damn you! Stop looking at me and *go!* You've made me despise myself, if it gives you any satisfaction—but I find that I hate and despise *you* much more!" I heard the strident note in my voice as it rose dangerously, and if there had been any kind of weapon at hand I would have seized it and killed him without a qualm if I could. It was sheer rage, and the bitter gall of knowing how easily I had forgotten both conscience and common sense, that rose in my throat and choked me into gasping silence even before I found myself

seized roughly and painfully by the arms and shaken until
my head swam.

"All *right,* damn you! You've said enough—there's no
need to belabor a point once you've made it. Or did you
hope to bring everyone within earshot to your rescue with
your fishwife screeching?" His cuttingly contemptuous
words exacerbated my already sore sensibilities, and I
felt—I felt as if I had first been set on fire and then frozen
into a statue of ice, incapable of feeling any emotion at all.

I stood still and almost limply in his hold until he released me with a softly violent expletive muttered half under his breath. I could read both frustration and anger in
his eyes and in the way his nostrils seemed to flare slightly
as he looked down at me with ridges of white tension showing along his jaw and at the corners of his mouth. For one
breath-held moment I felt as if I looked into his mind—but
whatever I had seen melted away like vapor as I released
my breath. Something broken, with jagged edges, rattled
about inside me—echoing inside empty space. Echoing . . .
like the sound of a door closing with barely controlled violence soon after Blaze Davenant swung on his heel and left
me—but not before advising me in a sarcastic voice to try
and make a habit of locking doors behind me when I truly
desired to be undisturbed.

I was still glaring at the door when Lilith rushed in on
the heels of her soft knock, carrying my newly pressed
gown over her arm. "They's almost ready to start in on
supper right now, Miss Trista! But if you let me I kin have
you all dressed an' ready in no time at all. I already done
tol' them you was taking a short nap 'fore supper, so nobody's goin' to say too much if'n you're a few minutes
late."

She had come in too soon after Blaze had stamped out in
a rage for her *not* to know, or at least suspect, what had
taken place, I thought as I let myself be taken over by Lilith's capable hands. Moving swiftly and efficiently, she
wrapped my damp hair in a towel before she proceeded to
dress me as if I had been a child, or a china doll. "You sure
got some pretty hair, Miss Trista! An' so much of it, too!"
Almost miraculously—for my hair has always been difficult to manage soon after I've washed it—she had it
smoothed in front and twisted into a heavy chignon at the

back, allowing a few loose curls to escape with seeming artlessness and cling to the nape of my neck and against my temples and flushed cheeks.

Papa had brought me a jade necklace from China once—and dangling jade earbobs shaped like teardrops to match. There was Chinese writing on each gold-linked piece of jade that formed the necklace and on the back of the earrings as well. And another time he had brought me a necklace of gold-clasped amber beads. I wore the jade that night and felt the earrings brush my bare shoulders. A certain amount of *décolletage* is considered permissible in the evenings. I had read something to that effect in the *Lady's Book*, I recalled. And Aunt Charity, who had impeccable taste, had chosen this green silk dress with gold lace flounces and satin rosettes with gold centers that were a deeper, more glowing green.

Lilith had already assured me that I would not feel I was overdressed. "It's not too often we've had a lot of comp'ny in some months now—not since Miss 'Rissa done left. Folks here are going to enjoy gettin' dressed up as much as they can, I 'spects! You looks jes fine, Miss Trista! Gonna have all the young gent'men's eyes startin' out from they heads when they sets eyes on you fer sure!"

The necklace was heavy. "Semibarbaric!" Aunt Charity had murmured when she first saw it in my small jewel case. And had added with a slight frown, "And hardly suitable for a child your age. Why is it that men don't stop to consider sometimes?" But I was sixteen now, not twelve—and semibarbaric or not, I knew that the jade necklace became me.

As it turned out, I did not have to feel embarrassed because of my tardiness when I finally descended the stairs with some trepidation. My first occasion—and I was late. It could not be helped. I would brazen it out somehow and not let myself think of *why* I was late, I thought feverishly as I forced myself to descend the stairway with my back straight and my head high. Hold onto the railing, I admonished myself. Be careful—lift your skirts a little higher—you almost tripped over them—and damn the dictates of fashion! Especially this ridiculous steel cage known as a crinoline! It's much more barbaric than a necklace of heavy pieces of jade embroidered with Chinese ideograms!

The famous Monsieur Worth of Paris must think that
women should still be encased in chastity belts like the unfortunate wives of the Crusaders in medieval times!

"Trista . . . Trista, wait for me! It would look much better if we made our late entrance together, don't you think?
At least I won't have to face my stepmother's frosty looks
alone!" Marie-Claire's breathless voice from behind me
made me feel as if I had been reprieved. Almost falling
headlong in her haste to catch up with me, she clutched
onto the railing just in time, swearing in gutter French under her breath before turning to me to say petulantly:
"Why were you *hurrying* so? We were so late getting back
from Amherst that I'm sure they will have held supper
back to give everyone enough time. But why are *you* late? I
thought you'd arrived *hours* ago."

I shrugged indifferently, continuing my careful descent.
"I suppose I've never been able to calculate time very well!
I had a hot bath and . . . fell asleep, I think. Do you know
which way we should turn when we reach . . . oh!"

"I expect the men were taking bets on just how late we'd
be!" Marie-Claire whispered, flashing her most brilliant
smile at the clustered group of well-dressed young men
who had suddenly fallen silent when they saw us. "The
intense-looking one with eyes that match his hair—that is
Farland. He is even more unprincipled than Blaze, and
much wilder; so be careful, and don't on any account be
taken in by him—or anything he might say!"

"I won't," I barely had time to whisper back before we
were surrounded by eager young men who begged for the
honor of being presented to Miss . . . ?

"You boys remember your manners, now!" Mrs. Hartford chided as she bustled up, tapping broad, masculine
shoulders with her fan to clear her way. "My dears—you
both look so lovely that I suppose I shall have to forgive
these ruffians for being so forward. But only if you promise
to *behave,* you hear?"

Later, I would try to match names with faces. But at
first all I heard was the strangely unfamiliar sound of my
own name ringing in my ears. "Miss Trista Villarreal . . .
Baton Rouge and New Orleans . . . related to the Natchez
branch of the De Marignys . . ." Aunt Charity or Papa,
making sure of my being accepted without question by

stressing my Southern background and connections. Villarreal—an arrogant-sounding name. I hated it already, even before I was told that one of the stipulations I had protested so fiercely was that I must take the family name and keep it—and my husband, if I decided to marry, must also agree to take the name of Villarreal to hand down to our children. Another small matter of expediency, for what man would not willingly change his name in order to gain control of a fortune? Or care if he took a wife if it meant he could better afford his mistresses?

That night, though, I had not yet had time to think too much about the sudden and startling change in my circumstances—nor to grow cynical and overly careful on whom I bestowed my smiles. I was still trying to get used to being called Miss Villarreal instead of Miss Windham—and attempting to erase from my mind the recollection of my earlier encounter with Blaze Davenant, who had used my body to suit his selfish whims and had made it clear to me afterward that I was no more than one of his fancy women. His *mistress*—to be taken and used as *he* pleased whenever it suited him, with no regard for *my* feelings or reputation.

No! I told myself almost frenziedly, managing somehow, by some instinct I had not known I possessed, to make all the correct responses that were expected of me and even to smile and show my dimple at the right time—and hide my pretended blushes behind my fan when I was expected to. I was a success! Even Marie-Claire had to admit it. And Mrs. Hartford, who had adopted me as her protégée, it seemed, took as much pleasure in my debut into society and the compliments she received on my manners and deportment as if I had been a favorite niece or adopted daughter. "You'll have all the other girls jealous, my dear! And their mamas twittering behind their fans! It used to be the same when my Clarissa was home. Never an evening passed without callers—and her beaux would stay for dinner and glower at each other across the table! And Mr. Hartford would sit there glowering too, while I wrung my hands wondering if there'd be a *scene!* But then—Clarissa knew exactly how to twist her papa around her little finger too!"

Taken firmly under Mrs. Hartford's motherly wing, I found myself introduced in dizzying succession to what

seemed to be half the population of the state of Virginia. It
was fortunate for me that at that time family names and
connections meant nothing to me, or else I might have
been completely overwhelmed. Every detail of my appearance was studied—especially by the sharp eyes of the older
ladies and the jealous mamas that Mrs. Hartford had jok-
ingly mentioned. "Oh, but I shall only be staying for the
wedding . . . only a few days, I am sorry to say . . . Oh yes,
how I wish we could stay longer so that I could see something of Richmond, but . . ." Once I had taken pains to
point out the briefness of my visit, the mamas and even
their daughters became quite cordial toward me, I could
not help noticing. And so did Mrs. Hartford, for at one
point during our promenade around the room she leaned to
me and whispered with a twinkle that I had certainly managed *that* very well indeed, and it was exactly what
Clarissa might have done.

I had begun to feel as if I were turning gradually into a
wooden puppet—moving on strings that made me incline
my head or extend my hand, or smile prettily or coyly, as
the occasion demanded. How easy it was to pretend I was a
silly, helpless, *brainless* butterfly who could not so much
as *think* for herself! I had even learned to *flirt*—partly by
observation and partly, I suppose, by pure instinct. Why,
flirting was like a *game*—played with eyes and fluttering
fans and tantalizing half-smiles. An easy, meaningless
game, and I became quite practiced at it before the night
had ended.

"So—my little sister has been magically transformed
into a beautiful butterfly! And I observe jealous looks cast
in my direction by your many admirers. Shall I prevent
them from challenging me by claiming my prerogative as
your . . . *brother*, Trista?" I had barely been allowed to sit
down and rest my aching feet when Fernando found me,
making his way through the gathering collection of young
men who begged to be allowed the privilege of bringing me
something to eat—or a glass of cold punch perhaps? Anything I might desire! And tomorrow, if I was not too tired
. . . I had actually begun to enjoy myself as I basked in the
warmth of all this masculine attention—and then Fernando had to saunter up and kiss my hand with exaggerated gallantry before he made his ironic little speech.

"Why—he can't be your beau; he's the bridegroom!"

"Gentlemen," I said with as much composure as I could muster, "may I present my *stepbrother*, Mr. Windham, to those of you who are not already acquainted with him? I'd have you know that Fernando was lucky enough to persuade my very best friend to marry him—and here he is, neglecting her already!"

"By no means, sweet sister! Marie-Claire is being held captive at this moment by a group of recently wedded matrons who are, I think, intent on giving her the best advice as to how she should deal with a husband!" I pretended not to notice the hastily stifled chuckles and knowing winks exchanged by some of my admirers, but could not help but be conscious of the pressure of Fernando's hand on my shoulder as he moved to stand behind my chair—every inch the protective brother standing guard over his sister's honor. And of course his hovering presence made everything awkward and strained all of a sudden, as he had known very well it would, I was positive. Even worse, he was subtly, and without being too obvious about it, making it clear that any plans or arrangements for my entertainment should have *his* approval first! "My father and my aunt have joined in a conspiracy with the Baron and Baroness—my poor Marie-Claire and I are mere pawns in their capable hands! And so, I have been delegated my sister's guardian and watchdog. . . . You're not too displeased, are you, Trista?"

"How could I be?" I had to force myself to respond, hoping that my smile did not look too artificial. "Why, Fernando's the most *understanding* of brothers—and not half the ogre he pretends to be! Are you?" Turning and tilting my head to gaze up at him, I almost shrank from what I could see, for an instant, looking out at me from Fernando's eyes.

"My sister knows me too well, I'm afraid!" he murmured with a laugh; but I felt at the same time the cruel, warning bite of his fingers on my shoulder, which made me suck in my breath quickly to prevent myself from exclaiming out loud.

I was thankful when the pressure eased, and I let the conversation that was initiated by Fernando flow about me and leave me isolated and ignored. It was exactly what

he had intended, of course; and if I made my excuses and
walked away *now*, it would seem as if I was acting like a
sulky, petulant child who could not bear *not* to be the center of attention. *Where* was Mrs. Hartford? And where was
Aunt Charity? I had not seen her since I had come downstairs—nor Papa either. If only I could be *rescued* . . . !
Even Blaze, who had rescued me once before from my stepbrother . . . And then I saw him—just as if I had conjured
him up by witchcraft with an unspoken thought. Only . . .
he was with Aunt Charity, and seemingly, he had eyes for
no other woman as he smiled down into her laughing face
and bent his head to whisper something to her that made
her laugh like a girl again.

Fernando interrupted my thoughts. "I think my blue-
stocking aunt has found herself a beau at last! They have
been 'strolling about the grounds' for the past two hours at
least!"

Suddenly, I could no longer endure what had become an
ordeal. I no longer cared what anyone might think—and I
did not feel as if I could bear to watch them together for one
moment longer. I could pretend fatigue—a headache—any
excuse would suffice! Perhaps some of the desperation I
felt showed in my eyes as I tore them away from that
which I did not wish to see, looking about the room for
someone I recognized. But how much of myself and my
feelings did I betray when I met Farland Amerson's
strange yellow eyes and continued to *look* at him straightly
instead of dropping my eyes demurely under his measured
regard.

"Hello, 'Nando! I've come to take your sister away. Gentlemen, my apologies—but I have been commissioned by
our hostess, who says that Miss Villarreal *must* meet some
friends who have not yet had the pleasure of being introduced. If I may?" I rose thankfully, shaking out my skirt
before I took his politely extended arm. I noticed that no
one—not even Fernando—made any objection to my being
carried off in such an abrupt fashion by the "wild" Amerson son I had been warned against.

Chapter 14 ~

"There's no need to feel anxious—if you are. I'm the best shot in the county—and they all know by now that if I fight a duel I shoot to kill. Anything else would be a waste of time, don't you think? And by the way . . . do they teach females to ride in Boston?"

"I learned to ride on half-tamed horses in California, Mr. Amerson. I was considered a good shot too—before I left to attend school in Boston. And by the way—thank you for coming to my rescue!"

"You will find, perhaps, that I never do anything out of purely altruistic motives—Miss Villarreal! You've heard about my evil reputation, no doubt? It's amazing that you aren't afraid of losing *yours*—or trembling with fearful anticipation of what I might do with you! I'm completely without conscience, you know!" His dark gold hair glinted under the light of a crystal chandelier as Farland Amerson looked down at me almost challengingly.

I found myself capable of a genuine laugh, enjoying the feeling of being challenged . . . or was it *tested?* "Are you trying to frighten me? Then you cannot succeed, I'm afraid. I had been made to feel uncomfortable when you came to my rescue; but that was only because . . ." Why was I speaking so frankly and freely to a man I had just met? I hesitated slightly, and Farland finished my sentence for me.

"Because your stepbrother lusts for you?" And then he smiled down at me crookedly before saying with something almost like amazement underlying his words: "What a pleasant surprise to find that you're not shocked by my bluntness!"

"Is that why you probe at people? To shock them? I must admit you're quite perceptive, Mr. Amerson, but I am not easily shocked unless—I suppose, unless I am supposed to act that way! Shall I manufacture a fit of the vapors? Or swoon as gracefully as possible? I would prefer to swoon, I think—if I could be sure that you were gallant enough to catch me in your arms!"

This time he actually gave a short laugh. "My dear Miss Villarreal—I have to admit that you are right! And quite *refreshing!* I would like to see you again—if your family permits it. I have a little Arab mare who is still only half-tamed. Do you think you will be able to ride her?" I was left uncertain whether I was being challenged or tested, finding myself left in Mrs. Hartford's care soon afterward. What a very strange and unusual man Farland Amerson was—and yet I discovered, to my surprise, that I could actually *like* him and feel comfortable with him, because there was no need for pretense or playacting. He was the first male *friend* I ever had . . . or missed, for that matter. And perhaps the only man to know me as I really am under the glossy surface I have since learned to present to the rest of the world. Farland, my cynical friend . . . where *are* you?

During the days that followed I spent, defiantly, almost all my time in Farland's company, until everyone stopped shaking their heads and warning me to be very careful, and began instead to speculate about the outcome of our relationship.

To tell the truth, I did not care what anyone thought—and neither did Farland. I rode his half-wild mare without being thrown, and I practiced shooting at a target and then at clay pigeons without disgracing myself too badly. As long as I was with Farland I did not have to think about anyone else—or fear them either. And I was careful to lock my door whenever I happened to be in my room alone.

"You have certainly managed to make quite a conquest! Farland Amerson, of all people! Has he proposed to you yet?" Marie-Claire kept pressing me for details, and I noticed how she licked her pink lips avidly before whispering: "Tell me—have you two . . . well? Did he mind that he was not the first?"

I refused to admit or deny anything—and in the end Marie-Claire gave up sulkily after advising me that I should try to be more discreet, since I was already being "talked about."

"Am I? How flattering!"

At least, I could think when I was alone, there would be no more confrontations with Fernando or with Blaze either. I was safe with Farland, even if only he and I knew it. But *that* was something I did not confide to anyone else—not even to Aunt Charity when she approached me worriedly.

"Trista, my dear . . . you *know,* I think, that I have never been narrow-minded or . . . I hope you can believe at least that my only concern is for *you,* and not for what other people may think or say! But you're still so young and inexperienced that I . . . well, the last thing on earth I would want is for you to be *hurt.* Men can be . . . well, sometimes they might say certain things, or act in a certain manner—and be truly sincere *at that moment!* The only thing is . . ."

I had been standing at the window with my back to her, and for an instant I found myself wondering: Supposing I tell her that I have already been made to realize that? Supposing I should say that I am not as innocent and inexperienced as she thinks I am . . . and that *she* is in more danger of being taken in and having her most sensitive emotions torn apart and crushed cynically underfoot than I?

I was glad, when I turned about, that the light was behind me, making it hard for her to read my face as I managed an uneven laugh. "Dearest Aunt Charity! I *promise* you that you need not have the slightest uneasiness or apprehension where I am concerned! If it is Farland Amerson everyone is wondering about—we are only *friends,* that is all. I give you my word on that. We . . . he is the only man I have ever been able to *talk* to quite freely, and we enjoy each other's *company*—that is all!" I could not resist adding: "Are they saying that I am in danger of being *compro-*

mised by spending so much time with Farland? I *like* him,
Aunt. And I trust him. He has never as much as suggested
anything in the least *improper*, as a matter of fact! And I
don't care in the least what Farland's reputation has been,
or *is*—it's only what other people say or want to believe, I
think! He's . . . he puts on his air of arrogance and cyni-
cism and not caring about anything and anyone, don't you
see? Underneath . . ." And then I stopped short, feeling
the cold prickle of goose bumps all over my body as I gave a
sudden shiver. For I had been permitted to see, once, into
the twisted, tortured depths of Farland Amerson's soul,
and had felt ice crawl up my spine.

"Oh, dear! I didn't mean to . . ." Aunt Charity's warm
hands touching my shoulders broke me out of the coldness
that had suddenly enveloped me, and I heard myself release a shuddering breath. "You have depths—and a kind
of *perception* of other people that so many of us lack. It is
just that . . . only promise me that you will be careful?"

It was the day before the wedding, and I was going out
riding again with Farland. I looped the hem of my riding
skirt over my wrist and said lightly: "I promise! And I *will*
be back in time to change for dinner at the house of your
friend Miss Van Lew. Will Papa be going with us too?"

"No . . . he and some of the other gentlemen are supposed to go into town for a game of cards—probably in some
den of iniquity!" And then, with the wry note in her voice
disappearing, Aunt Charity said in a different, almost
studiedly casual tone: "But Blaze has promised to escort us
tonight, since he too has been invited to dine."

I felt as if I was seething inside, and kept biting my lip
until Farland told me cuttingly to stop it at once. "If you're
in the mood to throw a tantrum, there's no need to *mutilate*
yourself when you could just as easily throw yourself off
the horse to kick and pound your fists against the earth!
Or would you like to shoot off a gun instead and shatter as
many empty bottles as I can find?"

"Ohh! Oh *damn!* I wish I had never been forced to leave
California! I wish I could . . . I wish I could escape from
everything and everybody and be . . . somewhere else! Be
on a storm-driven ship—ride with the wild Bedouins across
an endless desert—or . . . exploring some uncharted river

in a canoe! Even, like Miss Nightingale, going to nurse the poor wounded soldiers in Crimea! To be *doing*—learning—*experiencing* life instead of merely *existing* like . . . like a vegetable!"

"Bravo!" Farland applauded in his usual cynical drawl. "I admire your taste for the dramatic, my dear Trista! And I truly hope that once you have made up your mind you will reach out and find whatever it is you want. One suggestion, though—why go no further than nursing? Why not study medicine and become a doctor? Not many females have been strong enough to face *that* particular challenge, I believe!" And then, shrugging, he challenged me to a race.

I had already changed, as usual, from my cumbersome skirts into breeches and an old shirt of Farland's that had shrunk sufficiently to fit me well enough. And riding astride I had managed several times to *almost* beat him. This time, amazingly, I did, and flung myself triumphantly off the little mare to lie in the shade with my arms crossed under my head and my legs cocked.

"I'll be damned if you couldn't pass for a boy right now! Where are your feminine curves and graces?"

I made a face at him. "You're being mean because I beat you! And I don't care if I don't have 'feminine curves and graces.' I feel so much more comfortable and natural dressed this way." I turned my head to look at his handsome, impassive face and said more soberly: "You know, I'm really going to miss all this when I have to go back. And especially your friendship. And don't lift your brows at me in that infuriating way, Farland Amerson! I mean it."

"Perhaps you really do! And God knows that you've probably learned more about me in less than a week than—the people who imagine that they have *known* me for all of my life!" He lay stretched out beside me but not touching me, one arm shielding his eyes from a stray shaft of sunlight; but in spite of his relaxed pose, his voice was so bitter that I had begun to put my hand out to him when he said in a different and almost offhanded fashion: "But you don't *have* to go back at once, you know! I have been thinking that it might prove convenient for both of us if we were to announce that we have fallen madly in love with each other and wish to become engaged before you leave. A *long* engagement, of course, since we have only known each other such a short time, and you are still in school. Long enough for you to make sure of your feelings—or to change your mind without being thought fickle and heartless!" Farland suddenly turned his head to look at me, but I could not read the expression in his shadowed eyes, even when he added dryly: "I did not mean to render you *dumbstruck* with the shock of my proposal, dear Trista! But since you seem incapable of *speech* at the moment, you might at least give some thought to my suggestion before you give way to cruel peals of laughter and cause irreparable damage to my deepest sensibilities—not to mention the poor heart I have just offered you on a platter, like John the Baptist's head!"

"And now I *know* that you are only being ridiculous and trying to pull my leg!" I said crossly, annoyed at myself for having actually taken him seriously for a few moments. *"Honestly,* Farland . . . ! John the Baptist's head indeed! Unfortunately, I cannot quite see myself as a Salome draped with diaphanous veils; so do stop teasing before you make me angry!"

"But I *am* quite serious, dammit! Couldn't you see that?" Farland sat up abruptly; and as I met his shadowed yellow eyes there was an instant when I thought I saw through them and behind them to twisted things and thoughts that chilled me in spite of the fierce heat.

I think I knew already what I would say in the end, in spite of the objections I felt impelled to produce. "But your *parents,* Farland! They won't like your getting engaged to *me* when you might have had any of the prettiest Southern belles available! And then . . . well, there is—"

He cut me off to say without emotion: "Why, as to my *parents,* I can assure you that my mother would positively swoon with delight and relief because I have decided at last to settle down; and my father will clap me heartily on the back and offer me a drink while he congratulates me on having finally come to my senses!" And then he said in a completely changed voice: "And if you were thinking of—of Jessie when you began to stutter . . . dear *God!* Don't you understand that this is the *only* way for us both? *She* understands. She has always *had* to. And she's lived too long with fear and always *wondering* and never knowing *when* it might happen. Hearing a knock on the door one day that isn't mine, and—"

"Farland! Stop!" I didn't realize that I was shaking until I heard my voice quiver and almost break. "You can't keep *thinking* that way. Such black thoughts . . ." Trying to silence him, I clutched at his arm and almost shook it.

"Why, Trista! Did I really manage to frighten you with my black thoughts? But my dear—your blushing consent to our betrothal can rescue me from the darkness of . . . not being able to *hope*—and make me the happiest of men as well!"

Even after Farland had taken me back to Hartswood and left me with a light brush of his lips against my cheek before he kissed my hand more formally, I could not shake off the feeling I had of unreality. As if I were a mist-shape moving through an insubstantial dreamland—reacting only when I was required to do so. Even when I was sitting before a mirror while Lilith attempted to arrange my hair into some semblance of decorum, I kept thinking: After the wedding tomorrow—or perhaps the day after—there will be a formal announcement of our engagement. At this moment, probably, Farland is preparing his parents before he talks privately to Papa—perhaps later tonight, after dinner. "A convenient arrangement" for us both, Farland had said. Freeing us both from certain constraints, and . . .

"Miss Trista! Ef'n you don't sit still fer a while, this here hot iron is goin' to *burn* you!" Lilith, usually stolid and impassive, let a short sigh of exasperation escape her. "Why, I swear I ain't ever seen you with such a case of the nervous fidgets before, Miss Trista—an' they's goin' to 'spect you down for dinner in less'n an hour, with you not even dressed yet!"

"I'm sorry, Lilith. I'll try to sit still—I promise!" I moved restlessly on the satin-cushioned stool the next minute and had to remind myself forcibly to keep still, angry at myself for fidgeting so, like a—nervous bride! None of this is *real* —although only Farland and I know it. And when it's known that we are engaged, I shall be *safe* at last; and *protected.* From Fernando, the bridegroom, with his eyes that seemed to *consume* me whenever he looked at me—and especially from Blaze, who uses my own weaknesses against me and *reduces* me. Without conscious volition, as I looked back into my own almost unnaturally huge eyes in the mirror, I thought: I wonder how *he* will look when he hears? Or if he will feel anything at all? But then, as I stared fixedly into my reflected eyes and suddenly imagined that I saw *other* reflections, moving and wavering like shadows on wind-rippled pools, I looked quickly away and had to catch my breath to bring myself back to where I was and who I was.

"Miss Trista, you sure is a picture tonight. And you goin' to have all the other young ladies bitin' they lips from bein' jealous!" Lilith stepped back to admire her handiwork while I looked at myself in one of the full-length oval mirrors that had been hung on each of the two doors leading into Clarissa's dressing room. Another enormous mirror covered the wall at the far end of the narrow, closet-lined room, so that I could see myself from three different angles if I chose. I knew I *did* look almost beautiful tonight with my hair parted in the middle and caught up high in the back with a jade and ivory comb that allowed loose curls to escape down past the nape of my neck and brush past my ears to my shoulders. For jewelry I wore again my favorite jade earrings to match the beautiful new gown Papa had surprised me with only that afternoon.

I had never been vain about my appearance, having accepted long before that I could never aspire to being known as a beauty. But that evening I found myself spending far too much time studying my triple reflections, hardly believing that I was seeing myself dressed in an exquisite gown of ivory-gold brocade, silk-patterned all over in glowing shades of green. Every tier of the skirt that belled out from the tight-waisted bodice was trimmed with a wide band of green silk; a narrower band of matching silk trimmed with ribbon bows outlined the dipping neckline. Devoid of the elaborate frills and flounces and lacy trimmings that were considered the height of fashion, my gown was still—I hesitated over words and suddenly thought, why, it's *elegant!*

With an exuberant burst of self-confidence, I whirled around in front of the mirrors just once more as I asked Lilith again: "Do I *really* look . . . ?" And then as I looked up, giddy and breathless, the rest of my question was trapped in my throat.

"You look ravishingly lovely tonight, Miss Villarreal!" Blaze Davenant murmured in a slow, lazy drawl, his amber-green eyes looking me up and down in an insolently appraising fashion that brought the blood rushing to my face even before he added with a sardonic lift of an eyebrow: "But you are also late for dinner—or had you forgotten all about it while you continued to admire yourself in those mirrors?"

Chapter 15 ⌒

"Your eyes look like twin thunderclouds discharging
bolts of lightning!" Blaze observed in the ironical tone of
voice he seemed to reserve for *me*. "Perhaps you should try
to veil them with those long eyelashes you have learned to
flutter so becomingly while you make your excuses for
being late—or you might frighten off people who don't enjoy storms and tempests."

If I had not been forced to hold on to his arm while we descended the stairs, I would have showed him what the fury
of a hurricane was like—and I still might, at that, I
thought vengefully. But I had learned already that losing
my temper, and my self-control along with it, only served
to put *me* at a disadvantage; and so, instead of letting him
bait me again I managed to give him a scornful look as I
informed him in an icy tone that I did not in the least need
either his advice *or* his comments on my appearance, before adding: "And I wish I *could* call down a bolt of lightning to strike you down and reduce you to—to nothing but
cinders! You, Mr. Davenant, are not only unscrupulous
and unprincipled—you are completely amoral! And, if
you'll excuse my blunt speaking, you are the very lowest of
the low—as you proved to me earlier. Human—*slime*,
that's what you remind me of!"

I suppose I *did* become quite heated as my emotions
overcame me, but that was no excuse for a rude and *loud*

burst of laughter that made several people who were standing near the bottom of the staircase break off their conversation to look up at us.

"*Slime!*" Blaze said in a choked voice. "No, no—but that's too much! I have been called many things before, but never—oh God! *Slime!*" And then, adding to my angry embarrassment, he had to give vent to another raucous burst of laughter, making color flame in my cheeks even before he looked down at me with the laugh wrinkles still etched deeply at the corners of his eyes and mouth to shake his head and say again wonderingly: "*Slime!* But are you *sure?* Mud—dust—dirt under your feet—anything but—"

"That's enough!" I made an attempt to lower my voice before I continued with suppressed fury: "Perhaps you can curb your amusement long enough to remember that . . . that . . . ," and then, unable to prevent my rage from breaking through, I almost hissed at him: "*Damn* you! Everyone's looking at us now, while you—you force me to stand still while you—make a *spectacle* of yourself, and of *me* as well, you—you . . . !"

"I think they are only staring because you are Beauty itself tonight, modest child! But if I might just venture . . ." I was compelled, seething inside, to keep still while he pretended that the flowers Lilith had just pinned in my hair needed to be fastened more securely. "There! And now you are—perfection." I had imagined, of course, that for just an instant the amusement left his voice and it sounded changed, almost a husky whisper. He had never said anything he really *meant* to me, after all! He only enjoyed playing teasing, cruel games . . . so that he could *laugh* once he'd succeeded in making me lose my temper . . . my control over myself.

Why did I have to meet his eyes just then? Or find myself thinking quite suddenly of deep green bayou waters gilded by the sun? What nonsense, I told myself a caught breath later. It is the effort of trying to keep my temper while he *provokes* me that makes me feel so—unbalanced! Why else would I hear myself say in a shaken whisper: "Blaze . . . *please!* Please don't . . ." for no reason at all? And there could be no other explanation for the strange paralysis that kept me standing there as if I had been stricken; even when I felt his fingers take my chin and lift it—just as if he meant to kiss me where I stood, halfway down the last flight of stairs and in full view of more than a dozen pairs of interested eyes.

It was such a *relief.* I thought soon afterward that he had recollected himself sufficiently at the last moment to make an exaggerated show of studying my face from every possible angle, tilting it this way and that and even sighing loudly before saying in an overly dramatic manner: "Ah, Miss Villarreal! You are, indeed, Beauty without Blemish—and I should think myself the luckiest man on earth if only you would condescend to allow me to make *some* poor attempt to capture your dazzling loveliness on canvas! Do I dare to ask if you might at least—*consider* sitting for me? Can I—*hope* perhaps?"

He was back to playing his games again—and I came back thankfully to reality as I caught angrily at his wrist to push his hand away, feeling as if I could not *bear* the touch of his fingers burning through my skin . . . no, not even for one half-second longer!

Afterward, I had no clear recollection for a while of either names or faces, as I was guided with unnecessary firmness through what suddenly appeared to be an unusually large room, stretching for what seemed like miles in front of me. Nor when, along the way, I was given no choice but to pause while I was either being introduced to someone I simply *must* meet immediately or who had been *longing* for an opportunity to be presented to *me.* I think I managed to fend off far too many extravagant compliments and had to endure having my hand kissed far too many times before I began to recover myself somewhat—feeling healing, cleansing rage begin to surge hotly through my veins to rise and keep building until I felt I might erupt like a volcano at any moment; perhaps the very next minute, if I had to meet just one more person! And *then* let him try and think of an excuse or a clever subterfuge to explain my irrational behavior, if he could!

Perhaps it was just as well that Farland came to my rescue when he did! And I can still picture the quizzical, almost surprised glance he shot me when I rushed to greet him with an unusual degree of enthusiasm.

"Farland! Please *do* say you are here to look for *me.* Why, if you only knew how *happy* I am to see you, and to know that when I have to face all those *looks* I am bound to get I will at least have some *support!*" I clung to Farland's arm with both hands as I spoke, acting as if I had forgotten the existence of everything and everyone else since I had set eyes on him while I continued brightly, "And now, at last, I am able to release poor Mr. Davenant from his *obligations* so that he may return thankfully to his dinner partner!"

"Oh?" Farland drawled, cocking one eyebrow. "Well, in *that* case—I presume there's no need for me to call Mr. Davenant out, at least! But is there anyone else that I *should* challenge? After all, you've been gone such an unconscionable time that everyone had begun to worry in case you had forgotten the way!"

How much had been teasing—and how much had not? I think that was the first time I came face-to-face with the realization that even if Farland and I both knew that our "engagement" was only a sham, both his pride and his honor would actually make him *obliged* to defend my name against even the slightest hint of suggestion that might be construed as a slur on my character—true or not. Good heavens, he had actually *meant* it when he asked me if there was anybody that he *should* challenge! The thought actually frightened me into being rather subdued for a little while—or at least until Blaze managed to make me fume with anger again with his *acting,* as he played to the very hilt the role of a foppish, even slightly *effeminate* dilettante who enjoyed sketching, and daubing paint on a canvas occasionally. It was as if he was playing a *joke* on everyone who allowed themselves to be taken in by him— how despicable of him, and how utterly contemptible! I could have almost wished that I had not intervened when Farland seemed on the point of *challenging* him—except for Aunt Charity and how *she* might feel if her beau was shot to death in a duel over *me!* As it was, I had my rage as well as two strong arms to sustain me while I made my excuses and abject apologies, feeling almost guiltily that I had been forgiven far too quickly and almost too easily before we finally sat down to dinner.

I remember feeling as if every course took an interminable time before being served and even longer before the plates were cleared away at last to make room for the next

course—*and* the one after that. But at least Farland had
been seated next to me; and I felt much more comfortable
than I might have if I had found myself sitting between
two strangers, attempting to make polite, meaningless
chitchat. At least I could carry on a sensible, intelligent
conversation with Farland—and find it easy to ignore both
my stepbrother Fernando's dark, almost glowering looks
and even the questioning, almost inquisitive glances Marie-Claire sent in my direction from time to time. I would
not—and for some reason *could* not—let my eyes wander
across the table to my left, to where Blaze Davenant and
my aunt sat side by side, engaged in some deep conversation that seemed to engross them both to the exclusion of
everything else. Why, he hadn't glanced in my direction
even *once* since he had led me directly to my hostess to beg
her pardon—and he had actually behaved as if he was relieved to be rid of me at last. Since then, whenever I happened by sheer accident to look in that direction, he
seemed incapable of removing his eyes from my aunt's
glowing, suddenly youthful-looking face and the smiling
curve of her lips I had never noticed before then. And . . .

"Dearest Trista!" Farland said softly behind the napkin
he raised to his lips just then. "Must I really fight a duel
with your aunt's *beau cavalier?* Your flashing glances in
that direction are beginning to be far too obvious not to be
noticed, I'm afraid—and the blushing bride-to-be puts on a
smug, *knowing* kind of expression whenever she catches
you at it. I hope she doesn't know *too* much?"

"I have been . . . oh no! I didn't even . . ." I felt my face
grow hot with shame as I made myself meet Farland's yellow, expressionless eyes and bit down on my lip before I
said in an uneven whisper: "I had no idea that—I was
being so transparent! Thank God you pointed it out to me,
for I would die with mortification if *he*—if anyone *else* had
noticed as well! Oh Farland, I'm *sorry* if I have . . . that
is . . ."

"Why don't you make a pretense of gazing soulfully into
my eyes while you beat your breasts and tear out handfuls
of hair, so to speak? Or better still—think how *jealous* you
could make him! And how much *happier* you could make
my parents at the same time—unless you prefer to think

that you are doing penance for all the grievous sins you have committed!"

I could not help smiling almost unwillingly in response to Farland's wryly ironic speech that put everything into its proper perspective—and saving me from making a perfect *fool* of myself. He was right; there was no point at all in breast-beating and hair-tearing for something that was done and over with. It was only the future that I should concern myself with from now on—and making sure that I would never again find myself too uncomfortably, far too *dangerously*, close to Blaze Davenant if I could help it. *Never*, I vowed to myself. I will never let myself be forced again into having to face my own hateful weakness; and when my engagement to Farland is announced formally— well, that will be the end of *that!*

"Farland—when do you think you will speak to Papa?" I leaned toward him as obviously as I could without risking being labeled either fast or too forward. When he lifted one quizzical eyebrow at me, I smiled back at him as sweetly and ingenuously as I could, fluttering my lashes in an exaggeratedly flirtatious manner that forced the beginning of a smile from him before I breathed: "Would you think me too bold if I admit how—how *impatient* I am to be—your betrothed? To be—oh, Mr. Amerson!—to be . . . *yours?* Why . . . my heart is beating so fast at the thought that I . . . that I could easily *swoon* away from sheer *happiness* and—and wild, soaring . . . *ecstasy* at the very thought of . . . of . . ."

"Enough, I beg of you!" I had actually succeeded in coaxing a quite natural and unfeigned laugh from him for almost the first time, surprising even me as he continued with mock severity: "At least, madam, I hope that you will manage somehow to *control* your 'unbridled ecstasy' for as long as possible—or at least until *after* dinner?"

Impulsively, I touched Farland's arm and whispered: "Do you know that I really do *like* you, Mr. Amerson?" And during the rest of the meal I gave all of my concentrated attention to Farland and our whispered conversation without even once permitting myself to steal a glance at Blaze so that I could observe his reaction—not even when I sensed his eyes on me like sudden heat against my skin.

"A magnificent performance—I'm proud of you," Farland commented later when dinner, thank goodness, was almost over at last. He gave me a rather twisted smile then, before adding in his usual bored drawl: "But you realize of course that in the eyes of our raptly attentive audience we are now both considered . . . well, *compromised?* I suppose I had better ask to speak to your father tonight, before that scowling stepbrother of yours becomes too belligerent! It would never do, I suppose, to kill the groom on the eve of his wedding and *then* beg permission to become betrothed to his sister. No—I suppose not! Not unless . . ." And then, almost casually, Farland said: "Not unless you want me to kill him for you, Trista."

Farland, in spite of his deceptively indifferent manner, seemed to notice almost too much sometimes. But I never knew him to say anything he did not mean—and I wondered at the time what might have made him think that I might want to have Fernando *killed* of all things! After all, Fernando was to be married the next day and he and Marie-Claire would be leaving soon afterward to spend their honeymoon in Europe, while I—I would return with Aunt Charity to Boston and a quieter, more sober manner of living. And more than likely, I would not have to see Fernando again for a long time—and by then they would be comfortably settled, probably with a houseful of squalling infants—although I could not help smiling at the thought of my frivolous friend coping with children, and I wondered if *that* part of being married had even entered her head.

But then, the thought that I might end up being engaged to be married to a man I had known for barely a week had never entered *my* head either when I had journeyed from Boston in order to attend a wedding! Any more than I could have guessed or even dreamed that my life would never be the same afterward and neither would I.

Chapter 16 ⁊

EXCERPTS FROM A DIARY

PARIS, FRANCE
1861

. . . Changes! Why is it that life has to be made up of so many *changes* and that nothing stays the same when you most want it to be that way? Places and people and things and a whole way of life—even the weather changes without warning, like my own moods of late. I was suddenly depressed this morning while I was trying to pack as few and yet as *many* of my belongings as possible into three small trunks and one rather large portmanteau, which I will probably have to carry myself if my luck runs true to form. It was then that I suddenly rediscovered all my battered diaries, buried away in the bottom of my old "schoolgirl trunk," as I have always called it. Why did I have to be foolish enough to begin leafing through the pages of the very first volume I happened to pick up? After a long and painful struggle, I am finally a doctor of medicine—a surgeon. One supposedly acquires some immunity as an adult to the childhood diseases you've already *had*. Or, like a gangrened limb, you simply have to sever it as cleanly and as efficiently as possible, and sew up the bloody, gaping wound very quickly before the patient bleeds to death; and if he is still alive after a week or so, it is considered that the operation has been a success. But the scar remains, and the feeling of loss—and memories.

How ridiculous of me, a rational, cool-headed *adult*
twenty-one years of age, to have suddenly and almost too
vividly remembered everything I thought I'd forgotten—
and to have felt, with a sudden rush, all the confusion and
the agony I thought, at sixteen, could hardly be *borne!*
Thank God Jessie happened to come in at that moment
asking if she could help, and then remarking worriedly
that I looked quite *white* and far too drawn and needed to
breathe some fresh air.

Jessie can be quietly but firmly insistent when she feels
she must be at times; and usually I waste my time by trying to argue with her so that I don't feel as if I am giving in
without protest. But on this occasion I surrendered so
quickly and with such eagerness that her smooth forehead
puckered slightly as she frowned—giving me a questioning
and almost suspicious look before I convinced her that I
had just been thinking the same thing myself because the
atmosphere seemed so stuffy indoors this morning.

"It's probably because the barometer's falling—whatever *that* means aside from rain and a return to cold and
damp weather after all the sunshine we've enjoyed. That is
why I thought that *you* might like to enjoy what might be
your last sunny day in Paris before you have to leave. Why
don't you drive yourself to Mr. Worth's *atelier* on the Rue
de la Paix to pick up the new gowns you ordered? I'm sure
you are bound to cause quite a stir, and you know just how
much you've always enjoyed doing *that!*"

Of course Jessie was right—as she usually is! My mood
changed once I was outdoors and felt the sunlight warm
me while I enjoyed the sudden surge of excitement and
pleasure I got from taking my new phaeton out for a spin
with the top folded back and the breeze snatching stray
tendrils of hair from the confinement of netting and pins to
blow wildly about my face while everyone I passed either
stared or swore when I demonstrated how well I could handle the ribbons by passing them neatly and swiftly—
sometimes with only inches to spare.

Monsieur Worth, as usual, seemed to surpass even himself as he made tiny, fussy adjustments while I tried on my
very latest wardrobe—two riding habits, one a very dark
green with black trimming and the other a burgundy-

crimson with silver-gray braiding. "To match madame's eyes, of course!"

The walking gown, two "town dresses" for shopping and tea afterward or for afternoon calls—they have already been carefully packed away, protected by layers of tissue. But my new "evening toilette," as M'sieu Worth called his creation when it was almost worshipfully unveiled by two of his assistants, almost took my breath away when I first saw it—and still lies draped across the bed I have not yet slept in. "Only *you*, madame, could carry it off—and be daring enough to wear a gown that is destined to release women from their cages and hoops for the very first time; and before this new style has already become the rage, as they say! And now—if you will observe how *different* and more flattering it is?"

The shades of gold melting into sea-greens and palest copper overlaid with silver catch the light from the lamp I write by and seem to keep changing with every movement of the flames that are brighter and leap higher since I have added more coal to the fireplace. Ah, but my spirits were so high at the opera tonight, with everyone staring while pretending not to—including the Emperor himself (and quite boldly too, I might add, with the Empress Eugenie smiling daggers at his side). And then, because she hates Eugenie and is ready to like anyone who manages to make her feel *outshone,* I received a nod and a conspiratorial smile from Princess Pauline de Metternich, who occupies a box across from ours.

"My dear, lovely child, you are the success of the evening—as I am sure you're aware of by now!" she said to me after I had been summoned to visit her box for a glass of champagne during the first intermission. Looking me over once more from top to bottom, the Princess actually smiled again with a twinkle reaching her eyes. "The estimable M'sieu Worth, of course? I shall rap his knuckles for not showing his latest new style to *me* first—if he is not too busy supervising our 'Empress Crinoline's' brand-new wardrobe, that is!"

"I think—I am not *sure*—that I have been approved of!" I whispered to Jessie, who sat beside me looking as calm and as beautiful as she always is. "But *not* by her Imperial

Majesty, I think! It is probably just as well that I shall be sailing for California tomorrow evening!"

Sailing for California on the evening tide . . . it sounds like a line from a poem. Even as I was writing those words I felt as if I were mechanically copying lines out of a book. It still does not seem quite *real* to say to myself, "I am going back home to California!" I feel, suddenly, that I *have* no real home—that perhaps I never have had after all! And I want—I had *thought* to stay here in Paris for some time longer, and to travel about Europe and spend more time enjoying myself and my newfound freedom from books and lectures and hospital wards filled with the sick and the dying whom I must try to think of impersonally as cases. Well, by God—I survived it, didn't I? All four years of nothing but hard, grinding *work* that kept my mind totally occupied and my body so tired I almost fell across my bed and slept dreamlessly until Jessie would wake me up with steaming hot *café au lait* with an egg beaten into it and plenty of brandy to revive me enough to face another morning and another day that lasted into the night.

But it's *over!* Even if I had to learn to swagger and boast and smoke cigars to masquerade as a man in order to be accepted by the conservative École de Médicine in Paris, they've all had to admit afterward, no matter how grudgingly, that I have *earned* the precious piece of parchment that announces to the world that I am a doctor of medicine and have won the right to place the letters M.D. after my name. I have *won*, after all! Why do I feel as if I have to keep repeating it as if I needed to convince myself of something?

I think it must be the sudden damp chill in the air and the rain that seems as if it might keep dripping down like this forever that has suddenly turned my mood of almost feverish gaiety into a gray depression—and keeps me awake when the chiming of the clock on the landing warns me it is almost dawn.

My new set of leather-bound diaries—a thick volume for each month—was a surprise *bon voyage* present from Jessie when I returned to the apartment this afternoon. "I thought that since you don't have to fill pages and pages with copious *scribbles* any longer, you might go back to practicing better calligraphy by keeping a diary again as

you used to before you became too busy. At least . . . you'll
remember everything that has happened and be able to report it faithfully when you write to me—and you *will*,
won't you? Please, Trista—it is the *only* promise I will ex-
act from you!" Oh, Jessie! If you only knew how very much
I will miss you, my loving, supportive, *dearest* friend! You
see—I have already made a beginning tonight; while I am
still here in the warm and comforting surroundings that
have grown so familiar to me. I can hear Justine's faint,
querulous cry for your attention as she wakes up hungry
and unpleasantly damp—and now as her crying stops, suddenly I know you have taken her from the nurse and will
keep her with you in your bed until she wakes again.

Oh <u>damn</u>! Yes, why shouldn't I underline the word!
Damn this mood of mine, and my selfish reluctance to go to
those I love and who love me when I am needed! I should be
happy and full of anticipation at the thought that I will actually be in California again and see everything I used to
remember and long for when I was in Boston and still in
school. And I will see Papa again and be able to tell him
my news in *person*—and Marie-Claire. . . .

I wonder if it was seeing Le Comte et Comtesse de Martineau at the opera house tonight that made my mood of gaiety and liveliness change so abruptly to thoughtfulness.
Or perhaps it was the story of the opera *Tannhauser* combined with Richard Wagner's almost sublime music that
seemed to collect and combine and *express* almost every
human emotion possible that caused this melancholy feeling I cannot shake away; and makes me think, suddenly,
that the windblown gusts of rain sweeping against my
windows and dripping from the eaves sound like voices repeating words I have fought to make myself forget.

Why can't memory be erased as easily as writing on a
slate? Oh *damn* and damn again! I've pretended to be a
man for so long that I must be careful now to stop myself
from using much *worse* words when I am angry or upset.
And since I have tried again to fall asleep and cannot, I
have decided that I might just as well put everything I feel
and *fear* into writing. Perhaps I might feel relief from
doing so—and put *all* the past to rest at last with repetition.

First a letter from Marie-Claire, who longs to see me and

is devastated that I have not written to give her *all* of the
news and the very latest gossip. She has two babies already and hopes that there is not yet another squalling in-
fant on the way, although of course she has always had a
wet-nurse to take care of them soon after she has delivered
so that she is by no means tied *down* and is able to attend
almost every function and festive occasion that is worth-
while attending in San Francisco; for they own a house
there now, for convenience, and she stays there for most of
the time because there is always something going *on* there
. . . "and Fernando, of course, is still a doting and indul-
gent husband who makes no objection to my attending any
important social events that count—even if he has to go
away or is preoccupied with silly politics and his friend
Judge Terry, who killed Senator Broderick in a duel and is
now drumming up support for the Southern Cause everywhere in California! Fernando thinks that all the old land
grants that were so cruelly and unfairly snatched by the
Yankees from their rightful owners will be restored after
the war ends (as it soon must, from all I hear) with a victory and a vindication of the brave Southern states who
have dared to defend their rights under the Constitution!
Why, I'm sure that by now you, since you have been living
in Paris, must have heard that not only the English but
the French as well are more than sympathetic to the Cause
and are soon expected to give it their open support! But
now that I have written something serious as Fernando
asked me to, please do remember every detail of how fashionable women dress now, and wear their hair. . . ."

Why did I never realize how shallow and empty-headed
Marie-Claire really is? Why, if she isn't dutifully repeating what someone else has told her to say, she'd talk of
nothing else but herself and her giddy social life! We never
really had anything in common before, and now it is going
to be even *worse* while I spend all my time trying to be civil
and curbing my unruly tongue!

I have suddenly thought, not being able to help smiling
to myself, what Marie-Claire's papa or her formidable
belle-mère might be writing to her—or may already have
written, for all I know! I fear I have become quite *notorious*
in Paris for my "daring escapades," as the sensation-
mongers would have it, ever since it became known ex-

actly *how* far I'd dared to go to graduate with honors from
the best medical school in Europe as A. T. Villarreal, physician and surgeon. *Merde!* Fernando, who sounds as if he
has turned into an affable and settled family man, will
never like it unless Aunt Charity has already smoothed
the way for me. If not for her unusually short and almost
terse letter that says only that Papa has been ill and I am
urgently needed now in California, I would not be leaving
Paris tonight on Her British Majesty's Ship *Sunflower*.
But at least Aunt Charity herself will be there too. Only, I
can't help thinking, *why* did her letter have to sound so
cryptic? And why wasn't it *postmarked?*

No—there's no point in worrying ahead of time! I would
have to go home in any case to claim my mysterious inheritance, now that I am twenty-one years of age, or . . . or perhaps I can make a show of the stiff-necked Villarreal
arrogance and pride, and turn it down *scornfully!* After all
. . . And now I remember that night when everything happened and my life was changed irretrievably—and remember that I have promised myself to write everything down
in order to forget, while the sky beyond my windows and
behind black, streaming-wet chimney tops seems to fade
almost imperceptibly from dark to slightly lighter shadings of gray and my cheerful fire falls in upon itself with a
sudden explosion of crimson-gold sparks before settling
into a sullen heap of glowing red embers.

So many things and so many other explosions of words
and emotions leading up to *this*. What I have made myself
achieve for the sake of forgetfulness—and what I have become. At least I am no longer that silly girl of sixteen having fun playacting as she played on emotions for spite. Yes,
I can admit that much at least!

The rain still sounds like distant voices . . . or perhaps
they have been hidden away in my mind for all this time,
clamoring to be heard again—to make me understand
what they were really saying that night. . . .

"You cheap slut! You're your mother's spawn all right,
aren't you? So you've slept with the gallant *fool* to make
sure of a conquest—and a match all the other women here
will envy you for! Isn't *that* it, bitch? Well? Are you afraid
or ashamed to answer me? *Puta . . . !* Whore!" Fernando's
hands on my shoulders suddenly shaking me out of sleep—

the heaviness of his body over mine, holding me down
while he continued to hiss filthy obscenities in my ears and
all my attempts to scream or even to protest were pushed
back into my throat by the painful pressure of one hand
and the other groped roughly under the flimsy silk shift I
had decided to sleep in because of the heat and oppressive
humidity that night. "Were you expecting a lover tonight?
Or do you leave your bedroom door unlocked every night
for any man who might decide he wants to use your wanton's body you enjoy flaunting? Tonight, whore, I shall find
out for myself if you have been used before or not!"

I still find myself shuddering and crossing my legs
tightly under my night-robe when I remember what it felt
like to struggle impotently with my wits vanishing into
stark, unreasoning terror, trying uselessly to scream
against his smothering hand as I tasted blood in my mouth
and beat wildly against his shoulders while I felt fingers
find and probe and stab so deeply, so hurtfully into me that
I moaned like a wounded animal and arched and writhed
against that invasion with all the frenzied strength of a
madwoman—biting and scratching now in an almost
mindless frenzy until he couldn't hold me any longer; he
cursed at me furiously and drew back the hand I had just
bitten as if to strike me when, thank God, I heard Papa's
voice, saying with a note in it I had never heard before:
"Fernando!" and then—everything seemed to stop and become suddenly still except the sound of my gasping, sobbing breathing and Papa's voice again, saying something
else in the same *terrible* tone before I felt Fernando's body
lift and relieve me of its weight before he left my room and
closed the door behind him without saying a word.

"Oh God—my little Trista! My poor little . . . daughter
of my heart, I . . ." I realized only then, when his voice
strained and broke, that I had never, ever before seen Papa
crying—or seen his face twisted into such a mask of sheer
agony that I could not endure myself the pain and grief he
felt because of *me!* His "little Trista" whom he had called
the daughter of his heart and thought of as an innocent
virgin, when I was not—as Fernando had already discovered for himself. When I had already, and of my own free
will and *wanting,* given to a hard-faced stranger who . . .

Yes—be honest with yourself at least, Trista! A man who

only took a *body,* shamelessly and wantonly offered; and what normal man with normal sexual urges could turn such an offer down without feeling less of a man if he did so? And then . . . then I had to make everything even worse by crying hysterically on my aunt's shoulder after Papa had sent her to me—and blurting out between sobs everything I should have kept to myself. The *truth* I felt I must confess as some kind of expiation for my own guilt; without thought of the hurt and disillusion I might inflict on *her,* when she already had more than enough to bear.

Crying over spilt milk, it's called. Shifting your own guilt onto the shoulders of those who love you enough to suffer because of you. How could I have been so thoughtless?

I suppose she must have spoken to Blaze—I *know* she did; to force him to come to me soon afterward with his hair still rumpled and his face a mask of fury that made me shrink back against the pillows that propped me up. He had been in bed—*whose?*—and undressed, for he was barefoot and was still tucking his shirt into his wrinkled pants when he erupted into my room, all but slamming the door behind him before he controlled himself for long enough to *lock* it deliberately behind him before he turned his glinting, *raging* eyes on me with a look that made me feel as if I were shriveling up as I was forced as if mesmerized to look into molten fire that would destroy me.

At least I wasn't deceived by the barely controlled softness of his voice, which was like the warning growl of a tiger who has stalked his prey for long enough and only draws his lips back from his life-destroying teeth just before he leaps for the kill. I remember the white lines of anger outlining every tense muscle in his face—and, still incredibly, that his chest was bare, and even there I could see the muscles move and strain against his self-control.

"Well? And how much more of an upheaval do you mean to cause before your selfish, greedy little mind is content with *enough?* You surely cannot be quite as foolish as to take the risk of demanding marriage from *me* now that you've spread your favors around thinly enough so that *I* seem the only likely prospect you have left?" His short, ugly laugh was almost as painful to bear as a savage blow across my face—and just as stunning; even if the calcu-

lated cruelty of every word he had chosen had not already
paralyzed me into petrified immobility.

I wasn't capable of defending myself against the things,
the untrue, unfair accusations he hurled at me with such
contempt while all I was capable of doing was to shake my
head in dumb protest while I was slashed at and cut into
ribbons of bleeding flesh by more harshly caustic words
meant to hurt and injure and render me even more vulnerable and helpless while he laid all my nerves bare with
every knife-edge word.

"I didn't beg for what you offered too easily and too eagerly, remember? And if I had not been unlucky enough to
be where I was when you blundered into me . . . But what
in the *hell* did you think you'd gain by telling Charity the
whole sordid little tale? I'm only here because I won't have
her hurt. Why don't you take Farland Amerson instead if
he'll still have you? Or you could take the stepbrother
you've always lusted for instead, sweeting. Even if you do
cause a resounding scandal, I'm sure Marie-Claire will
survive it and feel herself lucky in the end!"

Oh—coward or not, I cannot force myself to write down
any more of those snarling, contemptuous words that
flayed me alive any more than I can bear to let myself
remember—even though I tell myself over and over that I
was still almost a *child* at the time, and no match for him
at all. Not *then,* at least!

"I . . . You *flatter* yourself if you could . . . could even
think that I would *ever* want to . . . I'd rather *die* first, do
you understand? I'd rather . . ." And then I made the ultimate, the crowning mistake of choking into his granite-
hard face: "In any case . . . in any case . . . Farland
Amerson has asked me to . . . to be his *wife,* and I . . . happen to *love* him! Never *you!* Couldn't you tell, in spite of
your stupid male *conceit,* that all *you* were to me was . . .
was the only available man I could find to . . . rid me of . . .
what had become an *encumbrance?*" And then, lifting my
head with a desperate kind of defiance, I flung back at
him: "Why, I only said something to my aunt because I . . .
I couldn't bear that *she* should be another of your . . . victims! Do you think I haven't realized already what kind of
. . . of low-down *scum* you are? Why, I have found out since
the last time you *forced* yourself upon me how"—and, trying

to steady my shaking voice, I added venomously—"how *poor* a lover you are in comparison to . . . to the others I have experienced since then to *wipe* away the *taint* of your loathsome touch!"

Like Fernando, after he had been frozen by the disgust and hurt in Papa's voice only a few hours earlier, I watched with almost horrified agony as I saw his face actually grow *pale* with fury under the darkness of his skin before he, too, turned abruptly and in smoldering, seething silence began to jerk at the handle of the door as if he were on the verge of tearing it off before he recalled that he had locked it himself.

To this day, I will never know what strange, unnameable impulse made me say suddenly, just when he had the door unlocked and open under the white-knuckled grip of his fingers: "Do you really *love* her, Blaze? Or as much as you are capable of loving *anyone?*"

Halfway out of the door and my sight I saw him pause as if I had jerked him to a halt somehow; and then he said without even turning his head and in a voice suddenly devoid of any emotion: "Yes—with the kind of love that *you* will never know or understand!"

And then—then I was staring at the blank face of the door . . . and I have never set eyes on Blaze Davenant since. Not even at the wedding. Not even at the reception given two days later by Farland's parents. I knew, by then, that whatever had been or I had imagined there had been between us had been broken and lost forever—and I would never find such a pulling of the senses to another man, in quite the same way, again.

But at least, I can tell myself now as I stretch and shiver slightly in the chill that seems to have crept into the room since I let the fire burn out—at least I tried to make amends by telling Aunt Charity that he had actually admitted to me that he loved *her*—"almost too much." And I feel that *then,* at last, the contentment and glow of happiness came back into her face as she hugged me and whispered how *happy* she felt to know that I had discovered in Farland my real and only true love.

Chapter 17 ～ん

EXCERPTS FROM A DIARY

AT SEA

This is *too* much! I should have stayed in Paris and could have been enjoying the warmth of Andalusia or Sardinia by now instead of violent storms and numerous delays because of putting in for shelter at the nearest available harbor, and constantly picking up new passengers and . . . but what point is there in making a list of my grievances all over again? I suppose I should feel relieved that I am still alive—that the crew did not mutiny and cast us off in one of the tiny lifeboats to make the best of the heavy seas in *spite* of our surly, unpleasant captain, who has continued to remain completely indifferent to the well-being or protests of even those passengers who, like myself, have been foolish enough to pay more than double the usual fare for the so-called *privacy* of a tiny cubicle known as a cabin—without having to be crammed in with at least three other people, as I have just been reminded of by His Majesty our captain's first mate, the despicable Mr. Simmons.

"I won't mince words—and don't believe in wasting them either!" I was told bluntly while the mate's arctic-cold eyes looked me over with obvious dislike and—yes, *contempt!* Even now I find it difficult to breathe, as I try to fight back rage and frustration. To think I must put up with being treated this way without being able to do anything about it!

"Any cap'n's like God when he's commanding his own

ship, miss! He's got the right to pick and to choose who he takes aboard—and especially *this* one! If I'd known you was a *female*—beggin' your pardon, miss; a *lady,* that is—I'd have said so before, when the gentleman—your friend?—came to pay for the ticket! After all, miss, all *I* got was your last name and your *initials* in front of it! You can't blame me, can you now, for never thinking it was a lady, and not a *gentleman* I wrote this here ticket out for? First class. Single cabin. Why, if there was anything in the world I could do, miss, I *would,* but Captain McCormick is the best skipper we've got, and the most experienced, so you might say his word, miss, is law! And he'd never take a woman traveling by herself on any ship of *his!* Sorry, miss, I'm sure, but . . ."

"But if A. T. Villarreal happened to be not a young woman traveling alone but a *man*—as everyone seems to have taken for granted?" I knew what the outcome would be, of course, from the sudden avaricious shine in the man's eyes as soon as I casually began to fold over and over the ten-pound note I had agitatedly produced from my reticule along with a lacy handkerchief.

"A—a *man,* miss? Well of course, if it was a gentleman like everyone expected . . . I mean . . . well . . . no one ever thought it could be anything *else,* of course."

"I am sure that when I inform Dr. Villarreal how helpful you have been, he will be *more* than generous with his expressions of heartfelt gratitude! *Thank* you, Mr. . . . Simmons, is it? And since it would not be proper to kiss you, you must at least allow me to shake your hand!"

While he was still stuttering over the "doctor" I could not resist throwing in, I extended my hand graciously—and that was that! I would not allow myself to be thwarted because of some bullheaded, woman-hating sea captain, I remember telling myself. I've pretended to be a man before—and after all this time it will only be for a month or so!

. But this time I could not bring myself to cut off all my hair again—not when it's only just grown long enough again to hang past my shoulder blades when I dare to free it from the two tight braids I wear wrapped closely about my head and covered always by a hat or cap of some sort. No—it couldn't be that! And I haven't indulged in any conversation except for the usual exchange of pleasant civilities when I have chanced to encounter my fellow passengers on board—which has been seldom enough, since almost all of them have suffered terribly from the *mal de mer,* poor creatures! How then, and in what possible way, could I have given myself away? Because, from the time I encountered those freezing eyes, I knew that Captain McCormick was aware of my real sex. Even before he ordered me to keep away from the men—at least those under *his* command. I still find it hard to believe!

I still find it hard to discipline myself, to *force* back my unruly temper and make myself *write* all this down instead of losing control of myself—as the captain hoped, no doubt, that I would so that he could make me feel the power of his authority over every unfortunate human being on *his* ship.

Yes—that *is* what he wanted; and I know it—although I don't know *why* yet. Keep away from his crew indeed! All I have done is tend to sore backs when that devil had one of them flogged for some minor infraction or even for being too *slow* at following barked-out orders no one could hear over the sound of howling winds and crashing seas. And he calls this deliberate cruelty discipline!

"Sailors don't need mollycoddling to make them soft, or the kind of tender care that might give that sort of crude, rough men certain *notions*—and I don't want *that* kind of trouble to deal with! So I'll be asking you to try and keep your kindness for your friends in California—if you're still so anxious to see them—and leave me to tend to *mine.* And you'll be understanding what I'm saying, I'm sure? Good! I have already asked the steward to see that your meals are brought to you in your cabin—and he'll see to anything else you might be needing that you've paid for, I'm sure! And—oh yes—there was one more thing I had almost forgotten. We are to have one or two more passengers join us when we stop for fresh water and cargo at the port of San Diego tomorrow; and I was sure, as tenderhearted as you are, that you'd never mind sharing your cabin with another gentleman for the few days it'll take us to get to San Francisco! Well—and now I've said my piece, I'll bid you good evening, shall I?"

I can hear every word he said—just as I have written

them down. Even the tone of his voice and the slight curl of those thin, mocking lips while he watched my reaction to every word, each deliberate innuendo. If I had flown at him in a rage, or picked something up off his desk and thrown it at him as I was sorely tempted to do, I have no doubt that he would have invoked his almost godly prerogatives that give him the power of life and death over any soul on board *his* ship, and had me clapped in irons—or worse!

I cannot help being agitated, being angry! Not only has it been very clearly implied that I should keep to my cabin and not even emerge for meals; but now I must also put up with a companion—a *male* companion of course—and no doubt someone who snores and is not only crude in his manners but the worst and lowest kind of scoundrel the captain can find to add to my punishment. I suppose that since he cannot *dare* go so far as to have me flogged on some pretext like one of his unfortunate crew members, he has chosen to torment me in as many other ways as he can, to punish me for taking him in at first. How on earth could he have *guessed* when he has hardly as much as glanced in my direction before? I should have noticed if he had, I'm sure . . . oh, damnation! How much longer will I have to tolerate this insulting and unfair treatment?

We have put in at San Diego—not for above four hours, the disgustingly obsequious steward has informed me before he left me my dinner and *two* bottles of wine as well. I could not help noticing how his eyes watched me—slyly, measuringly; making me feel as if . . . no! I refuse to let my imagination get the better of me and put me into such a state of nerves that the captain will find me easy prey. I have nothing, *nothing* to be nervous about. I am not one of his crew, after all; I am a first-class passenger—and entitled to the privileges I have paid an extremely high price for. And to *courtesy,* at the very least! He is *not* some demigod or Eastern potentate, this Captain McCormick, whatever *he* may consider himself to be—and there is no reason in the world why I should allow myself to be intimidated by him!

And now that I have written it down and underlined every word for emphasis, I feel as if I have regained my senses again and can, in fact, almost feel sorry for the ridiculous *little* man whose whole empire is this ship he is in charge of, which does not even belong to him but to the company that employs him. How *silly* I've been! Just as if I were still only sixteen instead of over twenty-one and adult. Yes—*adult*—although I'm not sure why I should suddenly have to keep reminding myself of it. Is it because I am going back to California at last after all these years? Why do I suddenly have to feel as uncertain and as unsure of myself or what might lie ahead of me as I did as a very young child? As if . . . as if . . .

After all the storming and the feeling of being flung upward in a cloud of foam before falling down along a green wall of water and then being tossed high again and bobbing from wave top to wave top, this slight swell that merely rocks and almost cradles this ship seems strangely soothing, in a way!

So we have sailed past Mexico! And this is San Diego—or all I can see of it through my porthole—only a few clusters of wavering orange lights that seem to huddle together for protection against the vastness and empty darkness of the night sky with only a few star-pricks of light showing against velvet black.

I wish I could go ashore! To take one of the lifeboats and row it myself toward those little, shivering lights until I feel the bottom scrape against coarse sand—and then I will climb out and wade the rest of the way to shore, and to whatever adventure waits for me there! Every wildly reckless impulse that I would have given in to without *thinking* only five years ago urges me to turn and run to the door this minute! To run, blindly, until I suddenly blunder into some unknown place that I neither know nor understand, and where I might find myself even more helpless than I feel I am now! But—I am not, thank God, that same sixteen-year-old girl who understood nothing. I am a mature woman of twenty-one who has learned enough self-discipline to think dispassionately instead of being driven by something primitive and mindless into—some exceedingly foolish and pointless action that will have been anticipated or *hoped* for already, I'm sure!

BOOK TWO: *Blaze*

Chapter 18 ⁓

I'll never let that icy-eyed martinet intimidate me again, Trista thought, as she turned away from her tiny porthole and the almost too-tempting prospect of freedom and—why did she have to think "safety"? There were only a few more days and nights to be endured before they arrived at San Francisco at last—and once she had thought out some clever plan of embarrassing the captain before every other passenger and showing how little she cared for his veiled threats . . . why, the prospect was quite worth smiling to herself about—and worth, even, a bland smile for the steward, who had just sidled in to clear the table of the food she had not deigned to touch.

"You may leave the cheese—and the wine that the captain was thoughtful enough to send me, of course! Convey my thanks, won't you? And you may say, of course, that I am quite looking forward to this gentleman he has chosen to share my cabin with me. It will be quite a change to talk to another intelligent human being again, I'm sure—and of course Captain McCormick, with his unerring knowledge of people, must have chosen, I'm quite sure, someone with whom I will find myself compatible and will feel quite comfortable with, since I am in disgrace and denied all other company for a time! But you will tell the captain I hold nothing against him, I hope? And that I—quite understand?"

Pocketing the pound note he had just been handed and wondering at the young gentleman's smile and sudden air of composure, Mr. Pruitt ducked his head before he carried out the tray with the dishes on it rattling; just like his nerves!

Poor Mr. Pruitt's nerves were in an even worse state by the time he had plucked up enough courage, after swallowing dryly a few times, to knock timidly and unwillingly at the captain's door, quaking inside his boots all the time. Gawd—what if 'e decides to 'ave me skin taken off me back this time? Or—but it ain't *my* fault, is it? I done everything I was told—follerin' orders to the letter, I was—that's all!

Captain McCormick had just taken a final, impatient look about his quarters to make sure his fool of a man had left everything spotless and exactly back in place. Damn all inefficient, frightened fools who couldn't do anything right and whined their excuses afterward! And if that idiot Pruitt didn't show his slimy self before he was obliged to join his first-class passengers at dinner . . .

"Ca'pn, sir—I did just like you told me, and I can swear it by me sainted mother! Took in the tray with dinner—with the best cut of meat, steaming hot soup, even that boneless piece of the fish Mr. Brown caught yesterday! And when I brought dinner in he was writing in them diaries, and real pale in the face too—shaking with pure funk he was too, sir! But when I went back for the tray . . ."

"Well?" Captain McCormick snapped the word out, his jaw set tightly and jutting out with annoyance that made Pruitt quake. "Stop staring at me with your mouth gaping, you brainless idiot, unless you want a taste of the bos'n's cat to remind you of your duty!"

"Oh no, sir! *Please,* sir! I mean—you might say, sir . . . that is, I was only looking for words to put it the way I could feel 'ow it was, sir! Like—well, like suddenly, from bein' all scared and shakin' almost, the young gentleman turned about from starin' out of the porthole and—and told me 'e didn't want anything left but the cheese and the wine, sir! And to be sure and tell you 'e thanked you for the wine and that 'e didn't—'old nothin against you, sir!"

"Oh? And that is all?"

"N-no, not exac'ly, sir! The young gentleman did say, real happy like, almost, that he was looking forward to sharing his cabin with . . . with another intelligent human being, sir! And 'e thanks you for your thoughtfulness . . . sir!"

"Does he indeed! A most perspicacious young man, wouldn't you say, Pruitt? And now you can get out of my way and back to your duties, before I'm tempted to let you feel my boot where it would do the most good!"

After Pruitt had scuttled out of the way, Captain McCormick paused for a brief moment to adjust his gold-braided cap and brush off his jacket with the stripes proclaiming his exalted rank, letting his thin gash of a smile show for an instant before he set his face into its usual sternly forbidding expression. Pruitt was a fool, but at least he observed almost everything. And in spite of his outward nonchalance, the young Señor Villarreal remained obediently in his cabin . . . *waiting?* Well, let him wait a few more days, and wonder . . . !

While Captain McCormick presided over dinner that night, Trista considered locking the cabin door at first and then, shrugging, decided against it, finally sleeping with a loaded two-barrel derringer (which the gunsmith in Paris had assured her was "the very latest thing") under her pillow and the comforting thought that she knew how to use it very efficiently if she needed to do so—and on *anyone,* including Captain McCormick himself!

Chapter 19 ~

Later, Trista confided to her diary, her pen scratching angrily against paper:

At *least* I can be almost certain that I will not be attacked in my sleep—nor kept awake by loud snoring or loud, vulgar conversation. In fact, all I have *heard* from the "companion" Captain McCormick has chosen for me were some half-smothered and very obscene swear words when he all but staggered in when it was almost morning and decided to sleep on the floor instead of attempting to grope his way to the other bunk across the room. And, thank God, he had disappeared by the time I opened my eyes late this morning.

That slimy toad Pruitt, whose hair is as oily as his manner, has hinted that the "other gentleman" seems to be occupied with cultivating and plying with liquor the foolish and unsuspecting husbands of the women he means to seduce—as a kind of *hobby,* I presume! But at least *I* can feel safe from this Casanova while he is aboard, I suppose . . . even if it means that I have to be patient and contain myself until he has disembarked at San Francisco. Perhaps I might be fortunate enough not to have to encounter him at all! It is almost worth my remaining in voluntary seclusion in this tiny space—until he's *gone,* and I can finally prove to our godlike captain that he was mistaken for once in thinking he had me cowed and frightened into submission by his blustering and his threatening *hints!* I should have remembered what Farland Amerson told me—was it really *five* or only four years ago?

It doesn't matter *when* he told me as long as I never again forget what he said. "Never show fear—even animals can sense it if you're afraid of them! You've got to learn, my dear Trista, to look an antagonist straight in the eye and face him down . . . always remember the *eyes*—watch them—you'll find that it throws most people off, actually!"

I think, sometimes, that I miss Farland almost as much as Jessie does, even if I am angry with him for—for going counter to everything he taught me, is what! How *could* he? Especially with the baby to think of, if he couldn't think of his *wife.* Farland the bored cynic—and he's off like any other silly, idealistic *idiot* to fight for something he doesn't even *believe* in! Jessie says she understands, but *I* never could. Damn men and their stupid, senseless causes that they're prepared to die for even when they *know* they're never going to change the world—to change *anything,* in fact, by *dying!* Oh God—I couldn't bear it if Farland is silly enough to get himself killed! I . . .

The ship heeled to one side, unexpectedly under the onslaught of suddenly gusting winds, and ink spilled all across the page she had been writing on and stained the cuff of her white shirt—the last clean shirt she had left. "Damn!" Trista exclaimed aloud, trying to blot up as much of the damage as she could with her blotter; she added several other words she had learned in various languages.

"Oh dear me! And I was just sent by the captain himself to warn you that what with the fresh wind and all it might turn out to be a bit rough! Such a shame, sir, when you spend so much time on your *writing*—why, all day and half of the night, as I've noticed! And if I can be of some little *help* . . . ? This napkin 'ere—now *that* should blot some of it up! And I'll be sure and bring back another inkwell for you right away, sir!"

Thank goodness she had placed the blotter over the

page, because of course the oily little wretch was longing to read as much as he could! And at *this* particular moment, at least, Trista thought balefully that she had had more than enough!

When she stood up to look the unfortunate Mr. Pruitt over in a manner that made him suddenly stumble back with his eyes popping out of his head, he *quailed*. He flinched when he found the napkin he usually carried over his arm snatched from him while he was almost impaled by a pair of cold, narrowed gray eyes; with a *look* to them, as he was to think later, that was enough to make one's blood run cold!

"Why *thank* you, Mr. Pruitt! How fortunate that you always seem to turn up *just* when you're most needed! But—you're not needed any longer, Mr. Pruitt! And if you *ever* walk into this cabin again without knocking first and asking my permission, I am afraid that I might accidentally discharge my pistol at you!" And then, with a wicked smile that made the unfortunate steward almost fall against the door in his hurry to be gone, Trista added in a regretful voice: "And I'm afraid that I have the quite notorious habit of *killing* anyone I shoot at! I should hate to deprive Captain McCormick of such a faithful and *helpful* lackey—Mr. Pruitt! It's my uncontrollable temper, once it has been roused . . . you understand? Why, I *knew* you would!"

As Mr. Pruitt fled, and the door banged with unseemly haste behind his back, Trista sank back in the chair and laughed almost hysterically before she managed to control herself once more. Good God! I would actually have done it too—and without a moment's hesitation. And all this time I have never been quite sure that I could be capable of *killing* another human being—even a wretched, worthless creature like Pruitt. But it's quite easy, after all . . . to kill without thinking.

The ship had begun to rock and heel from side to side as it flew before the wind—as fast as a China clipper and without any need for steam to help her along. Looking through her salt-encrusted porthole, Trista watched the foam flying wildly in their wake from the white-crested waves that rose to hug the sides of the vessel and fall behind as its sharp bow cut through wind-ruffled blue sea.

About the only thing that could be said for Captain Mc-

Cormick was, she thought grudgingly, at least he was a good sailor! And now, riding with the wind, he would be on the bridge of course holding the wheel steady while he barked his orders at the unfortunate men who must clamber up the rigging and hope to survive the wind that tried to dislodge them while they had to hoist or lower the sails at his command. But while Captain McCormick was busy with his precious ship and all his timid passengers were hiding safely below deck . . . he'd never have time to notice if someone dared to venture out on deck. And even if he *did*—why should it matter?

She could almost feel the salt kiss of the sea against her face and the urgent tugging of the wind in her hair, driving it wildly about her. Witch! That's what they'd think, whoever happened to see me! she thought. A black-haired witch of the sea—cast up by the waves and wind—only to disappear like a fragment of foam that dissolves as soon as it touches the deck. She began to rummage in one of her trunks until she found the cloak she had been looking for, a heavy black wool with a hood—what could be more suitable, or more witchlike?

She had managed to scare Pruitt away from his task of *guarding* her, obviously—and there was no one about who dared venture out on deck to face the challenge of the wind and the sting of sea spray against their cheeks! Clinging to the rail with both hands, Trista leaned her head back without caring if the hood of her cloak was blown backward by a sudden violent gust of wind that sent her heavy cloak swirling about her body.

Without thinking or knowing why she did so, she put one hand to her head to pull off the woolen cap she had worn, and to snatch and scatter the pins that held her hair in confinement. There! And then the braids—her body balancing and swaying with every movement of the waves and the ship that rode them; purely by instinct and without thinking of what she was doing as she put both hands up to her hair and let her fingers unbraid it and set it free for the wind to take and the salt wet foam . . .

The woolen cap, as she flung it, seemed to sail and skim over the water for a while as the wind toyed with it—and then sank, suddenly disappearing. So much for disguises! Trista thought, leaning back her head and her body as her hands held on to the wet rail again and she let her eyes close while for a moment she only *felt*—nothing else.

"Flinging your cap to the winds—is that significant or only symbolic? And is it possible that you are real?"

There was an instant when she was almost petrified with terror as if she had with no more than a thought crossing her mind managed to conjure up a demon. No. No! Just as if she had suddenly been trapped in a nightmare, Trista found that her feet couldn't seem to move in spite of the frantic commands of her mind that said, "Run! Run!" For one wild moment Trista thought of flinging herself over the rail, into the embrace of the sea waves that reached up to her—vastly preferable to *this!* No! she thought again despairingly, before she managed at least to snatch her hood back protectively around her head, shielding her face—while the warmth of his body against her back was like the heat from a forest fire, burning through her skin . . . burning *into* her everywhere as his arm, closing about her waist, gathered her even more closely against him so that she felt again that frightening sense of being melted and dissolved against him and into him just as he seemed to penetrate into *her*—so deep, so far inside every part of her that she tensed all over and flung her head back with an inarticulate, almost primitive cry that came from her throat without any conscious volition; and then she heard him say in a harsh but almost *wondering* voice: "Oh God! And now I know that I have imagined you into . . ." Just before he spun her around roughly and kissed her. And kissed her—savagely, exploringly, hurtingly, tenderly—in every conceivable way, it seemed, that it was possible to be kissed and to feel *taken* by a kiss alone, that was both rape and seduction at the same time.

Afterward, Trista could never remember how she had suddenly found the strength to wrench herself away from him and *flee,* almost blindly—as if all the demons in hell were pursuing her.

He hadn't followed her, at least. She must have run, like a doe before a forest fire, the whole length of the ship or more before she regained her senses enough to find her cabin and almost *fall* into it, slamming the door shut behind her and locking it before she fell across her narrow bunk sobbing with exhaustion and . . . I don't want to *know!* her mind screamed at her. You have been imagining something that doesn't exist—something quite impossible. The Demon Lover—it was the book of poems I had been reading . . . I didn't even *see* his face, if he *had* one after all! But at least I didn't say one word. . . . How could I? And he didn't make the slightest effort to come after me either—so it could have been one of the sailors, who became afraid after he realized how bold he had been. Of *course!* And by now the poor wretch, his mood of wind-spawned bravado having left him, must certainly be consumed with anxiety in case the mysterious lady all hooded and cloaked has complained to his captain!

Cloaked . . . ! She had lost her cloak, feeling it snatched from her shoulders by the wildness of the wind at some time during her mad, panic-stricken flight along the slippery deck, and had hardly noticed or cared at the time. She didn't even care *now.* Let it follow her cap as a sacrifice to wind and sea! To Poseidon, worshiped by the ancient Greeks as God of the sea—in return for her protection. But from what? Or worse—from *whom?*

No! She had already allowed her imagination to go too far as it was. She might just as well imagine that she had summoned up Poseidon himself by letting the wind and the sea have her for those few minutes. By tossing her cap to the winds, he had said before . . .

I won't think about it any longer—at least, not now; not until I have changed out of these wet clothes and have dried my hair! Trista told herself as a sudden chill made her shiver uncontrollably. It would be the last thing in the world I need at *this* point—to catch a chill—or even pneumonia!

Naturally, her clothes were ruined by the salt spray, but Trista was in no frame of mind to care about that *now.* She would have to bundle them up and stow them away somewhere for the moment. The pleated shirt she had worn felt wet and sticky against her skin, showing her nipples and the curve of her breasts quite clearly. She had not bothered to bandage them tightly since she had been confined to her cabin; and now Trista thought with a shudder: Well, at least I did not encounter the captain! I wonder what *he* would have done? Or *Pruitt?* He would probably have screamed with terror and fled from the windblown appari-

tion I must have appeared to be with my hair streaming
behind me and blowing across my face. I certainly look
witchlike enough at the moment!

Grimacing at her reflection in the mirror, Trista tugged
her comb almost viciously through her still-damp hair as
she tried to restore some order to the riotous confusion the
wind had created. Perhaps she *should* have cut it short
again! And then . . .

And then it would not have gone swirling and whirling
about my head like a storm cloud, to draw attention to
me—or whip against my face and into my eyes to blind me,
so that . . . so that for some minutes I became blind and
lost to everything but mindless *feeling* and the wild, uncontrollably passionate side of my nature that I thought I
had managed to subdue and had almost forgotten about.
Until today, when a man who could have been *any* man, a
stranger whose face I couldn't even *see,* came up behind me
and held my body against the length and hardness of his
before he turned me about and kissed me in a way that
made me feel as if—oh, God—as if he were already *in* me
and making love to me! Until I felt that burst of feeling
and the weakness after it that I used to feel when Blaze . . .

Abruptly, Trista turned away from the mirror she had
been staring into unseeingly, angry at having allowed herself to dwell on what was much better forgotten—except as
a reminder of certain weaknesses in herself that she must
remember to guard against from now on. It could not possibly have been Blaze Davenant, of course. Not after five
years—not here, on this ship! What happened this afternoon had been nothing but a reaction to her natural tension because of everything she had been forced to endure
for too many miserable weeks; culminating with being virtually *imprisoned* in this tiny cabin where there was
hardly enough room to *turn* or stretch her legs in comfort.

And the cold-eyed Captain McCormick, who gloated at
being able to play cat-and-mouse with a frightened victim—or so he thought! Yes—she'd much rather think about
having her revenge on the captain and the pleasure she
would gain from it than dwell on her own folly, Trista
thought as she began to braid her unruly hair again, remembering suddenly that the obnoxious Pruitt would
probably knock at the door any moment now to ask what

the "young gentleman" would prefer as the main course tonight. What would his reaction be when he was told that all the "young gentleman" wanted was several large mugs of steaming-hot eggnog laced with large quantities of brandy? With perhaps a bowlful of soup before, to coat the stomach. After all, it was a physician's privilege to heal—herself, in this instance. For tonight, at least, with her mind wandering in too many strange, unwanted directions, the bought oblivion of alcohol seemed well worth the price of a wretchedly pounding head the following day! Or so she told herself recklessly at the time, without considering the fact that she would first have to become *drunk* in order to numb her senses into blank forgetfulness. So very drunk that she might not realize what she was doing—nor *care*, either!

Chapter 20 ~

Mr. Pruitt would say afterward that he had always had a strange feeling about that young person! And clear his throat portentously as he prepared to relate his story—after making quite sure that Captain McCormick was not within earshot at the time. He had never in all of his born days seen nor heard of anything like it! The captain almost beside himself with rage—and not being able to do anything about it either! Why, there was hardly a poor sailor on board who wasn't given a taste of the cat during the days that followed—or else the feel of the captain's boot, which could be even worse, depending on *where* he decided to place it when he kicked you. Even if it wasn't your fault at all, because you'd asked him first if it was all right . . .

"It was at least three eggnogs with more brandy in 'em than egg or milk! And then more brandy, and another eggnog with rum in it because I couldn't find no more brandy without 'aving to ask the cap'n for some of *his* private stock. And 'ow was I to know what would 'appen soon after? Gawd—I thought for sure I must be seeing things, I did at first! I go in to clear up, and instead of a young gent lying stone drunk and snoring across his bed, there's only his *clothes,* mind you! He's made himself drunk enough to jump overboard, I thought, and I run down to the dining room to tell the cap'n right away . . . and *that's* how I saw *everything!* All them faces—with their mouths open and

154

eyes staring like—like it was a ghost that they was seeing. Even . . ." Mr. Pruitt always lowered his voice and looked fearfully over his shoulder before daring to continue his tale. "Even the cap'n hisself! Only one in the room cool as *her* and not lookin' surprised at all was that gentleman who'd come aboard at San Diego—the one with a Frenchy-sounding name. *He* just kept right on drinking his wine with the kind of smile that'd make your blood run cold if you'd seen it, and—just *watching* her, that's all! While *she*, that bold, lying, scheming *hussy*—wearing a fancy, shiny kind of gown that showed most of her *bosom* and her bare arms and shoulders as well—such as no *respectable* female would dare to be seen wearing in *public*, if I might say so quite frankly . . . why, *she*, being *quite* intoxicated by then, *naturally*, she stood there just *laughing* at first, before she said . . ."

What Trista had said, after she had been able to stop laughing at the *sensation* her sudden and rather unsteady entrance had caused, was: "Oh goodness! I hope I am not *too* late to join everyone for dinner!" in an innocently questioning kind of voice—before beginning to laugh helplessly again at the choking noises that were the only response to the spontaneous and quite brilliant opening lines she had delivered as she walked—strolled? *swayed?* (that might be easier)—onstage as herself for the first time so that they could all find out at last what a brilliant performance she was capable of giving—brilliant enough to take everyone in, the captain included!

The captain—how very *angry* he must be at being *tricked!* Well, the nasty, overbearing *martinet* deserved it, for having tried to frighten her with his threats and his *orders*, just as if she were one of his cowed, unfortunate *slaves* he enjoyed having flogged for any pretext at all, just to show his absolute power over them. She would have enjoyed seeing the furious glower on his face at that moment if only everything about her had not seemed so blurred and fuzzy for some peculiar reason.

But it wasn't fair that anyone should be angry with *her* and not with the captain himself, who had *forced* her into pretending to be a man again! Nobody had *said* anything yet, or as much as drawn out a chair for her to sit in, especially since they *must* know she was feeling quite dizzy—

and so coldly clammy all of a sudden . . . and who was
applauding her? Why didn't the only appreciative member
of her audience help her to a seat at least? Did they imagine that she was one of those men who enjoyed dressing in
feminine attire and not a real *woman* at all? Perhaps if she
showed them . . .

"You don't believe me, do you? But I can prove it—see?"

"I think that's enough!" Blaze Davenant suddenly exploded, on a note of quite unreasonable fury as he seemed
to almost *erupt* across the room to twist her wrists painfully and with unnecessary force before she had managed
to rip her tightly fitting bodice down the front to prove to
them all that she was a female, with *breasts!* He caught
her just before she would have fallen, and almost the last
thing Trista could remember of that particular night was
feeling as if she had suddenly been swooped up and carried
off to sea on the crest of a tidal wave; and the sound of his
hateful and too-familiar voice that echoed and echoed and
seemed to fill her head until everything, even thought,
was drowned out and disappeared into thankful blackness.

"*I'll* take care of her now!" Blaze flung curtly over his
shoulder before he carried her suddenly limp body through
the doorway without waiting for a response—barely missing striding over Mr. Pruitt before he scuttled out of his
path just in time.

And *now* she'll probably be sick all over me, the silly
little bitch! She probably got herself drunk on purpose as
an excuse for exhibiting her breasts for the benefit of
everyone who cared to see them—and not for the first time
either, I'll be bound! I should drop her overboard if I had
enough sense—or if I could forego the pleasure of *telling*
her exactly what I think of the loose, wanton *slut* she's become, once she's sober enough to listen!

Blaze swore violently and much more explicitly when he
found himself obliged to halt in midstride before he had
reached her cabin in order to lean her over the rail so that
she could be sick—as miserably sick, he hoped grimly, as
she well deserved! Holding her head up by the hair, he
found himself tempted to tear it away from her scalp in
handfuls; and might even have done so if he thought her
capable of feeling pain. Unfortunately, in her disgustingly
drunken stupor she would probably not feel *anything*—

much less be able to hear all the cutting invectives he ached to throw at her while he was telling her, with unsparing bluntness, exactly what he thought of her and her complete lack of *any* morals whatsoever!

"Goddammit, you drunken bitch! Makes me wonder what in the hell you've learned these past five years—unless it's to make a public show of yourself! And if you don't stop your twisting and struggling about while I'm trying to—I'm going to slap you across that pointed little witch's face of yours, by God! Do you hear me?" Damn her! By the time he'd managed to get her, *and* those ridiculous, crinoline-swelled skirts of hers, through the cabin door, Blaze found himself breathing as hard as if he'd been running up the side of a steep mountain. Not only was he annoyed at himself for almost letting his temper get the better of him on *her* account, but he regretted now that he hadn't sat back in his chair and just *let* her show everyone what a trollop she really was, enjoying the display she had been about to put on along with every other man in the room!

Unfeelingly, he let her drop onto her unmade, rumpled bed, disregarding her protesting moans while he lit one of the lamps and made sure the door was locked. She was half on and half off that narrow bunk that was not designed to accommodate hoopskirts and crinolines, and she kept making those little moaning sounds that reminded him of a kitten in pain. Damn her—was she going to keep *that* up all night and keep him from his well-earned rest? Especially after *last* night! In spite of himself, Blaze couldn't help grinning as he looked down at Trista. She might be a little bitch, but she was obviously a clever one! Fooling everyone, even Captain McCormick, into thinking that she was really a young man—with a tempting, rounded little bottom that had felt deliciously firm under his hands. Would it still look and feel the same? As strutting youth, she must have caught the eyes and the fancy of all those men who preferred young boys to women—and someone had whispered to him with a wink only this evening that he happened to be sharing a cabin with "Captain McCormick's latest fancy boy." Surely even *she* would not venture *that* far? Or had she? The look on the captain's face tonight had been a study in fury and frustration when she'd made her grand entrance, laughing uncontrollably

until she'd had to lean against the doorjamb in order to
stay erect. Well . . . , he thought almost unwillingly,
maybe not—not that it mattered to *him* in the least!

Later, Blaze told himself that it was only because she
was Charity's stepniece and because she had looked, suddenly, as if she were still only sixteen years old and far too
vulnerable. And far too eager to experience as much as she
could as well, he reminded himself, angry at his own weakness for going so far as to wet his clean handkerchief with
water from the carafe on the washstand to wipe off her
damp, sweat-beaded face, scrubbing it roughly enough in
spite of her incoherent murmurs to bring some color into
her pallid cheeks and lips. And it was only because of the
way she was breathing, in short, shallow gasps, that he undressed her before she rolled off the bunk—swearing to
himself as he had to fumble with innumerable hooks and
buttons and clumsily knotted ribbons while he wondered
how in the hell and *why* in God's name women allowed
themselves to be imprisoned within this ridiculous, cagelike contraption that was nothing more than a modern version of the medieval chastity belt. *Not,* he reflected grimly,
when he'd finally got her freed, that *some* women didn't
need to be restrained for their own good!

Obviously *she* didn't believe in wearing any more than
was absolutely necessary, he discovered—feeling as if he
were unwrapping a Christmas package as he peeled off
first her gown and then her layers of petticoats before finally unlacing her tight-fitting corset, which had left deep
red welts on her too-pale skin. *No* underwear. Not even the
frilly, lace-trimmed pantalettes that most women wore for
decency's sake at least—even if they were meant to be
taken off by a man! But then, *she* would probably consider
any kind of underwear a needless impediment to her promiscuous pleasure seeking!

He had thrown each garment he had removed with unnecessary violence across the room, where they made an
untidy pile that *she* could damn well pick up whenever
she managed to pry her eyes open. Blaze found himself
scowling down at her, wondering why he could not keep
his eyes from lingering on her body and wondering how
many other men had had their hands on her and had been
granted the license to explore it and use it familiarly for

their pleasure—and hers. Just as *he* had those times that seemed so long ago. She lay sprawled out on her stomach with one leg dangling off the bed, and lest she fall off it, he turned her over roughly and grabbed for a blanket to cover her nakedness before he had time to wonder why he had taken the trouble to do so. After all, judging from the way she had acted earlier and the ease with which he had been able to undress her first and turn her onto her back to lie there with her legs spread like a cheap waterfront whore, without even an involuntary attempt to cross them . . . dammit! There ought to be no doubt in his mind by now that she must be quite used to lying sprawled out this way—legs readily open and her nipples hard little points of excitement—that wild black cloud of hair spilling across the pillow while she licked her parted lips with anticipation and those silver witch-eyes of hers darkened to the color of pewter with lust.

And for how many lovers? Did she care who or what they were as long as they could satisfy her insatiable desires? And what in the *hell* business was it of his, anyhow? Disgusted at himself for suddenly beginning to desire her in spite of everything, Blaze yanked the blanket up to her neck before turning his back on her and beginning to take his own clothes off with angry, impatient fingers that had already ripped half the buttons off his white lawn shirt before the sudden idea struck him, holding him still for a long moment as a particularly unpleasant and cynical smile curled one side of his mouth downward. He had just been thinking that some of her lovers ought to see her as she was just now, even more yielding than usual as she lay in a drunken stupor, the little slut! Perhaps *she* ought to see herself, for that matter!

And why not? Perhaps, if she happens to be sober at the time, it might even give her something of a shock to see a sketch of herself as she is now. Or perhaps I'll do more than just sketches of her this time—perhaps I'll paint her full-length portrait in oils and exhibit it! It's just what the bitch deserves. Still fuming, Blaze jerked the blanket off her body and turned the lamp up higher, turning every contour, every curve of her body and her side-turned face into shadings of gold and shadow—except for the dark, silken triangle swooping down like an arrowpoint between her legs as if to emphasize her sex—those pretty, pouting lips, dark rose pink and delicate; sweet-petaled opening to drowning whirlpool deepness. . . .

But dammit—not for him! Not even if *this* was the only way to exorcise the spell of the sorceress—by making her mortal with her lewd, pictured image.

Chapter 21 ~

"I will see the *gentleman* first, and that—*creature* after I have dealt with him. By God, I'll have no whores plying their trade on my ship, nor any of my passengers or crew wallowing in the filth of harlotry! Do you understand me, Pruitt? Good! Because I am leaving it to *you* to explain exactly what I have just said to Mr. Davenant—*and* that—that vile Jezebel who has been parading herself so brazenly in our midst as a respectable young *man*—a doctor of all things! Why, I have every right to . . . get out of my sight, you abominable *slime!* What are you standing there for?"

Pruitt, white to the gills and terrified almost to the point of incontinence, was only too glad to turn and flee from the sight of the captain's red face and the veins standing out like knots along his neck and his forehead. He'd seen Captain McCormick angry before, but never in such a state of sheer *fury;* with his heavily bound Bible clutched in his hands almost like a weapon. Jesus! he thought, actually running in his hurry to perform his errand; better that dirty, lying little whore than *me*, who's perfectly innocent! Wouldn't be in *those* shoes for anything in the world. Although now he knew she was a female after all, he was almost sorry he hadn't got himself some of the stuff she was obviously used to giving out free and easy like—to judge from the looseness of her manner and morals. Maybe while

her latest gentleman friend was making *his* explanations
to the captain he'd get a feel or two in—after he'd taken
that little gun off her that, come to think of it now, she
probably didn't know how to use if she wanted to, the lying
strumpet! And after *he'd* had her one way—Pruitt grinned
like a ferret to himself as he licked his lips at the thought—
why, she'd probably end up wishing she'd never come
aboard before the captain got through with her—in every
way possible!

His being able to gloat over the discomfort of someone
else and how he might use it to his own advantage helped
bolster Pruitt's courage by the time he paused before the
closed—and *locked*, as he discovered—cabin door. Aha!
They're probably hard at it, he thought; considering it's
been at least two hours or more that they've been locked in
here alone! He was so lost in the lascivious pictures his
imagination had already formed, that his knock was only
perfunctory before he put his key in the lock and turned it,
pushing open the door in almost the same movement.

Afterward he was to tell himself painfully that he
should have remembered to go on his first impressions of
the "artist gentleman" who was always sketching this or
that ever since he'd come on board—if he wasn't romanc-
ing up the ladies. Dark complexioned and hard faced, with
dangerous eyes that reminded one of some ferocious beast
lying in wait. No—soon after the gentleman had come
aboard with his Spanish friend, he had suddenly seemed to
be quite a different person; and even the captain had
treated him with barely concealed contempt.

How should *he* have known that in trying to deliver a
message from the captain he might almost get himself
killed? And for just doing his *duty,* no more! "Just *pounced*
on me, 'e did! Why, I'd 'ardly 'ad time to open the door—
following Captain's orders, I was, too—'ow was *I* to know
what was what?" All Pruitt remembered afterward was a
great deal of pain—not to mention the unpleasant feeling
of not being able to stop retching—while from somewhere
above him he heard a falsely regretful drawl inform him
that he really *should* remember to ask permission before
he entered a private cabin, it could be quite dangerous for
him otherwise.

"Feel grateful, Mr. Pruitt, that you are still alive! I've

had to train my reflexes in order to survive wars and revolutions and remain alive in order to send in my sketched impressions to my editor. I usually *kill*—without even thinking to ask questions. I do hope you have a very good reason for this intrusion?"

After Pruitt was able to gasp out enough to make himself understood, he was only too happy to stumble away as fast as he possibly could, hoping only that the captain would not be sending for him again too soon. And as to what might happen between the surprising Mr. Davenant and Captain McCormick —he was sure he was much better off not knowing!

Trista, sunk in the dreamless black oblivion that had suddenly swallowed her, knew nothing at all of what was going on, or what was about her either. She slept without even knowing she was sleeping, or where she was or what day or time it was or even how she had arrived there—wherever "there" was. In fact, when she finally started to surface with strange, disjointed dreams that first stirred her into half awakening, she was not even aware of her sighs and restless movements because she was still not quite aware of awareness; her mind wanted to stay drowned in nothingness while her senses seemed to function of their own accord and she responded instinctively to *feeling,* even before she had begun, consciously, to *think.*

Unfamiliar feelings only half remembered of warmth and being encircled and held; and unfamiliar heaviness over one leg that kept her from moving from her side onto her back . . .

Her dreams had to do with words and things and times she had almost managed to forget that came slow-bubbling from some primeval deeps to burst in short-spanned dream images.

The swamp water and the island and the ageless old woman who had warned her with words from the mind that did not need speaking aloud: "You have a power in you, young one, that can draw to you what you may think you want—but remember always if you can that all feeling of power is deceptive; for once you use it for yourself it uses you . . . !" And the words went around and around like rings spreading out in a depthless pool of the deepest

black-green that took on all colors and shades of colors
with every spreading ripple, so that she spun around and
around until she was part of all and was all—center and
circling ripples and colors and rising depths and molten,
liquid flame rising to the sky and beyond, and . . . suddenly she was frightened. Dreams mixing in too-dark
sinking darkness and too-bright blinding light—both swallowing and consuming her in some way—so that she was
desperate to escape, escape! And felt herself held and
pinned down by her own feelings—by . . .

"Ahh—no! No!"

"What . . . ? Damn it, stop squirming and be *quiet*, for
Christ's sake! You've turned out to be quite enough of a
nuisance already! Do you hear me?"

All that Trista could think of for the next few moments
was, Why couldn't this have been only another nightmare
after all? Why does it have to be *him* that turns up out of
the depths of hell I consigned him to? She was quite
naked—so was *he*, for that matter—and what was Blaze
Davenant doing in *her* bed anyhow? Oh God, if only her
mind was not so—so *fuzzy* that she could not think or even
remember very well.

He should *not* have said, in that patronizing, *complacent*
tone of voice: "That's better! And since I'm sure you have
the headache you really deserve, you might as well lie
down again and get some sleep. We'll be disembarking a
few hours from now."

In spite of the fact that her head *did* ache and pound in
the most disconcerting fashion, Trista felt everything pent
up inside her explode in a spontaneous burst of screaming
fury.

"You—why, you—bastard! Unspeakable—*vermin!* You
beastly cad! How dare you take advantage of me while I
was *asleep?* Is that the only way you can make sure a female won't reject your—your loathsome advances? Oh—
ohh! If I only had my gun or a knife I'd—I'd . . ." What
infuriated her most was the way he'd turned on his back
and crossed his arms under his head, grinning at her while
she screamed invectives at him, and only quirking one
dark brow occasionally at a particularly descriptive word.
Any man who had the very slightest vestiges of decency
left in him would at least have shown some signs of

embarrassment—but not *him*, of course! And to make matters worse, when she ran out of breath he actually laughed up at her. It was too much to tolerate! "Bastard! You—I'd like to *kill* you!" And she began pounding on his bare chest before deciding to claw that mocking grin off his hateful face—only to find her wrists seized so suddenly and with such force that she had no choice but to fall on top of him with her face only inches away from his; almost weeping with frustration as he held her wrists as far apart as possible to either side of him, making it impossible for her to do anything but squirm impotently against his warm, naked body.

"Well, well, well!" He drawled infuriatingly into her face. "Just like old times, isn't it? But, sweeting—you didn't have to go to such lengths to jog my infernal memory, you know! All you had to do was *ask*—as you did before—and so charmingly too! Did you really think I'd forgotten?"

"Oh God! You *are* utterly despicable! I should have remembered *that!* So vile—so *low* that in spite of all your nasty, cruel little innuendos, you had to—to rape me while I *slept*, of all things—having *bribed* your way in here, I suppose! I wouldn't put *anything* past you! You—did you have that slimy little steward make sure I was safely drugged first? Who took my clothes off? What *else* happened while I—I was . . ."

Trista gave a cry of alarm when, without warning, he brought her wrists forward and together between their bodies and in the same swift movement used them to push her roughly over onto her back, straddling her with his body so that she could hardly breathe.

Blaze said slowly, between gritted teeth: "What *else?* You drunken, depraved little bitch! I suppose you'll tell me next that it was I who encouraged you to get yourself thoroughly inebriated before you decided to bare your breasts—such as they are, I might add—to everyone in the dining room! The talk was that you were advertising your wares for the highest bidder! And *then*, I might add, you were disgustingly sick over the rail, and if *I* hadn't been fool enough to hold on to you, you'd probably have fallen over—and good riddance it would have been! Christ! The trouble you've put me through tonight while *you* lay here

in a drunken stupor! And let me tell you—no, it's no good
struggling or trying to defend yourself until I've finished,
since I heard *you* out just now—and a foul-mouthed little
slut you've become, too! If I didn't let you fall over the side
I should have let Pruitt or Captain McCormick have you—
although you might not have liked what the captain had in
mind, after he'd chastised you for your unexpected change
of sex! Dammit—any man on this ship could have had you
and you wouldn't have known or cared!" Not giving her a
chance to gasp out a refutal of all the ugly, cutting things
he was saying, Blaze said with a snarling kind of laugh
that only curled and lifted his upper lip slightly: "Waterfront doxies, especially when they're drunk, have never
appealed to me, my dear—and the only reason I'm sharing
your bed is because you must have spilled half a bottle of
rum or wine all over mine, and I don't fancy sleeping in
sopping-wet sheets! Do you have all that *clear* in that
alcohol-befuddled mind of yours yet?"

"No—no, you're lying—you're *lying!* Do you think I'd believe *you* of all people? You're only trying to put all the
blame on *me* for your—your . . ." Trista thought for a moment when she felt his weight shift that he was preparing
to leave her without further ado; but he had only moved to
reach down by the bunk to snatch up some thick sheets of—
And then she felt the blood drain out of her face when she
saw what he had drawn. How he had seen her . . . a sleazy
trollop, her lips parted, her legs sprawling open . . . oh
God, no—he made it up—that isn't—that wasn't really
me . . . ! He . . . and then she remembered those other pictures, and *they* had been real enough; but these were cruelly detailed—they were . . . did they show how she really
saw her now? He'd kissed her that time on the deck—she
knew that now for a certainty. And he hadn't wanted her
physically last night—*that* much too she was certain of,
now that she had seen the way *he* had seen her. Why didn't
he go now and leave her to her misery and shame? If only
she could say something without . . . without making
more of a complete idiot of herself by bursting into tears?

Staring down into her white face and the eyes she'd
squeezed tightly closed like a child, Blaze had begun to feel
against his will that he *was* as vile and despicable as she
had named him. Dammit! He'd only meant to teach her a

lesson at first, but he might have had a change of heart and torn them up without saying a word if she had only shown the slightest sign of remorse instead of accusing *him* of being responsible for her state. She had no *right* to look so *injured,* so stricken—as if he'd struck her a mortal blow! And why in the hell . . .

He *hated* goddamn sniffling females! Especially those sly bitches who could pretend to force back tears and let one escape anyhow to trickle forlornly down . . . damn her! Now he *knew* she had to be a witch after all, or he would not be taken in by her acting; wouldn't feel as if he wanted to comfort her, as if he *wanted* her in spite of everything he knew or could guess about her, in spite of *anything*—including the warning signals that kept going off in his mind. Blaze swore softly and violently under his breath. Now that he'd proved his point, he ought to keep the advantage by leaving her to her own conscience!

Instead, almost involuntarily, he bent his head and kissed her eyelids very gently—and then that damned solitary tear before it trickled off the side of her face, tasting its salt against his tongue before he turned her face to his and kissed her cold, trembling lips until they warmed and parted under his with a long, shuddering sigh.

And for some time, all he did was kiss her, moving his mouth in infinitesimal fractions over hers to explore the feel and texture and shape of her mouth—of each of her lips and the corners of her mouth and the tiny hollow that marked the curve of her upper lip—before kissing her damp cheeks and her still-closed eyelids again and then her temples, lingering against the tiny pulsing veins; there, and on each side of her neck—feeling the sudden fluttering in the hollow at the base of her throat as her breathing began to quicken.

If I say one word—even if I move—it will break the spell! She didn't really want to think either, Trista thought from a distance away. *Only to feel and experience what was happening at this moment between them. Don't wonder why or how everything changed quite suddenly to this— and we know each other and are as familiar with each other as if we have been lovers forever, knowing exactly how to please and pleasure one another. . . . Don't think!*

His body moved so slowly down hers and against hers as

his mouth continued to explore slopes and hollows and throbbing peaks and . . . her hands caught in his hair as she moaned and her body arched upward as his exploring lips and tongue found and touched and tasted every secret, hidden part and place of her until she thought she would die, die from sheer feeling and pleasure—and could not stop shaking and sobbing for a long time afterward as if she had experienced an earthquake with a myriad after-shocks that would not stop rocking her with shudder after shudder as she clung to him tightly with her face pressed against his shoulder and cried out against him over and over—almost screaming when he went into her at last and stayed in her; feeling the contractions and the rising and falling like tides deep inside her. Stayed, holding her, before he began to move very slowly, very gently; holding her, touching her, kissing her until it started again—all over again—something that started from deep, deep down inside of her, rising and bursting and spreading through-out her whole body until even her skin seemed to burn—burn—and she didn't care if she burned or died at this moment when he was hers and she was his, for there was no separation after their willing, wanting joining had made them one.

Trista felt his body shudder against hers at almost the same instant and felt him swell even larger inside her as she opened to take all of him and tightened again—over and over again, hearing him gasp and then, instead of withdrawing, go still deeper and further inside her and they lay there not moving, only holding each other closely and remaining part of each other for a flame-wrapped eter-nity in time and space.

But after all, a dream that seemed to last an eternity could, when you woke up and blinked at the clock, only have lasted a scant second! She must have slept again, somehow; perhaps she'd really only dreamed everything she thought she'd experienced—and *felt*—Trista told her-self sternly afterward. The only thing that was real at all was that she seemed to be saddled, whether she liked it or not, with Blaze Davenant's obnoxious presence for a time; although *he* had taken pains to assure her that he didn't enjoy being saddled with *her* either, and they'd both just have to make the best of it for the time being.

If there had been any dreaming, it had been all on her side or in her imagination. He'd insulted her in every possible way first, and then—no doubt because she'd challenged his manhood—he'd seduced her very artfully indeed; which of course only went to show how much practice he'd had—and how much *she* needed in order to hold her own in future. As she packed the few things she had left out, Trista almost wished she could have continued to masquerade as a male. She hated the dress that *he* had taken the liberty of choosing for her to wear today—not being gentlemanly enough to forbear from mentioning that "after last night's exhibition" she needed to look "subdued." What he had meant, of course, was like a poor governess; and it was a good thing she hadn't brought along a gown of black bombazine, or that would no doubt be what she'd have had to end up wearing to suit *his* peculiar set of morals!

Gray—"dove-gray" the *vendeuse* had called it, clasping her hands together soulfully. "It matches mademoiselle's eyes so beautifully! So correct for shopping and for morning calls . . ." Trista grimaced at her wavering reflection in the mirror. Gray silk that looked almost regimental—trimmed with darker gray cords at the wrists and shoulders—white collar softening the uncompromisingly high neck. And silver buttons all the way down the front . . .

Trista remembered with a sudden flash of anger that Blaze had raised one eyebrow in that infuriating way he had and given her a lopsided smile as he commented: "Quite convenient, all those pretty, shiny buttons—wouldn't *you* say, my love?"

"Damn you—I am *not* your "love"! And you had better leave my buttons alone—*and* me! What is more—" But it seemed as if he would never let her finish a sentence, for he had interrupted her again to shrug and say impatiently:

"For God's sake, let's not get into anything like *that* again! Believe me, both you and your buttons are quite safe from me . . . ," and then the wretch had added wickedly, "at least for the moment!" And then, having issued his commands to her, he had left her to finish *his* packing as well as hers, reminding her quite unfairly that she could choose between San Francisco and *his* doubtful escort or that flinty-eyed Captain McCormick and . . . what-

ever he might have anticipated doing with her once he
thought he'd had her thoroughly frightened and cowed.

Trista turned quickly away from the mirror, not really
wanting to think further. For once, she had actually believed what Blaze had informed her of with unnecessary
bluntness, so that she hadn't been able to prevent a cold
shiver from running through her body, making her flesh
prickle with apprehension. No! Even the thought of being
escorted to San Francisco by Blaze Davenant was certainly better than being at the mercy of the captain. Better
the known evil than the unknown, she thought—never
imagining that there would be a day when she would find
herself proved wrong.

Chapter 22 ～

Blaze Davenant was more furious than he had ever been in his life—except with *her*, he qualified grimly. From the time he had first met her with her arrogant nose-in-the-air attitude, he had disliked her: for all that he had reminded himself several times that she was still a *child*, with a great deal to learn. And then she had managed to make him want her—first by her startling offer of herself for the first time, and later by the fact that she obviously learned extremely fast; how else could she have managed to graduate from one of Europe's leading universities with a doctorate in medicine?

He had thought himself immune to her, knowing what he had learned of her; but then, finding her alone on the deck with her cloak and her hair blowing wildly behind her as if she were a figurehead on the prow of a Viking ship, he'd felt that strangeness that drew him to her in spite of himself make him feel impelled to touch her to make sure she wasn't an illusion, and to turn her around and kiss her until he felt her inevitable surrender—until she'd torn herself away from his arms and *fled*, running wildly like a panic-stricken animal and not even noticing when her cloak blew off and almost caught him in the face. She didn't know yet that he had saved it. Cinderella's slipper! Except that she was no innocent Cinderella by now;

and all they had in common was—their mutual *lust* for each other. Nothing more than that!

Blaze was in a foul mood by the time he had banged his way back into the cabin they had been forced to share without being aware of the fact—angry both with Trista and with himself for giving in to his so-called gentlemanly instincts (which in any case *she* didn't believe he possessed), and rescuing her from the consequences of her drunken folly the previous night as well as from the clutches of the ship's master, who would probably have forced her to pay very dearly for having taken him in with her clever deception first, before making sure everyone else on board knew of it. She had no sense at all—and obviously neither did he, or he wouldn't have weakened because of a tear and a few sniffles of self-pity!

"And who in the hell did you think you were locking the door against *now* when almost anyone who felt so inclined could have had Pruitt use his key—and had anything they wanted of you while you were lying inebriated and dead to the world?"

She had turned her back on him deliberately once she had let him in, but now Trista swung around to face him with those silver-gray eyes of hers seeming to shoot icicles at him while her lips firmed and hardened. "I'm afraid the door seems to lock itself when it's closed. And as for the rest of your ranting, I doubt that anyone *else* could have taken advantage of my—'stupor,' did you say?—while *you* were already quite busy doing just that—as you took such pains to *prove* to me a short while ago! Although I suppose that after you had finished amusing yourself you *could* have amused yourself even more by inviting your friends and acquaintances in to share with you in taking *advantage* of an unconscious female!"

Although he had not said one word to interrupt her while she was speaking, Trista could see from the way his jaws clamped together and white lines of tension suddenly stood out against the darkness of his angry face that she had probably gone far enough for the moment; but in spite of that, she let her eyes meet and clash with his, almost expecting to see sparks fly from their encounter before she gave a deliberately indifferent shrug and turned away to make an elaborate show of pretending to test the padlocks on her trunks and portmanteau, saying over her shoulder as she did: "But I suppose there's no use in recriminations *after* the fact! I shall know better than to imbibe too much alcohol on an empty stomach in the *future*, at least! Are we close to San Francisco yet?"

She could almost *feel* him breathing fire down the back of her neck, ready to consume her at any second—especially if she should be foolish enough to turn and face him again. Trista thought suddenly: I'm afraid of something I don't really want to understand! Why is it that I can always *feel* him without his actually touching me? Or know, without having to turn my head, that he's in the same room?

It was only with the greatest difficulty that Blaze managed to retain some measure of self-control while she was delivering her cutting, deliberately provocative little speech. And when she dared turn her back on him before throwing that final, patronizingly resigned final line at him over her shoulder, it was all he could do to restrain himself from throttling her into silence before he treated her as she deserved and obviously *expected* to be treated—like the cheap, easily accessible slut that she really was! He should have slapped her a few times and forced *her* to make love to him while he lay back and told her exactly what he expected of her, instead of being fool enough to show her any tenderness or consideration. And right now, he was more than half-inclined to take himself out of her annoying presence and her life as well, without so much as a word of explanation, leaving *her* to deal with the problems that she had created for herself, the ungrateful little bitch!

"How long before we get there?" Trista repeated her question petulantly, with a pretense of being unconcerned at his ominous silence as she attempted to peer through the salt-encrusted porthole without quite daring to turn around yet. She heard him suck in his breath before he answered her coldly.

"In three to four hours, I believe. If we still have the wind behind us. But I thought that while it's still light outside, my dear, we might take a promenade about the deck to watch the sun go down. I'm sure some fresh air will do you good after you've been cooped up in this airless little hole all day—and for quite a few days before yesterday, as I heard it. It's really too bad you had to be tactless enough to force our skipper to keep you confined to your quarters—although you can count yourself lucky, I suppose, that he didn't have you put in irons belowdecks! Shall we go?"

She had not been left with any *real* choice at all, Trista was to reflect bitterly later. In fact, he had practically *forced* her to accompany him on a painfully slow and leisurely promenade along the whole length of the deck and back again, holding his arm (with *loathing,* she whispered to him fiercely), while she was obliged to endure the stares and whispers of the ladies and the embarrassed coughs and half-hidden grins of the gentlemen—*all* of whom, obviously, had witnessed her making an utter spectacle of herself the previous night.

Trista felt that she could easily have thrown herself overboard if she did not die of mortification first, and she prayed for the deck to split open and swallow her—or for a tidal wave to engulf them all. How could anyone, even Blaze Davenant, be so brutally cruel and so coldly heartless as to subject her to such an ordeal? And—making matters even worse—bend his head down to hers to whisper with a smiling pretense at tenderness: "Hold your head *up* and keep a *smile* on your face, damn you! You made a fool of yourself, and now you have to face them down, d'you hear? Incline your head very slightly—that's better. After all, you've always been such a good little actress, haven't you? Might as well face up to facts instead of trying to cower away from the truth, sweeting! Brazen it out. It's the only way left to you now if you want to save some small shreds of whatever reputation you have left, you know. That'll take *them* aback—to see you act as though nothing had happened. . . ."

The worst humiliation of all she had to force herself to swallow was knowing he was right. At all costs, she had to hold on to her pride and pretend to be nonchalant, even arrogantly indifferent to their looks, their curious eyes, most of all their *opinions*.

Blaze had already reminded her that even if *she* didn't particularly care about what other people thought, she might at least give some consideration to her family, since most of their fellow passengers also would be disembarking at San Francisco. "And I might as well tell you, I suppose, that several of the gentlemen present have whispered to me that you are well known, in your *female* guise at least, as a famous Parisian courtesan whose favors can only be bought by the richest and most discriminating men in Europe—and that the poor fools have actually fought duels over you!"

"Really? Why, I hardly know if I should be flattered or insulted by such a rumor!" Somehow, Trista managed to shrug lightly with a pretense at bored indifference to his barely veiled insinuations. It was so much easier, she discovered reluctantly, to look up challengingly into that dark, unreadable face of his as they fenced with words, instead of being forced to meet all those *other* faces with their varying expressions that she could very well imagine. Better the known devil . . . or was it? She thought suddenly that she must have been insane to allow him to talk her into the ship with him staying on. After all, what could the captain—or anyone else, for that matter—actually *do* to her? Especially now that she had shed her disguise and they all knew her real sex, it did not really matter what they thought of her or guessed about her morals (or lack of them, more likely); the fact that she was a woman would at least protect her from any bodily harm. And in any case, she was tired of being forced to promenade from one end of the deck to the other as a penance for some "sin" she hadn't committed in the first place! If anyone was a sinner and a hypocrite, *he* was; using any method he could think of to take advantage of her—the bastard!

Trista suddenly halted in midstride, reminding Blaze of a mule digging in its heels—and of the only remedy that worked in such a case. So far he had, almost miraculously, managed to retain some measure of self-control; but if she pushed him any further than she already had . . .

"I've changed my—," Trista had begun, at the same time attempting to jerk her arm free, when Captain McCormick advanced upon them with his thin lips stretched into a travesty of a smile that did not extend to the arctic blue of his eyes.

"Ah! So here is our culprit—if I may say so? Madam, as I have already told your husband, I should really be *most* annoyed, you know! And you have thrown everything and everyone into a state of confusion with your mischievous prank—or a wager, did you say last night, Mr. Davenant? You are lucky, madam, to have so understanding a husband, I'm sure!"

Husband! Husband! How he dwelled upon that particular word. *Husband?*

"My dear Captain McCormick!" Trista heard Blaze say in that slow Southern drawl he could affect so well when it suited him, "I thought, dear sir, that my wife's little escapade did not need to go further than—well, the *three* of us, I suppose!" And then, turning the surface amber-green of his eyes on Trista, who felt literally paralyzed, he added with a shrug and an unnecessarily painful squeeze of her arm: "I'm sorry, sweetheart, but after your little escapade last night I felt *obliged* to confide in our good captain here, and some of our confused fellow passengers as well—just so nobody could misunderstand you, of course, my love, and these little theatricals you are so fond of in order to make me ravingly jealous! A devilish plot you succeeded in, as you well know!" Taking advantage of the fact that Trista was still quite stunned with shock, he smiled down at her charmingly before adding with a pretense at reproachfulness: "But, my dearest—it was not really necessary for you to run away from me as you did, you know! After all, didn't I promise to give up all of my mistresses for *you* if you would only submit yourself to my instruction and become everything I could ever need or want in a woman?"

Trista could feel the heat rising in her face and spreading all over her body as she listened, almost unbelievingly, to his falsely deprecating words. She *tried* to speak a few times, but although her mouth opened, the words she longed to utter were trapped in her throat and almost choked her with sheer fury at having to endure his lies— his hypocrisy—his insolent taunts! If only—if only there was some way she could strike back at him and prove to him that he had meant nothing more to her than a casual *fling,* not to be taken *seriously* in the least . . .

Why had he "informed" the captain that they were *married,* of all things? Why, he disliked her and had made it clear—almost as intensely as she disliked him. She could look after herself well enough, he didn't have to. And then quite suddenly, as she met Captain McCormick's ice-cold eyes, Trista felt their iciness run down her spine, chilling her, freezing even the white-hot rage she had felt only seconds earlier.

Without quite realizing what she was doing, her fingers tightened over Blaze Davenant's arm and her body pressed closely against his as she leaned into him as if she suddenly needed reassurance—or protection?

Not that it mattered in the least what *she* needed or pretended to feel, Blaze found himself thinking furiously a few seconds later, after he had been forced to listen to the rest of Captain McCormick's speech with an air of studied amusement combined with incredulity. Damn and blast! He should have known better than to imagine that the captain would give in quite so easily; especially after he'd been both duped as well as frustrated in his designs—and too many people either knew or suspected that fact.

He'd announced, out of a mistaken sense of chivalry, that the little cheat was his runaway *wife*—and at the time the captain had had no choice but to accept his statement . . . or so it seemed until now. He was trapped because of his own stupidity—and perhaps his ridiculous sense of guilt over a loss of a maidenhead that would have been awarded to the first available and willing male the bitch had come across while she was in heat. Why hadn't it been Fernando instead of *him?*

But unfortunately, it seemed as if there was no way out of the ridiculous situation short of admitting that he'd lied—and he wasn't about to admit anything of the kind; especially not to this Captain McCormick whom he had disliked from the moment he had set eyes on the man; and liked even less after he'd learned certain things about him.

Trapped, Goddammit! Because neither of them could produce a marriage certificate, and as the captain had said: "After all—now that you have been reconciled with your *wife,* a second marriage ceremony on shipboard, performed by me, would not only reinforce and remind you both of your marriage vows but put an end to the questions and the—forgive me if I am too frank—the gossip among the rest of my passengers; which I am sure none of us would want spread about San Francisco and even further?"

Trista's eyes seemed to widen—that was all. Silver witch's eyes that only reflected light and had no depths that could be discovered. *She* might have said something— anything, in fact, that might get them both off the hook. It was up to *her*, after all, as a woman. But she had said nothing at all . . . leaning against him as if she had been turned into a statue, and only turning her face up to his once so that her eyes caught and captured his for seconds that seemed to stop in time while he could almost feel himself pulled in to drown in those unknown, unplumbed depths.

"Madam—*you* have no objections to this symbolic little ceremony, I hope?" The captain's voice sounded unctuous, although his eyes remained dry-ice cold and just as burning as hot coals.

What in the hell was the matter with her? Why couldn't she say something *now,* when she had always been *too* ready to flash back at *him* with some cutting response? "Well, my love? I know you will not care to go through a ceremony that obviously means objectionable *ties* all over again, but . . ."

He had given her a way out. It was up to her now, Blaze thought, waiting impatiently for her to take her cue. But when she spoke, her murmured words almost stunned him with their unexpectedness.

"Objectionable? Oh no! How could you think that I would still feel that way after you have taken such pains to persuade me otherwise? I think it is such a *romantic* idea— don't *you?*"

Chapter 23 ~⅞

How in the world was she to know what she was getting herself into with her provocative words that had only been meant to annoy him—and perhaps even teach him a lesson?

Trista had been quite confident all along that Blaze would in the end manage to wriggle out of the awkward situation that Captain McCormick had hoped to put them *both* in. After all, Blaze had always excelled at doing just that in the past. He'd find a convenient way out, all right—and until then, let *him* find out how it felt to be backed into a corner for a change!

She had thought so, at least—until suddenly it was too late, and what she had believed impossible was actually happening, like something out of a bad dream she would wake up from at any moment, sighing with profound relief. An unreal nightmare, Trista kept telling herself all through the brief ceremony performed by the thin-lipped Captain McCormick—and witnessed by every other passenger on his ship, as well as most of his crew—until she heard a ragged sort of cheer go up and realized that the captain had just pronounced them man and wife, suggesting immediately afterward in a sarcastic, wintry manner that the groom might just as well kiss his bride, since they now had the sanction as well as the blessing of every passenger on the ship.

Reality had become a blur. Perhaps because it was something she did not want to acknowledge? Blaze kissed her with an almost *hating* violence mixed with passion—she remembered that part of the mockery, at least! Yes, and she remembered feeling as if her neck were going to snap, and her spine as well, as he bent her backward as if everyone were not watching them and they had been completely alone. And then someone—she thought it was his friend who had come on board with him, Señor Cuevas—called for champagne and plenty of it; the best they had, naturally! And she drained her glass in acknowledgment of every toast—did she or didn't she throw her glass overboard each time?

There was far too much that Trista found she could not remember later, except for certain scattered patches of lucidity—certain faces and voices that stood out from the rest even after all the champagne she knew she had to have consumed during the past few hours.

She *did* remember being literally carried off the ship. Yes, because she had attempted to struggle free, and had been warned harshly that if she persisted she could easily end up being *dropped* into the water and left to sink, swim, or damn well *drown*—which was what she really deserved for being a sly, drunken little slut with a vicious sense of humor—if it could be called that!

"And *you* are being just as unfair and unreasonable as usual! Blaming *me* for an unfortunate predicament that *you* brought about by your interference in my affairs—and your damned male vanity that insisted on a public proclamation of your—your *property* rights over me, once you found you were sharing a cabin with a *female*—one you happened to know!"

"What a spirited young woman, to be sure! And what a challenge to *any* man, eh, my friend? A—hmm—a *constant* challenge and a series of surprises, I would imagine—which is probably exactly what you need from a woman, especially since . . . no, I won't say more! I have come to recognize that particularly dangerous look on your face by now. Not one word more, I assure you!"

Señor Gerardo Cuevas was really quite a *nice* man after all, Trista had already decided; even before he gave her a mischievous wink. And he was a gentleman too, in spite of his unfortunate choice of friends. At least he continued to treat her like a lady, even when she was suddenly and unceremoniously handed over to him like some unwanted package that had grown too burdensome—*dumped* into his surprised arms was more like it, Trista thought furiously, as Blaze said over her head in a gritty kind of voice: "But since you have already expressed your sentiments, my friend, perhaps *you* can cope with whatever challenges and surprises a spirited young woman might come up with, while *I* make an attempt to placate her glowering brother, who would probably have shot me to death already if his pretty little wife hadn't been hanging on to his arm. Damn! I suppose I should have expected something like this!"

"Well, you needn't . . . ," Trista began to say indignantly, her words only a trifle slurred; and then as realization penetrated through the mildly pleasant alcoholic fog that had blurred reality for a while, she blinked her eyes to focus them and found herself looking for an instant into Fernando's narrowed, furious eyes.

No, not just furious—there was *hate* in them that almost made her flinch and close her eyes against the ugly force of it while a trickle of coldness down her spine made her shiver involuntarily. I mustn't be afraid—I mustn't ever let myself be afraid—refuse to countenance it—grow stronger from inside. Old, old words as old as the swamp that was forever and always.

She heard Blaze's voice, all Southern drawl, making lightly worded explanations that were all too obviously meant to "protect Trista's reputation"—what else could a Southern gentleman do after discovering he'd shared a cabin for the past few nights with a young man who then later made sure everyone on board knew she was no man but a female? The—the mealymouthed, hypocritical bastard! Why, she'd give them *all* an earful, her reputation (whatever shreds remained of it, thanks to *him*) be damned!

Poor Señor Cuevas, who had stood there rooted without having the least idea what was going on, suddenly found a struggling spitfire in his arms, who threatened in a choked voice to scratch his eyes out if he didn't put her down *immediately*.

"I hope, my dear, that by now the fresh air has cleared your head somewhat and you are able to *stand* instead of falling over? I'm sure Fernando and Marie-Claire have already had more than their share of unpleasant shocks for one afternoon without your making a spectacle of yourself in front of everyone here; not to mention our ex–fellow passengers!"

"Why you . . . you . . ." While Trista searched for words that were expressive enough and *biting* enough, she suddenly found herself enveloped and rendered breathless by Marie-Claire's embrace that took her off guard and almost made her lose her balance soon after poor Señor Cuevas had hastily deposited her back on her feet.

"Oh, Trista! Oh, dearest, how *could* you? This isn't France, you know—and you really ought to have remembered how people here love to *gossip,* especially when—but oh, how thoughtless and selfish of me! All I meant to say was how very glad I am that you are back at last—and you *must* bring me up to date on *everything.* . . ."

"I have arranged for accommodations at the Lick House for tonight, since the last stage to Monterey has already left," Fernando pronounced in a suppressed kind of voice, adding: "Marie-Claire, my dearest, perhaps you and Trista might be more comfortable waiting in the carriage while Mr. Davenant and I see to my sister's baggage?"

There was no help for it, with Marie-Claire's arm already hugging her about the waist while she kept up an endless flow of questions without pausing long enough for answers. Damn him! Trista thought furiously as she was led away willy-nilly—before she had been given a chance to tell Blaze . . . to tell him without mincing words exactly what she thought of him! The look she gave him was as sharp and dangerous as a silvered sword, meant to cut and kill; but he merely gave her an exaggerated bow and a mocking grin before turning his attention again to Fernando, who was making almost too obvious an effort to keep his rage from showing.

There were too many curious eyes on them at the moment, Fernando knew, and to let his anger explode would only cause talk. But when he got the cheap little slut alone . . . well, he'd teach her a lesson she wouldn't forget in a hurry! The whore—bitch. Just like her bitch-mother and

just as false. And now she had to go and commit bigamy on
top of everything else! And as for this Davenant fellow . . .
why in hell did *he* have to keep turning up around Trista so
often? He was too glib tongued . . . for all that Gerardo
Cuevas seemed to like him. Well, he'd find out in the end!
And since neither Blaze Davenant, who professed to have
"rescued" Trista by going through a farce of a marriage, or
Trista herself for that matter knew what *he* already
knew—that her *real* husband was in San Francisco, on fur-
lough and staying at the same hotel . . .

Fernando's manner grew almost affable as his mind
began to skim over the almost limitless possibilities. Trista—divorced for adultery—a disgraced woman—a *fallen*
woman. Then she'd have to grab thankfully at any marriage prospect at all or any likely prospect for that matter;
and think herself damned lucky, at that! Yes, he'd make
sure that Major Farland Amerson was informed (reluctantly, of course) of *everything* his wife had been up to in
Paris and on the ship that had brought her here. That
would leave a man of honor no choice but to divorce the
woman who had cuckolded him so openly—or face contempt and ridicule. No, Amerson, quick-tempered South-
erner that he was, would have no choice, especially when
the gossip and the rumors began going the rounds and his
touchy honor was at stake.—*Then* they'd see! Oh yes, he
had lots of plans for his *puta* of a stepsister with her air of
arrogance that proclaimed her sureness of getting away
with any kind of vice, any type of outrageous behavior.

"And your *padre,* 'Nando?" Gerardo Cuevas was saying,
his concerned voice suddenly recalling Fernando to the
moment. "He is very much better by now, I hope? Your sister seemed very much concerned. . . ."

"Was she? She sometimes has strange ways of showing
her feelings, I am afraid!" Fernando's voice had an underlying harshness that caused Señor Cuevas to wonder at
the cause of the obvious tension between the two. Jealousy? Or something else?

He said quickly, "I'm sorry if I have said something tactless! Your *padre,* he is not . . ."

"No, my father still lives—but it is a living death. The
other doctors who have seen him say that there is nothing
more to be done but . . . to wait on God's mercy." Then,

making a visible effort to control himself, Fernando clasped his old friend's arm before saying with a return to his usual, half-sarcastic manner of speech: "But there's no need for *you* to be sorry. How should *you* know? Now that my sister the *doctor* has deigned to return, perhaps she might have learned some new methods of helping to ease the constant pain he suffers! But enough of depressing subjects for now, eh?"

In spite of the fact that Blaze Davenant had strolled off to retrieve his luggage and had with a martyred sigh offered to fetch his "wife's" bags as well ("After all, I suppose they'll all think it is a trifle strange if I get mine and not *hers* as well!"), Fernando lowered his voice after glancing around them to make sure he could not be overheard.

"There's a meeting tonight at the Bella Union. We'll have a private room upstairs, of course. You might find it interesting—or have you become disinterested in political affairs here since you have been living in Mexico? What are you doing back here anyway?"

"Settling the affairs of my Uncle Ysidirio. Since he died my aunt has written to say there are Anglo families who talk of "homesteading" on the best sections of the *rancho*. So you see . . ." Gerardo spread his hands palm up as his shoulders lifted in a shrug. He added cautiously: "But who knows—after I have had time to recover from being tossed about day and night on that damned ship—perhaps some gaming, some entertainment, and a lesson in politics might prove interesting before I must leave for the *rancho*."

Later, in their hotel room, Gerardo Cuevas explained almost apologetically to Blaze:"My friend, I do not at all like this feeling of being a kind of Judas—or a traitor to my own kind, you understand? I have known 'Nando since the time when we were boys, although we were never very close as friends, but all the same . . . he told me that this Judge David Terry of the Supreme Court would make sure that my aunt will not be bothered again. The same Judge Terry, do you think, who is supposed to have . . . ?"

"Not supposed to have, my dear Gerardo. The same man who challenged United States Senator Broderick to a duel and murdered him—*and* managed to get away with it too. He's the leader of the Copperheads—the Knights of the

Golden Circle, they call themselves grandiloquently—in
these parts."

Blaze Davenant, having seen to his luggage, had returned to pour himself a glass of bourbon from one of the
bottles arrayed on the doilied dresser. "Want one,
Gerardo? or do you still prefer tequila?"

"*Gracias! The tequila, if you please.* Even without salt
and lime. And before you give me that scowling look and
embark on more lectures on local politics—yes, I've already agreed to go to this damned meeting and make up
my mind if I think they are to be taken seriously or not,
these so-called knights! It sounds like a schoolboy secret
society to me, *amigo!* But—I must admit that I'd rather
share a bed with some soft, yielding female tonight rather
than with *you!*"

Sēnor Cuevas drained his glass and set it down with a
thump. "And you?"

"Me? Sleep, I guess. *I* haven't been invited to any Cop-
perhead meetings—and I haven't had much sleep these
past few nights either. Maybe after dinner I'll gamble
awhile—the Bella Union, you said?—and perhaps do some
of the sketches I'm supposed to hand in to *Leslie's* and
Harpers Weekly this week, before I turn in." Blaze answered his friend's quizzical, rather suspicious look with a
bland smile.

I wonder why I don't ask him why his "wife" of a few
hours is supposed to have had a husband already, Gerardo
Cuevas wondered.

But then—Blaze Davenant was not the kind of man one
asked such personal questions of. Under his sometimes
foppish and mild exterior (when he chose to present himself so), Blaze could be as dangerous as a coiled rattlesnake
when it was disturbed or challenged.

Indeed—did Trista really *know* the kind of man she had
married? *If* they were married, that was!

Chapter 24 ～

"You don't mind, do you, Trista, if Consuelo comes with me? I can't possibly get out of these stays and petticoats without her help—and in any case, *you* will have your Farland to help you undress, won't you? You're so lucky to have such an *understanding* husband, aren't you? Fernando has turned out to be so *boringly* jealous—and he's hardly ever at home any longer what with his new group of friends and these everlasting meetings he has to go to. . . ." Marie-Claire's voice trailed off as she smothered a yawn before adding with an attempt at brightness, "But we *will* talk tomorrow, while you're getting ready to leave for Monterey, shan't we? And you must be exhausted too. You look quite peaked and almost haggard, my poor pet— being forced to go through a sham marriage, and then running into your *husband*, of all people, quite by chance . . . Heavens, what an evening this has been after all—and I must admit I'm glad it's over and I can lie down! It'll probably be ages before Fernando comes back, so maybe I'll get a decent night's rest for a change!"

Marie-Claire leaned forward to give Trista a light kiss and a sleepy, "Well, good night then—Farland must be quite impatient to come upstairs to you!" without noticing the ominous silence with which her friend had received her flow of light chatter and innuendo. It was at that mo-

ment that Trista decided she did not really *like* Marie-
Claire—and never had!

What an evening indeed! It was all Trista could do not to
slam the door behind her with a resounding bang that
would probably awaken everyone in the adjoining rooms—
if any of them had elected to go to bed at such an early hour
and forego the variety of pleasures and entertainments
that San Francisco's nightlife had to offer. She would
much rather have gone out somewhere—to Maguire's Opera House, or even to the notorious Bella Union, which offered (so she had heard Señor Cuevas mention to Blaze
during dinner) decidely risqué cabarets. And off he'd
gone—her "husband" of only a few hours—with a casual
announcement that he was off to experience and sketch
the best and worst of the saloons and theaters of San
Francisco.

He'd given her a sardonic grin and a mocking travesty of a
bow before wishing Farland a *very* pleasant and *productive*
(and what exactly had the unfeeling brute meant by *that?*)
night before he took his leave of them all, while the other
men were still smoking their cigars and sipping their port.

"I hate him!" Trista exclaimed aloud, wishing she could
scream the words into his mocking, grinning face as she remembered his words upon leaving the table:

"I did the best I could, under the circumstances—what any
gentleman would have felt to be his *duty!* In fact, I gave our
little charade my *all*—did I not, Gerardo? Although your suggestion that I should carry Trista off the ship was, I think,
overdoing it rather—besides being a trifle *wearing.* As romantic as it may sound, it wasn't easy! Sorry, Farland!"

"Sorry," was he? She'd make him sorry in the end! With
an extremely obscene French oath, Trista threw her reticule across the room, barely missing knocking over a lamp.

She hated Blaze Davenant and she was furious at Farland Amerson, her supposed "real" husband, for suddenly
turning up in the lobby of the Lick House, of all places—
although she had to admit in all fairness that he couldn't
have known that his supposed "wife" had just arrived
from Europe and would be spending the night in the same
hotel. The unfair part was that Blaze Davenant had run
into Farland first, and prepared him; whereas *she* had
been taken completely off guard.

At least the shock of seeing Farland had dispelled most of the champagne haze that had made her feel drowsy and impervious to Fernando's barbed comments and Marie-Claire's pretended, honey-sweet concern over her rather tipsy condition.

"I'm afraid that it was the only way I could go through with it—that mockery of a wedding with all the rest of the passengers looking on and whispering and the captain . . ."

"If my friend Gerardo Cuevas had not told me the whole story and assured me that this so-called marriage was forced upon you, I would not have believed such nonsense!" Fernando's voice had been full of barely suppressed anger and something else that Trista, in her rather nebulous state at that moment, could not quite make out. "Your reputation—or what is left of it after your open flaunting of convention in Paris and elsewhere—would have been irreparably ruined; surely even you must realize the consequences of your wild, reckless behavior? And if, as usual, you don't care for the opinions of others, you might at least show some concern for the feelings of those you profess to care for! This is California, not Paris or Rome—and the decadent habits of your friends there are not accepted *here!*"

"Oh, Fernando, my love—I'm sure Trista regrets everything by now, but can't you see she's not feeling quite well? Do give her a chance to rest first, and I'm sure she'll be able to explain everything . . . isn't that so, *chérie?*"

"I'm not unwell; I drank too much champagne in order to—to make myself *numb,* that's all! And I don't feel that I owe anyone any explanations—so if you were expecting me to pour out my sordid story and beg your forgiveness . . . I'm sorry, Fernando, but I won't do so—not to *you;* especially when you have already made your accusations and your judgment of me in almost the same breath! Please don't bother to say another word—and pray do think what you will, for *I* don't give a damn!"

All in all, with Marie-Claire trying to soothe Fernando and motion Trista to silence, it had not been a very pleasant ride from the dock to their hotel; and the simmering atmosphere had not been helped at all when their carriage was overtaken, with only a few inches to spare between the two vehicles, by a stylish English phaeton, reins expertly handled by an equally stylish blond woman who waved mockingly as she passed them.

"And who is *she?* That woman who seems to know you—that cheap-looking *poule* who almost overturned us just now?" When she was angry or jealous, Marie-Claire was all French. "Well? She must know you, *hein?* Your friend Gerardo Cuevas was riding with her—and your *petit ami* Blaze Davenant as well. What do you think of that, Trista? Her customers for the evening, no doubt! She must have been expecting them. Were *you* supposed to join in the fun and games this evening, 'Nando? Is *she* your meeting tonight?"

"Haven't I told you before that acting like a jealous shrew doesn't become you, my dearest wife? And as for your ridiculous suspicions—that show-off of a female is no acquaintance of *mine,* I assure you! She's probably one of Gerardo's many female friends—he always seemed to enjoy the company of the pretty gambling girls since he's a gambler himself. And now we will drop the whole sordid subject, I think!"

So that had been Blaze after all! No doubt he and Señor Cuevas meant to enjoy everything that San Francisco had to offer them while *she,* on the other hand, having been both wed and casually *discarded* like an unwanted piece of baggage within the space of a few hours . . . she must now listen to domestic bickering, pompous sermons and probably advice she didn't want. Damn all men anyhow! Why hadn't she been born a male with all the attendant privileges of manhood?

It's not fair! Trista thought rebelliously. Why shouldn't *I* have some fun too? I've been accused of much worse by dear brother Fernando—yes, even by that sanctimonious, hypocritical bastard I happen to be *married* to, damn his hide! I ought to . . . oh, I'd like to see the look on all their faces; Farland too. . . . Perhaps I *will* after all; why not?

In her agitation, Trista had flung herself facedown on the narrow bed; but now her layers of clothing and the cagelike crinoline she was forced to wear in order to be fashionable seemed almost unbearably constricting, so that she could hardly breathe. Hemmed in and held in—dragged down by the weight of her clothes under slimy-surfaced green water while her lungs tightened and tightened and breathed the smell and the taste of swamp-water and absorbed and became

part of the dark, primeval soul of the ageless swamp itself
and everything it took and gave back.

Held motionless for a few seconds while she heard herself panting from a distance away and felt the sweat
pouring down her face and trickling down between her
breasts; and then, almost in a frenzy, she began ripping at
the high, demure collar, tiny black jet buttons scattering
in every direction, bouncing off the opulent carpet. There
were buttons all the way down her tightly fitted basque—
down to the veed waist; and she ripped and tore at them,
needing to free herself, to be able to breathe deeply again,
feel *light* again.

By now silk was tearing under her fingers as Trista
ripped at her newest gown and her many lace and silk petticoats and her hated iron cage, the ridiculous crinoline
contraption that she would never wear again—even if she
was considered a dowd!

And corsets be damned as well—stays digging into your
ribs and waist and cutting off your breath . . . Why do
women put up with such discomfort in order to look ridiculous? If only she could tear her tightly laced corset off her
body as easily as she had managed to rid herself of the rest
of her garments!

But of course, the laces were hopelessly and firmly knotted behind her back where she could hardly reach them;
and Trista uttered an unladylike French expletive out
loud when she remembered that *he* had been the one to
lace her in—had it only been *this* morning? *He* had made
sure she couldn't possibly free herself without help. Did he
have the effrontery to think that she'd have to wait for him
to unlace her, no matter what time in the morning he
might choose to return?

I'll find someone *else* to do it, that's all, Trista told herself defiantly. And why not? The best cure for whatever
unholy weakness ailed her when Blaze Davenant put his
hands on her would be to establish a standard of comparison—to experience being made love to by another man. A
stranger . . . no, she couldn't take that risk. Someone . . .
someone she knew and could like? Quite suddenly, it came
to her, and Trista could have laughed out loud. Blaze's nice
friend. Gerardo.

Three doors down—and he had announced that he intended to retire early, that the thought of his bed seemed infinitely inviting all of a sudden. Poor Gerardo was alone and *she* was alone also—and it had turned into one of those fog-cold San Francisco nights when you needed a fire in every room to keep the cold from sinking in through every pore . . . "a shivery-freezy night," Aunt Charity used to say when Trista was still a child.

Why sleep alone without the comforting warmth of another human body to snuggle against? Even Farland, her "official husband," had deserted her tonight for the flesh-pots of San Francisco without a qualm; without consideration for poor Jessica and their son. Why were all men such rutting animals?

Why *think?* It was so much easier not to—let instinct and the body take charge—to *do* rather than hesitate.

Trista closed her mind to thought while she snatched out the pins and tiny combs that had held her hair in place, letting her wild, tangled black mane of curls fall heavily over her shoulders and down her back. Not troubling to pick up her hairbrush, she only paused to run impatient fingers through her hair before snatching up from the back of the chair the silk-fringed cashmere shawl she had worn down to dinner earlier, wrapping it around her near-naked body in the fashion of the women of the Sandwich Islands and Polynesia.

No voices or footsteps outside—it's late, and no one will be about. In any case, his room is only a few yards down the hall from mine, and if I run very fast . . .

I won't lose my courage—I *will* do it, Trista reminded herself fiercely as she opened her door to peer down the deserted corridor before her bare feet carried her swiftly to the door of Gerardo Cuevas's room. *Don't* hesitate, not now, her mind warned her before she knocked on the door softly—and then rapped on the wood panels again more imperatively. She thought she heard a sleepy mumble that might have been a Spanish expletive before the sound of voices on the stairs made her suddenly nervous . . . and thank God that he hadn't locked his door! she thought, feeling the knob turn under her cold fingers, letting her slip safely inside its sheltering darkness before she closed the door behind her quickly.

Was he asleep already? Now, at the last moment, a sudden fit of nerves assailed her—making her want to turn back and run for the comparative safety of *her* room before he could discover exactly how bold she had dared to be. But it was already too late—the voices she had heard had grown louder as they passed by; and she heard an ominous clicking sound that made her freeze before she was able to whisper in a shaking voice: "I hope you are not going to *shoot* a frightened woman, señor! If I had known you were asleep already I would not have disturbed you for the world—but I find—I mean, I have found that I—oh, I am so terribly embarrassed!" Why couldn't he respond in some way? Say something to make her feel less awkward? Trista thought she might have heard him swear again in Spanish under his breath before she rushed on, not daring to lose her earlier sense of bravado: "Please—I don't know how to say this, but I—I couldn't really fall asleep for feeling that my breath was quite cut off and I was suffocating! I haven't been used to wearing corsets for quite some time, and now I . . ."

"A *corset*, señora? *Descuide usted—déjelo por mi cuenta!* I never imagined I'd be so lucky as to have my dreams turn into sweet reality! And to think that I might actually have fired this pistol at you, not knowing . . . *Válgame Dios!*" He had spoken to her in Spanish, his voice a soft, *passionate* whisper that made Trista unaccountably nervous once more, so that she had to remind herself that this was, in fact, what she had hoped for, wasn't it?

"I'm sorry—I really shouldn't be here at all, and I beg your pardon for this intrusion, señor! I could not have been thinking—and what must *you* think of me? I wish you would try to forget that—that this foolishness ever . . . ohh!"

How had he contrived to get out of bed and cross the room to her without her knowing it until suddenly she felt hands on her shoulders, turning her around—the shawl dropping to the floor almost unnoticed at the same time that he whispered from behind her: *"Con su permiso . . . bella señora?"* And as she stood motionless, just as if her bare feet had suddenly taken root, she felt warm fingers brush against her skin as knots came apart unerringly in the darkness and lacing came undone; and suddenly there was nothing between his hands and her tingling skin but the thinnest veiling of silk that only made the sensation and feeling of being touched infinitely more exciting and sensual than anything she could have imagined—the feeling of an unseen stranger's hands touching and stroking and exploring her body familiarly and boldly while she felt as if she was incapable of either moving or resisting— *entranced,* leaning helplessly back against the hardness of his body, and unable by now to deny him anything he demanded of her—anything at all. . . .

Trista heard herself gasp softly as he lifted the heaviness of her hair to kiss the hollowed nape of her neck while with one hand he caressed her breasts and belly before moving with tantalizing slowness to touch her between her legs, although still through silk moving and sliding with indescribable eroticism against and along her almost unbearably sensitive flesh—touching a peak before sinking into narrow deepness of depthless canyon.

The harshly whispered words in Spanish were almost muffled against the slender, bent nape of her neck, although there was no mistaking either their meaning or implacability.

"*En el piso, mujer! Arrodíllese . . .*" What was there to mistake, since she knew Spanish? "On the floor, woman," he had said. "On your knees . . . ," while at the same time the hands that had caressed her were suddenly pressing her downward to comply with his demand, pressure against the small of her back making her arch it like a cat as her silken protection was snatched out of the way just before he entered her with one unexpected and almost brutal thrust that seemed to penetrate all the way inside her and into her womb itself; and she cried out aloud before sinking her teeth into her lip, with her face pressed hard against the rough scratchiness of the worn carpet while he went into her and into her until quite unexpectedly what had started out to be agonizingly painful had turned into pleasure that was much more intense and more violent than she thought she had ever felt before—wave after rising shock wave that made her keep vibrating over and over without being able to stop; both inside herself and over every inch of the surface of her skin—crying out turning into crying sobs that continued to shake her whole body without ceasing, in spite of every effort made by her *will* to fight against something separate and removed from it and uncontrollable.

Was *that* the precise moment when she knew with her instincts and in her soul who he really was, or had she always sensed the truth from the very beginning?

It was only after she had (*partially,* at least) recovered

from her temporary derangement that Trista found herself able to think in an *almost* rational fashion, realizing that in spite of what *her* senses had discovered, *he* obviously thought that she still believed him to be Señor Cuevas and that it was his *friend* she had yielded to so easily and so willingly. Did he really imagine that his softly whispered Spanish phrases had duped her? Well—let him think so! At least for the sake of her own self-respect and her *pride* that he had all but succeeded in destroying. Yes, why not let *his* insufferable male vanity suffer for a change?

He had kept her pinioned under him, although he had shifted his weight slightly to one side, his quickened breathing far too warmly disturbing against the side of her neck. He had taken her on the *floor*—ordering her onto her knees as if she had been . . .

Sighing exaggeratedly, Trista murmured in a breathless fashion: "Ohh—Gerardo! I think I sensed from the first time our eyes met that as soon as you touched me I would forget everything—*anything* else—and that I would feel so . . . *transported* by just the pleasure of knowing it was *you* to whom I was giving myself . . . only to you . . . and of my own free will, without coercion. . . . I kept imagining your dear face all the while you were making love to me, Gerardo! Only for you would I submit—and *enjoy* what happened between us!"

Ah yes! With vindictive pleasure, Trista had already felt the tensing of his whole body that still lay so intimately entwined with hers, even while she found herself holding her breath as all of her senses warned her of the sudden surge of purely primitive fury emanating from him that could easily explode into violence at any moment. Even the silence that stretched between them seemed to vibrate like the strings of a harp under clumsily impatient fingers. What had she meant to do or to provoke with her deliberately artless-sounding speech? Why did she feel almost impelled to make him angry?

He was angry enough to kill her—in fact, Blaze realized suddenly, he had actually come to within a hairsbreadth of strangling the life out of her. *Her*—night-haired, moon-silver-eyed *bruja* he'd been damnably stupid enough to *marry* of all things—only to have her deliberately search out a friend of his to cuckold him with just a few hours after the ceremony.

God, what a promiscuous bitch she had turned into—a little slut who took her pleasure whenever she felt like it without showing the slightest signs of guilt or remorse even afterward. Obviously she was completely amoral, and had always had that tendency; and *he* had been the first fool she had taken in with her clever acting. He really *ought* to kill her, Blaze thought; and with the thought his hands spanned the slenderness of her neck almost consideringly, with deceptive gentleness, feeling the tiny pulses that fluttered agitatedly under his fingers.

Why in hell didn't she *move?* Try to jerk herself free—beg for mercy—*do* something instead of lying there against him with her body still and—poised; as if she was *waiting.*

Waiting for *what?* Bitch! What else did she want, beside his balls? He'd like to . . . but why not do exactly as he wanted to with her now that she was here and yielding and obviously wanting even more than he'd already treated her to? She enjoyed being taken almost by force, then? Almost anonymously, from behind, by a man she was scarcely even acquainted with, of her "own free will . . . ," wasn't that how she had put it? Perhaps it was time she found out that women who gave themselves as easily and *zestfully* as she did deserved to be treated as they should be and *would* be by most men who weren't as understanding as *he* had tried to be where she was concerned. She wasn't even worth killing, cheap little slut that she was!

From her neck, Blaze deliberately moved his hands down to her shoulders and from there to her breasts, squeezing and kneading them in a careless fashion before he slid one hand down her belly and insinuated his fingers between her legs to probe callously and almost perfunctorily up inside her in spite of her sudden resentful cry and her attempt to flinch away. Since she was acting like a whore, let her see how it felt to be treated like one!

"Gerardo . . . no!" she gasped, and he bit down with feigned gentleness on the soft nape of her neck, whispering in Spanish: "But you just told me how much you enjoyed submitting to me—to my wild passion for your body—and your very words have driven me even madder, *chica,* so that I desire to explore every part of your body, both *inside* as well as out! Come, there's no need for you to pretend modesty and embarrassment at *this* point, you know. I don't need to be teased into fondling and playing with you. There, do you like *this* better? You've been so uncommonly sweet and obliging that I'd like to return the favor if I can—or if you'll hold still long enough for me to . . ."

Losing his patience when she suddenly began to squirm and struggle, Blaze held her body down with the weight of one leg, taking his hand from her breasts to smack her thigh sharply, as if she had been no more than a recalcitrant mare in need of a taste of discipline. Ignoring her muffled cry of outrage, he deliberately drove his fingers even more deeply inside of her, exploring the warm, pulsating tightness of her that was slippery silken-smooth as wet silk. And now, quite inexplicably, he found himself beginning to desire her again—loins winning out over mind and rational thought.

Trista had begun to sob with a sense of humiliation and frustration when she found herself unable to escape from his intimately probing exploration of her—just as if, she thought ragingly, she had been no more than a—a—cadaver! It was only by sheer brute strength that he forced her to endure yet another form of degradation—punishment—or whatever he might choose to call this . . . this . . .

But what was wrong with her that in spite of herself she had actually begun to feel the stirring and gathering of sheer animal lust inside herself to match the stirring and heating and hardening that was the proof of *his* lust for her? When she was suddenly released from what she had at first thought of as torment, the half-choked, despairing moan that escaped her became a startled gasp as Trista found herself picked up off the floor as if she had been a bundle of dirty laundry, only to be dumped sprawling on her back on a bed and *mounted*—entered—*taken;* her legs trapped aching and immobile over his shoulders while he drove deeply and more deeply yet into her, first fast and then teasingly slow and then fast again and slow until she was screaming against his mouth and wanting, wanting, needing what he was doing to her, giving her, making her feel—and feel—and *feel,* until pure, mindless feeling blotted out thought and everything else.

Chapter 25 ~

There had been a certain point, during that night, when neither of them had made any further attempt to continue with the pretense they had started out with. It would have been impossible, in any case, after Señor Cuevas himself arrived rather drunkenly on the scene with a voluptuously proportioned *señorita* in tow, his mouth dropping open with dismayed embarrassment when he discovered the bed he'd thought of as his already occupied.

It was then that Trista had her moment, relishing it all the more after Blaze's grunted, "So your Gerardo has given you a rival—what are you going to do about it?" She'd *show* him what she was capable of, damn him!

Gerardo Cuevas had set down the small lamp he'd brought with him on the rickety side table; and now suddenly, before anyone knew what she was about, Trista had twisted herself free agilely and was on her feet—with not a stitch of clothing to cover her naked body as she walked calmly across the room to pick up her shawl and fling it carelessly about her shoulders before requesting, with a smile and an insouciant shrug, Señor Cuevas's permission to borrow a light to see her back to her own room.

The shawl hid almost nothing—a fact she was quite well aware of, the teasing little trollop, Blaze thought wrathfully as he was forced to watch her carry off her ad-lib performance with superb insolence; not to mention audacity!

Stalking stark naked across the room with other people
present while she acted as if she were cloaked in diamonds;
and then, while poor Gerardo and his entertainment for
the night still gaped at her in stunned silence, she actually
paused at the door to turn around and blow a mocking kiss
before she left—uncaring whom she might run into in her
state of near-nudity; shameless hussy!

Why did a cuckolded husband always seem to be a
slightly ridiculous figure? Especially if he suddenly found
himself occupying *alone* a bed that two other people obviously longed to share? Blaze found himself wishing that he
had followed his earlier instincts and killed the slut instead of fucking her, for if he had he would not find himself
in such a goddamned ludicrous position. No doubt *she* had
become quite used to shedding her clothes and walking
about naked in front of anyone, whether they happened to
be lovers or complete strangers. Damn her!

The woman with Gerardo had begun to giggle nervously
behind her hand, her curious brown eyes darting about the
room and not missing a single detail, including the discarded corset. . . .

"*Ah, perdón, Blas, mi amigo!*" Gerardo Cuevas stuttered in an embarrassed fashion. "If I could have known
that . . . if you had said something . . ."

"Said what?" Blaze snarled as he swung himself out of
the damp embrace of the sheeted bed. "She came here looking for *you, amigo,* and I made the best of what was at
hand, I must admit."

Had he, though? Afterward Blaze would curse his own
folly and his stiff-necked pride that kept him from going to
her—even if he had to break open her locked door in order
to break down the barriers *she* had purposefully erected
between them for her own reasons.

In this case, making the best of what was at hand once
Trista had left turned out to be making a bargain of sorts
with Gerardo—a sop to masculine pride—that ended up
with Blaze remaining to dally with the buxom and experienced Rosita while Gerardo, allowing himself to be persuaded after some time, went three doors down to discover
for himself the surprises and the pleasures that awaited
him there.

Quite clearly, Blaze realized, he hadn't needed to kick

his way through a locked door! And just as obviously, Gerardo had been greeted with a warm welcome—which was
why he was still contentedly lying abed wrapped in the
treacherous embrace of her twining arms and encircling
legs until long past noon—and how much longer yet? Blaze
wondered. She was a born whore—that much, at least, was
certain; and he ought to feel *sorry* for poor Gerardo instead
of giving way to his irrational, murderous instincts that
urged him to smash through that closed, locked door and
shoot them both—each bullet very carefully placed.

How dare she be so overtly blatant? And how was it that
his so-called friend hadn't even bothered to put up too
much of an argument at the suggestion of changing bed
partners?

Blaze himself had managed to extricate himself from
the clinging Rosita very much earlier, with the help of a
more than generous "gift" that would help her to support
her starving parents (or so she *said!*); and when he found
himself pacing back and forth before that ominously closed
door like an angry cougar with his thoughts dwelling more
and more on some pointlessly stupid act of violence that
would only show him up as a jealous fool as well as a cuckold, he was, quite thankfully, able to tell himself that he
had, after all, done his duty by the undeserving creature
for Charity's sake—by rescuing her from what could have
turned out to be a most unpleasant situation—and now
that she seemed so determined to go her own amoral way,
he might just as well go about the business that had
brought him here in the first place and forget about her
existence—ungrateful, ill-mannered bitch that she was!

Purposefully, Blaze strolled downstairs and in the
course of the next few hours made several new acquaintances and learned a great deal about the activities of the
Knights of the Golden Circle—especially since he was the
scion of an old and respected Southern family, even if, as
an *artist,* he was considered somewhat of a black sheep!

It was only very late in the afternoon that he happened
to encounter Gerardo Cuevas, who was looking for *him* by
this time, and appeared to be somewhat sheepish and apologetic about the whole sordid affair. Full of stammered attempts to *explain,* in fact, when none of it mattered to *him*
in the least, as Blaze tried impatiently to make quite clear

to his friend once and for all. Why in the hell should he give a damn what the little slut did or where she ended up? She was supposed to be Farland Amerson's wife. Let *him* worry about her open infidelities!

"Blas, amigo—I only thought since—well, I thought you might want to know. . . ."

"All I want to know is what this nest of Copperheads is cooking up. I hope you managed to find out something before you succumbed to the buxom charms of . . . whatever her name was. Well?"

Not being a stupid man, Gerardo recognized the steel under the icy Southern drawl that Blaze sometimes exaggerated deliberately. Especially when he was in one of his dangerous moods—white-hot lava simmering just beneath the surface and ready to erupt explosively at any minute. It was best to stay calm and stick to business when Blaze was like this. Much wiser, in fact!

It was not until after he had delivered his report and started to leave that Gerardo Cuevas remembered what he had been about to say when Blaze had cut him short with that deadly note underlying his voice.

He had been about to close the door behind him when he turned to say casually: "Oh yes, I almost forgot. I thought you might feel relieved to know that your—that the young woman has already left San Francisco on the coach to Monterey."

The jouncing, swaying movement of the Abbot & Downing Concord coach as it raced along the potholed roads was hardly conducive to resting, leave alone sleeping. It did not help her already exacerbated nerves, Trista discovered, having Fernando sitting next to her.

Marie-Claire was feeling poorly—and she missed the children besides. In any case, she was not strong enough to face sickness or death—her unwilling presence would only make matters worse; especially since Aunt Charity had no patience with her, and had told her bluntly that unless she could control her sniveling hysterics she should stay with her children instead of forcing herself to come to Monterey out of a sense of duty.

Fernando was full of excuses for his absent wife—but at least he had said nothing more to Trista about *her* tangled affairs. During a journey that seemed interminable, he allowed her some peace when she leaned her head back with her eyes closed, pretending to be asleep, even while her thoughts kept gouging into her mind and her nerves.

How selfish she had been—how unfeeling and full of her own ambitions, her own emotions, *herself,* in fact. She had taken too much for granted—Papa's unswerving love and understanding, his strength and support—while all the time he must have known, and yet said nothing of the pain he must have been suffering even then.

Thank God Fernando remained silent for the most part, leaving her to wrestle with her own conscience—and the power of her instincts—the burning lust and desire to experiment that had driven her to ask a man, a stranger she had thought at first, to satisfy her curiosity—to take her. Her fault—her fault! And it was much better not to think of *that* kind of thing—or of Blaze Davenant and his reactions when he found out that his "bride" of less than twenty-four hours had left him.

It's only his silly masculine pride that might be wounded! Trista thought; she quickly brushed away certain *other* thoughts that suddenly tried to crowd into her mind, but reminding herself that Blaze would probably be immensely relieved at being rid of the burden of a wife who was supposed to be someone else's wife. In any case, she had made up her mind that she never wanted to see or hear from Blaze Davenant again. Especially after the way in which he'd treated her last night, the bastard!

She must have fallen asleep, for nightmares crawled like worms into her mind until she forced herself awake once more and found that they had already reached the outskirts of Monterey.

The Rancho del Arroyo seemed just the same as it had always been except for the unusual, almost strange quietness that seemed to blanket everything, like the fog that shrouded all the old, familiar landmarks and made everything seem unreal and unknown.

It was better, even easier, to pretend that nothing had changed or happened during the past few years—for all their sakes, as Trista discovered.

She heard the remembered, constant sound of the ocean

that one could glimpse from the top of the bluff where the
old adobe house built by one of the earliest settlers who
had followed Father Junipero Serra to California still
stood.

From the porch (added on a generation later) one could
look across fields where horses grazed to the ocean, and
hear its incessant pounding against a crescent-shaped,
white-sand beach.

"He said . . . well, you know how much he loves the sea
and always has! He told me that . . . that when he dies he
would like the roaring of the ocean to be the last thing he
hears."

Aunt Charity looked older and more tired than Trista
could ever remember seeing her. Her hair had silver-gray
threads interwoven with its usual rich chestnut-brown.
And yet, her indomitable spirit and strength had not deserted her—nor her acerbic tongue that spared nobody who
made her impatient or insulted her intelligence.

"Well, thank God you've come at last!" had been the
first words with which she'd greeted Trista before taking
her aside and giving her a concise and unvarnished account of Hugh Windham's condition. Charity had made
herself accept that her brother was dying. Trista, for the
first few weeks she spent nursing him, could not bring herself to do so.

Days and nights became a blur and she lost sense of
time; did not want to regain it; wished she could go back
into time and make things different. Papa couldn't die!
She wouldn't let him! He was Papa, and he'd always been
there for her—her strength, her bedrock, her sense of being
loved and of belonging. Why hadn't he told her he was so
ill? Why hadn't he let her stay with him, close to him? She
was a doctor, and inured to all kinds of sickness and
disease—she had performed surgery and removed limbs
when it had been necessary, and had comforted friends and
families of the dying. But now at last she understood how
easy those glib, comforting words were; and how difficult
the experiencing of the death of a loved one. No words
could ever afford comfort when no hope was left, only the
suffering of watching someone you loved suffering while
he died in slow stages.

"You don't have to tell me what I know already," Char-

ity said the first day. "But it'll make him happier to know
you came—and you can help ease the pain. It's all he needs
now, do you understand? You have to be strong for *him*
now—and don't you dare let him see you weeping, d'you
hear me? Thank God that silly creature my nephew married decided not to come. I can't stand her! And as for you—
you'll get some regular hours of sleep and stop looking so
drawn or I'll send you packing—doctor or no doctor! You'll
find that he won't know you sometimes—or takes you for
someone else; best go along with it. It's better for him to escape from the present."

Aunt Charity was right; there were times when Hugh
Windham recognized her and managed a travesty of a
smile while he patted her hand with fingers so emaciated
that skin seemed to hang upon bones. And then there were
times when he seemed to be in another place and time and
would babble incessantly in a hoarse, hardly intelligible
voice to people and about places that Trista knew nothing
about. And sometimes, when she gave him the morphine,
he remained in a semicomatose state for hours on end.

Fernando came in and out of his father's sickroom, but it
was obvious he could not stand to stay for more than a few
minutes at a time. He made sure of obtaining without
question the medicines that Trista prescribed, but clearly
he was relieved at any excuse to get away from the Rancho
as often as he could, or else invent excuses to go to the
main house in the valley to make sure that everything was
being run smoothly.

"How long? Damn you, I brought you here to *do* something! What good did it do you to become a doctor anyhow?
A *woman* doctor! No one could take you seriously!"

Fernando caught her off guard one morning, after she'd
spent a sleepless night listening to the labored, stertorous
breathing and the involuntary moans of pain that made
her flinch and want to gasp with shared pain herself.

"I don't know—I feel so useless! He's . . . if there was
only something I could *do!* Please, Fernando, don't!"

"Don't what? What do you expect, eh? You've never
fooled *me,* you know, even if you managed to take everyone
else in with your little Miss Innocent act! You used to
throw yourself at my head only too obviously, as I recall—
but then you discovered it was more fun to tease, didn't

you? You led me on—and then you pretended I was raping you when all the time you longed for it, didn't you? Didn't you, you little lying bitch?"

He seized her by the shoulders and shook her violently, and Trista's already ragged nerves made her cry out protestingly as she attempted to wrench herself free of his hurtful grip.

"No! Let me . . . alone!"

"Fernando!" Aunt Charity's uncompromising voice rescued her on that occasion. "This is hardly the place nor the occasion for recriminations of any kind, I think. Trista needs to sleep—and *you*, dear nephew, are supposed to meet your brother within the hour, are you not? Or had you forgotten he was arriving this morning from San Francisco?"

Trista escaped, running on bare feet, to the comparative safety of her tiny, sparsely furnished room. Thank God for Aunt Charity's intervention! There had been something in Fernando's eyes that frightened her.

Why does he hate me so? What have I done to him? It's all because of my mother, of course! And then, as she burst into the tears she had held back for so long, Trista found herself thinking that Papa couldn't, mustn't die and leave her alone and abandoned without his strength and his love to lean on and trust in.

She knew she was overtired—lack of sleep could make the mind play tricks on you and produce illusions. But her unsaid wish was so strong and so fierce that it stayed with her even when she drifted, still sniffling, into the limbo state lying between daydream and sleep, and heard quite clearly in her mind the voice of the Ancient One of the swamps and even smelled the miasmic wet-mud and green-weed-water smell she would never forget.

"You have yet to learn, impatient child! You share in The Power but you are too occupied with striving to be still and think of what is the truth. The Power is not to be used . . . never to be misused . . . Be careful . . ." And then, as the voice she seemed to recognize and know so well faded and grew fainter, she imagined that, just before the silence that sank into her, she heard the softest whisper: "You will come to me when you really need—but not now . . . not yet . . ." And then she slept heavily and dreamlessly until Aunt Charity shook her into wakefulness.

"I'm sorry, my dear—I know you've had only too few hours of sleep, but—but he's worse. And in so much pain I can hardly bear it! Trista, you must . . ."

"I can give him some morphine—a hypodermic injection. It will ease the pain at least. I'll come right now—I have my case right here." Trista heard herself mouthing words—words! What good were damned words in the face of suffering and despair? What good was Power if you weren't supposed to *use* it, even to help and heal?

"Yes, bring your case—and the morphine. . . . How much do you have left?"

Trista had grabbed up her case, still in a half daze as she tried to keep up with her aunt. She could feel her heart pounding even while she strove for the calmness and detachment of manner she knew was essential. Was Papa *dying?* He can't die, he can't die! one part of her mind kept repeating stubbornly; while she said aloud: "I made sure to have more than enough morphine on hand to last two weeks or more. Aunt Charity, please—if Papa is worse . . ."

When Aunt Charity stopped abruptly, Trista would have fallen against her if she had not had her arm taken in a firm, almost harsh grip. "Worse? What could be worse than *this?* We both know he's dying . . . and he's dying by inches and spasms and in the greatest agony. Have you heard him pray under his breath for an end to this? Would we allow an animal we care for to suffer so? For God's sake, girl—would *you* want this kind of end for yourself?"

She hadn't understood or perhaps did not *want* to understand what Aunt Charity was suggesting. Morphine . . . so much to alleviate pain for a while and bring sleep . . . a stronger dose and there would be no awakening again to pain and suffering, only a slipping into oblivion.

"I . . . I can't! I've been trained to *heal*, to . . ."

"If you're not strong enough to release him, then I will, because I *must*—for him, for Hugh, my brother! As he would have done for *me* if necessary. I'd hoped that you might understand, Trista, but if it is your *conscience* that holds you back, let *me* do what has to be done."

Chapter 26 ❧

"What has to be done . . . what has to be done . . ."

The words kept repeating themselves in Trista's head like the tolling of the bells from the bell tower of the mission church founded by Father Junipero Serra.

Everyone wore somber black, even Aunt Charity. "He died, thankfully, in his sleep. I called Trista at once of course, but he had already gone . . ." Nobody doubted their story or questioned it. Trista, numb with a mixture of grief and guilt, let Aunt Charity explain everything to everyone.

She had cried so long and so hard that she could only speak in a hoarse whisper.

"You shouldn't take it so *hard*, for heaven's sake!" Marie-Claire told her impatiently when she arrived for the funeral in her brand-new black silk and satin gown trimmed with layers of ribbon and lace. Marie-Claire had no intention of staying on in dull, backward Monterey for a day longer than was necessary; and her impatience to return to the city made her sulky and irritable. Trista, she felt, was only being dramatic; for after all, she hadn't seemed to miss her stepfather while she was enjoying herself in Europe, had she?

"I suppose you'll be going to Boston with your dear Aunt Charity Windham now?" Marie-Claire questioned in a sugary voice just before she left the day after her father-in-law's funeral. "I've heard that they actually allow female doctors to practice medicine there—if that is *really* what you want of life! But if you want my opinion, what you really should do is to settle down and have children! I'm sure the Amersons would be overjoyed . . . and what about your *husband?* You're lucky he's such a gentleman and so understanding, *chérie!* But if you are not careful, some other woman might take him from you!"

Trista was relieved when Marie-Claire finally departed—to her children who always missed her terribly, she told them all. The fact that her husband made no objections to her hasty departure and practically ignored her during the day and a half she spent in Monterey did not appear to worry Marie-Claire in the least, as wrapped up as she was in herself and her own pleasures.

"I'm sure I do not have to tell you that I think that young woman is a vain, self-centered little . . . well, never mind!" Charity Windham's voice sounded grim as she continued packing the two small trunks she had brought to California with her.

Continuing to place layers of tissue paper between every garment, she looked up briefly at Trista, who sat on the edge of her bed watching her through those strange, dark-pupiled silver eyes that sometimes seemed too large for her pointed face.

"*You* had better come with me, you know! You *can* practice medicine in Boston—or you can teach other women who want to be doctors and can't, because the men don't want them to learn. *That* ought to be enough of a challenge for you!"

"I can't!" Trista hadn't realized that she'd already made up her mind until she said the words aloud, blurting them out. "Aunt Charity—I can't—don't you see? I have to make my own way this time; without help. I have to do something—to *feel* sure inside myself *of* myself. And I want to use everything I've learned—to feel useful. With this war going on they must need doctors. . . ."

"*Nurses* would be more like it, my dear! Think they'd accept a woman 'doctoress'? Hah! No, they'd take you as a nurse, but that's all. And you'd have to take orders from some fool of a man who calls himself a doctor because he's read a few medical books! Are you going to be content with *that?*"

The truth was that she didn't know what she wanted—and she wasn't prepared to think too far into the future yet. But, as she told Charity, she had to *try,* at least. And before then, she wanted to spend some time alone—to think things out.

"You always were a stubborn creature, even when you were under ten years old!" Charity had snorted in the end, giving up the argument. But then she added in a thoughtful voice: "Although, since you're bound and determined to be *independent,* and discover all of life's disappointments and pitfalls for yourself . . . do you remember meeting Miss Elizabeth Van Lew when we were in Richmond? Perhaps there might be ways, my dear, if you are willing to take some risks, that is, to be of help to the Union."

"As a *spy?* But that is not—"

"Not a spy, my dear! Not at all. All you need to do is observe and listen very carefully to all the gossip—and then I will arrange for you to pass whatever you have learned on to a courier. You can still practice medicine, of course—if they'll let you! And if they don't like the idea that you're a female, then you can always pass yourself off as a young man again, couldn't you?"

There were so many depths she had never even suspected beneath Miss Charity Windham's starched and staid and somewhat prudish exterior, Trista thought somewhat bemusedly later. Was she absolutely dedicated to the cause she believed in or completely ruthless when it came to her beliefs and her causes?

"Are you sure you won't change your mind and come with me? You might find it uncomfortable with my nephew Fernando hovering about—unless you still happen to cherish a certain *tendresse* for him! And if you do, my advice is to make the most of it while you pick up as much information as possible about this society he's a member of. The Knights of the Golden Circle, they call themselves; and they want to win or else *take* all of the Western states over to the South. Now there's a challenge for you, my girl!"

* * *

She had decided to return to San Francisco to accompany Aunt Charity and to see her off on one of the new steamships that was bound for Boston first and then for Europe.

At first, Trista didn't know if she was glad or sorry that Fernando had insisted upon escorting them as far as San Francisco. A male escort was always helpful; and Fernando was certainly protective of the ladies he was escorting, even putting his arm around Trista when the coach careened perilously around the curves leading up to the Pacheco Pass, so that she would not be flung painfully against the side of the coach. Fernando had actually been trying, of late, to be nice to her, Trista had to admit; but his disapproval had been almost palpable once he had learned that she did not intend to accompany Aunt Charity to Boston.

Fernando—member of some silly secret society? And even if he was—didn't all men enjoy such things? In this instance at least, Trista was certain, Aunt Charity was surely exaggerating the importance as well as the influence of the so-called Knights of the Golden Circle.

"Where you folks headed anyhow? Me, I've been traveling all the way from Los Angeles, and I'm plumb tired out!"

The woman who had spoken had a wide, friendly smile for all that she was flamboyantly gowned and hatted. With a withering glance at her companion, whose formerly florid complexion had turned pasty white, the woman turned back to Trista and said: "I could see that *you're* not scared any more'n I am! My first husband was killed by Indians right before my eyes, poor man; but at least he put up a fight before they got him! Not that we're likely to be attacked by those red devils *this* trip—it's only if you're traveling on the Overland Stage that you'd better keep your eyes peeled and carry a gun! I always carry a two-shot derringer—just in case, you know?" The woman gave a throaty chuckle before she leaned back, winking conspiratorially at Trista—much to Fernando's annoyance and her Aunt Charity's amusement. "A female needs to be able to look out for herself—especially in Virginia City, which is where I'm heading. I've heard it's wide open, and the pick-ings are great for a gal with ambition. You wouldn't be going there, would you?"

"I'm not sure yet where I shall end up! Do you think they will accept a woman doctor in Virginia City? A good one?"

"I don't know about *that*, honey—but I know they're sure looking for pretty lady gamblers there! You know how to deal faro? Poker? Twenty-one?"

Perhaps it was because she felt Fernando's arm go about her waist and tighten, like the expression on his face, that Trista answered with a laugh: "Not only those but roulette and baccarat as well! But I've never heard of Virginia City!"

"Honey—it's a silver town and a gold town—and it's *rich!* Except that right now there's a real shortage of women, if you know what I mean? You won't find a town that looks uglier and is much wilder than Virginia City! But they have them a real theater there and I've heard that Lola Montez did her Spider Dance there, and that Adah Menken played her *Mazeppa* role—horse and all! They had pokes of gold dust thrown onto the stage—and there were gold nuggets to go along with the flowers sent backstage."

The red-haired woman introduced herself as Martine Girard—and as soon as she discovered that Trista spoke fluent and idiomatic Parisian French and had only recently left France, she confessed to being somewhat homesick in spite of the fact that she was supposed to be in the land of opportunity. In French she told Trista with a *gamine* grin that if she ever changed her mind between being a dull doctoress and a gambling girl there was always the Silver Slipper in Virginia City—and she didn't have to do anything she didn't feel like doing either!

"An interesting woman," Aunt Charity commented later; adding with a glance in Trista's direction, "and a veritable mine of information as well—didn't you think so, Fernando?"

"My dear aunt tries my patience too often with her barbs and sarcasm!" Fernando ejaculated soon after they had seen Miss Charity Windham onto the steamer that was to take her back to Boston. "And as for that cheap tart that you allowed to engage you in a conversation that all but implied *you* were one of *her* kind . . ."

Tiredly, Trista protested: "Please, Fernando—can we *not* quarrel just for once? I think we are both naturally overwrought and unhappy for the same reason—but can't we declare a truce for now? Whether you believe it or not, I loved Papa—your father—more than I could ever have loved the man who was my natural father. Fernando— can't we try to be friends perhaps? For Papa's sake at least . . . I think he would have been happy at the thought."

"I suppose you're right. . . ." Fernando seemed to make the admission grudgingly, before he questioned her, typically, about what she intended to do *now*.

"Practice medicine—wherever and however I can. And if I can only meet the right people . . ."

"Listen," Fernando said gruffly, "I know I'm old-fashioned; but if you insist on going ahead with this stupid notion of yours that you can force the whole medical profession to accept female doctoresses—who am I to stop you? In fact, I'll even help you if I can—if only to show you how wrong you are to think that a female could ever be accepted as a doctor!"

As it turned out, Fernando insisted on introducing her to a friend of his who was a doctor also, and might be able to help her. "He's Turkish—and almost too intellectual for *my* taste. Ali Yuvuz is his name, and his house is on the way to ours in Menlo Park. I'll introduce you to each other if he's in—and then you can do as you please." Fernando gave a sudden, unexpected chuckle before he added with a sidelong look at her, "There's only one thing you must be tactful about with my friend Ali—he'll offer us his Turkish coffee that is as thick as molasses and just as sickly sweet, but you can't refuse it, mind you, because he'd consider it an insult. Just swallow it down like castor-oil and smile afterward—that should make him happy and—he could help you—if you're really serious about this stupid ambition of yours, setting up as a doctor!"

Fernando was actually being pleasant to her for a change—and meeting this friend of his might even prove helpful.

He was really making an effort to be *nice* to her, as if to make up for what lay in the past, Trista thought somewhat fuzzily. And the least *she* could do was to be nice in return!

She was charming to the black-mustached Turkish doctor, whose dark eyes studied her far too closely for all his surface politeness. And she drank the hot, sickly sweet coffee in two gulps, trying *not* to taste it or grimace at its bitterness. Manners! Politeness! But why did she persist in feeling so clumsy? Dr. Yuvuz was questioning her about her medical training in Europe, and while she tried to answer him vehemently, her tongue felt as weighted as her eyelids, for some reason.

She must have fallen asleep in spite of all her efforts to stay alert and attentive—how embarrassing! Vaguely, Trista could remember voices—the Turkish doctor's—Fernando's —apologizing for her. And then she was being undressed— divested, thankfully, of constricting stays and corsets while she sank into soft cushions deeper and deeper seeking total oblivion . . . dreaming nightmares that made her move about restlessly; trying to scream without being able to force a sound out of her throat; trying to run from some horrible, unseen peril without being able to move her feet; trying to ward off frightening creatures out of hell that kept swooping at her, attacking her, tearing at her and laughing all the while because she couldn't even seem to lift her arms to protect herself. . . .

"No—! No—no!"

It must have been the sound of her own voice that awakened her finally, her mind full of faded thoughts—blurred memories. Or only bad dreams? What was real, and what wasn't?

She thought she felt a needle prick sting her thigh and heard herself cry out again—forcing her eyes open and blinking them against . . . no! It could not possibly be reality! Shadowy shapes that were wavering outlines against leaping crimson and gold flowers—going higher and higher. Why couldn't she escape from this ugly nightmare into thankful reality? If she could only open her eyes! And then, all of a sudden, she did—only to find that the reality she had awakened to was much worse than any of her nightmares.

Even afterward it would all come back to her against her will. That time. Those days—some of which she didn't even know had passed, and could not clearly recall; and perhaps was better off *not* remembering.

She was somewhere—she didn't quite know where at first, except that she was confined and helpless.

They told her, with pitying headshakes, that she was "suffering from delusions"—and nothing she cried out in refutation was believed, or even listened to for that matter; except as a reason for more shaking of heads and whispered consultations among people she had never met or seen before.

"Hallucinations . . . ," they said. "Typical in this type of hysteria, of course . . . a derangement of the nervous system that sometimes occurs in highly strung females. . . ."

All false words strung together that made no sense at all, as she very well knew! Only—no one would *listen* to anything she said; ignoring her desperate please for attention while they continued to talk over her head—discussing her "case" as they put it.

"They" were (or called themselves) doctors. She was confined in a private sanitarium somewhere close to Sacramento; that much at least she was able to gather, because occasionally, forgetting themselves perhaps, the doctors spoke in French to each other.

Trista's later memories had jagged edges that would always continue to tear at her and make her shiver with the remembrance of pain and humiliation and helplessness.

If she attempted to ask for explanations or to scream out her protests she was gagged. If she tried to fight against being forcibly fed or handled as if she were no more than a mindless *thing,* she was "restrained."

"It's fer your own good, miss," the hulking man who was her "attendant" told her without inflection on such occasions. He had huge, bearlike shoulders and pale blond hair that was beginning to thin slightly at the edges—almost as pale as the washed-out blue of his expressionless eyes. Nordstrom—how could she ever forget?

She tried to remember little things, merely to keep her mind active and to convince herself of her own sanity, in spite of her surroundings—a dingy little gray-walled cell without even a window—a heavy wooden door with an iron grating set into it, through which she could be observed at all times—at *any* time they pleased.

Not only her free will but her privacy had been taken away from her; leaving her completely helpless and vulnerable.

"Stone walls do not a prison make, nor iron bars a cage . . ." Lines from a poem written centuries ago that Trista found herself repeating over and over again in her head—merely to keep herself sane in this place where cries and moans and anguished screams echoed and reechoed until they were abruptly cut off; continuing to beat like flapping buzzard wings inside her mind nevertheless.

Oh, by now she knew only too well how those pitiful cries for help must have been stifled—and had learned better than to question or protest—or even to display anything that could be taken for defiance in her manner or demeanor.

I will be looked for, surely—searched for. There will be questions asked—inquiries made, and then . . .

If she didn't keep reassuring herself that she would be rescued in the end from this hell she had found herself tumbled into all unwittingly, then she really *would* end up losing her sanity. But it was hard—dear God, it was almost too hard to endure! And why and for what reasons had Fernando done this to her? Would she ever find out?

It had turned cold, and the only garment she was allowed was an ugly, shapeless sack with holes in it for her head and arms that did not even reach as far as her ankles. One thin blanket was all she had for warmth; and Trista huddled under it on the narrow iron cot—her legs drawn up and her arms wrapped around herself while she imagined a fireplace piled high with logs that burned fiercely and hotly, sending tongues of flame leaping and licking all the way up the chimney. Oh, what a magnificent, beautiful fire she could conjure up in her mind! Towering column of red-hot flame spewing out molten embers that became a flowing, all-consuming river of fire—and ah, the heat, the heat!

"Well, up you get, miss! Got a visitor today, you have."

Was it possible that she had been asleep and dreaming everything that had seemed so real she could still imagine the stench of sulphurous smoke in her nostrils? Fire and smoke and loss . . .

But now there was no time to think as newly ingrained

habit made Trista scramble off the bed to cower against the wall—still in a kind of daze.

"I—I'm sorry!" she murmured automatically before her eyes focused properly and she saw who her visitor was— every nerve and muscle in her body suddenly going tense.

Fernando! He stood there grinning at her—his eyes traveling mockingly over her—from the tangled mass of her night-black hair to her bare ankles and feet; his grin broadening when instinctively Trista crossed her arms across her breasts—tongue moistening her suddenly dry lips as she forced herself to look back at him.

It wouldn't do to let him see how terrified she had suddenly become. She mustn't let him goad her into any display of temper or emotion of any kind, because then they would use that as an excuse to . . .

"Doctor Beck seems to think that with the right treatment and careful supervision there might be some chance of recovery from the unfortunate ailment that afflicts the poor creature," Fernando said in a deliberately condescending fashion to the impassive Nordstrom, who had stripped her cot of its one sheet and the blanket already, and had begun to fold the thin mattress into a tight roll. Did it mean that she was to be set free now that she had been punished?

"Hasn't given any trouble fer the last week or so at least, sir. She's been keepin' real quiet and doin' as she's told—as you musta saw fer yourself just now."

Trista stood frozen in place, her teeth biting into her lip as she forced herself to remain silent—even while she was being discussed over her head as if she weren't capable of hearing or understanding anything—as if she didn't even exist, for that matter.

She had dropped her eyes to stare down at the floor while she willed herself to remain unmoved, to remain still and mute, Fernando strode over to her; his fingers biting painfully into the softness of her flesh as he forcibly tilted up her face to make her meet his glittering eyes.

"Well?" he questioned her softly, still with that strange, half-mocking, half-gloating grin stretching his lips. "And have you really learned some self-restraint at last? Or are you merely playing a game of pretense as usual?"

How could she answer him with his fingers pressing cru-

elly inward on either side of her suddenly trembling
mouth? Tears sheened her eyes, making them more silver
than gray now; and somehow, her very silence and lack of
reaction to his calculated taunts hardened Fernando's resolve.

She was a bitch—in need of taming—born of a bitch!
Leading him on, teasing him, full of half-promises she had
no intention of keeping. Oh, but Marie-Claire had told him
a great deal about his wide-eyed and pretendedly innocent
little stepsister! The letters from his mother-in-law from
Paris had only served to confirm what he already knew—
and on top of that, what he had heard from Captain McCormick of her outrageously shocking behavior while she was
a passenger on his ship had been enough to bring him here
today. She was lucky he hadn't killed her before now; although before he was finished with her she would wish
that he *had* done so!

"You cannot—or *will* not answer me, eh? I have been too
patient with you, Trista—and you took my patience for
weakness, didn't you? Now, you are going to learn a lesson
you have needed to be taught for a long time—do you hear
me? And I'm going to make you admit to what you are—
and what you want from almost every man you encounter—you conniving little slut! You cheap whore!"

It didn't really matter what he *called* her—"sticks and
stones . . ." It was what he *did* to her after he ended the
ugly stream of abuse he almost spat into her face.

"Here—strip the bitch before you tie her down. *This* lesson, at least, is going to be one she'll never forget!"

A vicious, backhanded slap across one side of her face
sent her sprawling to her knees until Nordstrom yanked
her to her feet and effortlessly, while she was still dazed,
ripped her only covering off her body with one hand—
leaving her naked and exposed. Her arms were twisted agonizingly behind her back so that if she struggled too much
she knew they would break—and that they wouldn't care,
only laugh even louder than they did now while Fernando
pulled and probed at the most sensitive parts of her body—
taking obvious pleasure from the proofs of the pain he was
inflicting upon her—enjoying every gasp, every whimper,
every outcry he could force from her.

But as if that alone wasn't bad enough, Trista suddenly

found herself turned about and made to lie facedown and spread-eagled across the bed—her hips and buttocks elevated by the mattress Nordstrom had rolled up so meticulously—her wrists and ankles secured by metal cuffs that chafed through her skin and gouged into her flesh when she struggled and writhed against the unbearable pain and humiliation that she was forced to endure while she was being beaten without pity—even when she forgot all sense of pride and was reduced to pleading and begging for mercy—ready to promise anything to anyone to stop this torture that was being inflicted upon her without her being able to prevent it . . . or anything else they chose to do with her for that matter!

"You're a whore like your mother, aren't you? Admit it—I want to hear you say it out loud!"

Lightning streaks of agony like liquid fire burned between her thighs and into her most sensitive nerve centers, making her scream.

"You like that? You want me to use my riding crop on you *there* again?" He laughed at the incoherent sounds she made when she tried to repeat the words he had instructed her to say, and laughed again when he used the whip on her where he knew it would hurt most—enjoying hearing her scream out loud over and over, the arrogant bitch, while he took his time raping her at last, now that he was ready. And what was even better, and gave him more pleasure, she was ready to say anything he wanted her to say—anything at all, in fact—just like the born slut she was. A bitch, like her mother. No difference between them!

And then, after he had finished using her and had signaled to Nordstrom, who had been watching impassively all the while, that *he* could use her too if he chose, Fernando was struck with a notion that made him grin all over again as he thought—why not? Why the hell not? Like mother, like daughter, as the saying went. And Trista, by now, could only sob brokenly and submit as the hulking animal of a man who was her "keeper" proceeded to thrust himself into her. She'd probably not need to be tied down the next time—or the time after that. *Her* kind usually ended up enjoying being abused—and *used!*

Chapter 27 ~꘎

Marie-Claire had grown plump and petulant—and bored to *death*, as she put it, with the cloistered life she was forced to live in California; especially *now*, with this ridiculous war between the states that had all the men so excited.

Married life hadn't turned out to be anything like she had expected it to be; and even if Fernando had presented her with the costly jewels she had always craved, he had also given her children—one after another—squalling, nasty-smelling little brats she was only too glad to hand over to wet-nurses and nannies. And what good were jewels when she had so few opportunities to show them off in public?

Fernando was more occupied with politics and the silly secret societies he belonged to than with living a *social* life—and people were so old-fashioned here that she was not supposed to attend any social functions on her own—no, not even to go to the theater, unless she wished to be *talked about!* Wasn't it ridiculous?

"But *you* can escort me, I daresay, since you're a friend of the family! And you will, won't you, Blaze? *Please*—for everyone who is anyone will be at the Metropolitan to see that scandalous creature Adah someone-or-other in *Mazeppa*—and besides, it's the kind of thing that *you*, like any

other man, will be sure to enjoy too—hmm? Like *this*, that
I can see that you enjoy very much—and *this* as well . . ."

Marie-Claire had lost none of her expertise in the art of
lovemaking, as Blaze had already realized during the
hours they had spent together—and now, under the caress
of her darting, flickering tongue and then the greedy onslaught of that full-lipped, pouting mouth of hers . . .

She could almost succeed in making him forget his
"wife" of less than a day, who had left him to run off with
the voluptuous Marie-Claire's husband, Fernando—for
whom Trista had always nurtured a secret passion, according to her best friend.

"Well of course they couldn't *marry*, since most people
thought of them as brother and sister!" Marie-Claire had
said with a shrug. "And me—I married Fernando because I
did not like my stepmother and I hated being imprisoned
in that silly girls' school that was just as bad as being
locked away in a convent!" Turning on her side in the bed
they were sharing for the night and rubbing her body
provocatively up against his, she had whispered: "But I
never cared—and I told her so—when they lay together.
Why should I? I do not even care that they are, the two of
them, probably doing at this moment the same thing that
we are doing. Does that thought excite you?"

He was better off letting go of his dark thoughts and
letting Marie-Claire's knowledgeable mouth and hands
excite him; taking him to that stage where pure sensuality
superseded everything else and there was only feeling
with his body—wiping out thinking.

Unfortunately, and infuriatingly, Blaze had begun to
discover that he could not—no matter who his bed partner
of the moment happened to be or how good she was—
completely eradicate certain annoying, nagging memories
from his mind; any more than he could stop himself from
thinking or wondering—or *breathing*, for that matter!

She was a perfidious *bitch*—Trista of the silver eyes and
lying lips—and *he* had made a fool of himself by going as far
as marrying her in order to rescue her from the consequences of her own impulsive actions.

What was worse, instead of showing any gratitude, she
had made a deliberate point of picking a friend of his as her
next lover within the space of a few hours; and then, add-

ing insult to injury, she had taken off without a qualm with the husband of her best friend.

Well—Trista was no business of *his* any longer, as long as she took care never to cross his path again—and right now and here, there was Marie-Claire—willing, eager, wanting . . . and *useful!*

Useful—he must remember that, Blaze told himself grimly while he spent a morning and most of the same afternoon sketching quick line impressions of different and typical San Francisco scenes—concentrating on the section that had become known as the Barbary Coast. Saloons, brothels, whores, pimps, and drunks. Gamblers with gold or silver stickpins in their elaborately tied cravats and derringers secreted in their vest pockets and scurrying Chinese with their pigtails bobbing.

Tomorrow he would be leaving for Sacramento by the river steamer, and from there to Placerville to catch the stage for Virginia City, where the Knights of the Golden Circle, headed by the ubiquitous ex-judge Terry and joined by representatives of that secret society from every individual group in the country would be meeting to decide on future strategy. He had learned that much in San Diego— and all there was to learn here in San Francisco, where there had already been eruptions of violence between Union and Secessionist sympathizers. Fernando Windham would be among the select group too, he'd learned from Marie-Claire, who enjoyed gossiping and grumbling at length when she wasn't occupying herself with other pastimes that kept her silent. Had he taken his compliant stepsister along to occupy his leisure hours? The hell with her anyhow! He hoped for *her* sake that he'd never be forced to encounter her again.

And then, when he looked down at his last, absent-minded drawing of a woman beckoning from a window at a passing sailor, Blaze swore violently under his breath as he ripped the whole page out of his sketchbook—crumpling it into a small, tight ball before he flung it away from him into the stinking, garbage-clogged gutter, which was exactly where *she* belonged; and his sketch of a woman with the face of a witch-enchantress. Trista's face. *Damn* her!

When Blaze returned to his hotel late in the afternoon, he was more than a little drunk—and still in a black, dangerous mood that wasn't helped in the least when the desk clerk, clearing his throat, informed him in a tactful whisper that "madame" was waiting for him in his room.

"Madame? Madame who?"

Catching a certain intonation in the gentleman's voice, the clerk backed off slightly, his Adam's apple bobbing over his collar. "Er—well, madame *said* she was—your *wife*, sir! And that she—that she wished to surprise you by her visit, Mr. Davenant! I didn't—that is to say—I didn't know what else to do, sir! Under the circumstances, you see—madame being quite *insistent* that . . ." The unfortunate man's stuttering trailed into silence when he realized that his guest was already halfway up the stairs before he could finish his excuses. "Never noticed his eyes before," he was to confide to one of his cronies later, with a slight shudder. "Reminded me of one of them Bengal tigers like we saw at the circus that time, that look. It gave me the chills, I'll tell you! And I didn't know if there'd be murder done upstairs in twenty-eight or even *worse,* if you know what I mean!"

Blaze Davenant, his long legs taking the stairs two at a time, *did* in fact feel an almost murderous rage mounting in him with every stride. His *wife?* Surely even *she,* promiscuous slut that she'd turned out to be, would hardly have the audacity to face him again after what she'd done? There wasn't a jury anywhere in the world that wouldn't applaud him for killing her as she justly deserved!

Expecting Trista and finding Marie-Claire instead, cozily ensconced in his bed, made Blaze come within a hairsbreadth of killing *her* instead.

"What in the *hell* are you doing here?"

Marie-Claire had *almost* fallen asleep when the door burst open to positively *crash* against the wall, making her sit up with a startled exclamation—covers falling away to reveal her nakedness. She'd thought it a deliciously daring idea—that he'd be pleasantly surprised and *excited* at finding her in his bed. But instead, he stood there glowering at her in a frightening fashion and all but *snarled* at her between his gritted teeth.

Never having seen *this* side of Blaze Davenant before, Marie-Claire's mouth dropped open with surprise, while at the same time she instinctively seized the bedcovers and held them up against herself protectively.

"Well?" he snarled in the same nasty voice, and this time, seeing the look in his narrowed amber-green eyes, she could not help cowering back as far as she could while she stared like a mesmerized rabbit into his stony, suddenly frightening face. And those eyes—she had never noticed before how they could change color from one moment to the next. She had never seen him so *angry* before either.

"I—I didn't think you'd be *angry!* I thought . . ."

"It's obvious that you're not in the habit of *thinking* at all! For God's sake—don't you realize what the consequences of this indiscreet whim of yours might be for both of us? *I* have no particular wish to be named as corespondent in San Francisco's latest scandalous divorce case, *ma belle;* no matter how desirable you might be as a lover!"

At any rate, he *did* find her desirable! Marie-Claire, her hurt feelings slightly mollified, was able to pout at him sulkily through her sniffles before she started to sob noisily, causing the cruel, unreasonable *beast* that he was being right then to give vent to an extremely rude oath before he did exactly as she had hoped and wanted him to do—sat down on the bed beside her instead of continuing to stand there *towering* over her.

Once she had wrapped clinging arms tightly about his neck, tugging him down against her undulating body— then he was hers! Or for the time, at least. Having suddenly seen a very different, almost dangerous side to this man whom she had only thought of as a very good lover and an understanding listener, Marie-Claire had begun to feel a strange, different kind of excitement inside herself as she found herself wondering half-fearfully how far she dared go with teasing and sugar-coated taunts before the violence hidden and held back deep inside him might erupt to consume her. It was like poking a stick at a sleeping tiger through the bars of a cage . . . and what if, once the beast had been aroused to blind fury, the cage proved not strong enough to contain the animal within?

"So—underneath what my husband used to call the 'effeminate softness' you are really *un bâtard*, aren't you? I have the feeling, *now,* since I have seen how fierce you can be, that you are something of an *aventurier*—an adventurer, as they say. Are you? You have made me a little bit frightened of you, Blaise Davenant . . . although you wouldn't have gone so far as to *kill* me, would you? Just because I chose to take a few risks and be *daring* for a change? San Francisco has become so dull of late!"

Marie-Claire, because she was French, always used the proper French pronunciation of his name, instead of the Americanized version *he* preferred to use. But at *this* point . . . Why in the hell did some women have to keep *talking?* He didn't give a damn what she said he was or thought he was—he had managed to regain some measure of his self-control after he realized how terrified he had made her, and now all he sought was forgetfulness, not talk!

"Tais-toi!" Blaze snarled before he made sure of silencing her by placing his mouth over hers to smother any further speech on her part. All he wanted and needed of her for the moment was movement in response to movement—murmurs and incoherent sounds in place of words, and feeling instead of thinking. If she had been the silver-eyed witch that he had expected he would have . . .

Marie-Claire was like a snake—a she-python wrapping arms and legs like coils about him to pull him deeper into herself until he slapped her smartly about the hips and made her turn about on the rumpled bed and onto her knees, to finish taking her that way; if only to prevent her damn clinging and pulling at him. And because, mounted from behind, there was usually not too much difference between one woman and another; except for the fact that some of them were less honest than others!

But then, Blaze was forced to admit wryly to himself later, how could *he* presume to judge anybody else for lack of honesty when he himself had been practicing subterfuge of one kind or another for so long? He had used people and he had used weapons of one sort or another if he felt it necessary, and would do so again if he had to; but to tell himself it was only because of a principle or an *ideal,* as some would call it, could not justly be used as an excuse. There was no point indulging in either excuses or regrets; but all the same he was angry at himself for his own loss of control, although Marie-Claire had seemed to enjoy the harsh way in which he had used her. Unfortunately for his peace of mind.

If only she had been a whore he could have dismissed with a large tip and a smack on the bottom so that he could be left to sleep alone with his suddenly morose thoughts! But she, it seemed, had different ideas of her own that didn't include his getting too much sleep.

"But you were so very angry with me for being *indiscreet* by coming here to you—so how can I possibly take the risk of sneaking out of here at *this* time of the evening when *everyone* I know will be out in their carriages taking the air or on their way to dinner—or the theater?"

When she had retired behind the screen at the far end of his room to use the washstand, Blaze had thought with relief that she was making preparations to leave. But no—it seemed that she had every intention of staying longer; and *he,* no doubt, would be expected to put on a repeat performance of what had just taken place between them. Shit! What did it take to get her tired out and satiated? What did her *husband* give her besides children—and several of them within a few years, at that?

By now, in spite of his noncommittal grunt as he turned on his side, Marie-Claire had already insinuated herself into his bed again—the abundant curves of her body pressing against the length of his resolutely turned back, while her hands went wandering all over him, alternately teasing and demanding until he grabbed her by the wrists and almost tore her greedy, seeking fingers off his body— ignoring her pained, querulous cry of protest as he did so.

"Ohh! Blaise, why are you so cruel to me suddenly? What . . . ?"

Before she could finish her question, he swung himself around to face her, those strangely colored eyes of his suddenly seeming more gold-hard than depthless green.

"And what, sweet temptress, if your husband should return unexpectedly and decide to come looking for you? Not that I can blame him in any way for being madly jealous of such a prize! But—you see, I'm merely an artist, not a duellist; and the thought of being shot to death by a jealous husband who catches me naked in bed with his wife appeals to me even less, I'm afraid!"

Reassured, Marie-Claire gave a throaty giggle. "But he is far too busy with other things, I tell you!" And then she laughed again. "Like getting little Trista safely married off to that friend of his from the Valley who isn't even capable of getting hard any longer! That is—after Fernando has finished with her, of course. It's something to do with her being an heiress, of all things, I suppose . . . but I don't really care about all that, do you? I don't care who my husband sleeps with so long as he has the decency, in return, not to interfere with *me!* And really—we get on quite well together. He tells me a great deal about his affairs because he knows that I am very understanding, you know? And above all—*practical!* As you are too; are you not, *mon cher Blaise?*"

Oh yes—he was eminently *practical* all right—hadn't he always been, every since he had begun making his own decisions and following his own beliefs? Idealistic dreams perhaps—but what of it? "The end justifies the means. . . ." "You have to fight fire with fire. . . ." "Beat 'em at their own game. . . ." Every cliché was based on a truth, after all!

Blaise Davenant (as he had been christened after his French grandfather), for all that his outward appearance did not too obviously betray his Indian ancestry, often used to feel that inside himself he was more fiercely, unforgivingly Apache than even his half-Apache mother. But then, his grandfather, for all that he had been a mountain man and a trapper, had come of a good family—and he had made enough money from furs first, and then trading with the Indians, to send his daughter to a convent school for her education. She had been married off to his father, a young widower, when she was barely sixteen—and without being allowed to choose for herself. She was very beautiful, with her light olive complexion and her amber eyes contrasting with her straight black hair; and she was still so young looking and so lovely, carrying herself erect and proud like a queen always; her voice never raised in harshness or in anger. Even her sullen stepchildren had in the end learned grudgingly enough to respect her, and even to confide in her. It was *he* who had been jealous of them, and of the time his mother spent concerning herself with *them*—and they, of course, had hated and resented his very existence.

"Injun brat—dirty little 'breed'!"

"Papa—I *can't* have *him* at my party and have everyone *talk!* I'd rather not have a party at all!"

"If he wants to learn how to ride, let him learn from that goddamned Injun kin of his, not me—although he's more likely to learn to *eat* horses instead of riding them, I guess!"

How clearly he still remembered! The happiest times in his life were the times he was allowed to spend with his grandfather—meeting all the other tough old mountain men and listening wide-eyed to their tales—some tall and some not. And discovering that he had two uncles who had chosen to live with the Apache and *were* Apache in every way—and through them, learning the Apache ways and customs, competing with young Apache boys his own age and being tested in the way that they were tested. Those had been his real learning years and times—not the times he had spent in schools and academies learning to be a gentleman.

He had learned a great deal more as well—how to carry off a pretense of being someone and something he wasn't— weakling, foppish dandy, even a coward if it became necessary. And to kill wearing a smile if he had to. In Europe, where he'd gone to study art, much to his father's fuming rage and open disgust, even the best-known and most reckless duellists tried to stay out of his way because, as one outspoken English friend of his put it:

"Davenant doesn't *give* a damn—y'know? Stands there with that infernal little smile of his that tells you it's all the same to him—live or die—*you* or him!"

But that was Europe—and art wasn't the only thing he'd studied when he'd met the passionate nationalists and revolutionaries of the day or dreamed of freedom and free men. And he believed and continued even now to believe that there was no injustice greater than enslavement—of the human body, mind, and questing spirit. In *owning* other human beings like a horse or a dog and treating them even worse than a pampered pet by denying them the existence of feelings and emotions—not to mention the capability of rational thought.

By the time he was twenty-five or so, Blaise Davenant had traveled and lived in almost every European country—

and had also visited a great many exotic-sounding ports
and places as well. India—Shanghai—Java—Egypt . . .

"Won't it seem rather—well—*boring,* old man? Going
back to the staid, respectable life at the old homestead, I
mean? Or is it the gold fever that's got you? Poor little
Samantha will be positively *devastated,* you know! Not to
mention Francine, and . . ."

Although the Viscount Nowell had sounded quite sol-
emn for once, his friend had burst out laughing.

"Oh damn! I'm sorry Pel—but when you mentioned
going back to the staid—what was it? *Respectable? I,* my
friend, am the equivalent of your remittance man—the
black sheep of the family, you might say." To his friend,
Davenant's curling back his lips and showing his teeth
had seemed more like a tiger's snarl than a smile, even before he had continued in the same softly *snarling* way:
"But of course I wouldn't miss my dearest stepsister's wedding for the world!"

That event had been Blaise Davenant's formal introduc-
tion to the close-knit "upper crust" circles of Natchez—and
later Charleston, Savannah, and even Richmond, Virginia.

He had bedded his stepsister on her wedding night while
her husband lay on the floor of his dressing room in a
drunken stupor; and in Charleston he had established his
reputation as a duellist and at the same time ensured his
entrée into the very best drawing rooms of that aristocratic
city by challenging (and killing) the man reputed to be the
best shot in four states after the so-called gentleman had
made a derogatory remark about "Frenchies and Texi-
cans."

Blaze (as he had begun to call himself by now) had met
Miss Charity Windham soon after that particular incident—and had encountered her again and then had sought
her company many times after that when he returned to
Charleston some months later from Texas. And that was
when it had all started—his involvement in the Underground Railroad and his present assignment as a special
agent and scout in the west and southwest territories—
directly responsible to President Lincoln himself.

Like Marie-Claire, who with husky, sensual murmurs
against his flesh and her stroking, teasing hands and fin-

gers was proceeding all over again to make him ready for
her—he too had learned to be a pragmatist. He had much
more important things to do than to allow his mind to
dwell angrily and for far too long on a false, night-haired
witch who deserved everything she brought on herself—
and if she was ready to commit bigamy at the drop of a hat,
that too was *her* problem and not his any longer! She was
out of his life, thank God; and from now on, he was determined to put her out of his mind as well.

Chapter 28 ~≈

Engulfing red-splashed darkness in patches divided by lines of light. The passing of time stamped on her mind like a repetitive pattern—like the words she must learn and had to repeat over and over until she could say her speech exactly right—thin threads running through the uncertain borders dividing pain and pleasure . . . or was this "pleasure" merely an expression of relief from pain? Whatever the case, she had learned by being *taught*—or rather, *instructed*. And Trista had always been told that she was an exceptionally good student who learned very quickly.

After that first "lesson" Fernando wanted her kept for himself alone—and the only pleasure Nordstrom had of her after that was from beating her if he was told she needed it, or humiliating and degrading her in other ways.

Until it was over at last—her sojourn in hell—and she was pronounced "cured" of whatever type of disorder or madness she was supposed to have been suffering from when she had first been committed to a so-called Exclusive Private Sanitarium for the Mentally Deranged. And by then, of course, she had been cured of everything—her former willfulness, her arrogance, her stubbornness, and above all her illusions.

She had made her well-rehearsed "confession" to the two pompous, self-styled doctors who ran the institution she had been confined in; with the proper air of abject humility and regret for having allowed her weak female nature get the best of her and lead her into sin and wickedness. She had, in fact, "admitted," with a certain amount of detail, having engaged in sexual relations and other lewd and lascivious acts with a countless number of gentlemen whose names she could not even remember, for money, jewels, and "other considerations." She had been a whore and a kept woman—a scarlet woman. And she'd even signed a legal-looking document that stated she admitted to all those things of her own volition.

She *had* no will of her own by then; only knowing without daring to question that she now *belonged,* as if she had actually been a slave, to her stepbrother Fernando; and that he, according to his whim of the moment, could choose between awarding her either pain or pleasure—whatever he felt like.

She was *his*—his possession, his *slave,* actually; and he had made very sure that she knew and accepted this fact while he forced her to wait upon his visits, his whims, and his moods—caught always between dread and anticipation as she wondered fearfully and could not think of anything or anyone else but *him* and how he would look at her and treat her when he next came; and how she could please him and satisfy him and prove to him that she did not need to be punished any longer. She was "reformed," she had been taught to be humble, she was by now unquestioningly obedient. And just like a trained circus animal who was required to jump through hoops, she too had learned to do what was expected of her. To *perform,* in fact.

Fernando preferred to call her Teresa in front of other people—sometimes when they were alone. And by this time, her performance polished, she was able to cut off the thinking part of her mind while she did, and *was,* whatever he wanted her to be.

"You understand now, don't you, why I had to have you punished—to bring you back to your senses? It was for your own good, my little *puta!*" Fernando laughed as he felt her press the length of her body more closely up against his— rubbing herself against him just like a little cat, he thought indulgently as his fingers stroked her soft skin with casual possessiveness, pausing and playing wherever he chose to enjoy her purring, throaty murmurs of response and her small gasps when he chose perversely to tweak or thrust to bring her to the threshold of pain. But she didn't try to pull away now—she not only knew better than that but had even learned to enjoy whatever he gave her. His *puta*, his little tame pet whore, who needed only to be shown who her master was!

"Well?" he persisted, fingers suddenly giving a sharp tug on the silky dark curls that shadowed the joining of her thighs at the same instant that he pulled cruelly on a nipple made erect by his earlier and more gentle caresses.

"Ahh!" she exclaimed, and he felt her shudder against him with the pain he was inflicting, for all that she had learned enough not to dare pull away. And then, pushing her rounded buttocks up against his thighs, she said in a broken, breathless murmur: "Fernando—I'm sorry! Please . . . ? But I thought that I had said so already—I mean—that I know everything was meant for my own good—and because—because I deserved to be punished—I *needed* to be corrected before—it was too late for me to—ahh! To change . . ."

Still holding her painfully and enjoying his power over her and the shivers he could feel running under her skin, Fernando nipped at her earlobe before he questioned almost teasingly: "Are you quite sure you mean what you say? After all, you have already demonstrated that you're far too easily swayed by facile speeches and languishing looks—not to mention the *comforts* of life, eh? So—do you still love me? Would you do anything at all for me, even if I did not have a piece of paper that could have you jailed as a common prostitute at any time I choose?"

"Yes—I know that. And I think that *you* have always known my feelings—even if I had too much pride to display them openly, I was jealous; you must have known that!"

"Were you indeed? And now—what would you do for me *now*?"

She responded with a sudden burst of spirit that amused and in a way titillated him. "What would I do? Get rid of Marie-Claire for one thing! And then—" She turned to face him and pressed her face against his shoulder while she murmured between quick, almost teasing kisses: "Oh, Fernando! Couldn't you see how enraged with jealousy I was?

I wanted only to strike back at you because of it—and then
to draw back and *tease,* so that you would notice me and
chase after *me* for a change; like I used to chase after you
before—don't you remember? Haven't you forgiven me
yet?"

He had started to laugh at the sudden fervor in her
voice; but when her hands began their journey along his
shoulders and back, and one hand, fingers moving lightly
and almost teasingly, explored between his thighs and
then between their bodies to hold and play with his sudden
hardness . . .

Then, although she reminded him far too much of Laurette at that moment, he could not resist her challenge and
temptation—and her final surrender. Yes—in spite of everything he had forced her to endure, the little bitch loved
him—like all bitches who had felt the whip and cringed under it. He had made her admit it quite freely and of her
own volition at last. He had completely conquered her!

Get rid of Marie-Claire indeed! He intended to make
sure that the two of them did not run into each other
again—at least, for a very long time! And since his little
stepsister was not only willing but eager for him, no matter what pain and punishment he had inflicted upon her
. . . well, the thrill of pursuit and conquest was gone, and
the only difference between *her* and all the others he had
taken and abandoned was that she, Trista, was the false
and fickle Laurette's daughter.

Laurette—had she only been playing with him from the
very beginning? How young and gullible he had been,
trailing after her in much the same way that her wide-
eyed daughter used to follow him around, much to his annoyance. She had been infatuated with him—and then she
had somehow learned to play flirting, teasing games, just
like her mother—for which he had punished her and could
punish her again at any time he chose to.

He rode her body savagely and harshly, slapping her
thighs as he did so to make her cry out; and then he made
her turn over and finished that way—imagining that she
was Laurette. Laurette—tame and willing and no longer
in charge. No longer the tantalizing instructress but his
slave—gasping and then moaning out loud with a mixture

of pain and pleasure—helpless beneath him and helpless to resist him.

After all—who could or would help her? There was no one to count on or turn to now but herself, and not a single person that she dared trust, either. I don't care—I don't *care!* Trista told herself fiercely as she moved and spoke and smiled purely by rote.

She was free and she was not. And she was far too frightened of Fernando to try to escape from him and risk being sent back to That Place. In any case, there was nowhere and nothing and no one she could escape to—ever since she had been told with brutal bluntness by Fernando that he had been appointed her guardian until she was married or reached twenty-five years of age.

"He was *my* father and not yours—and I think that he had realized before he died how unstable you are—what a wild bitch you are and always have been!"

She dared not refute his statement, for he would have her beaten again if she did; but she felt his words pierce like daggers into her heart—even worse than the pain inflicted on her body.

Especially when Fernando had said with an ugly laugh: "I told Papa that I didn't think you were coming at all because you were having far too much fun in Paris—and that's true, isn't it, *puta?*" And then, with another short laugh: "But never mind—in the end—in the end I was able to persuade my father to change his will and appoint *me* as your guardian until you are twenty-five years of age. So you see, I have every right to discipline you—as you should have been a long time before this!"

It's a lie—it's another lie meant to hurt me! Trista's mind cried out; although she dared not say so aloud. The only words she uttered were those demanded and expected of her, for she had taught herself to *act*—and to keep her thoughts to herself behind a blank face or an artificial smile, no matter how painful they might be.

I've taught her well! Fernando told himself. The promiscuous slut, with all her arrogant airs! How quickly they disappeared once she had been shown her place—usually on her hands and knees, pleading for mercy. He thought again, as he had thought so many times before: Laurette! If it could have been Laurette instead of her daughter I've taught to love me and cater to my every wish! I want Laurette to know what I've done with her brat and to understand what I think of *her*. They're both whores!

But now that the damned little bitch had been finally tamed and was ready to lick his hand or to do anything else he demanded, she was no longer the challenge she had once seemed. Worse—she had actually begun to pout if he didn't spend enough time with her, and even to question him jealously about the time he spent *away* from her—even if it was, as he said, with his wife and children!

It was time, Fernando thought, to get rid of the slut—and of the encumbrance she had turned into by now; especially since she had begun to cling. It was time indeed, now that he had tired of her too-easily available body, to make use of her. It was called "having your cake and eating it," he believed; for he'd be sure to let her imagine he'd be back to visit her often—and would punish her if she hadn't done exactly as he instructed her.

Virginia City—mushrooming, woman-hungry, silver-rich. And his friend Judge Terry was there, stirring up more support for the Southern cause. A great deal of useful gossip could be picked up and passed on—especially by an attractive and *talented* female who had been well instructed in the art of pleasuring a man while she asked him questions without seeming to. A woman with some modicum of intelligence, like his little love-slave Trista, could glean a great deal of useful information if she followed orders—as she would, of course. Fernando had not doubt of *that!*

And so it began . . . for Trista, at any rate. Hope—while she carefully schooled both her face and her manner in order to present an outward attitude of subdued obedience and gratitude at being released from the hell of her enforced captivity. She was only out on parole, she had to keep reminding herself. On a leash, like a half-tamed bitch, so to speak. Because Fernando could have her committed and contained again at any time he chose—she must never forget that while she was being tested and tormented by the sharply pointed prodding of his sarcastic words and his contemptuous treatment of her—even in public.

She was a whore—*his* whore for the moment: Hadn't she

been "induced" to sign a legal document to that effect? What good would it do her to deny it? He even made her *dress* like a whore, in low-cut gowns of garishly colored silks and satins ornamented with gold or bright silver lace; the necklines dipping so daringly low in fact that it was easy for him to slip his fingers into a tightly cut bodice to fondle her breasts and play with her nipples quite openly, without any regard for who might be watching.

He did it in the lowest type of gaming houses in Sacramento and Placerville—and even on the Wells Fargo and Company Concord stagecoach that was taking them over the new Placerville Road to Virginia City, Nevada.

"Smile, *puta,*" he would whisper as he bent down to her ear. "Smile back at the gentlemen who are envying me as they watch your nipples grow hard under my fingers until they strain to burst through the thin silk of your gown! Let them see how much you are enjoying my caresses, eh? Don't you like it? Let's see you smile provocatively at each one of the staring gentlemen who are licking their lips and growing hard for you . . . let's see how well trained you are, my little pet bitch!"

In the end she learned to touch his arm and whisper back to him: "Of course I'm yours—all yours, Fernando! But I'm so jealous of *you* and the way other women watch you that I'd rather smile provocatively at *you* instead!"

And then he'd laugh, grinning down at her with self-satisfaction sometimes; and at other times awarding her daring with a sharp pinch or a smack on the bottom before he said warningly: "You had better remember then that since you belong to me it is for *me* to command—*comprende?* Now *smile*—and flirt—but only if I tell you so! All the gambling ladies are good at such teasing games, and I intend that you will soon become known as one of the best! *That* is how you will please me, my *puta-bruja*—and I won't tolerate any jealousy from *you* either—you'd better get that quite clear!"

During her years of masquerading as a man, Trista had learned to gamble as well as any of them; and all the knowledge and cool-headedness she had managed to acquire helped her now. She could, indeed, play faro, and *rouge-et-noir, vingt-et-un* and even poker. And the provocative smiles and flirtatious manner that Fernando de-

manded of her certainly served to distract their attention
from the game at hand.

Almost constantly, Trista could not help wondering
what he intended to do with her—why he had suddenly decided to set her free—even if it was under his careful
guardianship. At least he had not offered her casually to
some other man; not yet, although he would always make
a point of reminding her that she was his whore and his
slave.

And I'm learning to be such a *good* whore! Trista would
tell herself bitterly sometimes. I've learned every trick in
the book—and I don't *feel* anything at all; even though I've
found out how well I can *act*.

Like any whore, she had no past and dared not think
ahead to the future. It was enough to survive—one day at a
time. She had, in fact, almost inured herself into not *thinking* at all while she was performing—playing to the hilt the
role that Fernando expected of her. There was no one now
that she could depend on or trust but herself; she had been
taught *that* lesson among too many others, and a shield of
hardness had begun to build itself inside her to hide away
all her real feelings and emotions, growing layer by layer
until she was only what she had to pretend to be—a gambler concentrating on winning a game that meant surviv-
ing—or not. And nothing, she would tell herself fiercely,
could be worse than being forced to endure the horror and
agony and despoliation of her most sensitive, private, inner self and her innocence as well as of her hopes and
dreams. Corrupted—corrupt—what difference? She was,
now, what she had become.

To become even more corrupt than the corruptors—to
beat them at their own game, in gambling parlance—yes,
why not? She had nothing left to lose, and her freedom
over herself to gain. Why not, indeed?

Nothing to lose that she had not foolishly squandered or
had not been taken from her—or that she had not been
forced to give whether she liked it or not.

"So *this* is what you were really like all the time, eh?
Even more of a *puta* and a bitch than your precious mama!
All heat underneath while you teased and promised and
drew back at the last minute—and now look at you! Enjoying everything I choose to give you, and rubbing your-

self up against me like a little cat soon after!" Fernando laughed shortly, but his laughter had a strange sound beneath it that Trista chose not to hear as she continued to be someone else who was a stranger to herself—a well-trained courtesan who could play any role that was required of her without thinking of what she was doing. And now she knew what she had to say—her well-rehearsed lines.

"But Fernando—I've *told* you I was only waiting for you to—to take me in spite of myself! I thought it was *you* who deliberately teased me and so I tried to make you jealous— and you see, now I am so jealous of you . . ."

"No more of that nonsense, do you hear? Or I'll have to beat you again to teach you your place—like *this*, and *this*—and stop squirming or it'll be worse!"

His open palm cracked down smartly against her bare flesh as he held her down with her wrists twisted up against her back, and Trista could not help the soft whimpers of pain that escaped her in spite of all her efforts to remain silent.

"There!" he announced as he released her as suddenly as he had seized her. "Let that teach you a lesson—that you're nothing more than my whore of the moment— understand? Your only purpose is to serve me—and to do whatever I say. And if you have fallen in love with me since I happen to have been the first man who's shown you who's master and who's bitch—that's all the more reason for you to try to please me instead of annoying me with your stupid jealous tantrums. And now—turn over so that I can mount you as a bitch should be mounted—on your knees, *ramera*—and beg for it, since you want it so badly!"

It was true that he could not help desiring her, especially when he had her like this, and in the most degrading ways possible, Fernando thought angrily; but she was not his false Laurette—Laurette who had taught him everything and made him crave her and even *love* her, damn her witch's soul! And then had left him without a word— without an excuse—with nothing but a hate that kept festering and growing in him like a cancer. Sometimes he would imagine that Trista was Laurette—but they were too unlike; and Laurette would never have allowed herself to be conquered so easily—no, she would have turned everything around so that *she* was the conqueror, and his queen. No, Laurette would never have submitted to such treatment—she would have died first—or smiled at him in that certain way that . . . but he wouldn't think of Laurette, not yet! His revenge on Laurette would be much more subtle. While as for Trista, clinging bitch that she had become, he was already tired of her—especially since she never resisted or protested any longer, no matter how much he humiliated or hurt her. In fact, he was beginning to think she actually enjoyed whatever he did to her—choosing to believe that the attention he paid to her, no matter how brutal, was a sign of *love*, of all things!

Laurette had loved him for a while at least—he was certain of that. The risks they had taken! And that little wild-haired daughter of hers who now writhed and moaned and tried by biting on the back of her hand to keep from screaming out loud from the pain he was deliberately inflicting on her—she had always kept following him—watching him—making a damn nuisance of herself. From the time Laurette had deserted him, he had planned what he would do with her little swamp brat as soon as she grew old enough to touch and take. He'd had to wait longer than he'd anticipated, thanks to his interfering aunt and to Trista herself—but now—now there was nothing he could not demand that she'd dare deny him. And he wanted Laurette to know that. He wanted Laurette to see her daughter this way—his willingly submitting whore. And she would. *Por Dios*—yes, she would—and would know then that this was his revenge on her for her betrayal of their love. *Damn* her!

Fernando used her, and hurt her even more while he was doing so, than he had done for a long time—and Trista knew why. Her mother—always her mother! But she was someone else—separate—and as she had finally managed to do before, her mind removed itself from her body that belonged to someone else—an actress in some unreal melodrama playing a role that had nothing to do with reality. Reality would catch up with her later—long after the performance was finally over.

Chapter 29 ～

They called her Silver because she only shook her head and smiled when someone asked her name—and because her eyes were a silvery gray that almost matched the sparkling silver trimmings that always set off the clinging, low-cut black gowns she always wore. Besides—Virginia City existed because of the silver that was mined from the Ol' Virginny and the Ophir—and the gold under Gold Hill.

There was a real shortage of women in Virginia City, except for the whores and the pretty waiter girls and the entertainers who put on shows at places like the Melodeon; and very few men could afford to send for wives, sisters, or families unless they had really struck it rich.

There were very few wives in Virginia City in these early sixties—but plenty of prostitutes; some high-class and some just cheap whores. The waiter girls fell somewhere in between; but Silver, now—no one could exactly figure her out, for all that she was a "gamblin' lady" and worked downstairs in a fancy house. One of the fanciest, in fact—but the men who clustered about her table soon discovered that she had a cool manner about her that discouraged any crude advances; and that she would never go upstairs with any man, no matter how much money she was offered. And dammit—she happened to be a good-looking young female too, with her night-black hair she always wore piled up at the back of her head with long, curly ringlets that seemed to have escaped by pure accident to cascade riotously down along her neck and shoulders and brush against her temples.

Silver. There were a lot of men who daydreamed and fantasized about her and the air of mystery that clung to her while they worked deep below the earth in heat that was almost unbearable. She talked like a lady and she acted like a lady, in spite of everything. There were some men who said they had seen her in a variety show at the Melodeon playing Lady Godiva and wearing nothing but her hair—but in a wild, bawdy town like Virginia City, it wasn't anyone's past that mattered. Only the present and how they acted. And Silver never did cheat a man, for all that she'd tease and flirt a bit sometimes. Hell, who cared? Here, everyone lived for the day—and if you were rich one day, you spent it and felt like a king; and you spent the money you had grubbed for on anything at all you pleased.

There wasn't a man in Virginia City who wouldn't have paid everything he had to take Silver upstairs and have everyone else envy him for it. Even if all they did was *talk*—sit on the edge of her bed—it didn't matter, he'd be envied by everyone who watched, and who heard about it.

She wasn't a whore—or at least she acted like she wasn't; and she wasn't *altogether* what a man would call a lady. She was a puzzle, and a question and—a challenge! And at the same time, if any brash newcomer, any outsider, had dared insult her he would be lynched or beaten to death by boots and fists.

For Trista, now known as Silver, this was a searching period in her life. Searching for answers or explanations perhaps. And at least as long as she remained in Virginia City where Fernando had brought her and had left her (thank God!), she was safe from him. Safe for the moment, at least.

How easy it had become to lose herself and to *become* another personality who was not herself at all. She had become Silver—remote, aloof, mysterious. And all because she neither demanded nor offered anything at all. Perhaps because she had learned, painfully, not to expect and not to trust. Not to believe in anything or anyone but her own strength and herself.

"I'm leaving you here with friends," Fernando had said

as he stroked the back of her neck with false tenderness as if she had in fact been a pet cat. "They'll look after you and keep you safe for me. But don't forget what you're supposed to do. Find out all you can about the Union troop movements—anything at all that might be of use, you understand? For *me, chiquita.* And I will be back as soon as I can to make sure you're still my good, obedient little whore. A *self-confessed* whore—but I'm sure that is something you won't forget, will you?"

No—how could she forget it? Or anything else he had forced her to say or do either?

She had managed to survive, somehow, by closing her mind off to reality by choosing pretense and unreality instead—being an actress giving a performance that would soon be over. Ah, how many roles she had learned to play, and how many lines she had learned to repeat by rote! But never again—no, never again. No one would dare touch Silver, the unattainable toast of Virginia City—not even Fernando. *Especially* not Fernando.

In Aurora, a boomtown almost wilder than Virginia City and the new meeting place of the Southern sympathizers who called themselves the Knights of the Golden Circle, she had been "married" off in a mockery of a ceremony with everyone naked to an old and all but senile man who had already made Fernando his heir; and all for the sake of her so-called inheritance that might not even exist by now. Like a shipboard wedding that had been both a lie and a farce.

What choice did she have? What choice did slaves have? She had only made a feeble protest that was carefully phrased as a question before she was slapped into sobbing acquiescence.

None of Fernando's friends seemed to notice that her face was red and swollen as they celebrated her "wedding" and hatched their plots—but she had been profoundly thankful at least that after she had been deposited in bed with her "bridegroom" he had promptly fallen asleep. And the very next morning they had set out for Virginia City, where she had been deposited like an unwanted package in the care of a man and a woman she had never met before and knew nothing about—except that at first glance she neither liked nor trusted either of them, even though

Vera, the woman, had attempted to be falsely and overly kind at first.

"You go upstairs with anyone who can give you any information, you hear?" Fernando whispered in her ear before he left her—with the madame of a parlor house and her current man friend, both of whom looked her over as if she had been a prize cow they had just bought.

"Isn't she just the *loveliest* girl? I'd get awful jealous right now, sweetheart, the way my Robert is giving you the eye, if you weren't so darned cute! Isn't she the cutest thing you've ever seen, Bobby? That hair, and those eyes—why, I'll bet she'll have all the men crazy about her, and ready to give her just about anything she asks for!"

At least Bobby came right to the point, which meant that he grunted disparagingly before he said:

"Don't think her tits are big enough fer her to do that Lady Godiva act—but I guess she'll have to do fer this one night at least or we'll have a riot on our hands after putting up all them posters and all. Just make sure you kinda push 'em up with one hand while you cover yer pussy with the other, huh? An' you better know how to ride a horse like you said you did, too. Well?"

She was, for that one night, the act that was supposed to outshine and outdo Adah Isaacs Menken's famous *Mazeppa*. Adah at least had worn flesh-colored tights when she was strapped onto her tame horse, but Trista had been permitted nothing but her hair and her hands with which to attempt covering her nakedness as her white mare ambled across an endless-seeming stage.

It was only the fear that Fernando might be watching to make sure she was still obedient that made her submit to that final public humiliation. It was bad enough to have had to strip to her bare skin under the appraising eyes of both Vera and her "man friend"—but to parade in the nude before a mob of cheering, shouting men was more than she could endure!

Especially when afterward Vera commented petulantly that she really shouldn't have hidden her face under that mass of hair—if she hadn't, there'd have been more pokes of gold dust and silver nuggets thrown at her. To make matters worse, Vera's hands seemed to travel all over her body while she pretended to help Trista on with the thin wrapper she'd been handed after her ordeal. And after *that,* she felt that she would not—*could* not endure anything more. No—no matter what they threatened her with or tried to do with her—this time at least she would fight back with all the strength of desperation.

Vera had bright red dyed hair and an overly abundant figure in addition to halitosis. And her hands were far too predatory; almost like Fernando's. Following and forcing themselves upon her even when Trista attempted to move away.

"My dear—I know too well what brutes men can be! They hurt and are so harsh, as we women know too well—but women—we know what pleases us, don't we? Exactly what pleases us . . ."

"No!" Trista heard herself say sharply as she caught Vera's plump wrists and held them away from her. "No—I'll make my own choices in my own time from now on—do you hear me?"

Trista saw and recognized the fear that had suddenly come into Vera's eyes as she attempted almost desperately to free herself, whimpering as she was shaken mercilessly until her breath came in protesting gasps.

Good! Now someone was afraid of *her* for a change! Still holding Vera's wrists in a tight, twisting grip that made the woman moan with pain, Trista had to fight back some ancient, primitive instinct that almost overwhelmed her—urging her to strangle Vera and watch her choke for breath while her fingers tightened about that plump throat—thumbs feeling for the carotid artery. . . .

"I could kill you right now, without a qualm! You know that by now, don't you?" Trista gave a harsh, contemptuous laugh at the expression on the woman's face and the paling of her normally florid complexion before she added in a softer and harder voice: "And tell your man—your Robert with his pawing, sweaty hands—that he had better keep his distance from now on, for I'd take pleasure in killing him if he ever tries to touch me again—understand? I belong to no one but myself, and *I'll* decide from now on what I will or will not do! You had better get that clear before I'm tempted to break both your arms!"

"Magnifique, chérie! But what is the reason for such a violent exhibition of rage? And please—try not to break my

poor Vera's arms while you explain your behavior; or I
might be forced to shoot you with this little pistol I am
holding."

A few minutes before, Trista had felt herself swept away
from thinking or reasoning by the bursting out, in an explosion of sheer, primitive fury, of all the pain and anger
and frustration she had been forced to keep pent up within
herself. But now, all of a sudden, she was almost coldly
calm as she released her grip on Vera and sent the woman
staggering backward with a contemptuous shove before
she turned around with deliberate slowness to face the
woman who had just spoken from behind her in an
amused, slightly accented voice she remembered and recognized only too well.

Her mother. Still slim waisted, still lovely, and still a
stranger. Trista heard herself laugh—a harsh, dissonant
sound that jarred her own eardrums. "Why not go ahead
and shoot me with that pretty little pistol of yours,
Maman? It would save us both the trouble of having to explain our peculiar relationship, won't it? Or did you know
already that your stepson, whom you took as your lover
under his own father's roof, made your daughter his
whore—and the whore of any other man he chose—because
I was unfortunate enough to have been born your daughter
. . . and because of his unsatisfied lust for my mother! The
idea should flatter you, *chère Maman!"*

Like eyes looked into like eyes—silver-and-steel spark-
ing as they clashed together before Laurette shrugged and
said with a half-sigh: "I think I have always known that
this would happen at some time! And so you are Trista . . .
and you are much prettier now, of course, than you were as
a child!"

"But *you* have remained quite unchanged from the way
I remember you! Beautiful and cold and unfeeling like a
marble statue seen at a distance—at least, by *me*, your
ugly, disappointing girl-child!" To her utter horror Trista
felt her eyes moisten and she had to fight to keep her voice
from shaking before she managed to add lightly: "However, you've been a good example to me—especially recently. And I've been taught well—by my stepbrother, who
told me that *you* taught him! Did you watch my performance tonight? Do you come here often, *ma mère?"*

"I *own* this place—and a few others beside. Some of the fanciest houses and gambling saloons in Virginia City. Right now I'm living with a wild and very rich Scotsman who has built me a mansion and gives me expensive jewels." Laurette gave a slight shrug and arched her brows expressively as she paused to light the slim cheroot she had fitted into a gold and ebony holder, watching for an instant the different emotions that chased each other across Trista's face. One day, perhaps, she would learn not to show others any emotion at all . . . that is, if she was wise enough to learn!

Laurette's face was a half-smiling, unreadable mask as she exhaled and continued in an almost casual voice: "But the thing is, that after your *striking* appearance as Lady Godiva, Charlie is *determined* to make your acquaintance . . . and to present you to some of his friends—for an evening of . . . what *he* refers to as "fun and games." I'm sure you know what I mean and what *he* meant by that? No—it does not matter; for I am going to make up some excuse for you to take his mind off ideas of "fun and games" tonight! And I'll provide one of the new girls who hasn't been used too much yet for Charlie's friends."

Trista noticed that her mother's smile had turned into what looked like a twisted grimace before she turned her face away to stub out her cheroot impatiently as she said over her shoulder: "In any case, my dear—I am really not sure that I *want* anyone to know that you are my daughter . . . and a far too grown-up one at that! It might prove embarrassing as well as awkward for both of us, I think!"

Trista had begun, stiffly: "I assure you that I have *no* intentions at all of . . . ," when there was what sounded like a tremendous crash as the door was kicked open by booted feet; and several impatient gentlemen surged inside almost hungrily, trapping her against the wall, their eyes and lascivious grins making her far too much aware of the one, thin garment which was her only and very scanty covering.

"Hell, Laurie! We just got too damn tired of waiting around! And she's one of the new gals, ain't she? Not as if you hadda spend this much time tryin' to *talk* the little charmer into bein' obligin' to my friends, huh? Not as if every man in the place didn't get a real good look at her already—so what's the difference?"

The red-haired man who had just delivered a heated speech about her lack of morals and easy virtue had to be her mother's latest paramour, of course. Charlie the Scotsman who was wild and very rich and had too many friends.

No doubt Charlie was willing to pay very handsomely for his friends' recreation! But it surprised Trista, in some strange fashion, to discover that her rediscovered mother seemed to be engaged in a furious, low-voiced argument with her Charlie. Jealousy perhaps? Certainly *not* because she was attempting to defend her daughter's *virtue!*

Trista had just thought that, when one of the men touched her—groping for a breast as he clumsily attempted to free it from its thin silk covering. Animal! They were all like crude, rutting animals wanting only to mount her and use her body and hurt her without caring that they did, or caring for her feelings. Perhaps they thought she had none left by now! Animals! Dirty, unwashed bodies pressing closer and closer to hold her trapped and pinned against the wall like a broken-winged butterfly . . . helplessly immobilized . . . No!

She had not realized that she had almost screamed the word aloud as the side of her hand chopped down as fiercely and hard as a knife blade striking into the wrist of that pawing hand, finding the most sensitive place where it would hurt and almost paralyze. And even as he fell back, crying out with pain as he clutched his wrist, she brought her knee up into the next comer's groin while she struck at the bobbing Adam's apple of the other man to his right.

As they backed away from her, eyes moving almost unbelievingly from Trista's pale, coldly hard face to their groaning companions, she said composedly: "I am very much afraid that you—I can hardly call you gentlemen after your crude exhibition of bad manners, can I? But you *men,* whoever and whatever you are, had better understand *quite* clearly that I am not for sale . . . and I will, if I choose to do so, make my own decisions and my own choices—but only after I have first been *asked.* Nobody takes me—I give if I want to! You understand?"

"I'll be goldurned if she don't have claws—and a way of

talkin' just as sharp too! Damn, Laurie, you shoulda warned us!"

Trista ignored them all and their surprised, gaping looks as she walked stiff-legged and stiff-backed to the door and outside, refusing to look back or to notice the stares she was getting now, or even to *think* while she held tightly on to her anger and her stubborn pride—all she had left to sustain her.

Chapter 30 ～⌒

"You'll never catch the real flavor and essence of Virginia City and these times we're living in until you've visited all the best bars and bordellos—where you meet everyone worth knowing, or sketching, for that matter!"

"Such as . . . ?"

"Such as the mystery woman known as Silver for instance. Now, there's a puzzle for you—and every other man, I suppose! Does she—or doesn't she? Will she—or won't she? You must admit that's intriguing! And so is *she*, the infernal female; like a constant question and a constant challenge—for all that rumor has it she arrived here with a "protector" who used to hire her out, so to speak, as a whore. And then she outdid La Menken's *Mazeppa* by playing Lady Godiva, and became the talk—not to mention the *toast*—of the town! Fascinating creature—always dressed in black and silver when she presides over her faro table at the Silver Slipper."

Sam Clemens, a reporter for the *Territorial Enterprise*, had certainly proved to be an interesting and informative guide to the fleshpots of Virginia City; and Blaze Davenant's bulky sketchbook had only four blank pages remaining in it by the time they made their somewhat unsteady way into the opulently furnished Silver Slipper, which, Clemens had informed him, combined gambling

248

and drinking until all hours downstairs with *private rooms* upstairs. "Always save the best for the last!"

The best? There were the usual mirrors and portraits of voluptuous nudes hung everywhere, and the usual tinkling piano in the background being ignored while most of the customers clustered about the gaming tables. Well—thank God it was the last saloon he'd have to visit tonight, as tired and half-drunk as he was, Blaze thought impatiently. All he really needed was a bed to *sleep* in tonight before he had to start traveling again tomorrow. Going south this time . . . too close to home and to old memories still as bitter as gall and old loves and old hates he thought he had long since forgotten or shaken off.

"Indio!"

"Hey—Injun brat! How long was it you lived with them savages, anyhow?"

"They say your pa bought your mother from *her* father—and *he* was an old French squaw man—*everyone* knows that, hear?"

Words from the past. Why did he have to remember? And what in the hell did anything in the past mean *now,* when he was long past being a confused boy on the verge of adolescence, and already imagining himself in love with a young woman several years older than himself? Half-Mexican, slimmer and taller than other girls of her age, she had seemed irresistibly lovely and infinitely desirable—and his hunger and his lust for her had become not only unbearable but close to becoming uncontrollable when he was abruptly returned to his father and forced to adapt to a completely new and different way of life that he hardly remembered or understood. Her eyes had been the color of the drink he was staring down into . . . wide and black lashed.

Forget! She was probably fat and ugly and had lost most of her teeth by now. The first infatuation was the hardest to get over—much more pleasant to think about Charity Windham instead. Charity, sweet Charity; loving, giving friend who had taught him caring and restraint and even how to be tender—sometimes. He should have married *her*—and he'd asked her several times; argued with her and even once or twice had come close to pleading with her, but she'd always shaken her head and reminded him

that they both had too much to do to think of such things—
and they were both far too independent and set in their
ways to take kindly to *ties* of any sort.

And then he had been fool enough to allow himself to be
seduced by Charity's hot-blooded young niece—and had
stupidly gone even further by *marrying* the amoral little
slut to save the "reputation" she neither had nor cared
about! Running off with her precious stepbrother and
flaunting their adulterous relationship in the eyes of the
whole world . . . making *him* look like a fool as well as a
cuckold. If he ever ran into her again he'd probably end up
breaking her neck—faithless, lying bitch that she was and
always had been!

In his moody, angry state of mind Blaze had not even noticed that he had already downed three whiskeys and had
slid back his glass to have it refilled until the bartender reminded him with an apologetic cough that he already owed
for the ones he'd had before.

Damn all unneeded, unpleasant memories anyhow!
Blaze flipped a gold eagle across the counter at the fat bartender, who had already begun to smile widely as he actually produced a clean glass before filling it with a different
and much better brand of whiskey.

Money always talked loud—anywhere in the world. It
had helped transform a savage into a so-called gentleman
with manners and education, hadn't it? And where in the
hell had Clemens disappeared to—upstairs with one of the
pretty gambling girls? Oblivion of another kind . . . and
Blaze didn't need to get drunk and insensible to obtain it,
either. He needed a woman to *forget*—warm, yielding,
opening flesh receiving him and holding him for an hour or
two perhaps. Sensation and physical release without feeling—forgetfulness in fucking.

"The woman dealer who's known as Silver and always
wears black and silver—where will I find her? Which
table?"

For some reason the bartender's smile had disappeared
as if it had been wiped off his face, and he stammered uncertainly as he answered with obvious unwillingness: "Er
. . . arh . . . well . . . it seems like . . . That is, Miss Silver—she's dressed up kinda different tonight . . . and I
hardly reckernized her myself at first! In that red dress

Mr. Charlie . . . Mr. Donelson, that is . . . he ordered it special for her an' then he bet her she'd never be bold enough to wear it out in public . . . an' so naturally she took him up on his bet—just like he knew she would! But mister, if I was you I wouldn't be jumping to any wrong ideas about that little gal, not if you value your hide, that is. An' she'd never go upstairs with you or any other gentleman no matter what she's offered, either!"

"And she makes her *sole* living dealing faro? Tell me— who is her protector? You, or this Mr. Donelson who buys her red dresses? Never mind—for now I have to see this unusual female paradox for myself, since you've managed to arouse my curiosity about such an unusual woman. She does not have hair that's dyed bright red or sport a mustache, does she?"

Of course she had to be the center of attention at the table around which most of the customers were closely crowded, elbowing and jostling each other while they exchanged muttered oaths and threats as they fought to get closer to the woman known simply as Silver.

She was probably not worth the expending of his energy, of course. Men in these primitive frontier towns were notoriously lacking in either taste or discrimination when it came to females—especially the kind good at playing helpless and silly and *dependent* as soon as some man turned up conveniently. This woman who called herself Silver probably had the acquisition of just that in mind when she named herself, and was most likely just another hard-faced, fortune-hunting bitch. So why bother?

Perhaps the only reason he did was because the bartender who had been smiling and friendly a few minutes ago had warned him in a suddenly expressionless voice, as he began polishing the mahogany bar with deliberate concentration, that strangers usually had to find out for themselves—and how much change did he want back?

Turning away from the bar and the suddenly silent, stony-faced bartender, Blaze Davenant told himself that there were many green-baized gaming tables in this same room; and just as many pretty dealers who would be more than willing to "go upstairs" and keep a man company after they were through with their regular duties in the gambling salon downstairs. Why then did he find himself curious about this one woman, who could not be very different from any of the others if she worked in a place such as this? Just another scheming whore who had learned that playing teasing games only made men more eager and willing to pay higher prices; and if he had not promised his friend Orion, who was Sam Clemens's older brother, that he would be sure to look up Sam who would have all the latest gossip—not to mention useful information—he probably wouldn't be spending a boring night here in Virginia City and actually thinking of battling his way through a crowd of eager admirers just to get a look at a female who called herself Silver!

"Ah! Here you are after all, Davenant—I was hoping you'd be kind enough to forgive my breach of manners for leaving you so abruptly, but I was impelled to follow up a story I am writing for the *Territorial Enterprise* next week—bread and butter—and just enough spice to excite and make 'em lick their lips waiting for more. But I don't need to tell *you* that!"

Sam Clemens had an infectious smile and a way with words; his own brother Orion had said so—almost *warningly,* Blaze recalled a trifle grimly even while he shrugged and assured Clemens politely that he quite understood what it was to be a member of the press.

"Well—thank God you're an understanding kind of fellow! And believe me, I'll make it up to you! In fact . . . I know what I can do! I'll introduce you to Silver, that's what!"

Silver—all polish and shine on the surface like the metal she had named herself after. Silver eyes and a mane of curly black hair no brush or tight chignon could keep decorously controlled enough to prevent curling tendrils from escaping riotously to brush against the nape of her neck . . . her temples and her flushed cheeks.

Trista—wanton witch with surface-sheened eyes that revealed nothing of what might lie behind and beneath their lamplit glitter.

The low-cut, flame-red dress she wore was trimmed with gold ribbons threaded through black lace—outlining every flounce of her full skirts; and ribboned bows on each ivory-colored shoulder were all that kept the tightly fitted bodice of her gown within the realms of decency. Quite obviously, whoever had bought this gaudily spangled dress for her had to have known her measurements very well indeed! Perhaps he had been present to watch it fitted on her naked body—this Mr. Donelson who must be her latest lover. How many others before *him?*

Blaze found himself tempted to violence by an unreasonable fit of fury that almost made him forget himself and the reasons for his being there in the first place.

Seductive little Trista with her silver-eyed witchery and her eagerly yielding, too easily given body. The sly, conniving bitch he had actually been stupid enough to make his wife in order to "save" her. It must have seemed quite humorous to her; and to Fernando as well until she had decided to discard him for another, richer man—and *that* one for another, and yet another! Why, she was nothing more than a scheming whore at heart—one of those women who was a born whore and grew up knowing by instinct all of a whore's little tricks and clever stratagems designed to take in fools and chivalrous idiots!

Sam Clemens, who seemed to know everyone in Virginia City, had managed to push his way through the men crowded about her particular faro table; but Blaze had had the chance to observe *her* and her falsely smiling face before his new friend could obtain her attention and attempt, sketchily, to "introduce" them to each other.

Looking up suddenly, Trista felt all the color drain out of her face before she felt her cheeks heat with a sudden rush of blood. Oh God—not Blaze! Rage and hate from his amber-green eyes striking into hers with all the deadliness of a water moccasin . . . paralyzing her . . . almost *killing* her, as her senses knew he wanted to do.

"Why, ma'am—I could surely swear we've already met— in Virginia, was it? Or on board a ship bound for San Francisco? I hope you'll pardon my uncertain memory for *some* things!"

Underneath the exaggerated Southern drawl he could affect when it suited him was cold steel. Daggers, meant to pierce and cut into her—deeply enough to find the essence of her—her soul. Worse than boiling, molten fire consuming her was the white-hot hate and rage in his eyes; holding her still and pinioned until she suddenly thought, without knowing why or how, that the same liquid fire

that had melted them into each other had bound them together forever—and the same fire consumed them both,
even *now.*

Her dream-thought had flashed across her mind in less
than a second and was gone when she blinked her eyes
once—feeling *life* rush suddenly through her on the one
long breath she took before she was able to answer him
with distant, indifferent coolness: "Oh have we? Well,
perhaps—it's quite likely, I suppose, because I—move
around so much!"

"Oh, I'm sure you do, ma'am! Must be quite *wearing* on
a delicate female constitution like yours, all this . . . moving around!"

How she hated him! Wanted to dismiss every trace,
every memory of him from her mind as well as her body!

They had both become oblivious to the sudden hush
around them—or to the fact that they were surrounded by
a growing crowd of onlookers and listeners while they
duelled with words.

Words sharper and more deeply wounding than swords.
Words meant to inflict hurt and kill any feelings that
might still be *there* for each other. Why say them? And yet
at the same instant she thought that, Trista heard herself
say cuttingly:

"What a low bastard you are! I should have seen it long
before!" She pushed her chair back abruptly as she stood
up, almost knocking it over with the gale of her sudden anger.

"You, in fact, are the one person I had devoutly hoped
not to set eyes upon again! Please excuse me, gentlemen—I
find myself suddenly indisposed!"

It was as if a collection of goggling-eyed, openmouthed
statues had suddenly come to life—questioning and protesting; and some even threatening toward the stranger
who was the reason for Silver rushing off like this. Why—
they'd lynch the bastard if he tried to force himself on *their*
gal, who was a real, honest-to-God doctoress too!

"Too indisposed to go upstairs with an old and *very* familiar acquaintance who has enough money now to afford
even *your* price?" Long fingers, tightening about her wrist
until she thought he actually meant to break it, held
Trista a prisoner—halting her headlong and ignominious

flight from him and forcing her to meet his ugly, hateful
look again.

And then suddenly and instinctively she knew how she
could fight back and injure. Smiling as she fluttered her
eyelashes in a deliberate caricature of coy flirtatiousness,
Trista questioned:

"Do you really have enough money to afford *me?* Goodness! I hope you'll forgive my natural amazement, by the
way, considering the *littleness* of what you had to offer me
before! Perhaps your . . . umm . . . assets have grown since
then? And there's really no need to try and break my poor
little wrist, I assure you, sir—now that you have managed
to arouse my curiosity. Do leave go—there's really no need
for a display of your superior strength, you know!"

There were angry murmurs that swelled into audible
threats from the bearded, rough-looking men who surrounded them; and Sam Clemens, who had been taken as
much by surprise as the rest of them, tried frantically to
explain things away with a shrug, a forced laugh, and a
joking speech. But it was Silver herself who calmed rising,
volatile tempers when she said quickly: "It's really all
right, boys—you know I can take care of myself, don't you?
And after all . . ." Her fingers stroked teasingly and ca-
ressingly down Sam Clemens's stubbled cheek, stunning
him into sudden silence before Trista added huskily: "After all, you won't mind waiting awhile, will you, darling?
Mr. Davenant happens to be an old—*business* acquaintance—and I'm quite sure he won't keep me for too long!
You were always so *quick* in finishing off . . . your business transactions, weren't you, Blaze honey?" The smile
she turned on him was honied too, and as false as the brittle porcelain mask that hid everything real behind it. Had
the bitch ever said or done anything that was truly *honest?*

"How many men do you usually take upstairs with you
each night?" Soon after he had almost snarled the question at her, Blaze regretted displaying what *she* would
probably take as a sign of jealousy, damn her!

She had been leading the way upstairs, her skirts lifted
high enough to show off ridiculously high-heeled red silk
shoes and silk-stockinged ankles; but she paused for a moment to look over her shoulder at him as she replied composedly: "As many as I please to take, of course!"

How dare she flaunt herself so obviously and openly as a whore, selling her body over and over again to whoever offered her the most money? *Silver*—how very appropriate; although Trista was more like quicksilver, and just as difficult to pin down in place, Blaze thought wrathfully. Even the law recognized the right of a betrayed husband to slay his promiscuous wife, after all!

"Well—here we are!" Trista announced in a brittle voice after she had closed the door behind them. "It's rather a pretty room don't you think?" she went on in a rush of words (*any* words at all, she thought desperately, watching Blaze's dark, dangerous face), and laughed with the sound of breaking crystal. "Red and gold—and if you care to look, there's even a mirror over the bed! It excites some people, you know. Watching themselves while they . . . but goodness! How remiss of me to babble on so before asking you if you'd care to make yourself *comfortable* first! Please feel quite at ease to do so, for we are very informal here! And if you will tell me what your choice of liquor is, I would be happy to—"

"How much? I recall that we struck a bargain without mentioning prices—and I always insist on knowing how much I'm paying for a whore and what I'll be getting for my money *before* I use her. So—why don't you strip for me first and serve me naked? A glass of bourbon—in case you had forgotten!"

Blaze laughed harshly and sarcastically at the sound of her indrawn breath as he tossed two heavy gold coins on the dresser, barely missing her.

"Well? Will that do as an advance payment? Take your clothes off and let your hair down—Lady Godiva! And then, if I'm still inclined to try you, you can ride a man instead of a horse and watch yourself doing it in your damned mirror! So? What in the hell are you waiting for?"

Trista flinched inwardly at every word he stabbed her with; but she had learned while she had been Fernando's plaything to school her features so that they showed no emotion at all. Why had she come up here with him at all? So that they could hurt each other and learn to hate each other more?

In spite of her strangely jumbled thoughts and the wounds he continued to inflict on her, Trista found herself

able to utter in a lightly questioning tone: "But what are
you waiting for, sugar? Surely you must have known when
you came upstairs with *me* that I only give the orders—
never take them! And now that we finally understand each
other—do be quick about taking *your* clothes off, won't you,
Blaze dear? You may have a whole hour because I happen
to be sentimental at times—but you will try to remember
that I might have other customers waiting?"

Now he *would* probably kill her by choking off her
breath! Hadn't she already read that thought in his eyes
and in his mind? And yet she forced herself to hold her
head up and to return his murderous tiger-glare defiantly
instead of trying to escape or avoid it; standing her ground
instead of backing off fearfully or snatching open the door
to run from him and from the threat he represented because of her own damned weakness.

Hate him! Trista's mind told her. Let him see how much
you hate and despise him! Never give in or let yourself be
duped again—learn to fight back, you fool!

But then, even as she readied herself for battle, Blaze
gave an exasperated shrug—his expression suddenly unreadable. "Shit! You mean to say that I'm expected to pay
for the privilege of removing my own clothes while *you*
merely stand back and watch? Sorry, honey—but I'm more
used to having it the other way around, if you understand
what I mean? But maybe your next customer might prove
more obliging and willing to spend money on a whim—or a
forbidden fantasy! Not I, I'm sorry to inform you, sweeting." His smile was more like a sneer or a snarl—a slight
upward curve of his lips that showed the white gleam of
his teeth. "All the better to eat you with, my dear!" Why
did she suddenly feel like Red Riding Hood?

"Since I haven't had the satisfaction I had expected from
the highly recommended and overpriced tart you've become, I'm sure you'll have to agree that I'm entitled to
have my money back?" The short, ugly burst of sound that
accompanied his equally ugly speech was supposed to be a
laugh—leaving echoes in the silence between them until
with a quirk of one eyebrow Blaze added mockingly: "No
argument, I take it? After all, my dear, you have surely
learned by now that when a man pays through the nose for
his pleasure, he should get his money's worth before he

has to give way to the *next* customer! Don't you agree?"
The gold coins he had flung down contemptuously earlier
clinked as he picked them up and dropped them negli-
gently into his vest pocket.

"You have your money back—now *leave!*" Trista's voice
sounded tight and constricted, rising into sharpness as she
said fiercely: "Did you hear what I said? Get out—at once;
or I'll have you thrown out! I owe you *nothing* . . . understand? And damn you and your gold you thought you could
buy me with, Blaze Davenant! Nobody will ever own me
. . . or any part of me; do you understand? And least of all
you—hypocrite that you are to dare accuse me and judge
me without question; because you'd *prefer* to think the
very worst—isn't that so? Well, you can think whatever
you want to—it doesn't matter to me; for I hope I will never
have to set eyes on you again, you—you despicable *cur!*"
Turning her back on him, Trista held on to the edge of an
ornately carved dressing table, her knuckles white from
strain. *"Will* you get out?" She repeated again. "I think
that now you've got your money back and said what you
had to say, we have settled accounts between us! You no
longer have any reason to—"

"No? But even if a man cannot buy his own *wife*, he is
entitled to conjugal rights—if he chooses to exercise them.
You must know that, surely? I don't need to *pay* you in order to bed you, after all; especially since I have the legal
right to take you whenever I please . . . *if* I so please!"

Trista caught her breath as she actually *felt* the heat of
his body against her stiffly held back. All the same, she
forced herself to swing about and to face him.

"No! Even *you*, as vile as you have shown yourself to be,
would surely not—"

"No? But then, my dear—since you have already named
me a 'vile beast,' you shouldn't be too surprised if I act the
part, should you?"

He had her pinned back against the dresser, its carved
edge digging painfully into her diaphragm as he deliberately placed his palms on the dresser on either side of her
so that she was kept an unwilling prisoner within his
arms.

"Well? You must have learned a lot since we last encountered each other! And was Fernando a good teacher,

by the way? But now's your chance to show me whether
you're worth the high price you demand—or not!"

It had been a long time since she had felt . . . trapped,
and surrounded and helpless. How could she have forgotten all the hard and painful lessons she had been forced to
learn? But—*Blaze?* And why?

Feeling him lean over her and the hard pressure of his
body against hers, Trista closed her eyes while she attempted to close her mind to any feeling or emotion that
might betray her. This was a man—*any* man. He had been
an adventure and a fantasy once, but that was long over
like a half-remembered dream; and *this* was the present,
and harsh reality. Inside herself she wanted (and perhaps
needed) to cry bitterly; but at some time and somehow, she
had forgotten how. Instead of releasing feeling, she had
learned too well how to hide by crawling inside herself and
living there, while her other, outside self acted and reacted
as it had to in order to survive.

It was purely her instinct for self-preservation that
made Trista twist her face aside to avoid his kiss on her
mouth as she murmured fretfully: "Well, for goodness'
sake, Blaze! There's no need for you to break my back, is
there? I know very well you're much stronger than I am;
and you've reminded me that we are supposed to have
been wed . . . but in any case I'm in no mood to argue with
you, since you seem determined to . . . claim your conjugal
rights, did you say? Whatever excuse you choose to employ
this time—"

"Christ!" Blaze interrupted, with barely controlled violence, as he put one hand under her chin to force her face
around and upward to confront him eye to eye whether she
wanted to or not. He was tempted, in fact, to break her
neck rather than lower himself by finding a suitable answer to her bored, barbed, and indifferent little speech that
showed her up for what she had willingly become. An easily available whore who asked far too high a price for the
use of her much-used body. Why hadn't he steered clear of
her from the beginning? Left her to take her chances with
Captain McCormick?

"Have you ever been taken fully dressed and standing
up, with your skirts lifted?" Blaze demanded abruptly,
and saw those silver-gray eyes of hers suddenly open

widely—just as if she had actually been shocked by his question! "That's how most of the waterfront whores fuck their customers, you know."

"Stop—please stop! Haven't you said enough and . . . and insulted me enough yet? You don't know . . . God damn you—you don't *know* me at all, do you? And yet you dare to *presume* . . . to . . . to . . ."

"I think I know you well enough, sweeting! *Far* too well to be taken in by dramatics, I'm afraid. So . . ."

"You . . . !" Fury overcoming her, Trista brought her fisted hands up to strike out at him wildly; but as she might have known, he was able to seize both her wrists far too easily—grinning sardonically down into her anger-flushed face while he twisted them painfully behind her back until he had forced an involuntary cry of pain from her between her clenched teeth.

"Harlots who like to waste a man's time by teasing and playing at being coy might appeal to some poor deluded fools, my dear *wife*—but I've never enjoyed playing charades; or any other silly parlor games—and especially not with *you!*"

I won't cry out—I won't beg for his pity or try to explain—ever! Trista's mind repeated almost frantically as she felt his free hand go under her skirts, pushing them up and out of the way together with her crinoline and petticoats so that she was bent backward and almost smothered under their stifling weight.

By now, since he had rendered her powerless to fight back, Blaze had released her bruised and aching wrists—only to tear her hair ruthlessly loose from the restraint of innumerable pins and ribbons in spite of her half-smothered, protesting exclamations of pain and frustration. And then, to her even worse discomfort, he pulled his fingers through her hair until they were tangled in the wild, black, rioting masses of curls—forcing her head back so cruelly that she began to think that he was bent on breaking her neck as well as her back.

She wore only one thin lawn undergarment—and he made short work of it before she was forced to endure the rough, hurtful probing of his fingers exploring deeply inside her, making her draw in her breath sharply before she released it with a pained "ahh!" as she felt *him* enter her now, with no regard for her unpreparedness—driving, piercing all the way inside her with all the fury and fierceness of a thrusting sword.

He *wanted* to hurt her. He *meant* to hurt her with every brutal, pitiless thrust that seemed to penetrate deeper and deeper into her with each rhythmic movement of his loins.

What had happened? Why? Through her tightly closed eyelids Trista could see only red and crimson sparks like burning tongues of flame—rising and falling, rising and falling—burning flame inside of her and wrapping about her: Consuming her and him until . . . until?

"Ah, there is the unfolding snake inside you, that some call *power* and some *knowing,*" the Old One of the swamp had said into her mind. "But be careful—what has been gained can be lost too easily; and what has been given can also be taken back. Remember!"

But she did not *want* to remember; for certain memories and half-felt dreams were far too painful and were much better forgotten or kept locked away in the very deepest recesses of her mind—explosions that filled the sky with burning sparks that came raining down on billows and gusts of vile-smelling smoke, even before the molten-hot rivers of fire flowed downward in a burning flood that took and destroyed and ended everything that had been up till then. A whole known world . . . existence . . . ah, God! Even loving!

"No—no! *Never!* Hear me! I will *not* accept! I . . ."

She seemed to have suddenly gone crazy! Words suddenly erupting from her as her voice, not even sounding like hers any longer, rose in a wild, almost strident scream of defiance.

The only way to silence her was to jam his mouth savagely down over hers, before she aroused everyone within earshot—the cunning, calculating bitch! His bitch—her stepbrother's bitch—anybody's bitch if they paid enough. But no matter what his furious thoughts were, Blaze found himself starting to *kiss* her instead of being intent only on quieting her—kissing her open mouth and tasting the hot saltiness of tears; feeling the heat of her naked thighs burning against his—feeling suddenly and quite without volition on fire himself with desire and need for *her;* the inside soul-mind of her opening willingly and wantingly to him. God damn her for being a witch who knew and must always have known only too well how to cast her sly, insidious nets of power in order to trap and ensnare any man she chose as her victim. And damn his own folly for allowing himself to become one!

He should have continued to *use* her body without feeling any qualms at all. Fucked her and forgotten her once he walked away from her. So why the hell didn't he do just that right now instead of lifting her off her feet and carrying her to that damned whore's bed of hers?

Chapter 31 ⟡

The wavering, low-turned lamplight created constantly
moving and changing kaleidoscope images in the mirror
overhead as sweat-sheened bodies turned and twisted
against crimson satin sheets to form, in smoothly fluid
motion, a myriad different patterns and positions that
kept changing—rising and falling like flickering tongues
of fire-flames.

This was drowning in molten heat—and not caring for
anything but the assuagement of the burning, spreading
need inside them both—fire leaping to meet fire until they
were both caught and consumed in an uncontrollable,
uncontainable conflagration of passion.

Lust—that was all he had felt. That, and a certain curiosity to find out how much she had learned or had been
taught during the past few months. In any case, he had always preferred seduction to rape, since a yielding, willing
woman would usually give a man a great deal more pleasure and entertainment than one taken by force.

Christ—she was a bitch and a wanton for all her lies and
her *acting* that might fool most men—including *him,* at
one time. But never again—now that he knew and recognized her for what she was and always had been probably—damn her black witch's soul that could make a man
crave her body over and over again even while he hated
her!

She lay over him where he had lifted and held her so that he could *see* as well as feel the almost unconsciously rhythmic movements of her tautly rounded buttocks as she began to clutch at him, with the dark, tumbled masses of her hair falling down about his shoulders and almost blinding him in the end. Or had he actually closed his eyes when he felt those convulsive inner contractions closing about him like a silken scarf being drawn tighter and tighter until the pressure inside himself was almost too much to bear and he felt the building up and rising before release as she cried out incoherently—cries ending in gasping moans before she let her body collapse against his.

Oh God! Trista found herself thinking over and over again, almost in a daze. Don't let him . . . not *now!* Don't let him say something ugly and cruel yet . . . *please* not now when I have no defenses left because I've allowed him entrance into *me*—the only *feeling* part of me that's left. *Please!*

She wasn't aware that she was actually weeping noiselessly against his shoulder until Blaze gave an impatient exclamation and pulled her head around by the hair unfeelingly so that he could look far too closely into her tear-stained face, for all that she tried to squeeze her eyes tightly shut against him.

"Ah shit!" Blaze said in a disgusted voice—more to himself, actually, than to *her.* Women's tears! All the bitches needed to do was to cry, or pretend to, in order to have every male in sight pulling out handkerchiefs and putting protective arms about them while attempting to *comfort* the poor dears!

Comfort indeed! She had certainly *acted* as if she had been pleasurably satisfied a few seconds ago! And now, at the very next minute, she was dissolved in a flood of tears that trickled all the way down from his shoulder to his . . . what the hell was the matter with her, anyway? Maybe he should have settled for raping her after all, as he had meant to do in the first place. It was what she would have preferred, probably; and better than she deserved—especially in view of her open and unabashedly scandalous behavior since she had elected to leave his protection and insult his name by running off with her precious stepbrother whom she had pretended to hate; and going from him to one man after another!

"For God's sake—if there's one thing I cannot abide, it's a sniveling female!" Blaze said harshly, wishing angrily at the same time that those damned silver-sheened eyes of hers didn't catch and reflect the flickering lamplight so that he could almost see in them a thousand particles of gold dust—fiery sparks that could burn and reduce flesh and blood to ashes. He could almost see it and feel it— white heat—showering down of fiery sparks—liquid-gold rivers of flame.

She *was* a witch. *Bruja!* Blaze heard his own sucked-in breath in the sudden silence that had fallen between them while he continued to look, as if mesmerized, into her widely opened eyes and the flickering, fiery images he suddenly saw in them for one timeless and time-held instant before he exhaled and moved his gaze very deliberately down to her mouth.

Trista felt a shudder run through her body as he suddenly turned over onto his side, taking her with him and keeping her captive with the weight of his leg across her body and the warning tug of fingers tangled in her hair.

She had thought—had imagined, perhaps—that for a few moments they had known and recognized each other! He had called her a witch in his mind—and then . . .

"Are you weeping because your hungry, greedy little body hasn't had enough yet? What does it really take to satisfy you, sweet slut? Is it gold, and lots of it—great nuggets thrust up inside you between those legs you part far too often and too easily? Isn't a man's cock enough for you any longer?"

"No!" Forcing her eyes to glare contemptuously into his, Trista almost screamed the word at him, feeling his body grow stiff with anger. But she didn't, couldn't care any longer—nor submit to any more of his filthy, vicious assumptions and insults she didn't deserve.

"No . . . damn you! No—it isn't enough for me and never was . . . merely to have a . . . a . . . 'man's cock,' as you crudely term it, forcibly pushed inside me whether I want it or not . . . hurting . . . moving in and out of me like a . . . like something mechanical, without feeling, without caring, without . . . without even wanting or knowing or

needing the person who is *me*—or who *was* me! Have you
ever been used and emptied into like . . . like a *privy*,
Blaze? *Forced* to do and submit to anything and everything without daring to protest or question? Do you *know*
—you with your noble ideals and causes and rhetoric . . .
how can *you* possibly know what it *is* to be owned . . . to be
a slave . . . a *thing* to be used and handed about and
abused and kicked or beaten whenever your master feels
so inclined? You damned, bloody, mealymouthed hypocrite, you! Of course you don't know and you can't know because you've never . . . you've never *been* someone's
chattel, have you? God damn you! How *dare* you presume
to pass judgment on *me* when you don't . . . you don't know
anything at all about me and you . . . you bastard . . . you
choose to believe only what *you* want to . . . don't you? Bastard, bastard, bastard! I despise you! I hate you!"

She would have screamed more invectives into his still,
almost wooden face if she could; but Trista found her voice
had grown hoarse and choked from strain and an excess of
tears, so that her words tumbled out in a voice that was
barely above a whisper, leaving her sobbing and gasping
for breath—feeling all the more frustrated when Blaze,
who had stayed motionless and almost ominously quiet
throughout her furious tirade, rolled away from her before
he swung his legs off the bed in almost the same motion.

Their clothes had been hastily flung aside or dropped, so
that they were scattered all about the room with careless
disregard. Speechlessly, Trista watched Blaze reach for his
pants and pull them on. She had managed to get rid of his
odious presence at last, then! All it had taken was a few
home truths. But why didn't he *say* something? *Anything,*
damn him! Surely he wouldn't dare to get up and *leave* her
after he had used the vilest epithets on her before proceeding, with brutal nonchalance, to *rape* her—before he
changed his mind and took her to bed in order to humiliate
her even further with his diabolical caresses that brushed
feather-light over her skin before touching her exactly
where she wanted to be touched and explored and reaching
into the very depths of her to find nerve endings and make
her discover and rediscover sensations she had never
dared to give in to and enjoy experiencing before.

"Let yourself *feel* with your senses and your body only,

sweeting!" he had whispered to her while his fingers
played with her and found her everywhere until every
nerve in her body was as taut and tightly strung and vibrating as if she had been a harp he was playing on. An in-
strument to be carefully tuned and made ready for the
plucking of his fingers, creating music for *his* pleasure.
"Like this now . . . my wild wanton witch! And now like
this! You are an orgy of delight and an unexplored continent in yourself . . . you are every fantasy I create or
dream . . . and Christ . . . you can almost have me
believing in it, and in every fairy tale in which witches
transform themselves into fair and innocent-seeming
virgin princesses . . . aching to be taught what it is they
ache and long for . . ."

Words! A calculated pattern of words woven about her
senses and her eyes to blind her to reason while she
watched her body and his forming and reforming other
patterns in the mirror above them—and watched and felt
and tasted everything he did with her and made *her* do for
him . . . *wanting* to . . . the pure sensuality of feeling and
giving . . . Pagan . . . like satyrs conquering their frightened nymphs by making willing victims of them, as *she*
had been!

Her fault. *Her* weakness! And he was preparing now to
leave her without a single word, just as if she really had
been some cheap whore he had picked up and paid for an
hour's use of her used body. But then, that was how he
thought of her, wasn't it? "Sweet slut." Harlot. Whore!
And he'd cling stubbornly to his preconceived opinions
rather than *listen* to her or try to understand anything at
all. Well, she didn't care! He . . .

And then, just as he had begun buttoning up his shirt,
Blaze abruptly and surprisingly swung about to face her
with a glowering frown drawing his brows together while
he studied her for some moments before he said quietly:
"I'm sorry, Trista—as feeble and meaningless as it might
sound to you now. Because you're right, of course—and I
have no right and am in no position to judge you or anyone
else, for that matter—especially considering my own weaknesses and vices, dammit! And I admit I've been both unprincipled and unfair with you as well. Are you satisfied
yet, or do you want to see me grovel on my knees as I ask

for your forgiveness because I, like any other jealous fool, imagined the worst and thought only of hurting you in order to avenge my stupid, wounded *pride?* Oh Christ! Pride and honor—every man's vulnerable Achilles' heel—and his fatal weakness. Some lying, crying female who . . . ah, shit! The hell with it—and you too, my dear, for all that you might be a silver-eyed enchantress whose charms might be difficult but by no means impossible to resist!" His voice had become harder and more harsh as he deliberately goaded her with his carefully chosen words—as if to refute the weakness he had already admitted to.

Sitting up in bed without deigning to pull the crumpled covers up to hide her nudity, Trista forced herself to look levelly back into those dangerously narrowed eyes that had invaded both her dreams and her nightmares for too long as it was.

With an effort, Trista managed to keep her voice coolly expressionless as she said on a sigh that was real: "You told me just now that you were *sorry,* Blaze; and so am I. Sorry and *sad,* because . . . because somewhere and somehow both of us seem to have lost something that we had—*once!*" Her sudden, high-pitched laugh was as brittle as her voice when she looked away from him with a casual shrug to add carelessly: "But after all, there's no use dwelling on what's past and done with, is there? We're different people now, you and I . . . or at least *I* am! Don't you think so, Blaze darling?"

He had lost half the buttons off his shirt in his hurry to get rid of it so that he could bed her and take her the way he wanted to—naked flesh against naked flesh. What he should have done was *use* her as he had intended to in the first place! But no—instead he had been stupid enough to let certain memories and a certain faint sense of regret weaken him enough so that he had actually apologized to the calculating little bitch who sat there laughing inside herself, no doubt for having taken him in once again with her emotional speeches and tears that welled up far too easily into those deceiving silver eyes of hers that gave back only reflections of what a man hoped or wanted to see; and showed nothing at all of the thoughts and the secret self of her that hid behind those mirrored shields.

God! Why had he ever put his hands on her or lain with

her to become corrupted by the corruption of her writhing, arching, eagerly opening and easily taken wanton's body? She had even been clever enough to transform rape into seduction tonight, Blaze thought wrathfully, as his mind actually toyed with the idea of killing her right then—choking her to death with his bare hands without giving her the chance to cry and lie again.

It was only by a tremendous effort of will that Blaze Davenant managed to retain his self-control after those first few breath-held seconds of silence that seemed to vibrate tautly between them until he shrugged—letting his eyes move with contemptuous deliberation over her naked breasts before he said in a bored voice: "Of course you changed, sweeting! You're an even better piece than I had remembered, and your latest instructors are to be commended, I must admit. In fact, you are almost worth the inordinately high price you must ask for!"

He turned away from her to begin hunting impatiently for the rest of his belongings—making it only too clear, Trista thought with a mixture of pain and anger, that he didn't give a damn about what her reaction might be to his caustic words that were meant to *flay* her, of course! And if he hoped that she would attempt to *defend* herself or to *grovel* . . . never! Let him think whatever he chose about her, and dear God, let him leave quickly . . . and never want to see her again! Then, with the passing of time she would surely forget him and whatever had taken place or whatever feelings might once have existed between *her* and between *him*, with his amber-green eyes that reminded her too much of tall grass waving under gold sun-gleams that melted into deep greenness—fooling the unwary into thinking they would be walking safely on dry land until it was too late and they were lost and helpless to extricate themselves; sinking . . . while the swamp gurgled its pleasure as it sucked another victim down into its dephthless depths to lie enshrouded and embalmed forever in sinking-soft primeval mud.

Fire and water! Hadn't people believed less than two centuries ago that the only way to kill a witch was either by drowning or burning? Was it the unexplained agony inside herself like burning brands thrust into her heart and belly that would kill her, or would she be drowned in a self-

created, salt-teared sea of sorrow? Oh . . . *damn* words!
Thrown at each other with deadly, painful accuracy like
sharp-edged stones meant to maim—or to destroy. *Why?*

Blaze noticed angrily that she had suddenly become as
silent and immobile as a stone image—so that he could discern no emotion or reaction at all in either her blank eyes
or her still, impassive face . . . not even when he casually
tossed two gold double eagles into her lap before he stalked
out—closing the door between them once and for all with a
final, satisfying slam.

BOOK THREE: *The Western Wind* ⤳

"Western wind, when will thou blow,
The small rain down can rain?
Christ if my love were in my arms
And I in my bed again!"

Chapter 32 ❧

ENTRIES IN A DIARY

1863–1865

It has been a long time since I have attempted to put down on paper my feelings, my confused thoughts, and all that I have experienced and—I hope—*learned* during the past year and a half. I am not sure, even now, if I am quite ready to face myself—or even the recent past; but if I do not allow myself at least *this* form of release from strain and tension, I will certainly go quite mad from wondering what I am doing here in what seems to be the middle of a vast nowhere scattered with broken, bleeding bodies and disembodied legs and arms thrown out to lie in bloody heaps while the screams of agony and fear never cease, and fill my ears even now.

Dear God! What *am* I doing *here?* Why did I ever think that being a doctor meant *healing*—never thinking of the *hacking* and hurting I might have to inflict on helpless, frightened victims staring with dumbly pleading eyes that beg for miracles or magic to piece back together shattered limbs and skulls—and sewing up huge, gaping wounds from which their organs protrude and trying to lie to them—especially the ones you know are past help—as you hurry past and try to avoid those eyes—get on with it—to the next patient—lie again and again and try not to feel when you cut through flesh and bone—try not to *hear* the pleading words rising into cracked screams of anguish. . . .

I wish, now that it's too late for wishing, that Aunt

Charity had never come all the way to Virginia City to
find me and remind me gently of such things as "duty"
and "loyalty." I was stricken with guilt at the time; for I
knew very well how perilous travel by the Overland Stage
could be—especially during such troubled and violent
times. And then, of course, I was, as I still am now, plagued
by my own conscience and regret at my thoughtless stupidity.

She *loves* Blaze Davenant, bastard that he is! I heard her
voice soften when she mentioned his name; just as her face
did. And she asked me, eagerly, if he had "called on me" as
he had promised her he would—if he had left any messages
for her. How could he be such a low-down hypocrite? How
many times, I wonder (and hate myself for doing so), has he
made love to my aunt and called her "sweeting"? What
promises has he given her? And if only I could have
warned her, without hurting her, of his perfidy and his lies
and the underlying violence that lies hidden behind his
smile and that effete, almost foppish manner he can affect
when it suits him! Does she have any idea of the kind of
man he really is and what he is capable of, I wonder? Or
perhaps it is only with *me* that he shows the dark side of
his nature, for after all, he took it for granted that I was a
whore—and treated me like one too, the despicable wretch!
Even now, if he's not making a far too obvious point of
ignoring my presence or *sneering* in my direction before he
turns his back on me, his loudly expressed opinions regarding the weakness and frailty of the easily swayed female
sex make me long to stick a knife in him—or challenge him
to a duel with pistols and shoot him in the heart instead.
Damn the unhappy quirk of fate that brought us together
again—and the Sanitary Commission as well! Otherwise, I
would not find myself here in this sun-baked purgatory—
and I would never have had to experience the horror and
ugliness of tending to the dead, the dying, and the maimed
remnants of what were *men* in the aftermath of some stupid pointless battle in a war where countless lives must be
lost in order to win a victory.

Reading history books and stirring poems and litera-
ture, I have found, does nothing to prepare one for the reality of actual experience. I am quite sure that Aunt Charity
could have had no idea, when she obtained through the in-

fluence of President Lincoln himself the piece of paper that resulted in my being here—and narrowly escaping death on numerous occasions as well! I was, as the first woman to receive official recognition as a qualified surgeon and doctor of medicine, given my Letter of Appointment through the Sanitary Commission—entitling me to be attached to any *volunteer* unit as a fully qualified *doctor,* instead of being relegated to nursing duties only. Hah! And the California Column, to which I am still officially attached (and in all probability labeled a deserter!), was never expected to become embroiled in any *real* skirmishes with the Rebels—and *I* was meant to represent an inspiring example to other women, I suppose; or a useful ornament like the traditional daughter of the regiment.

I hate him! *Him*—Blaze—how dare he suddenly and *conveniently* recall that we are supposed to be married as an excuse to carry me off like a piece of merchandise? And I do not care if he *does* read this journal! All the better, for then he will be reassured regarding my true feelings toward him . . . my utter dislike and disgust when I am forced to endure his presence and his caustic, sarcastic words that are meant to prod at me and force me into some angry reaction—only so that he might demonstrate his superior *physical* strength and his "rights" over my body. Oh, how I dislike and despise the man and can actually pity the unfortunate women who have allowed themselves to be taken in by his gentlemanlike manners and his glib lies!

"Promise a woman everything and you can get anything from her, my love!" he said callously to me only yesterday, with that strange, twisted smile of his that I have grown to hate and mistrust. And then he added, as if to thrust the knife edge of his words even deeper: "But I'm sure you've found this out for yourself, haven't you? What a great deal you promise and expect in exchange for nothing more than a few practiced twists and turns of your body! I've known Turkish belly dancers who perform much better—and for much less!"

"Indeed?" I managed to answer him disdainfully. "Then I'm surprised that you should waste your time in raping a—a block of wood, I think you compared me to before?

Why not stick to these Turkish belly dancers who *respond* to your kind of advances and leave *me* in peace?"

Unexpectedly, he laughed—shortly, harshly, looking me over as if I were a slave up for sale; and I could not help the warm rush of blood that stained my cheeks, making him laugh again before he ran his thumb down one side of my face and said in a provoking, nasty-teasing kind of way: "But I don't think that you really *want* to be left in peace, as you put it. Not at all. But then, I happen to know, sweeting, what an accomplished little liar you are!"

Damn him! Why do his words have the power to pierce and penetrate deeply enough to force a reaction from me? Too much like the way he takes me physically in fashions that seem to uproot and tear out of me against my will every weak emotion I had thought armored in steel and so carefully hidden away that they could never be found or reached again. And then I forget my aunt and all the other women he's used and uses just as he is using me . . . God, yes—to my everlasting shame I forget everything except *that* which starts to happen between us like fire-flames joining and rising out of control—burning and consuming everything; will, thought, reason, and even conscience— along with ourselves.

What is it? *Why* is it? How is it that I can hate so fiercely at one moment and love as fiercely the next? I am afraid of this wildness that seems to leap out of some dark depths within myself to meet something similar in *him.*

How can I be so damned weak as to continue to want, physically, a man who has lied to me and deceived me and—yes, why not admit it?—has *played* with me and used me without any consideration for the person that is *me;* or for what *I* might feel, or might or might not want? Ah yes—I *hate* him! and I despise myself for allowing him the diabolical power he seems to have over my body in spite of all of the right and rational objections my mind can produce; and the cutting words I can still summon up on occasion—if only to *try* fighting back, perhaps for the sake of my pride alone. But I can never tell if my words are capable of hurting him or not, no matter how viciously I use them to strike back at him—damn him! I can drive him away with cutting, hateful words, sometimes—but then it is I who tosses and turns and suffers sleeplessly for hours on end while my mind conjures up pictures of what he must be doing with the woman he has gone to from *me*. Paquita—his first love, who was considerate enough to marry his best friend! But then, men are always stupid enough to invent excuses for anything when it suits them; and why should *I* care in any case? Blaze can have his childhood sweetheart, now that her husband is conveniently dead and they are actually considered *married* according to Apache custom—and his *chief* wife to boot!

I should have let him die from blood poisoning or gangrene; or cut off his leg and watched him bleed to death, rather than be subjected to this humiliation! I, a surgeon and an M.D., am forced, in order to survive, to act the part of his *squaw*, when it was *he*, Blaze Davenant, who forced me by trickery and threats to become his *legal* wife, although now that I am trapped here in some remote mountain fastness where I am a virtual prisoner on this Apache *rancheria* I am only his *second* wife, and of hardly any importance except to wait upon him and submit to his *other* needs when he decides that he wants the use of my body. And if I do not give in with an appearance of willingness, the unprincipled wretch has told me cheerfully that he can always *sell* me or give me away to his friend Running Wolf who has offered to make me his *chief* wife and is willing to overlook the fact that I am no longer a virgin!

I have been so agitated of late, especially since I do not know quite where we are, and *he* has been gone for at least two weeks, leaving me under Paquita's supervision, that I have forgotten to keep this journal in an orderly fashion and to record events (especially those that brought me here) in their proper sequence. But whenever I think of doing so I have wondered where I should start. With Aunt Charity's unfortunate idea that I should make use of my medical training, which ended up with my being attached to the California Column under the command of General Carleton, who, like General Sheridan, "did not like skirts." And since I had already discovered that skirts, besides being impossibly unwieldy and a hindrance, could be dangerous during times of crisis, I found myself wearing breeches again—much to my relief at the time.

I suppose now that part of the reason for my going along

so easily with the plans that Aunt Charity had made on my behalf had to do with my guilt for having let myself slip into an easy kind of life—and then, I did not want to have Fernando suddenly turn up either; disrupting everything and making me fearful and terrified all over again, like the puppet he had forced me to be for him. There was also the awkward fact that Charlie Donelson had, of late, started to become more and more protective and concerned about me, and my welfare—and I had begun to feel uncomfortable about accepting the gifts and "little surprises" that I suddenly found myself receiving almost constantly.

So, in the end I thought it best for us all that I should leave—with a noble excuse for doing so! I think my mother was a trifle relieved too, for all her casual insouciance. I wonder what she would think if she knew the position I find myself in *now*—and its cause? Laurette (I could never call her "mother"!) would probably laugh her husky, amused laugh as she lighted up another of her special little cheroots, and tell me that I should make the best of an exciting adventure, and enjoy as many new experiences as I can.

"And why not?" I can almost hear her say with a shrug and a raised eyebrow. *"Ciel!* You are a woman by now, are you not? Enjoy whatever you can, while you can, my dear—and turn it to your advantage too—if you are clever enough, or have learned anything at all from life—or the men you have known!"

I wish, now, that I *had* known as many men as I have been accused of sleeping with! I wish that I could learn that certain art that my mother must have been born knowing—the smiling power to make a slave of any man while feeling no emotion at all; making use of a man by allowing him to make use of your body while you hold back your self and move without feeling, like a wound-up mechanical toy. After Fernando, I thought I had learned that much, at least. So why did Blaze Davenant have to put his hands on me again, that hot day, when I had just been relieved from duty after more than twelve hours of makeshift "surgery" sawing off living limbs and trying to push protruding intestines into place—staunch the blood gushing out of gaping wounds I had to sew with my fingers wet and slippery with blood while I tried to close my mind against smells and screams . . . Why did he have to be there just *then*, when I was unprepared for him—his fingers closing about my arms to pull me around and against him—invoking far too many wild and uncontrollable feelings from the deepest primeval depths I have discovered within myself? I have endless "whys" to which I've found no answers yet, and a few casually bestowed "reasons" I can neither understand nor accept.

Dammit! I did not graduate as a doctor from one of the best schools in Europe to end up as a misused and abused squaw in an Apache village on the wrong side of the border! It seems unbelievable sometimes, even to me, as I force myself to think back on the chain of events that ended in my finding myself *here*—a virtual prisoner.

I should never have been foolish enough to pay heed to any of his lying, persuasive speeches in the first place; let alone trust in all the gallant words and promises I would be faced with later. And above all, I should *never* have softened in my resolve to *hate* him and let him know it! Or to have let myself become soft and stupid enough to nurse the bastard back to life instead of allowing him to bleed to death or die of blood poisoning as he deserved.

He took advantage of my tiredness, my every hidden weakness, and even the shock I would naturally feel when I felt myself grasped by the arms without warning and turned about to face him—the last person in the world that I could ever have expected or wished to encounter. Shock—I must have been numbed and overwhelmed by it to allow myself to be kissed into breathlessness while whisker stubble burned my face and my cap was snatched off my head to permit brutally hurtful fingers to run through and release the heavy and unwieldy tangle of hair I had to try so hard to conceal. My mind screamed, "How *dare* he," even while my treacherous body pressed closer against his, allowing and even enjoying the further indignity of the way his hand moved far too familiarly down my back to mold and caress my buttocks after slapping them lightly and almost playfully—forcing my body even more closely into his in a fashion that made the rising hardness of him pressing up and between my thighs far too obvious

to be denied by either of us at that moment when crude,
unthinking desire overrode sanity.

The wild, thoughtless surge of feelings I had thought
long suppressed made my head spin; and were intensified
when Blaze whispered fiercely and harshly against my
ear: "Why in hell do you try to hide that witch's mane of
yours? Thank God you did not cut it off this time at least!
Circe . . . Medusa! You make me hard as stone and as
heedless as a rutting boar of all else but my need to take
you and fuck you right here and right now—even if the
whole world watches, and even though we both know too
damned well how bad we are for each other in every way
but *one* way—you bewitching bitch-sorceress!" And then I
thought he growled beneath his breath: "Christ! If only I
could forget you!" But I could have been mistaken . . . and
in any case I was not capable of thinking too clearly at that
moment, or of retorting either; with the breath all but
crushed out of me by his roughness and the insistent proof
of his urgency and determination to *have* me without de-
lay, willing or not. And he was capable of doing exactly
that, too—uncaring of the consequences to *me,* of course.

That thought was all that persuaded me to let him all
but drag me along with him—under the interested and curious eyes of a number of soldiers; some of whom, I know,
had not been aware until now that "Doc" was actually a female. As usual, I remember thinking resentfully, Blaze always contrived to turn up at exactly the wrong time, and
to ruin everything for me, including my peace of mind.

"What do you think you're doing? How did you get
here?" I demanded breathlessly as I tried to resist the cruelty of his grip and the heartless way he *pulled* me along
with him, forcing me to try and keep up with his long
strides. He was no better than an animal, for all his pre-
tensions of being a gentleman, I reminded myself angrily
as I stumbled forward—almost tripping several times.

"I'm a newspaper correspondent—don't you remember?
I draw pictures and take photographs of battle and car-
nage—the dying and the mangled; and empty faces with
staring eyes reseeing countless horrors afterward. The so-
called survivors, my dear—like you and I! Does that answer one of your questions? And as for the other . . . why, I
thought I had made myself quite plain! You're my wife—

you are a woman, are you not? Because I happen to feel the need for a woman to fuck—and you happen to be here and available! Wives have their uses sometimes, I have to admit." And then he added with a snarl in his voice, "Even if they share the pleasurable intimacy of the same quarters with no less than four virile young men!"

I am thankful now that he did not notice the tears that almost blinded me although I would not and did not let them escape to trickle down my cheeks and shame me. I think that I deliberately managed to make myself as numb as if I had inhaled the dream-sleep of ether or given myself an injection of morphine. Perhaps it was sheer exhaustion that made me, after the painful poison darts of his words, not *care* any longer where he took me or what he did with me, or what he chose to think about me either.

Or so I thought, until . . . Oh God, even now I can feel my face burn with shame and anger when I remember the manner of his *using* me—there is no other word for it—without any regard for my feelings or for *me* except as a convenient outlet for his animalistic urges.

"There's a small clearing in the brush here, if I remember right," he said tersely before giving my sore wrist a sharp tug that made me cry out protestingly with pain before I stumbled over a rock and against *him.* Almost disbelievingly I heard his short, caustic laugh before he said, "So you're in a hurry too? Well then . . . why postpone our passionate reunion any longer? But take off your tunic first—it'll do for you to lie on; and I like to see you bare breasted and taut nippled. They haven't sagged, have they?"

Oh—cruel! Why the need to hurt and hurt me, when I've been hurt enough already? I remember thinking that and making some inarticulate sound as I attempted to turn and run from him—only to be pulled about and thrown down uncomfortably onto my back amid the prickly brush while he held both my wrists in one hand as he straddled my body and commenced to undo every button with slow deliberation, grinning wickedly at my squirming discomfiture as he did so—brute-beast that he is!

"There . . . there are sentries posted *everywhere* around here, for God's sake!" I remember gasping as he bent his head down to my naked breasts—his mouth and tongue and even his teeth playing and teasing each one in turn until I felt I could not bear any more of this subtle torment he was inflicting on me . "Oh *please,* Blaze—don't! You must stop . . . the sentries . . ." Losing all sense of pride, I actually *begged* the wretch for mercy; only to be answered by a sarcastic burst of laughter as he lifted his head for a moment to stare down into my eyes.

"Sentries? Well, let the poor young devils watch if they want to! Maybe they'll learn something from this—or at the very least it'll make their dreams more pleasurable! Ah!"

As he unfastened the very last button, I felt his fingers find me and plunge deeply inside me in spite of all the struggles I put up to evade him.

It was almost like the very first time—when I, in my stupid ignorance, had awakened the sleeping dragon and made of myself a living sacrifice to its fiery breath that could destroy me.

"No, Blaze—please, no!" I heard myself whimper even while my body was beginning to strain upward against his; in spite of his callous exploration of me and in spite of the thought that we might be watched . . . ah, damn him!

"What a ranting hypocrite you are, Trista! Lying, night-haired witch! You're like a black cat—bad luck to any man whose path you cross—rubbing yourself against his legs at one moment and all claws and spitting fury the next! 'No!' you protest unconvincingly while at the same time I can feel for myself how wet and ready you are! For *this,* and this, and this as well, my sweetly yielding wife—my eager little bitch!"

I could not help the gasps that escaped me at every deep, savage thrust of his body into mine while his fingers, abruptly withdrawn from inside me, and still damp with moisture, now played almost tauntingly with my nipples.

How could he treat me in this fashion? How could I *let* him? But thoughts are one thing and reactions another. My mind hated him even while my body responded to his and I could not stop what had begun to happen within me— that gathering and tightening and rising and rising until I writhed and cried out with the violence of that explosion that is also an implosion that bursts within myself.

* * *

Why must I remember all too vividly certain things and certain incidents I would much rather forget? This diary is meant to be a *solace*—not a recounting of every unpleasant experience I'd much rather wipe out of my mind and memory.

Memories and regrets! After what happened between Blaze and me on that hot and humid afternoon that crimsoned into evening before we were done, I should have left well enough alone, if I'd had any sense left. I should never have agreed to take the risk of crossing the border with him to visit his close friend who was sick and wasting away from some undiagnosed ailment that also caused him a great deal of suffering.

But then, after all, it was known to everyone by now that I was not only a female masquerading as a male but a *wife* as well. I suppose the only reason I was forgiven for having pretended to be a man was because it was generally believed that it was my unbearable *yearning* for my husband's presence and attentions that had forced me to go to such lengths. Why, I even heard the reprehensible villain *congratulated*, with sly grins and winks, on having such a devoted and loving wife. If they only could have known the truth about our relationship and the way I really felt about the suave, lying Mr. Davenant—I wonder now, would things have turned out differently—or not?

My Aunt Charity, to whom I owe so much and love so much . . . why did Blaze Davenant of all people have to act as courier for her? He had seen her, met with her, talked to her, and I cannot even now help wondering what else might have transpired between them apart from the passing of information and messages back and forth. Oh, there is no *decency* in him at all, nor honesty either! Is there anything but self-seeking that motivates him at all?

I suppose there is no use in my asking myself all these questions and no use in dwelling on my own stupidity and the mistakes I made. But when he actually threatened, grinning devilishly at me, to denounce me—*me!*—as a spy supposedly married to a Southern officer, and a known associate of one of the ringleaders of the infamous Knights of the Golden Circle who now rode with Quantrill and Bloody Bill Anderson . . . he knew the extent of the trouble and the danger he could cause me—what with all of the fast-flying rumors about female Southern spies such as "Rebel Rose" and Belle Boyd, who were able to fool Northern soldiers and even their commanders.

Better to have different rumors go about—especially after the gossip of what had happened between us started to spread. Between husband and wife? Ah, then of course it is *excusable* and *understandable*, they'd say; for a husband has his *rights* and a wife her *duties!* How I hate and despise the very idea!

If Blaze had not subtly *threatened* me in his smiling, hatefully soft-drawling fashion that only *I* could see through, I probably would not be here—caught in another, different kind of trap; one that confuses as well as frightens me too, because . . . because to my utter shame and self-hate, I do not *know*, positively, what it is I want in the end! To escape from the flames that draw me into them, mothlike—or to fly daringly and uncaringly into what could very well consume me?

I hate being free and not free—I hate, above all things, not knowing or even understanding my own instincts— myself. Is the answer something I *fear* or what I *need?* My head is aching, and I have written enough without finding either solutions or conclusions. . . .

Chapter 33 ❧

Long afterward, Trista was to remember that particular
time with anger and frustration bursting in her, even
without having to read what she had scrawled in her jour-
nals. Writing down her feelings at the time was one thing,
and a release she needed for herself; but memories that
combined mind-pictures with sounds and smells and sensations . . . these were, and always would be, so much
more real to her than words put down in a book; and it was
so even then, when she wrapped away her precious jour-
nals carefully in the small bag that also contained her
medical instruments and little vials that could bring forgetfulness and relief from pain—or even death, if they
were misused.

Remembering her stepfather, she suddenly wanted to
cry bitterly; but there was no time to give way to tears
when there was so much to be done yet. Women's work!
She had experienced the freedom as well as the risks of
being a man—and yet it seemed to her that there was more
pride and self-assurance in being a male. You might get
killed fighting a duel or in battle, but it was the women left
behind who got the worst of it in the end! Starved, seeing
their children slaughtered, or even worse, being forced to
submit to rape by their murderers as well. And yet, it is *we*
who are the strong ones, Trista thought strangely as she

turned away and hurried out to join Paquita, her *co-wife,* in helping to gather wood and herbs.

It was only too easy, she had found, to hate Blaze Davenant with a passion—but she could not hate Paquita, for all that she had tried to in the beginning.

None of this was Paquita's fault, after all—and the woman had certainly saved her life—and probably Blaze's as well. No—it was the Oath of Hippocrates that she had taken, and Blaze's "persuasion," that had led to her being here; in a hidden Apache *ranchería* where she was forced to perform the duties of a squaw rather than a doctor of medicine and a surgeon.

And yet, Trista had to admit grudgingly that there were certain things she had learned about wild-growing herbs and weeds and their uses that she could not help but find fascinating from a medical standpoint. Already, whenever she had a few extra minutes, she was writing these down—and Blaze of all people had actually deigned to make some sketches for her; even if it was with a sarcastically raised eyebrow, and he all but threw them at her.

"So you're actually learning something from—'these savages,' I think you called the Apache people? And that there are more cures than are listed in your *Materia Medica?* Maybe you'll even learn something of the nature of human beings someday, sweeting!"

"It was *my* medical knowledge that saved your damned, worthless life, you bastard!" she had ranted at him on that occasion, seeing the muscles in his face tauten for a single, dangerously still moment before he laughed harshly and chucked her under the chin before he asked her sardonically why she had felt impelled to do so, after all.

"Or have you asked yourself that yet, witch-doctoress? Perhaps you should!" And then, strangely enough, he had added almost under his breath in a harsh whisper with those swamp eyes of amber-green holding hers against her will: "Or perhaps *I* should ask myself . . ." And then, almost angrily, as if shaking himself free of some spell, he had let his hand drop away and turned his back on her without another word, leaving her with long strides that put distance between them while she stood there rubbing at her chin as if to erase his touch and feeling mutinous and frustrated at the same time.

She hated remembering certain things, certain incidents, certain times, far too vividly. Why did she have to?

"You will look for the herbs and berries by the stream, yes? I am better at finding the wood twigs we need for our fires." Paquita hesitated no more than an instant before going on to say in her even, matter-of-fact voice: "But you will be careful, Medicine Woman? The stream is deep in places, and you could slip on the green-covered rocks."

"I'll be careful—I promise!" Trista suddenly felt almost ashamed for having come close to hating this woman who was concerned for her safety even if they shared the same "husband" by some strange quirk of fate.

Trista's feet, in high, Apache-style moccasins, lightly found their way now down the narrow pathway that had already become familiar to her; the hot gold of the sun filtering through the leaves that moved slightly and sluggishly with every puff of heated breeze making her long for the cooling sight of the stream that flowed and wound its way here through narrow cracks and tiny crevices from its source-spring high in the snow-peaked mountains.

Think of the stream—think of healing cold—of anything but fire and moving, leaping flame, she told herself fiercely as she suddenly felt her steps begin to lag; as if mesmerized by the light patterns before her and falling all about her. No—not this time—no, for I'm stronger now—strong enough to . . . and speeding forward on the strength of that unfinished thought, she came out of the trees to all but fall down on her hands and knees at the moving water's edge.

A few tiny pebbles dislodged by her headlong flight made small ripples like circles dissolving into circles before they were caught up and disappeared into the constant motion of the stream, shining gold-sheened over green-depths as Trista looked down into it and *saw* without willing or wanting or being capable of *not* looking.

The Old One who spoke only with her mind—her face coming and going with every water-movement—telling her something about . . . about staying still enough and quieting her mind long enough to find inside herself . . . *herself?*

It's sunstroke—again! But *this* time—no, I won't be so easily hooked like a trout tickled and stroked gently until, once unaware of danger, it is easily captured and destroyed. Is that the how and the why of my being here, then? But I have a will and I have strength and I refuse to give in or to give way!

The Old One's face disappeared, but now another voice spoke in her mind, and looking up with difficulty, Trista saw the frail, dying Shaman who they said had lived for over a hundred and ten years. He sat cross-legged on the other side of the stream from her, and his face was an intricate, netted web of wrinkles. She had met him—or seen him rather—only once before, and then briefly; supported by his family. It was he who had named her Medicine Woman, knowing from that one glance they had exchanged that she knew as well as he the shortness of the time left to him. What was *he* doing here, forcing her mind to listen to his while his hooded, almost hidden eyes kept hers fixed and captive?

"I too am one of the Old Ones—surely you know? Just as you must know better, foolish child, than to expend and waste these precious things you call 'will' and 'strength' against that which cannot be withstood? You are wasting the energy granted to you by the Great Spirit with your futile struggles—and what is more, I feel you already know this yourself! You know why you are here and what you search for and will find only by stilling the turbulence and rebelliousness within yourself."

Was he really *there*, sitting across from her, or merely an illusion of light and shadow? There was too much light reflecting off the water, and when she looked into it, she saw too much she wasn't ready to see—Blaze's eyes . . . pain and bleeding and death. Paquita's husband, a man dying from cancer already, who had fought with a recklessness that welcomed the relief of death.

He, "another of the Old Ones," he had called himself, was *forcing* her to see and relive that horrible day again. An innocuous morning to begin with, it seemed, since the Rebs were retreating too fast, and apart from manning the forts they had taken, the Column was needed elsewhere. Why shouldn't she go for a short ride with her *husband*, as long as they were both careful about the "Injuns"?

She hadn't—couldn't have known that General Carleton had put a bounty on every Apache head or scalp brought in—encouraging anyone greedy or unscrupulous enough to try to claim that money—no matter by what means. She had thought about the Apache then as everyone else did—a name that meant "enemy"—a deadly foe not to be trusted, who killed and marauded and tortured indiscriminately. But what she had seen and experienced was so different from every preconceived idea fed to her before! Blaze, in whose veins the blood of the Apache flowed, had helped her to understand.

She had witnessed the heartless, purposeful massacre of human beings—women, children, men who were either very old or sick. And it was into *that* they had ridden—she determinedly following that silly, stubborn fool Blaze in spite of (or perhaps because of) his orders that she was to stay under cover and lie low; while *he* rode into the thick of it like a crazy man with, of all things, a bloodcurdling rebel yell. What did he expect her to do—*stay* there hidden in the brush? At least *she* had had enough sense to pick off a few of them calmly and carefully before she rode downhill in his wake with a scream of rage she hoped sounded just as bloodcurdling as his had been—and the presence of mind to command an invisible patrol to "follow me, men, but get as many as you can first!"

At least *she* hadn't got herself shot in the process of being a damned fool, Trista thought resentfully now. Binding his arm and leg up for him and saving him from blood poisoning or worse after it was all done; in spite of the fact that he had refused to acknowledge his bullet wounds or the pain he had to have felt until then.

He would probably have followed Paquita's man outside in that last crazy charge of his where, for a few telling moments, he had seemed invincible—before he fell face forward across the man he had just killed. If not for the bloody wound in his leg and her hitting him carefully on a certain spot at the back of his neck, Blaze would probably be dead too! And once she and Paquita had finished off the last twitching bodies of the attackers, she had given him enough ether to keep him quiet while she removed a bullet and cleansed and bandaged up his wounds.

"You are woman-warrior!" Paquita had said in her halting Spanish; and it was only then that Trista had noticed that her cap had fallen off and her tightly pinned-up hair had come cascading down her back and shoulders. She

remembered feeling numb, somehow, even as she reached
up with bloody fingers to knot it at the back of her head
while she wondered why Paquita did not show emotion at
the death of her husband.

"I am a doctor—woman or not," Trista said shortly, and
could not help adding, "and you, I think, are a warrior too.
Is there anything I can do for your husband? He was a
brave man."

"I know. Warrior is not afraid of death—but it is better
to die as a warrior should. *You* were not afraid?"

"Not *then*, while it was all happening. Now, a little, perhaps. Will they come back—or others like them, do you
think?"

It had been at that moment that Blaze reared up angrily, swearing at her in every language he could think of,
instead of showing gratitude, before he gritted: "Damn
right there'll be a lot more of them here—probably on the
way already. We've got to get out while the going's—good.
Damn!"

She had almost felt *glad* to hear him suck in his breath
before he swore softly at his own weakness. And then he'd
turned his head from her to speak to Paquita in the
guttural-sounding language she had come to recognize as
Apache, with his voice changing and becoming gentle and
almost tender.

How could she have known or understood *then* what it
all meant? *She* had helped bury Paquita's husband; and
she too had taken turns walking, since they could only find
one horse left tethered (and terrified, poor animal!) anywhere in the small village from which Paquita's husband
had once, as a young child, been taken captive—had come
to find his relatives and live—only to die with those he had
hoped to protect from "the soldiers."

She had not, Trista recalled with clenched-teeth anger,
received any explanations as to where they were headed,
or *reasons. She,* dressed as a man in a hated blue uniform,
could very well be (and almost was) shot by that first
fierce-looking Apache warrior who suddenly appeared
from behind a rock that seemingly could conceal no one.
Blaze was in a fever and close to being delerious as he muttered under his breath—and it was only Paquita's quick

thinking and authoritative-sounding words that must have saved them all, and especially *her!*

They had reached another small *ranchería;* and Paquita was half sister to the Chief as well as being the great-great-granddaughter of their medicine man, or Shaman. She was also Blaze Davenant's childhood sweetheart and first love, whom he had obviously never forgotten. It had been an excuse only—his trying to explain away his marriage to Paquita as an Apache custom just as it was for a woman to cut off not only her long black hair but her fingers as well when her husband died. And to make deliberate slashes on her face and breasts.

What a horrible, primitive custom, to be sure! Just as primitive and ridiculous as marrying the wife of a blood brother or very close friend; or the custom of allowing a warrior more than one wife. And then also, there were certain *other* customs that could still make Trista grind her teeth together with rage; especially when it was explained to her patiently that the reason they must build a second, smaller wickiup beside the larger one was because—during that certain time of *the moon,* a woman must stay apart from her husband, while the rest of the time they were forced into far too close proximity for *her* liking, at least, in a crude brush shelter smelling of smoke—lying on a "bed" made of hides while she hoped and even prayed he wouldn't decide he wanted her—the brute, the beast, the savage he had turned into! Paquita could have him and keep him if she could—all *she* desired was her freedom—the freedom he had promised her that one day. . . .

He had gone hunting meat, of all things—and with his wounds not quite healed yet.

"You—you *deserve* whatever you get! Meat—is it humans you're hunting again, dressed and looking like an Apache—you—you *renegade?* Is it? You're a predator—a liar—an ungrateful, conscienceless . . ."

"And *you* never run out of words meant to goad and cut, do you? You don't ask if you have questions worth asking—and you won't listen either—you *presume* to draw your own bloody conclusions, don't you? You're a bitch, all right, and I should have seen that from the first time I set eyes on you, damn your black witch's soul!" His hands had clamped down roughly and painfully over her shoulders, but as their eyes met and clashed and she refused to back off or look away, Blaze suddenly removed his hands from her as if her flesh had burned him, and said between his clenched jaws with a kind of grating softness: "Very well, *bruja*—what is it you want in return for saving my life? My body you've had—is it my soul you want now?"

"No! I want none of you, Blaze Davenant—and damn *your* black soul too! I want my freedom from this—this *bondage!* From this captivity I'm subject to because of *you!* Do you understand me?"

"Only too clearly, my dear. And you shall have your freedom, I promise you; as soon as I have discovered some place to leave you where you will be quite safe from the likes of *me!*"

"But are you safe, child, from yourself? And from those feelings that lie beneath the quickly spoken shallowness of angry words? Have you learned yet that what you once had is what you have now if you but recognize and grasp it? Learn—and gather your herbs of knowledge and wisdom—take for yourself what comes to you first—and my wings will shade you on your way back."

Trista felt herself as dazed, for some moments, as if she had actually been in a seeing-trance. She had dropped into a prone position while she looked into the water—her face so close to drowning that a few escaping curls trailed in the moving, murmuring stream and dripped ice-cold water down her neck and between her breasts when she raised her head and sat back on her heels.

The coldness revived her and almost brought her back to her senses as she shook her head to clear it before she dared to look over to the other side. Was he still there, or had water-drops flown into her eyes—blurring them to cause illusions of shapes and forms that weren't there at all?

"I am here . . ." She heard the voice in her mind before she saw him again sitting just as she had imagined him. "I am here and I shall watch you until you have gathered the herbs you came to find. And then the eagle's wings will shelter you." She thought he nodded slightly and that his seamed mouth smiled indulgently as he said again: "Go now and find what you came here to find."

Chapter 34 ～

It had all meant nothing—nothing! She had been tired and feverish, that was all—and the Shaman had sent his great-grandnephew with an infusion from the bark of a certain tree that broke her fever. He was merely a kind and very old man who had taught her about certain herbs and remedies that no physician *she* knew of would believe in! Or so Trista had to keep telling herself. She had had a fever—she had *imagined* that the Shaman had been there looking into her mind and communicating with her without words. It was the fever that had also made her imagine that the old man had turned himself into an eagle whose wings spread over her had shaded and shielded her passage back. It had been a cloud, that was all—nothing more than that! And perhaps the effects of the very small and very bitter tasting bite she had taken too daringly from the grooved buttonlike head of a gray-green, spineless cactus that Paquita, shaking her head knowledgeably and somewhat disapprovingly, told her was called "peyotl"— and was not to be tried by those who did not know of its powers or understand the visions it could bring out of the mind of the user.

Trista almost began to blurt out: "But the *Shaman* told me . . . ," before she halted her unruly tongue and said nothing instead; even though she wondered with some annoyance whether she had been meant to be the butt of some game—or a joke, perhaps.

Blaze came back from his hunting expedition with an antelope and eleven rabbits—and she had to help Paquita skin them and learn to smoke-dry the flesh that could not be used immediately, as well as cure the skins. It was sickening—the odors of entrails and blood reminding Trista too much of the operating theater.

"You're eating, aren't you?" was all he'd said brusquely when she started to protest.

"And cooking for you, and making sure *you* get served first—yassuh Massa Dav'nant suh!" Trista snapped back at him, turning to stalk away from his obnoxious presence, only to be caught and hauled around by her carelessly braided hair in a heartless fashion that brought tears to her eyes.

"If you're acting the role of slave wench, my sweet, why not play it to the hilt? I quite like hearing that 'yassuh Massa' from you—and since *you* chose your role . . . think about the fact that your 'Massa' *owns* you, and can have you beaten like any recalcitrant little hound-bitch—or *sold* to another master if you grow tiresome or boring! Running Wolf says he wants you and is willing to give a high bride-price for you, considering that you're a trifle *used* to say the least! Would you like me to sell you to him, Trista?"

Soon after he had said those words, harshly and bitingly and intentionally hurtfully, Blaze felt a stab of regret, much like the stabbing pain of both his wounds, that he would never admit to her; and especially not now.

Why, dammit, did they both have this compulsion to hurt and strike out at each other? He saw her face whiten and readied himself for her striking out at him wildly and furiously; but instead she merely put her fisted hands up against his chest and leaned away from him as far as possible until, half-ashamed, he released his deliberately cruel grasp on her hair.

"Blaze—I cannot live like this, and under such circumstances—and I think you know it. You must do as *you* wish, of course—but *I* must remind you of the promise you made to me. You owe me your life, like it or not, Blaze Davenant! You are in my debt—and you owe me my life back. I'm calling you, Blaze. Are you going to pay up or renege?"

She reminded him, as she tilted her head up scornfully, her nostrils flaring, of a wild mare scenting a stallion who would mount her—mistrusting and hating and fighting until the last, sweat-lathered minute when in the end she gave and gave . . . and *took* as well . . . God damn her little games!

"Oh, I'm going to pay up for sure! Takes one gambler to recognize another, doesn't it? I'm going to deliver you safely to what *you* might call 'civilization,' my sweet wife—why in hell would I want to *keep* you, after all?" His voice was hard; his smile a twisted grimace that mocked and derided. "Dear Trista—my much-used bride! Is it Fernando you want to go back to and be fucked by or Amerson, your so-called husband who didn't care to keep you company on a certain night I remember?"

He had *meant* to hurt her with every calculated word he threw contemptuously at her like so many barbed arrows; and he was rewarded now by her gasping exclamation of denial.

"No! Damn you . . . !" before he cut it off short ruthlessly with his mouth coming down hard over hers to silence all of her lies and her excuses—just as he had done almost too many times in the past when he'd needed to quiet her.

But this time it wasn't that easy, and she kept twisting her head from side to side making wild, angry, incoherent sounds as she sought to avoid his painful, almost smothering kisses and beating at him wildly until he felt the wound in his arm that had been almost healed open and start to bleed again.

"You can scream and yell all you want and nobody's going to give a good Goddamn!" Blaze snarled at her as he all but carried her, squirming and swearing and clawing like a wolverine bitch caught in a trap, to the piled-up hides in one corner of the wickiup and let her drop—with a shove for good measure when she would have tried to struggle upright again. "And if you think to kill me—better think about Running Wolf and the way *he'd* treat you if I wasn't around! Apaches tend to cut off the noses of adulterous wives—after they beat them, that is! You understand?"

Her every breath and every word she managed to force out sounded like a sob. "You—you! *Promised* . . . I *hate* . . ."

"You can hate me all you want—but I'm going to have you at least one more time before I take you back to wherever or whoever you can't wait to get back to! But for right now, you're *my* bitch—bitch! *This* one is for old times' sake, shall we say?"

She was wearing only the fringed buckskin gown that had been a present to her from Paquita; and she was too easily reachable, Trista knew despairingly even as he reached her and played almost mockingly with her while he asked her if she preferred this or that before he made her turn over and went into her—his fingers still caressing that tiny, sensitive peak in spite of her struggles until she was almost on the verge of screaming well before she felt his other hand stroke her buttocks with deceptive gentleness before his finger plunged deeply into her *elsewhere,* to make her bite on her knuckles hard enough to bleed rather than let him hear her scream with the mixture of feelings he was forcing her to feel, *making* her feel in spite of everything he was doing with her, until . . . until there was no holding back any longer and she *had* to . . . could not prevent that implosion/explosion that kept on happening and happening and kept her crying out with her whole body shaken by one tremor after another.

Was it only *her* body that shuddered over and over again from wave after wave of sheer *feeling*—or his as well as he lay over and against her? And had she imagined or not that he had whispered against the back of her neck: "Oh damn, damn, damn you for the enchantress you are—and my own cursed weakness for you!"

His weakness? It was hers for him, showing itself when she least needed to have it show, that damned *her* even while she was damning him.

"This is for you to remember me by—perhaps!" Blaze said in what sounded like a growl from deep within his throat as he turned her still-trembling body over so that she lay on her back now and he deliberately began to excite her with light, calculated finger-touches that brushed over her body everywhere—lingering and growing less light and more teasing as those diabolical artist's fingers of his made the tension inside her almost unbearable, even before he had the notion to use her body (soon stripped of its one poor garment) as a living palette that he painted on with his sable brushes and with his fingers themselves and with his lips as well—until she begged for respite and found none as her body's tides rose into tidal waves that rose and peaked and crashed downward almost crushing her; only to draw back and gather and rise again.

He knelt between her legs to keep them parted, and used the red Apache headband he had worn to go hunting to bind her wrists together while he played relentlessly with and on her helpless body—disregarding even her tears and sobbing entreaties to have done, for God's sake!

"It's blue-purple I see for your nipples—there, don't you like that? How erect and almost throbbing they are! And—gold for your navel, of course, with ruby-red right in the very center, like the fake jewel an Eastern belly dancer might wear if she does not have an admirer rich enough to afford the real thing. And—hold still and stop your wriggling for the moment, sweetheart, for I haven't yet reached—*this!* Vermilion, I think—don't you? Dark pink for those pretty, welcomingly open lips just below this little, rising point. I am using my finest sable paintbrush dipped in the color that emphasizes and suits it best—or so *I* think! I wonder if I'll be poisoned if I yield to the temptation of licking it off before I paint it on again. And here— raise your hips a trifle, my love—here is bronze and ombré. You agree?"

"Oh stop! You're a *monster!* Please—oh please stop this . . . this torture, Blaze! No—don't! Don't! Do anything else to me . . . not this . . . Oh God—no more! Whatever you want me to do . . . I'll *do!* Isn't that what you want?" Trista heard herself babbling almost incoherently without being able to prevent herself—feeling the wetness of the paint against her skin and the silken brushstrokes everywhere, driving her almost mad with feelings she had not believed herself capable of before this—before *now.* Too *much* feeling until it was almost worse than pain—an exquisite kind of agony she could not bear much longer while her body quivered and shook and she could feel her skin vibrating and the deep inside of her vibrating with every brushstroke—every lip- or tongue-touch superimposed over that.

"Don't you enjoy being painted and played with, my

lovely, bewitching wife? Didn't Fernando appreciate you enough?"

"Aaahh!" This time her scream was pain and hatred and frustration; exploding in his face and enough to arouse the whole camp as well, damn her!

Angry, and hardly thinking by now, Blaze covered her open mouth with his hand and felt her sharp, feline teeth sink into it—making him cry out this time with the unexpected pain and shock of her sudden attack.

"Goddamn wolf-bitch! Want to give me hydrophobia?" As he brought his injured hand up to his mouth to suck instinctively at the bleeding puncture marks her teeth had left on his palm, he slapped her open-handed with his other, uninjured hand, feeling and hearing the harsh crack of his blow against her face, swinging her head sideways.

For one terrible moment Blaze thought he might have broken her neck and killed her—and in that moment he felt a self-hatred and desolation inside himself he would not have believed possible as he leaned down to put his lips against the reddening and already swelling mark he had left on one soft, silky-skinned cheek.

"Oh Christ! Christ, Trista, sweeting, I'm *sorry!* Shit! Are you all right? Trista—dammit, I didn't mean to hit you or hurt you! I'll take you anywhere you want to go—I swear it. Trista . . ."

She turned her head around suddenly to look him in the eyes with *her* silver eyes from which tears were running— and *laughed.*

Her laughter was high and hysterical as she looked into his astounded, angering face and said through the sobs she suddenly could not control: "You *hit* me! But Fernando used to *beat* me, you see, or have me beaten by Nordstrom—and that used to hurt much worse! Oh—*much* worse! Have *you* ever been tied down and beaten like an animal, Blaze? Is that what you want to do with me before you invite your friends—or even your casual acquaintances—to *have* me? But I've already been tamed, you know! You don't have to beat me—because I'll do whatever you tell me to do—with anyone! Understand, Blaze? With *anyone!*"

Suddenly the sex-games that were really love-games

he'd been playing with her seemed sick and ugly and as painful to him as they must have been for her. He should have guessed from what Charity had hinted at, from what Trista herself had almost said before. Damn his own jealousy, he should have known and believed in what he had always sensed! And now? Too late. For either of them—at least with each other.

"You're hysterical—and no one can abide a screeching, hysterical female! I suppose that since a smack in the face hasn't cured you, there's only one other cure left that I can think of!"

Blaze Davenant's noncommittal voice gave away nothing of what he felt or thought within himself as he wrapped Trista roughly in one of the hides and carried her out of the wickiup and past staring eyes that were quickly and tactfully averted.

It was only when he dumped her, naked, into the icy coldness of the stream the Shaman had called the Stream of Life that sheer breathlessness stopped Trista's uncontrollable sobbing and made her scream again from shock and sheer fury; once she had struggled back to the surface and learned to breathe again.

"I . . . I . . . ooohh! Damn you—damn you for a devil bastard! Damn . . ."

Unfeelingly he pushed her head underwater; releasing her to come up choking and sputtering and spitting water and vituperations at him.

He preferred these reactions of hers to words wrenched out from the black depths of her soul, in which he could too easily drown. Witch or not—whore or not, Blaze knew then what he felt unwillingly he had always known since that first time he had put his mouth over hers to give her breath and get back . . . what did it matter? There was a poem he remembered from his difficult years at school—"La Belle Dame sans Merci." She had enchanted him—bewitched him—and he, for his own soul's sake, could never let her know it . . . if he wanted to keep her ephemeral self for a while at least.

While she was still sputtering and gasping and swearing at him, Blaze dragged her free of the waters that might have taken her first, and he repossessed her on the very edge of the murmuring stream itself; with her legs still

trailing and kicking in the water while he knelt over her—
straddling her and *having* her.

The Shaman knew what must and had to happen—and
Paquita, seeing, retired to the little wickiup because, as
she told them all, it was *that* particular time of the month
for her.

Trista, by now, didn't care. She was to be returned to
whatever was "home"—plucked out of this savage wilder-
ness where everything that was unfamiliar to her was
taken for granted; and she was no more than an object to
be taken or rejected by the man who *owned* her.

She had already been taken and used over and over
again without any consideration for *her* feelings. What did
anything else matter?

After what had erupted between them, Blaze hardly
seemed to notice her, paying much more attention to
Paquita. Sometimes Trista could hear them talking at
night when she was trying to sleep.

But at least he had *sworn* to deliver her safely to
civilization—had he meant what he had said?

She had to escape him—or be destroyed by him. He took
her when and as he pleased now—and she had no recourse
or rescue except to believe in his promise that soon—any
time now—she would be set free from this bondage . . . this
timeless bondage of the soul . . . and why must she think
that? He slept with Paquita too—she *knew* he did—the bastard!

Was Paquita with child too, by *him* as she had discovered that *she* was? She would never tell him—and neither
would Paquita, who would much prefer to have her out of
the way!

Trista pretended—but what she did not know was that
he pretended too. In his case it was almost all masculine
pride; and Blaze knew it even as he continued to pretend.

It was Paquita who *sensed* the truth before she *knew* it;
and brought matters to a head by telling Blaze bluntly
that he must make a choice between his women, because it
was obvious that his *other* wife was not happy with sharing a husband.

"Running Wolf will have me if he cannot have *her,* the
Medicine Woman. And now you must choose for once and

for all time," Paquita said to him—her eyes searching his without finding what she looked for.

She said, more strongly, as she sensed his indecision: "Do you think I have not seen where and in what direction your heart leans? You want *her*—the woman who made you well, and who can hurt you also! Once *we* wanted each other, you and I, but that was long ago, and our feelings were not strong enough to bond us together. So now—you must do whatever it is that you truly feel."

And what was it that he truly felt? Trista, silver-eyed black-haired witch who had chosen *him* instead of it being the other way around—was *that* the reason why he couldn't and hadn't accepted and taken her just as she was?

It was only too clear that she wanted her freedom, for all that he could, with certain cunning caresses, almost force her to feel and respond. But with her *body*—not her mind and all of herself.

"I want to be free of you!" Trista had often said, even while her body yielded to him.

"Where do you want to go? Or to whom shall I deliver you?" he mocked her with until, hating the responses he was able to force from her, she was able to say, even if she didn't mean it:

"Anywhere, damn you! And to *anyone* else!"

Chapter 35 ⌇

Had he gone back to Paquita? Trista wondered. Was *she* more than just another easily forgotten incident in his life? Forgotten and forsaken—uncared for and unimportant—that was all she was as far as *he,* Blaze Davenant, was concerned. Why should she worry about him or even *think* about him? Why should she care what happened to him, especially after the callous way he had treated her?

Damn him! How could he have left her . . . *abandoned* her so easily and without a qualm after all the ways he'd used her and all the words he'd whispered in her ear while he made love to her? Had he suspected or known what might happen to her after he'd left her here to find her own way back to wherever she desired to be?

"You're close enough now to New Orleans to claim your inheritance—or what's left of it. I'm sure you'll find General Banks sympathetic—he's more reasonable than Butler was; and more acceptable." He'd kissed her on the heels of his pragmatic speech—the bastard—leaving her too breathless to answer him or protest his high-handedness.

Trista paced almost feverishly back and forth in her cell-like room, feeling as if she were back in medieval times in some fortress. A protected virgin—a commodity useful for bargaining with . . . but she wasn't a virgin any longer—even if she *was* overprotected at the moment!

302

The Big House—his parents' home—was indeed close enough to New Orleans; but had been built across the Sabine River, in Texas, although the many acres Anthony Davenant owned lay in fertile Louisiana land between the Sabine and Red rivers.

"You might as well meet my parents—my mother understands me sometimes—my father never did. But he was a close friend to Sam Houston and their beliefs were the same."

How well (too well!) Trista remembered that *lowering* look on Blaze's face when he spoke of his parents. How well she remembered his offhand words and manner when he *produced* her, so to speak, like a magician's rabbit; while hounds barked and *vaqueros* stared.

"My wife—she likes to be called Trista because her several formal names are too hard to handle. Trista . . . my mother—my father." He had embraced his mother first, hugging her hard and almost lifting her off her feet until she protested, tears mingling with her laughter. His father had looked long and searchingly at Trista before he bowed formally and lifted her hand to his lips.

"Oh, it's legal—and we *are* married. She's an heiress, after all—aren't you, sweetheart? The only reason I married the wench, of course!"

How well she recalled those surface teasing, half-laughing words! Why did she?

Blaze had delivered her into his parents' keeping only to be rid of the burden she had become. Left her there in cumbersome, confining hoopskirts while *he* went off to draw his pictures and write inadequate, cursory words about the "Red River Campaign."

He was going . . . *she* should have been there! He had not warned her, of course, that she would be a virtual prisoner here; always carefully protected and *guarded*—like a precious possession. A Ming vase—or a Stradivarius violin to be played upon and enjoyed while he was in the mood for such pleasures of the senses. A *possession*—that was all she represented to him. And now, looking back, she would, contradictorily, much rather have found herself back at the Apache *ranchería;* where life had been much less complicated in some ways.

Where *was* Blaze? Why had he brought her here of all places—introducing her as his wife?

Trista found his father not at all as fierce as he had appeared to be in the beginning—and his mother somewhat like Paquita, and just as inscrutable at first . . . perhaps because she did not understand the suddenness of her son's marriage to a woman she had never met before. Perhaps Blaze had made the time to explain to his mother the circumstances leading to their marriage? *She* didn't care— she had already decided that she would seek and find her freedom again at all costs—Blaze be damned!

His mother had long, straight black hair with only a few streaks of silver in it when she set it free to hang down below her still-slender waist. She was a beautiful woman, even now; and Trista found herself wondering if she could manage to look as lovely when *she* was . . . whatever age the Señora Madalena might be.

"Do you love my son?" she had asked directly when she showed her new daughter-in-law to her room herself.

Now Trista wondered why she had answered yes to that blunt, straight question. Why, she hated him, and should have told his mother so quite honestly. Why had she blurted out a yes instead of a no? And why should it concern her at all what Blaze might be doing or what he might be risking?

He *knew* very well what the risks and the rewards were, Trista reminded herself impatiently. He wasn't going to take *too* many risks, because he was a survivor—a pragmatist who thought of himself first. Perhaps that *was* the real reason for their unfortunate and ill-timed marriage that had brought her too much bad luck already!

Blaze had at least informed his parents that his wife was a "doctoress" (a word that earned him a killing look) and had inveigled her way into the most famous medical colleges in Europe by masquerading as a young man.

"Yes, that's true—and *fortunately* so for my husband since I was called upon to tend two very nasty bullet wounds not too long ago! Didn't I, *dearest?*" Trista had looked directly at his father before adding: "And—as a surgeon and doctor with the Sanitary Commission, I have had to perform amputations and . . . try to alleviate the pain of soldiers wounded in battle. I can also ride and shoot a

handgun or rifle accurately enough, if I have to do so. I am
not a weak and helpless female, I'm afraid!" Her look was
challenging as she said: "I hope it does not shock you, sir!"

To her surprise, and the surprise of his wife and son as
well, Anthony Davenant, after a short, breath-held pause,
had laughed shortly and held his glass up in a toast.

"I drink to a woman with courage and convictions who
isn't afraid of telling the truth! I must say that I'm relieved that my son didn't choose a weak namby-pamby for
a wife—and that you can stand up to him and talk straight.
And so you're a female doctor, are you? Know anything
about ailing horses and cattle? Ever ridden a half-wild
horse?"

"Yes I have, as a matter of fact. My stepfather owned a
ranch in California, and I learned to ride soon after I
learned to walk! But skirts hamper me and I do not like to
ride sidesaddle."

"That doesn't bother *me!* Hah! My Madalena doesn't
like riding sidesaddle either—and never did—did you,
love?"

It was clear that when Anthony Davenant called his
wife his love, he meant it. But when *Blaze* said it to *her*,
there was always a mocking inflection in his voice. What
did she mean to him? Why did he continue reentering her
life at exactly the worst times—or when she had almost
started to forget his very existence? Trista felt her feelings
all mixed and muddled up when she thought about Blaze;
and wondered why the thought that he might have gone
back to Paquita could make her fume.

It's for your own safety that you must only ride out with
one of the *vaqueros*—even if you can use a gun. These are
not good times—and there are many evil men—renegades
who have no thought but their own gain and taking what
they want, who come through here on their way to Mexico.
So—it is best that we are all careful. You understand?"

Only today, as if she had sensed Trista's mood of frustration, Blaze's mother, who spoke better French than English, had explained this to her rebellious daughter-in-law;
watching Trista's reaction with hazel eyes that were almost too much like her son's.

"But I feel—I don't want to appear ungrateful, please try
to understand! I feel—useless! And—without purpose, I

suppose. I'd rather *do* than sit back and let happen!" She
walked restlessly and tensely from one end of her room to
the other—from windowed wall to door; not really knowing
why she did so and for what reason there was such an un-
easy feeling within her that urged her to motion instead of
stillness. She whirled about from the window she had been
looking out of to say: "I *must* have something to do! And I
have to be able to make my own choices! I—in California
they called me a *bruja*—a witch—and some of the servants
were afraid of me although I never did anyone harm consciously! It is only that I . . . when I feel certain things,
even if I do not *want* to, I must . . . I am sorry to speak this
way and to say such things, but I *know* that you of all people understand! Isn't it strange that I know this? Isn't it
even stranger that I . . . that I . . . Oh! I sound hysterical
and foolish, don't I? I really didn't mean to . . ."

Madalena, looking more Apache than French in that
moment, said quietly: "Why do you fight against your feelings? It is easier not to, as I learned myself. *You*, of all people, should know that—since you *are bruja*—and so am
I—or so my husband has always said! But there are certain
things—certain feelings and forces that even *we* cannot
fight against or overcome, *oui?* Such as a strong loving
that cannot be held back or contained. And do you think
that I would be speaking to you in this way if I didn't know
that my son loves you and that you love him—even if both
you stupid children quarrel with each other and pretend?
Ah—such foolishness and such waste of time!" Madalena
suddenly gave a mischievous-sounding laugh that almost
astounded Trista before she said: "Me—I made my husband think that it was *he* who took me and swept me off my
feet, while all the time it was the other way around! And
that is how we women rule our men; and how easy it is—
once you are sure of what you must have. You children!"

"But—but that's not . . . ," Trista began before her voice
faltered and she suddenly pressed her clenched fists
against her temples as she lowered her head in acknowledgment of the one truth she did not want to admit. She
didn't hate Blaze—she loved him. And if even his *mother,*
who had always been so close to him, said that *he* loved her
. . . but hadn't always known it?

Even while she damned him she'd always loved him—

the unfaithful bastard! At least, she was the one who had
done the choosing, whether he liked the thought or not.

And where in the hell was he *now*, at this very moment?
With Paquita? Or traveling down the Red River making
sketches and being shot at? Why were her nerves so much
on edge tonight?

She had gone riding with Madalena and Anthony Davenant earlier and enjoyed the feeling of a fresh breeze
against her face. "You are a damn good horsewoman after
all! How much do you know about cattle?"

"Nothing at all," Trista had admitted frankly, actually
earning the accolade of having explained to her the plans
her father-in-law had for joining some of the neighboring
ranchers in driving their half-wild long-horned cattle to
the nearest town, where they'd pay good money for meat
on the hoof.

"How about the army?" he asked her with a sideways
look that reminded her too much of his son. "Heard they're
short of meat—although I wouldn't sell any of *my* cattle to
damned Yankees!"

"But then, you wouldn't get top price, would you?"
Trista responded sweetly, with an innocent look. "I've
been given to understand that the Yankees have all the
money these days."

In spite of her daring, she actually elicited a smile from
under her father-in-law's grizzled mustache.

"You've got guts, haven't you? I like that in a woman.
And I suppose you like to have your own way too, don't
you?"

They'd had dinner early and retired early—it was as if
everyone else had had the same feeling of unrest that kept
her awake now, Trista thought. She could hear voices—
horses' hooves outside. But whatever was going on was obviously none of her business. She thought of writing in her
journal and then, impatiently, shook her head at her
own reflection in the lamplit mirror. Lace with ribbons
threaded through it—her chemise was made of thin cotton
that was easy to see through.

"I'd like to see you looking like a woman for a change,"
Blaze had all but snarled at her when he threw a mysteri-
ously procured package on the bed she had been forced to

share with him in a cheap border cantina on their way to his parents' home.

"Here—I must say I preferred you in that short buckskin dress with nothing underneath—but my father clings to convention and might not approve."

Oh, but she should have kept on hating him—especially after the way he had treated her; taking her as and when *he* pleased without consideration for *her* feelings—even under his own parents' roof. And the worst part was that he had always, in some diabolical fashion, made her enjoy his calculating lovemaking and the many different ways in which he touched and stroked her body.

It's not right and not fair that I should continue to want him in spite of everything—in spite of the fact that he's probably making love to another woman at this very moment, Trista thought, angry at herself as she whirled about from scrutinizing herself in the mirror; telling herself to forget both reflection and remembrance. It was easier to think that he had married her only for this mythical (or so it seemed to her) inheritance that might not even exist by now . . . not that it even mattered by now!

Trista threw herself across her white-sheeted bed—wanting for some strange reason to weep bitterly and yet not able to find the release of tears.

She wanted to go riding astride a wild stallion even in the blackness of this night. She wanted . . . God, she wanted to be filled and fulfilled and lift her hips to meet every long, calculatingly slow thrust of *him* penetrating her and . . .

"Trista! Trista—you are awake, I hope—saw the light under the door. You are needed—please."

Madalena, her voice kept low, but urgent all the same. Blaze! Something had happened, and that was the cause of her uneasiness. No!

She went to snatch open the door without troubling to put on a robe; the dark pupils centering in her silver-gray eyes dilated with apprehension until her mother-in-law put her hand out and grasped her shoulder strongly, shaking her head.

"It is *not* what you fear. It . . . there has been fighting and there are many wounded men—and no doctor. They are from the South—but I don't think it matters to you.

However, you must hurry, please! I'll help you dress . . . no skirts, eh? You can enjoy being a young man again for a while."

There had been a battle at Sabine Crossings, Trista learned while she hurriedly changed clothes and let Madalena help her wind her tightly braided hair closely about her head.

Of course she would not wear a uniform. She was a doctor—and it didn't matter on what side a wounded, hurting man had fought. It was only war and its effects she hated.

There were wounded Union soldiers too among the hordes of the maimed and the dying and the almost dead. And no other doctor could be found within miles, it seemed. It was her *duty;* and in this, at least, her mother-in-law was persuasively insistent—even offering, until her husband had positively forbidden her, to accompany Trista.

"You look kind of young to be a Doc—and I have a lot of men who are in a bad way—even if we did give those goddamn Yankees hell!"

"General—I'm sorry if I didn't take the time to bring you proof of my qualifications! I was given to understand that there were men who needed care urgently. Where are they?"

General Taylor was obviously not used to being answered in such a brusque fashion; and at first his eyebrows drew together as he frowned in a fashion that would have made any of his officers or soldiers quake. But Goddammit, he needed a doctor—young or not—and even if they *had* defeated the Federals again, it had been at a tremendous cost. How long could either side manage to cling to what they had managed so far to gain?

There was no time to hesitate or even to *think.* And, used to having certain medical supplies readily available, Trista found it hard to hide her shock at the miserable lack of almost every pain-staying drug or medication—even bandages! All those things that before she had taken for granted, she had to discover makeshift substitutes for, if she could.

"I will first take care of those who are in the most need of being taken care of—no matter what the color of their uniform might be. I am here to heal, if I can; and not to take sides in a cruel, pointless war!"

"If you were under my command, young man, I'd have you flogged for your impudence—as well as court-martialed!" the general had growled.

"But then—you are *not* my commanding officer, are you? Please! Allow me to do what I was summoned here to do, sir."

She had, by ignoring his fit of temper, subdued the general; and she had, by forcing herself to function without *thinking,* managed somehow to do the best she could, with as much help as could be mustered up from battle-weary men.

Trista felt almost numb with tiredness and reaction by now; and perhaps it was better this way—not to have to think or feel any longer.

But then, why did she have to *dream* when she finally got to sleep? Whirling shapes and faces—everything mixed up. And if they wondered why the Doc kept this jaunty cap on even while he slept—she didn't care by then!

Oh damn, *damn!* Why think at all? Sometimes it was easier not to, especially if you happened to be a valuable pawn in a deadly chess game—being moved back and forth at the whim of whoever desired to use her services, now that it had been proven that, young and fresh-cheeked or not, Doc knew what he was doing—thank God and the École de Médicine!

It was only Trista's blunt revelation the next day, that she was in fact a female that saved her from being "enlisted" and forced to join General Taylor's army.

"Damnation! I should have guessed it, I suppose! What ails you females who can't be content with sitting home? A female doctor—not that you aren't efficient enough—for a *female,* that is—but . . . !" General Taylor was in one of his famous rages that were capable of making his aides cower and try to stay out of his way; but Trista, who didn't *know* she was supposed to be terrified, merely shrugged as she ran her fingers through her hair, shaking it free, without showing any concern whatsoever.

"I'm sorry, General—but I understood that you needed a doctor—and I happen to have graduated from one of the best and most respected medical colleges in Europe; by masquerading as a *male* of course!" She faced him defiantly and almost challengingly now—ignoring his frowning glower. Let him intimidate the men under his command—he could not do the same to *her* now that she had told him she was a woman.

"And how in the hell do I know you're not a Union Spy? Answer me that, miss!" The general's face had become red and his voice was almost a parade-ground yell.

"Why do you think I am here? As I told you, General, I am a doctor . . . and I became one to save lives."

He pointed an accusing finger at her, his face still choleric. "Did you indeed? Couldn't get a man to marry you because of your independent, unfeminine ways? You seem more like a Northern Abolitionist to me—and I'm not a man who minces words—*madam!*"

"How admirable! For a *man*, that is! Really, General, you surprise me—*sadly*, I might add! Although I was brought up in California after my poor mother was widowed—her husband was a Louisiana Villarreal, you know?—I have *never* forgotten my roots. And I happen to be married to Major Farland Amerson—a Virginia gentleman—perhaps you've heard of him, sir?"

She should have been an actress after all, Trista thought, watching the general's face go from crimson to almost purple before he was able to recover himself sufficiently enough to tell her that she was dismissed—and he would make arrangements to send her back to her friends in Texas first thing the next morning.

"Sir—I thank you! And if I travel as a *lady* I will be escorted, I hope? Or shall I continue the pretense that the doctor is a male . . . because women are not supposed to be clever enough or strong enough to practice medicine?"

She was tired and tense—and pain ate at her like acid for what she had *not* been able to do, and the lives she had not been able to save. She should never have dared to speak so boldly and so brazenly to a general who was well known for the shortness of his temper.

He had a cruel mouth under a sharp hooknose—why hadn't she recognized the face of a predator?

"You have the tongue of a bitch—hardly a lady worthy of respect! Doctor or not—your words and your actions are those of a common camp follower—and I am sure that you

must be used to the kind of treatment such women deserve. Is that why you continued to stay here to taunt and
tempt me instead of leaving when I made it clear I had
nothing more to say to you?"

"So! Do I actually *tempt* you, sir, in spite of my bedraggled and masculine appearance? I have not tried to do so;
and by now it does not matter to me whether you believe
me or not! I only came here . . . for . . . for the *lives* I hoped
to save and the pain I wished to alleviate . . . Oh . . . oh
damn! I had thought myself past tears . . . and damn *you*
for driving me to them, general or not! I don't care what
you do to me—have me executed if that will help your silly
male pride! I only wish . . . how often I have wished I had
not been born a female!"

As much as Trista would have wished back her weeping,
she was not, at the moment, capable of holding back the
flood that overwhelmed her fit of temper and her will.

"You are hysterical, madam!" the general pronounced
sternly before adding, "But then—that is so typical of a
woman!"

Now that he had discovered weakness in her instead of
continuing defiance, his voice actually softened somewhat
as he went on forbearingly: "I've no doubt you meant well
enough . . . but why won't women learn their place? Masquerading as a male and living at close quarters with
males is no place for any decent woman—*doctor* or not—
especially one married to a gentleman and officer of the
South!" Clearing his throat suddenly, General Taylor
questioned abruptly: "I take it you *are* married? One of
these secret, quickly accomplished war weddings or not?
And you're from an old Louisiana family, eh? Well—if you
can stop bawling long enough to answer my questions, perhaps we can find a way out, eh? And in the meanwhile I'll
see if I can find you some halfway decent female garments—and put you under guard so you won't be mo-
lested!"

He had added almost soothingly (for *him*): "We'll see—
hmm? We'll see!" And then more strictly: "But don't forget that until I dismiss you, you're still under orders! *My*
orders, mind you!"

And what did *that* mean? By now, worn out both from exhaustion and weeping, Trista did not particularly care!

She accepted the general's offer of "a glass or two of red wine—to make up our differences with" without protest . . . and she was even, in a mind-dulled kind of fashion, thankful enough when he suggested she might, being a female, want to have first try at the makeshift bath his orderlies had prepared for him.

"I'd . . . I'd love it above all things! But not if . . ."

"My dear madam—now that I *know* you are such—I am a Southern officer and a gentleman, I hope!"

And *I* must only hope so too, I suppose, Trista told herself—feeling most of the strength she had possessed ebb out of her; too tired by now to refuse yet another glass of wine—or to protest when he joined her to splash playfully in the far-too-small hip bath.

"You are *not* a gentleman, sir!" she half-remembered saying in a slurred, drowsy voice; barely hearing his response.

"But then—neither are you *quite* the lady, my dear! That much is quite obvious, isn't it?" Had she only imagined that he had added a little while later: "However—if you are what you say you are, and who you say you are—then you might, as a woman this time, prove your loyalty to the South; and be of service to our cause—no matter what your *morals* may be! More wine here!"

Had his orderlies been watching everything—whatever had taken place . . . perhaps certain happenings she might neither choose nor want to remember? Or *could* not—because that thought was easier?

Whatever had taken place—or *not,* as she hoped—the general had turned suddenly affable, and had, he informed her, decided to take her along with them after all; just as if he were doing her a favor!

The truth was, Trista had to admit shamefacedly to herself only too early the next day, when she was aroused and ordered—*ordered!*—to report to the general's tent "on the double, if you will, . . . er . . . sir!" (and damn the grinning orderly as well as his general!) . . . well, the trouble was that she had grown more than a little afraid of General Taylor's choleric disposition and his capability of almost insane fits of rage, during which he was capable of anything.

"Don't worry, puss—I've already had one of my most reliable couriers take a message to these friends of yours in Texas! They'll have it by nightfall—and since they were loyal enough supporters of the Confederacy to persuade your presence here, disguised or not—I'm quite sure they'll understand. So—well—now that we've taken our bath— you'd better be off to your quarters and snatch some sleep before morning!''

That was how he had dismissed her last night—and now, feeling as if she hadn't had any sleep at all, she was summoned "on the double" into his Presence again this morning—to face God knew what else this time.

Should she go as a male or a female? Did it matter? All the same she heard all the familiar warning sounds of men getting ready to go on the move again—to battle again no doubt . . . but this time, even while with clumsy fingers she braided and pinned up her hair, she felt her nerves tighten with the strangest kind of—no, not fear—apprehension.

Chapter 36 ~

"You always know to look for something bad when you feel the black wing pass over you—worse, if it brush your face. But you strong enough to know what to do when the times come—got to fight that badness leaning over you with the brightness of the light shining from the deepest inside of you! Yes, your thoughts hear mine—yes. And when it's your ready-time you will remember how . . ."

"Aahh!" Trista heard herself cry as she sat up, feeling her body, even her gown, drenched with sweat—and hearing herself cry out simultaneously in the past at the same time.

But now she understood—and it had taken coming home to do it—and no . . . not to be consumed from the fires outside this time . . . no and no! For this was *her* place, *her* country of the heart—her learning place. And outside, dark green and sun-ambered sometimes, the bayou waited and *was*—as it always had been from the beginnings of time and always would be. The same. The bayous and the cypress swamps and the "shaking grass," as the Indians had called those certain treacherous places. Now she knew why she had had to come here—why all answers and endings lay in beginnings.

She was shaking all over; soaked to the skin—even her hair clung like snake-coiled tendrils about her face and her neck and her shoulders when Fernando burst into the room—his face ugly and angry until he saw her and stopped still.

Even to him, she looked like a holy terror—Medusa—a. . . what in the hell was the matter with the bitch *now?*

Before he could snarl out his questions, or better still, belt her across the face and breasts a few times, he heard her gasp out, to his horror: "It's . . . it's the . . . the bad swamp fever! See? See what it does? I need . . . I need my medical bag . . . you'll *all* die of it if *I* do . . . ! And I don't care! Don't . . ."

He didn't quite dare get close enough to slap her silent, just in case. But a second look at her, the way she was shivering all over with the only color in her pale face the feverish red patches outlining her cheekbones—damn the bitch! It would be like her to infect them all with whatever disease she had contracted!

"I'll get your damn stuff for you! But you *stay* there, you hear me? You just tell me what we're supposed to take and *I'll* see to it—and damn the prisoners—easier for us all if they die—a much easier way out for those goddamned spies too; don't you agree, *querida?*"

The shivers that rippled under her skin didn't stop; because it was her body's reaction to everything that had happened so far. Battles for bayous and tiny towns laid waste or burned in any case—"skirmishes" that left land that had once been fertile a barren waste. And then—Fernando, turning up as a courier from General Kirby-Smith, who had actually given the likes of Quantrill and Anderson commissions. Fernando, who had actually ridden with them in Bloody '63 and shared in the slaughter and the loot.

Oh, she could well imagine what he had told General Taylor with that smiling Spanish charm. She *was* an heiress—she *was,* in fact, his stepsister, and "married" so one heard to a Confederate officer listed missing or dead. However, she had always been loose-behaviored—had conceived an unfortunate alliance with a Carolinian who was also a Union spy, with whom she'd entered into a bigamous marriage on shipboard. Yes—no doubt she deserved to be shot . . . but on the other hand, she could prove extremely useful to the Confederate cause if she was held under close surveillance and *control!* She was not only an heiress but now owner of L'Acadienne Plantation on the Bayou Teche—a *Northern* lady could stop the Yankees in their tracks for a while at least—and prevent them from taking over on their damned Red River Campaign. And in the meantime, General Kirby-Smith thought they could store not only cotton but ammunition and prisoners there; while the "Northern lady" was held hostage not only by the guns at her back but by the thought that . . .

Blaze! Oh God, Blaze—damn fool! Why had he risked everything, including his life, to come after her? The answer wormed its way into Trista's already feverish, half-hysterical mind. Because he could no more stay away from her or forget her than she could him—in spite of everything—or anything either of them might say or do. Hadn't *he* said it himself?

They had converted *her* inheritance, *her* plantation that she remembered as peace, into a prison and a guerrillas' nest—a deadly minefield that could blow up the unwary—over which *she* must preside as chatelaine—with a Boston accent, of course! Not because of *threats*—not even Fernando's. Because of—old-fashioned bayou talk coming back—because of *her* man. Yes, *her* man—no matter how she might hate or swear at him sometimes! And to have to pretend, even after Fernando had shown her gloatingly how Blaze had been tortured and how he was kept imprisoned in what the guards called laughingly the "hot box"—*that* alone was almost too much for her to bear!

"You can talk to him—tell him he might as well tell us everything he knows—although the bastard might not have enough breath left in him to answer by now!"

"Then perhaps I can persuade him?" God! She'd been able to say that calmly enough *before;* and Fernando had laughed in his ugly fashion and said sarcastically:

"With words or *medication,* such as I remember so well? But *do* try, dear Trista—my sister and my whore! Eh? You remember *that* very well, do you not?"

"Very well—haven't I said so already? Please, Fernando, when will you believe me?"

Oh yes, she had even diminished herself into that other self that had pleaded and rubbed herself up against him even after she'd been beaten like the bitch he likened her to! It was time turned back—but not far enough—until now.

Perhaps it had been Fernando's vanity and self-assurance that had led him to "allow" (this in *her* house, *her* property) them a few minutes together so that she might use her powers of persuasion. Fernando knew, of course, that she would not dare to touch Blaze for fear of causing further agony as he hung suspended by hooks through the skin of his back like Sioux warriors undergoing the Sun-Dance ritual—his arms bound behind him and the soles of his feet merely brushing the ground.

His eyes had been closed, but he had lifted his head when he heard her involuntary gasp of shock and horror; and his eyes; his swamp-eyes had been feverishly bright as they stabbed and searched into hers. And then he'd said, in gasped-out whispers that cut into her heart: "It doesn't the hell *matter,* do you understand? I . . . would have had to find you anyway . . . any*how.* Silver Moon on silver water . . . save yourself, you hear? No matter . . . No—please, my love . . . don't touch me . . . I don't want to . . ."

And then she had seen with fury and hatred that they had lashed him too and his body was all lacerations; and she could have wept and screamed out loud except that *he* and something else rising and uncoiling snakelike up her spine kept her erect and her voice only a tremor less than calm when she said, with her eyes looking and locking into his: "I don't *need* to touch you, do I? Nor you me . . . once we've known?"

"Oh God, my Silver Moon, Silver Witch . . . you know . . . don't you? Knew . . . all the time, I guess! Please go now . . . it's about time for them to . . . For God's sake . . . my love."

"My love . . ." Ah, but she had seen into his eyes, and he into hers and at last . . .

"Madame—here is the black box of madame—and you are to prepare I am told a medicine to prevent them all from having the terrible Bayou fever—the yellow fever. . . ."

"It's one of your housekeepers—she says she's had it before!" Fernando shouted from the doorway, his eyes wild. "If you can stop shaking long enough, damn you, take a dose yourself and then give *her* enough for the rest of us—you hear? Do it!"

The door slammed and Trista said with her voice still shaking: "Tante *Ninette?* But I thought . . ."

"So phoo on what you thought! Everyone thought the same, eh? Poor Tante Ninette! She must be dead by now . . . poor spinster crow . . . Hah! I have ten sons and two daughters while my poor sister had only one! So now—you hurry up, yes? And do quickly what I know you are planning to do Madame Doctoress!"

At that point, Trista didn't pause to ask questions under her aunt's impatient look and tapping foot that she suddenly remembered from babyhood. "Hurry, hurry! You want that your man should die? Today—no food, no water—but me, I was able to give him a little. Hurry! I get keys, yes?"

Yes—hurry! Enough morphine, in a bitter-tasting elixer, not only to kill all pain but, when mixed with opium, to put into a deep and almost comatose sleep everyone who drank it.

"It will take some time. . . ."

"Yes, me I know—I can wait. So must *you!* And before *he*, the bad one, comes, you must mix something bitter for yourself and give me also something for the pain of your man."

What her aunt knew and *how* she knew, Trista did not bother to ask—she would find out later, when the time was right and not so tense. Also, the *how* of her Tante Ninette suddenly being here with all her clan to help . . . But that, of course, was the doing of the Old One—did she still exist? Had she ever existed except in a child's imagination? And what did it matter? Now was now, and there were things to be done.

Trista could not help pacing the floor of the tiny room she had been kept in—reminding her all too much of *her* "prison cell" where she'd been kept to be tortured and beaten and used for what had seemed like an eternity. Had it seemed like that to Blaze as well? Fernando liked to make people and even helpless animals suffer. She should close her mind against such dark thoughts and think instead of the bright beacon light of the future, where Fernando could neither reach nor hurt them.

Fernando! Once, as a child, she had thought him her knight in shimmering armor—the Lady of Shalott to his

Sir Lancelot. And yet it was Blaze, her destiny, not her terror and her destruction that she had chosen. Blaze . . . ah, they were each other's battlegrounds sometimes—but every battle had ended in either a pleasant truce or victory for them both!

I cannot wait any longer! her mind screamed desperately, and she pushed open the door and started to run equally frantically—wanting and needing only to be with him—even if it was only this one more time—this once-more coming together.

This is what love is—this is what love is—the pounding of her heart and the racing of her pulses told her. And if I lose him this time—if I lose him again, I will never want to live again—I will . . .

And then she ran straight into him and clung wildly to him until the sharp intake of his breath, even while his arms surrounded her, reminded her, and she drew back unwillingly; the salt of her tears smarting all his wounds and cuts although he would never for the life of him have admitted so—especially looking into her wet silver eyes and seeing the pain in them.

"We should leave now, I think, me! Hello—I am your Cousin Antoine. I have me a pirogue—but they will be waking up soon, and one of them I had to tap behind the neck to put to sleep—the bad one."

Blaze could barely walk, from being kept crouched up in the hot box—a hole in the ground covered with corrugated steel that was blazing hot under the sun and deadly cold at night. He had thought of the coolness of her silver lunar eyes in the heat—and of the warmth of her giving body when it became almost unbearably cold. Trista. Silver Moon he had called her once—Blaze didn't know how or why he knew that; perhaps it had been in one of the dreams he'd had when he was slightly delirious.

He felt slightly delirious now, too, as he stretched out his hand to hers; and had actually to lead her, as blinded as she was by tears.

Dammit, he might hurt like hell all over, but he could still walk; even at a half-run, once his cramped muscles got more used to the motion. And he had a bowie knife in his belt that the lady who had called herself Tante Ninette and was Antoine's mother had handed him soon after she had released him from the cramped-up agony he'd been forced to endure for what had seemed like a timeless eternity already.

It was only Blaze, even as he half-limped, half-ran to the waiting pirogue, who knew without knowing how he knew that Fernando would follow them no matter where they went or how far they went. He thought that perhaps Antoine knew too; from the glances he sent over his shoulder as he rowed with silent strokes through deceptively silken-looking, hardly moving water.

The bayou snaked about and around itself like a serpent—and Fernando would have to be faced. Not for anything to do with a goddamned stupid war, or even what had been done to *him;* but for Trista. His Silver Moon, who'd burned for him—and because of him.

"Which way will he come?" Blaze said abruptly; gritting his teeth between sickening waves of pain now, to which he wouldn't and *couldn't* succumb.

"From behind. He follow now, he. Come alone for kill. For woman, yes? For hate—this was seen by—she whose name shall not be spoken!"

"The Old One? The One who speaks into my mind with hers?" Trista had rested her head on Blaze's knee and now she reared up like a striking serpent, almost overturning the pirogue. *"I* am not afraid to mention names! *I* . . ." and then she began to weep again, seeing what must happen—like a play of dice—all her air of arrogance and certainty vanishing as she said in a numb, soft voice: "I'm sorry, Cousin Antoine—I'm sorry, Blaze my husband, my love. Antoine, if we may stop for a while to put moss and the spider webs on my man's wounds? For you are both right—there are things that have to be faced and overcome—usually by *men*—although women have the worst of it, with the waiting!"

EPILOGUE: *El Condor Pasa* ~

The ways of the bayous and the swamps were ancient and almost ageless—as were other ways and other lives lived otherwhere. But the Old Ones were Always and Everywhere.

After the application of the wet moss and the healing spider webs it was Trista herself who paddled the pirogue back; understanding even in her pain of *not*-understanding that there could be no worse enemy—nor fear—than that which is always at your back to keep you looking over your shoulder.

Whatever the outcome she must abide by it—the old, primitive battle of two males over a female that Antoine had already understood and the Old One had already seen. And *she*, the new and untried one, had already and painfully learned that the test of one's newfound power was in *not* using it—even if it broke your heart. . . .

There was a small island in the middle of the "shaking grass" and it was there that they met, while she waited with her heart shaking far more.

Because they were ill-matched—even though she had made Fernando throw away his gun by leveling one of her own. She could tell, though, that he liked the idea that she would belong without any holding back to the victor—to be his forever.

322

"Like mother—like daughter, eh?" Fernando taunted, while Blaze only listened; containing his strength; saying nothing. "Why—I've had you both, haven't I? Any way and every way I pleased! And you both loved me too, damn your black souls! You both *loved* me—and said so too, didn't you? And now, after I've cut the balls off this latest lover of yours—you'll be all mine to do with as I want to, won't you? You *promised,* bitch! Said you loved me too—didn't you? *Didn't* you?"

"Yes—yes I did. I did think I loved you, Fernando. I . . . Oh God!"

Blaze, Blaze! Be careful, love—I spoke only to distract *him!*

He had only a slight cut on his arm—but Trista, even while she sighed her relief, realized suddenly that *he* too had suddenly begun to hear her thoughts; from the sudden lopsided grin he gave her before he concentrated all of his attention on Fernando.

She had never really seen Blaze Davenant in a fight to the death before—leave alone a bloody knife fight. He had been tortured and beaten and close to dying not too long before—and she could see, agonizing over it without being able to show it, the care he was taking *now* merely to avoid Fernando's wild attacks and the taunts that grew uglier and uglier—staining her cheeks in spite of all her resolves.

"Artist-bastard! Think that knife you're holding is a paintbrush? I've ridden with Quantrill and Bloody Bill, and I've taken scalps—all kinds of scalps! Your mother's part 'Pache, I've heard tell. Might take hers too—after I've had my fill of this black-haired whore and passed her around enough times—like I have before! Didn't know that, did you?"

He lunged, and Trista had to put her hand before her mouth to keep from screaming as he did.

That time Blaze managed to evade him and keep his balance at the same time. He didn't say a word—not even in refutation of all the ugly, filthy, twisted-true-enough things Fernando was saying—*gloating* over.

"I'm going to stab you in the gut—and while you're sinking I'm going to fuck your woman right before your eyes—right here. . . ."

"I think not!"

They had been circling each other warily, Fernando lunging forward and Blaze always cautiously backing off; but now, suddenly, taking even Trista off guard, he leaped in for the kill—a desperate, cornered panther using the last of his strength as his one fisted hand struck Fernando's wrist that held the knife; paralyzing it; while his knife went straight for the heart—or had it been lower?—and ripped upward and then crosswise again before he pulled the bloody knife free and the shaking grass shook harder and the water was red-stained for a few moments before the swamp swallowed and took what belonged to it into its maw.

And the Old One smiled—and a sudden shaft of sunlight ambered the green waters of the ancient bayou and Trista felt her smile as she came to lie over her man as he thrust the red-stained knife into the damp, cleansing earth beside him as he let himself fall back to lie prone with one arm over his eyes as a dying sun suddenly turned the water and the world to bloody flame—but only for an instant, before it was gone.

They had burned for each other and with each other in a sea of lava long ago—but now—now they had rediscovered and at last recognized each other in this other time, this other place.

He was so still for some moments that Trista became terrified he had stopped breathing, and placed her mouth over his, to give him her breath.

And then gasped, half-laughing, half-crying, when both his arms closed over her to hold her demandingly closer as he whispered teasingly against her open mouth:

"And isn't *this* how all *this*"—telling her with his body now—"began? Since *you're* the doctor, my dearest, damndest, most infuriating and unforgettablé love of all my lives—hadn't you better continue what you've started in the way of . . . um . . . treatment?"

Being a doctor—his wife—and his lover—what else could she do, after all? It didn't matter where they went from here or where they ended up, as long as they would be together from now on.

THE MAGNIFICENT NOVELS BY
NEW YORK TIMES BESTSELLING AUTHOR
KATHLEEN E. WOODIWISS

Dear Reader:

If you enjoyed this book, and would like information about future books by this author and other Avon authors, we would be delighted to put you on the mailing list for our ROMANCE NEWSLETTER.

Simply *print* your name and address and send to Avon Books, Room 1210, 1790 Broadway, N.Y., N.Y. 10019.

We hope to bring you many hours of pleasurable reading!

Sara Reynolds, Editor
Romance Newsletter